P9-BZZ-902

An Audacious Plan

Balasar Gice had come to Acton with his best men, the books, the poet, the plans. The High Council of Galt had heard him out—the dangers of the andat, the need to end the supremacy of the Khaiem. That part had gone quite well. No one seriously disputed that the Khaiem were the single greatest threat to Galt. It was only when he began to reveal his plans and how far he had already gone that the audience began to turn sour on him.

Now the fate of all his work, the years of planning, of struggle, of battle, rested on what happened in the next moments.

The Lord Convocate spoke. "Fourteen cities in a single season. It can't be done, Balasar. Uther Redcape couldn't have done it."

"Uther was fighting in Eddensea," Balasar said. "They have walls around cities there. They have armies. The Khaiem haven't got anything but the andat."

"The andat suffice."

"Only if they have them."

"Ah. Yes. That's the center of the question, isn't it? Your grand plan to do away with all the andat at a single blow. I have to confess, I don't think I quite follow how you expect this to work. You have one of these poets here, ready to work with us. Wouldn't it be better to capture one of these andat for ourselves?"

"We will be. Freedom-From-Bondage should be one of the simplest andat to capture. It's never been done, so there's no worry about coming too near what's been tried before. I've found books from the First Empire . . ."

"All explaining why it's impossible." The old man's voice was almost gentle. It was a ploy. He wanted to see whether Balasar would lose his temper, so instead Balasar smiled.

"It all depends on what you mean by impossible. . . ."

Turn the page to see what people are saying
about *An Autumn War*. . . .

People Are Raving About *An Autumn War*....

"Thanks to the dignity with which Abraham invests his characters, and the exquisite sensibility with which he details their inner states of mind and emotion, their tragedy offers us the kind of catharsis that marks a superior work of art. I was deeply moved by Abraham's grim yet far from hopeless tale, whose conclusion in the forthcoming *The Price of Spring* I await with impatience." —*Realms of Fantasy*

"*An Autumn War* is, in its closing stages, heart-stoppingly surprising and exciting. Rarely does the penultimate volume in a series carry such a charge of its own." —*Locus*

"Daniel Abraham delighted fantasy readers with his brilliantly original and engaging first novel, *A Shadow in Summer,* and in *A Betrayal in Winter* penned a tragedy as darkly personal and violent as Shakespeare's *King Lear.* Now in *An Autumn War*, the third volume in the Long Price Quartet, Daniel Abraham has written a spectacular epic fantasy of much wider scope and appeal that will thrill his fans and enthrall legions of new readers." —*Fantasy Book Critic*

"Daniel Abraham gets better with every book. *A Shadow in Summer* was among the strongest first novels of the last decade, and *A Betrayal in Winter* was a terrific second book, but in *An Autumn War*, Abraham puts both of them in the shade. This book really blows the top off, taking the world of the andat and the poets in new and unexpected directions. *An Autumn War* will keep you turning pages and break your heart in the bargain. If there's any justice, this should be a contender for all the major awards." —George R. R. Martin, *New York Times* #1 bestselling author

AN

AUTUMN

WAR

>+<

Book Three
of the
Long Price Quartet

>+<

Daniel Abraham

TOR®
fantasy

A TOM DOHERTY ASSOCIATES BOOK
NEW YORK

AN AUTUMN WAR: BOOK THREE OF THE LONG PRICE QUARTET

Copyright © 2008 by Daniel Abraham

Edited by James Frenkel

Maps by Jackie Aher

A Tor Book
Published by Tom Doherty Associates, LLC
175 Fifth Avenue
New York, NY 10010

www.tor-forge.com

Tor® is a registered trademark of Tom Doherty Associates, LLC.

ISBN 978-0-7653-5189-0
s
First Edition: July 2008
First Mass Market Edition: July 2009

Printed in the United States of America

0 9 8 7 6 5 4 3 2 1

To Jim and Allison,

without whom none of this would have been possible

ACKNOWLEDGMENTS

Once again, I would like to extend my thanks to Walter Jon Williams, Melinda Snodgrass, Emily Mah, S. M. Stirling, Terry England, Ian Tregillis, Ty Franck, George R. R. Martin, and the other members of the New Mexico Critical Mass Workshop.

I also owe debts of gratitude to Shawna McCarthy and Danny Baror for their enthusiasm and faith in the project, to James Frenkel for his unstinting support and uncanny ability to improve a manuscript, and to Tom Doherty and the staff at Tor for their kindness and support.

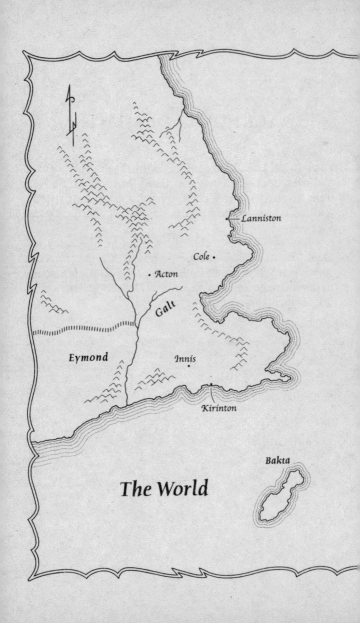

Lanniston

Cole

Acton

Galt

Eymond

Innis

Kirinton

Bakta

The World

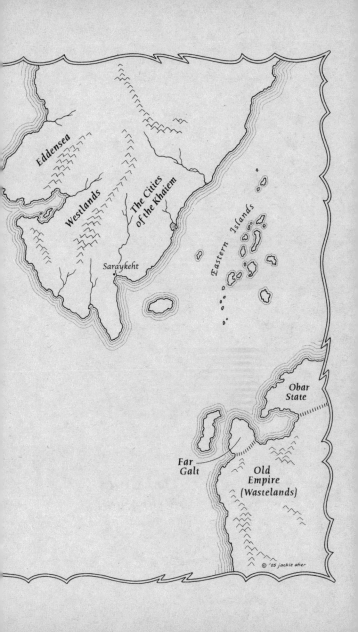

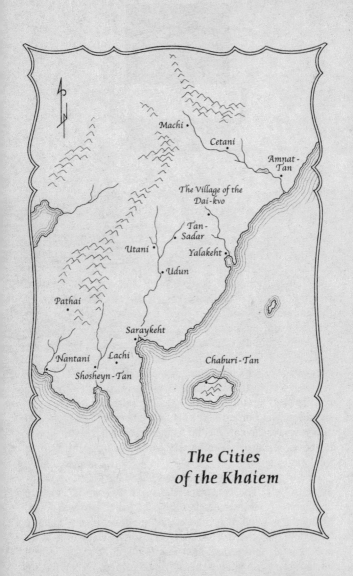

Machi •

Cetani •

Amnat-
Tan

The Village of the
Dai-kvo

Tan-
Sadar

Utani •

Yalakeht •

• Udun

Pathai •

Saraykeht •

Chaburi-Tan

Nantani •   Lachi •

Shosheyn-Tan

The Cities
of the Khaiem

Prolog

>+< Three men came out of the desert. Twenty had gone in.

The setting sun pushed their shadows out behind them, lit their faces a ruddy gold, blinded them. The weariness and pain in their bodies robbed them of speech. On the horizon, something glimmered that was no star, and they moved silently toward it. The farthest tower of Far Galt, the edge of the Empire, beckoned them home from the wastes, and without speaking, each man knew that they would not stop until they stood behind its gates.

The smallest of them shifted the satchel on his back. His gray commander's tunic hung from his flesh as if the cloth itself were exhausted. His mind turned inward, half-dreaming, and the leather straps of the satchel rubbed against his raw shoulder. The burden had killed seventeen of his men, and now it was his to carry as far as the tower that rose up slowly in the violet air of evening. He could not bring himself to think past that.

One of the others stumbled and fell to his knees on wind-paved stones. The commander paused. He would not lose another, not so near the end. And yet he feared bending down, lifting the man up. If he paused, he might never move again. Grunting, the other man recovered his feet. The commander nodded once and turned again to the west. A breeze stirred the low, brownish grasses, hissing and hushing. The punishing sun made its exit and left behind twilight and the wide swath of stars hanging overhead, cold candles beyond numbering. The night would bring chill as deadly as the midday heat.

It seemed to the commander that the tower did not so much come closer as grow, plantlike. He endured his weariness and pain, and the structure that had been no larger than his thumb was now the size of his hand. The beacon that had seemed steady flickered now, and tongues of flame leapt and vanished. Slowly, the details of the stonework came clear; the huge carved relief of the Great Tree of Galt. He smiled, the skin of his lip splitting, wetting his mouth with blood.

"We're not going to die," one of the others said. He sounded amazed. The commander didn't respond, and some measureless time later, another voice called for them to stop, to offer their names and the reason that they'd come to this twice-forsaken ass end of the world.

When the commander spoke, his voice was rough, rusting with disuse.

"Go to your High Watchman," he said. "Tell him that Balasar Gice has returned."

BALASAR GICE had been in his eleventh year when he first heard the word *andat*. The river that passed through his father's estates had turned green one day, and then red. And then it rose fifteen feet. Balasar had watched in horror as the fields vanished, the cottages, the streets and yards he knew. The whole world, it seemed, had become a sea of foul water with only the tops of trees and the corpses of pigs and cattle and men to the horizon.

His father had moved the family and as many of his best men as would fit to the upper stories of the house. Balasar had begged to take the horse his father had given him up as well. When the gravity of the situation had been explained, he changed his pleas to include the son of the village notary, who had been Balasar's closest friend. He had been refused in that as well. His horses and his playmates were going to drown. His father's concern was for Balasar, for the family; the wider world would have to look after itself.

Even now, decades later, the memory of those six days was fresh as a wound. The bloated bodies of pigs and cattle and people like pale logs floating past the house. The rich, low scent of fouled water. The struggle to sleep when the rushing at the bottom of the stairs seemed like the whisper of something vast and terrible for which he had no name. He could still hear men's voices questioning whether the food would last, whether the water was safe to drink, and whether the flood was natural, a catastrophe of distant rains, or an attack by the Khaiem and their andat.

He had not known then what the word meant, but the syllables had taken on the stench of the dead bodies, the devastation where the village had been, the emptiness and the destruction. It was only much later—after the water had receded, the dead had been mourned, the village rebuilt—that he learned how correct he had been.

Nine generations of fathers had greeted their new children into the world since the God Kings of the East had turned upon each other, his history tutor told him. When the glory that had been the center of all creation fell, its throes had changed the nature of space. The lands that had been great gardens and fields were deserts now, permanently altered by the war. Even as far as Galt and Eddensea, the histories told of weeks of darkness, of failed crops and famine, a sky dancing with flames of green, a sound as if the earth were tearing itself apart. Some people said the stars themselves had changed positions.

But the disasters of the past grew in the telling or faded from memory. No one knew exactly how things had been those many years ago. Perhaps the Emperor had gone mad and loosed his personal god-ghost—what they called andat—against his own people, or against himself. Or there might have been a woman, the wife of a great lord, who had been taken by the Emperor against her will. Or perhaps she'd willed it. Or the thousand factions and minor insults and treacheries that accrue around power had simply followed their usual course.

As a boy, Balasar had listened to the story, drinking in the tales of mystery and glory and dread. And, when his tutor had told him, somber of tone and gray, that there were only two legacies left by the fall of the God Kings—the wastelands that bordered Far Galt and Obar State, and the cities of the Khaiem where men still held the andat like Cooling, Seedless, Stone-Made-Soft—Balasar had understood the implication as clearly as if it had been spoken.

What had happened before could happen again at any time and without warning.

"And that's what brought you?" the High Watchman said. "It's a long walk from a little boy at his lessons to this place."

Balasar smiled again and leaned forward to sip bitter kafe from a rough tin mug. His room was baked brick and close as a cell. A cruel wind hissed outside the thick walls, as it had for the three long, feverish days since he had returned to the world. The small windows had been scrubbed milky by sandstorms. His little wounds were scabbing over, none of them reddened or hot to the touch, though the stripe on his shoulder where the satchel strap had been would doubtless leave a scar.

"It wasn't as romantic as I'd imagined," he said. The High Watchman laughed, and then, remembering the dead, sobered. Balasar shifted the subject. "How long have you been here? And who did you offend to get yourself sent to this . . . lovely place?"

"Eight years. I've been eight years at this post. I didn't much care for the way things got run in Acton. I suppose this was my way of saying so."

"I'm sure Acton felt the loss."

"I'm sure it didn't. But then, I didn't do it for them."

Balasar chuckled.

"That *sounds* like wisdom," Balasar said, "but eight years here seems an odd place for wisdom to lead you."

The High Watchman smacked his lips and shrugged.

"It wasn't me going inland," he said. Then, a moment later, "They say there's still andat out there. Haunting the places they used to control."

"There aren't," Balasar said. "There are other things. Things they made or unmade. There's places where the air goes bad on you—one breath's fine, and the next it's like something's crawling into you. There's places where the ground's thin as eggshell and a thousand-foot drop under it. And there are living things too—things they made with the andat, or what happened when the things they made bred. But the ghosts don't stay once their handlers are gone. That isn't what they are."

Balasar took an olive from his plate, sucked away the flesh, and spat back the stone. For a moment, he could hear voices in the wind. The words of men who'd trusted and followed him, even knowing where he would take them. The voices of the dead whose lives he had spent. Coal and Eustin had survived. The others—Little Ott, Bes, Mayarsin, Laran, Kellem, and a dozen more—were bones and memory now. Because of him. He shook his head, clearing it, and the wind was only wind again.

"No offense, General," the High Watchman said, "but there's not enough gold in the world for me to try what you did."

"It was necessary," Balasar said, and his tone ended the conversation.

THE JOURNEY to the coast was easier than it should have been. Three men, traveling light. The others were an absence measured in the ten days it took to reach Lawton. It had taken sixteen coming from. The arid, empty lands of the East gave way to softly rolling hills. The tough yellow grasses yielded to blue-green almost the color of a cold sea, wavelets dancing on its surface. Farmsteads appeared off the road, windmills with broad blades shifting in the breezes; men and women and children shared the path that led toward the sea.

Balasar forced himself to be civil, even gracious. If the world moved the way he hoped, he would never come to this place again, but the world had a habit of surprising him.

When he'd come back from the campaign in the Westlands, he'd thought his career was coming to its victorious end. He might take a place in the Council or at one of the military colleges. He even dared to dream of a quiet estate someplace away from the yellow coal smoke of the great cities. When the news had come—a historian and engineer in Far Galt had divined a map that might lead to the old libraries—he'd known that rest had been a chimera, a thing for other men but never himself. He'd taken the best of his men, the strongest, smartest, most loyal, and come here. He had lost them here. The ones who had died, and perhaps also the ones who had lived.

Coal and Eustin were both quiet as they traveled, both respectful when they stopped to camp for the night. Without conversation, they had all agreed that the cold night air and hard ground was better than the company of men at an inn or wayhouse. Once in a while, one or the other would attempt to talk or joke or sing, but it always failed. There was a distance in their eyes, a stunned expression that Balasar recognized from boys stumbling over the wreckage of their first battlefield. They were seasoned fighters, Coal and Eustin. He had seen both of them kill men and boys, knew each of them had raped women in the towns they'd sacked, and still, they had left some scrap of innocence in the desert and were moving away from it with every step. Balasar could not say what that loss would do to them, nor would he insult their manhood by bringing it up. He knew, and that alone would have to suffice. They reached the ports of Parrinshall on the first day of autumn.

Half a hundred ships awaited them: great merchant ships built to haul cargo across the vast emptiness of the southern seas, shallow fishing boats that darted out of port and back again, the ornate three-sailed roundboats of Bakta, the antiquated and changeless ships of the east islands. It was nothing to the ports at Kirinton or Lanniston or Saraykeht, but it was enough. Three berths on any of half a dozen of these ships would take them off Far Galt and start them toward home.

"Winter'll be near over afore we see Acton," Coal said, and spat off the dock.

"I imagine it will," Balasar agreed, shifting the satchel against his hip. "If we sail straight through. We could also stay here until spring if we liked. Or stop in Bakta."

"Whatever you like, General," Eustin said.

"Then we'll sail straight through. Find what's setting out and when. I'll be at the harbor master's house."

"Anything the matter, sir?"

"No," Balasar said.

The harbor master's house was a wide building of red brick settled on the edge of the water. Banners of the Great Tree hung from the archway above its wide bronze doors. Balasar announced himself to the secretary and was shown to a private room. He accepted the offer of cool wine and dried figs, asked for and received the tools for writing the report now required of him, and gave orders that he not be disturbed until his men arrived. Then, alone, he opened his satchel and drew forth the books he had recovered, laying them side by side on the desk that looked out over the port. There were four, two bound in thick, peeling leather, another whose covers had been ripped from it, and one encased in metal that appeared to be neither steel nor silver, but something of each. Balasar ran his fingers over the mute volumes, then sat, considering them and the moral paradox they represented.

For these, he had spent the lives of his men. While the path back to Galt was nothing like the risk he had faced in the ruins of the fallen Empire, still it was sea travel. There were storms and pirates and plagues. If he wished to be certain that these volumes survived, the right thing would be to transcribe them here in Parrinshall. If he were to die on the journey home, the books, at least, would not be drowned. The knowledge within them would not be lost.

Which was also the argument *against* making copies. He took the larger of the leather-bound volumes and opened it. The writing was in the flowing script of the dead Empire, not the simpler chop the Khaiem used for business and trade with foreigners like himself. Balasar frowned as he picked out the symbols his tutor had taught him as a boy.

There are two types of impossibility in the andat: *those which cannot be understood, and those whose natures make binding impossible.* His translation was rough, but sufficient for his needs. These were the books he'd sought. And so the question remained whether the risk of their loss was greater than the risk posed by their existence. Balasar closed the book and let his head rest in his hands. He knew, of course, what he would do. He had known before he'd sent Eustin and Coal to find a boat for them. Before he'd reached Far Galt in the first place.

It was his awareness of his own pride that made him hesitate. History was full of men who thought themselves to be the one great soul whom power would not corrupt. He did not wish to be among that number, and yet here he sat, holding in his hands the secrets that might remake the shape of the human world. A humble man would have sought counsel from those wiser than himself, or at least feared to wield the power. He did not like what it said of him that giving the books to anyone besides himself seemed as foolish as gambling with their destruction. He would not even have trusted them to Eustin or Coal or any of the men who had died helping him.

He took the paper he'd been given, raised the pen, and began his report and, in a sense, his confession.

THREE WEEKS out, Eustin broke.

The sea surrounded them, empty and immense as the sky. So far south, the water was clear and the air warm even with the slowly failing days. The birds that had followed them from Parrinshall had vanished. The only animal was a three-legged dog the ship's crew had taken on as a mascot. Nor were there women on board. Only the rank, common smell of men and the sea.

The rigging creaked and groaned, unnerving no one but Balasar. He had never loved traveling by water. Campaigning on land was no more comfortable, but at least when the day ended he was able to see that this village was not the one he'd been in the night before, the tree under which he slept looked out over some different hillside. Here, in the vast nothingness of water, they might almost have been standing still. Only the long white plume of their wake gave him a sense of movement, the visible promise that one day the journey would end. He would often sit at the stern, watch that constant trail, and take what solace he could from it. Sometimes he carved blocks of wax with a small, thin knife while his mind wandered and softened in the boredom of inaction.

It should not have surprised him that the isolation had proved corrosive for Eustin and Coal. And yet when one of the sailors rushed up to him that night, pale eyes bulging from his head, Balasar had not guessed the trouble. His man, the one called Eustin, was belowdecks with a knife, the sailor said. He was threatening to kill himself or else the crippled mascot dog, no one was sure which. Normally, they'd all have clubbed him senseless and thrown him over the side, but as he was a paying passage, the general might perhaps want to take a hand. Balasar put down the wax block half-carved into the shape of a fish, tucked his knife in his belt, and nodded as if the request were perfectly common.

The scene in the belly of the ship was calmer than he'd expected. Eustin sat on a bench. He had the dog by a rope looped around the thing's chest and a field dagger in his other hand. Ten sailors were standing in silence either in the room or just outside it, armed with blades and cudgels. Balasar ignored them, taking a low stool and setting it squarely in front of Eustin before he sat.

"General," Eustin said. His voice was low and flat, like a man half-dead from a wound.

"I hear there's some issue with the animal."

"He ate my soup."

One of the sailors coughed meaningfully, and Eustin's eyes narrowed and flickered toward the sound. Balasar spoke again quickly.

"I've seen Coal sneak half a bottle of wine away from you. It hardly seems a killing offense."

"He didn't steal my soup, General. I gave it to him."

"You gave it to him?"

"Yessir."

The room seemed close as a coffin, and hot. If only there weren't so many men around, if the bodies were not so thick, the air not so heavy with their breath, Balasar thought he might have been able to think clearly. He sucked his teeth, struggling to find something wise or useful to say, some way to disarm the situation and bring Eustin back from his madness. In the end, his silence was enough.

"He deserves better, General," Eustin said. "He's broken. He's a sick, broken thing. He shouldn't have to live like that. There ought to be some dignity at least. If there's nothing else, there should at least be some dignity."

The dog whined and craned its neck toward Eustin. Balasar could see distress in the animal's eyes, but not fear. The dog could hear the pain in Eustin's voice, even if the sailors couldn't. The bodies around him were wound tight, ready for violence, all of them except for Eustin. He held the knife weakly. The tension in his body wasn't the hot, loose energy of battle; he was knotted, like a boy tensed against a blow; like a man facing the gallows.

"Leave us alone. All of you," Balasar said.

"Not without Tripod!" one of the sailors said.

Balasar met Eustin's eyes. With a small shock he realized it was the first time he'd truly looked at the man since they'd emerged from the desert. Perhaps he'd been ashamed of what he might see reflected there. And perhaps his shame had some part in this. Eustin was *his* man, and so the pain he bore was Balasar's responsibility. He'd been weak and stupid to shy away from that. And weakness and stupidity always carried a price.

"Let the dog go. There's no call to involve him, or these men," Balasar said. "Sit with me awhile, and if you still need killing, I'll be the one to do it."

Eustin's gaze flickered over his face, searching for something. To see whether it was a ruse, to see whether Balasar would actually kill his own man. When he saw the answer, Eustin's wide shoulders eased. He dropped the rope, freeing the animal. It hopped in a circle, uncertain and confused.

"You have the dog," Balasar said to the sailors without looking at them. "Now go."

They filed out, none of them taking their eyes from Eustin and the knife still in his hand. Balasar waited until they had all left, the low door pulled shut behind them. Distant voices shouted over the creaking timbers, the oil lamp swung gently on its chain. This time, Balasar used the silence intentionally, waiting. At first, Eustin looked at him, anticipation in his eyes. And then his gaze passed into the distance, seeing something beyond the room, beyond them both. And then silently, Eustin wept. Balasar shifted his stool nearer and put his hand on the man's shoulder.

"I keep seeing them, sir."

"I know."

"I've seen a thousand men die one way or the other. But . . . but that was on a field. That was in a fight."

"It isn't the same," Balasar said. "Is that why you wanted those men to throw you in the sea?"

Eustin turned the blade slowly, catching the light. He was still weeping, his face now slack and empty. Balasar wondered which of them he was seeing now, which of their number haunted him in that moment, and he felt the eyes of the dead upon him. They were in the room, invisibly crowding it as the sailors had.

"Can you tell me they died with honor?" Eustin breathed.

"I'm not sure what honor is," Balasar said. "We did what we did because it was needed, and we were the men to do it.

The price was too high for us to bear, you and I and Coal. But we aren't finished, so we have to carry it a bit farther. That's all."

"It wasn't needed, General. I'm sorry, but it *wasn't*. We take a few more cities, we gain a few more slaves. Yes, they're the richest cities in the world. I know it. Sacking even one of the cities of the Khaiem would put more gold in the High Council's coffers than a season in the Westlands. But how much do they need to buy Little Ott back from hell?" Eustin asked. "And why shouldn't I go there and get him myself, sir?"

"It's not about gold. I have enough gold of my own to live well and die old. Gold's a tool we use—a tool *I* use—to make men do what must be done."

"And honor?"

"And glory. Tools, all of them. We're men, Eustin. We've no reason to lie to each other."

He had the man's attention now. Eustin was looking only at him, and there was confusion in his eyes—confusion and pain—but the ghosts weren't inside him now.

"Why then, sir? Why are we doing this?"

Balasar sat back. He hadn't said these words before, he had never explained himself to anyone. Pride again. He was haunted by his pride. The pride that had made him take this on as his task, the work he owed to the world because no one else had the stomach for it.

"The ruins of the Empire were made," he said. "God didn't write it that the world should have something like that in it. Men *created* it. Men with little gods in their sleeves. And men like that still live. The cities of the Khaiem each have one, and they look on them like plow horses. Tools to feed their power and their arrogance. If it suited them, they could turn their andat loose on us. Hold our crops in permanent winter or sink our lands into the sea or whatever else they could devise. They could turn the world itself against us the way you or I might hold a knife. And do you know why they haven't?"

Eustin blinked, unnerved, Balasar thought, by the anger in his voice.

"No, sir."

"Because they haven't yet chosen to. That's all. They might. Or they might turn against each other. They could make everything into wastelands just like those. Acton, Kirinton, Marsh. Every city, every town. It hasn't happened yet because we've been lucky. But someday, one of them *will* grow ambitious or mad. And then all the rest of us are ants on a battlefield, trampled into the mud. That's what I mean when I say this is needed. You and I are seeing that it never happens," he said, and his words made his own blood hot. He was no longer uncertain or touched by shame. Balasar grinned wide and wolfish. If it was pride, then let him be proud. No man could do what he intended without it. "When I've finished, the god-ghosts of the Khaiem will be a story women tell their babes to scare them at night, and nothing more than that. *That's* what Little Ott died for. Not for money or conquest or glory.

"I'm saving the world," Balasar said. "So, now. Say you'd rather drown than help me."

>+< It had rained for a week, the cold gray clouds seeming
to drape themselves between the mountain ranges to
the east and west of the city like a wet canopy. The mornings
were foggy, the afternoons chill. With the snowdrifts of winter almost all melted, the land around Machi became a soupy
mud whose only virtue was the spring crop of wheat and
snow peas it would bring forth. Travel was harder now even
than in the deadly cold of deep winter.

And still, the travelers came.

"With all respect, this exercise, as you call it, is ill-advised,"
the envoy said. His hands still held a pose of deference though
the conversation had long since parted from civility. "I am
sure your intentions are entirely honorable, however it is the
place of the Dai-kvo—"

"If the Dai-kvo wants to rule Machi, tell him to come
north," the Khai Machi snapped. "He can pull my puppet
strings from the next room. I'll make a bed for him."

The envoy's eyes went wide. He was a young man, and
hadn't mastered the art of keeping his mind from showing on
his face. Otah, the Khai Machi, waved away his own words
and sighed. He had gone too far, and he knew it. Another few
steps and they'd be pointing at each other and yelling about
which of them wanted to create the Third Empire. The truth
was that he had ruled Machi these last fourteen years only by
necessity. The prospect of uniting the cities of the Khaiem

under his rule was about as enticing as scraping his skin off with a rock.

· The audience was a private one, in a small room lined with richly carved blackwood, lit by candles that smelled like rich earth and vanilla, and set well away from the corridors and open gardens where servants and members of the utkhaiem might unintentionally overhear them. This wasn't business he cared to have shared over the dances and dinners of the court. Otah rose from his chair and walked to the window, forcing his temper back down. He opened the shutters, and the city stretched out before him, grand towers of stone stretching up toward the sky, and beyond them the wide plain to the south, green with the first crops of the spring. He pressed his frustration back into yoke.

"I didn't mean that," he said. "I know that the Dai-kvo doesn't intend to dictate to me. Or any of the Khaiem. I appreciate your concern, but the creation of the guard isn't a threat. It's hardly an army, you know. A few hundred men trained up to maybe half the level of a Westlands garrison could hardly topple the world."

"We are concerned for the stability of all the cities," the envoy said. "When one of the Khaiem begins to study war, it puts all the others on edge."

"It's hardly studying war to hand a few men knives and remind them which end's the handle."

"It's more than any of the Khaiem have done in the past hundred years. And you must see that you haven't made it your policy to ally yourself with . . . well, with anyone."

Well, this is going just as poorly as I expected, Otah thought.

"I have a wife, thank you," Otah said, his manner cool. But the envoy had clearly reached the end of his patience. Hearing him stand, Otah turned. The young man's face was flushed, his hands folded into the sleeves of his brown poet's robes.

"And if you were a shopkeeper, having a single woman would be admirable," the envoy said. "But as the Khai Machi, turning away every woman who's offered to you is a pattern of insult. I can't be the first one to point this out. From the time you took the chair, you've isolated yourself from the rest of the Khaiem, the great houses of the utkhaiem, the merchant houses. Everyone."

Otah ran through the thousand arguments and responses— the treaties and trade agreements, the acceptance of servants and slaves, all of the ways in which he'd tried to bind himself and Machi to the other cities. They wouldn't convince the envoy or his master, the Dai-kvo. They wanted blood—his blood flowing in the veins of some boy child whose mother had come from south or east or west. They wanted to know that the Khai Yalakeht or Pathai or Tan-Sadar might be able to hope for a grandson on the black chair in Machi once Otah had died. His wife Kiyan was past the age to bear another child, but men could get children on younger women. For one of the Khaiem to have only two children, and both by the same woman—and her a wayhouse keeper from Udun . . . They wanted sons from him, fathered on women who embodied wise political alliances. They wanted to preserve tradition, and they had two empires and nine generations of the Khaiate court life to back them. Despair settled on him like a thick winter cloak.

There was nothing to be gained. He knew all the reasons for all the choices he had made, and he could as easily explain them to a mine dog as to this proud young man who'd traveled weeks for the privilege of taking him to task. Otah sighed, turned, and took a deeply formal pose of apology.

"I have distracted you from your task, Athai-cha. That was not my intention. What was it again the Dai-kvo wished of me?"

The envoy pressed his lips bloodless. They both knew the answer to the question, but Otah's feigned ignorance would force him to restate it. And the simple fact that Otah's bed habits were not mentioned would make his point for him. Etiquette was a terrible game.

"The militia you have formed," the envoy said. "The Dai-kvo would know your intention in creating it."

"I intend to send it to the Westlands. I intend it to take contracts with whatever forces there are acting in the best interests of *all* the cities of the Khaiem. I will be pleased to draft a letter saying so."

Otah smiled. The young poet's eyes flickered. As insults went, this was mild enough. Eventually, the poet's hands rose in a pose of gratitude.

"There is one other thing, Most High," the envoy said. "If you take any aggressive act against the interests of another of the Khaiem, the Dai-kvo will recall Cehmai and Stone-Made-Soft. If you take arms against them, he will allow the Khaiem to use their poets against you and your city."

"Yes," Otah said. "I understood that when I heard you'd come. I am not acting against the Khaiem, but thank you for your time, Athai-cha. I will have a letter sewn and sealed for you by morning."

After the envoy had left, Otah sank into a chair and pressed the heels of his hands to his temples. Around him, the palace was quiet. He counted fifty breaths, then rose again, closed and latched the door, and turned back to the apparently empty room.

"Well?" he asked, and one of the panels in the corner swung open, exposing a tiny hidden chamber brilliantly designed for eavesdropping.

The man who sat in the listener's chair seemed both at ease and out of place. At ease because it was Sinja's nature to take the world lightly, and out of place because his suntanned skin and rough, stained leathers made him seem like a gardener on a chair of deep red velvet and silver pins fit for the head of a merchant house or a member of the utkhaiem. He rose and closed the panel behind him.

"He seems a decent man," Sinja said. "I wouldn't want him on my side of a fight, though. Overconfident."

"I'm hoping it won't come to that," Otah said.

"For a man who's convinced the world he's bent on war, you're a bit squeamish about violence."

Otah chuckled.

"I think sending the Dai-kvo his messenger's head might

not be the most convincing argument for my commitment to peace," he said.

"Excellent point," Sinja agreed as he poured himself a bowl of wine. "But then you are training men to fight. It's a hard thing to preach peace and stability and also pay men to think what's the best way to disembowel someone with a spear."

"I know it," Otah said, his voice dark as wet slate. "Gods. You'd think having total power over a city would give you more options, wouldn't you?"

Otah sipped the wine. It was rich and astringent and fragrant of late summer, and it swirled in the bowl like a dark river. He felt old. Fourteen years he'd spent trying to be what Machi needed him to be—steward, manager, ruler, half-god, fuel for the gossip and backbiting of the court. Most of the time, he did well enough, but then something like this would happen, and he would be sure again that the work was beyond him.

"You could disband it," Sinja said. "It's not as though you need the extra trade."

"It's not about getting more silver," Otah said.

"Then what's it about? You aren't actually planning to invade Cetani, are you? Because I don't think that's a good idea."

Otah coughed out a laugh.

"It's about being ready," he said.

"Ready?"

"Every generation finds it harder to bind fresh andat. Every one that slips away becomes more difficult to capture. It can't go on forever. There will come a time that the poets fail, and we have to rely on something else."

"So," Sinja said. "You're starting a militia so that someday, generations from now, when some Dai-kvo that hasn't been born yet doesn't manage to keep up to the standards of his forebears—"

"There will also be generations of soldiers ready to keep the cities safe."

Sinja scratched his belly and nodded.

"You think I'm wrong?"

"Yes. I think you're wrong," Sinja said. "I think you saw Seedless escape. I think you saw Saraykeht suffer the loss. You know that the Galts have ambitions, and that they've put their hands into the affairs of the Khaiem more than once."

"That doesn't make me wrong," Otah said, unable to keep the sudden anger from his voice. So many years had passed, and the memory of Saraykeht had not dimmed. "You weren't there, Sinja-cha. You don't know how bad it was. That's mine. And if it lets me see farther than the Dai-kvo or the Khaiem—"

"It's possible to look at the horizon so hard you trip over your feet," Sinja said, unfazed by Otah's heat. "You aren't responsible for everything under the sky."

But I am responsible for that, Otah thought. He had never confessed his role in the fall of Saraykeht to Sinja, never told the story of the time he had killed a helpless man, of sparing an enemy and saving a friend. The danger and complexity and sorrow of that time had never entirely left him, but he could not call it regret.

"You want to keep the future safe," Sinja said, breaking the silence, "and I respect that. But you can't do it by shitting on the table right now. Alienating the Dai-kvo gains you nothing."

"What would you do, Sinja? If you were in my place, what would you do?"

"Take as much gold as I could put on a fast cart, and live out my life in a beach hut on Bakta. But then I'm not particularly reliable." He drained his bowl and put it down on the table, porcelain clicking softly on lacquered wood. "What you *should* do is send us west."

"But the men aren't ready—"

"They're near enough. Without real experience, these poor bastards would protect you from a real army about as well as sending out all the dancing girls you could find. And now that I've said it, girls might even slow them down longer."

Otah coughed a mirthless laugh. Sinja leaned forward, his eyes calm and steady.

"Put us in the Westlands as a mercenary company," he

said. "It gives real weight to it when you tell the Dai-kvo that you're just looking for another way to make money if we're already walking away from our neighboring cities. The men will get experience; I'll be able to make contacts with other mercenaries, maybe even strike up alliances with some of the Wardens. You can even found your military tradition. But besides that, there are certain problems with training and arming men, and then not giving them any outlet."

Otah looked up, meeting Sinja's grim expression.

"More trouble?" Otah asked.

"I've whipped the men involved and paid reparations," Sinja said, "but if the Dai-kvo doesn't like you putting together a militia, the fine people of Machi are getting impatient with having them. We're paying them to play at soldiers while everybody else's taxes buy their food and clothes."

Otah took a simple pose that acknowledged what Sinja said as truth.

"Where would you take them?"

"Annaster and Notting were on the edge of fighting last autumn. Something about the Warden of Annaster's son getting killed in a hunt. It's a long way south, but we're a small enough group to travel fast, and the passes cleared early this year. Even if nothing comes of it, there'll be keeps down there that want a garrison."

"How long before you could go?"

"I can have the men ready in two days if you'll send food carts out after us. A week if I have to stay to make the arrangements for the supplies."

Otah looked into Sinja's eyes. The years had whitened Sinja's temples but had made him no easier to read.

"That seems fast," Otah said.

"It's already under way," Sinja replied, then seeing Otah's reaction, shrugged. "It seemed likely."

"Two days, then," Otah said. Sinja smiled, stood, took a rough pose that accepted the order, and turned to go. As he lifted the door's latch, Otah spoke again. "Try not to get killed. Kiyan would take it amiss if I sent you off to die."

The captain paused in the open door. What had happened between Kiyan and Sinja—the Khai Machi's first and only wife and the captain of his private armsmen—had found its resolution on a snow-covered field ten years before. Sinja had done as Kiyan had asked him and the issue had ended there. Otah found that the anger and feelings of betrayal had thinned with time, leaving him more embarrassed than wrathful. That they were two men who loved the same woman was understood and unspoken. It wasn't comfortable ground for either of them.

"I'll keep breathing, Otah-cha. You do the same."

The door closed softly behind him, and Otah took another sip of wine. It was fewer than a dozen breaths before a quiet scratching came at the door. Rising and straightening the folds of his robes, Otah prepared himself for the next appearance, the next performance in his ongoing, unending mummer's show. He pressed down a twinge of envy for Sinja and the men who would be slogging through cold mud and dirty snow. He told himself the journey only looked liberating to someone who was staying near a fire grate. He adopted a somber expression, held his body with the rigid grace expected of him, and called out for the servant to enter.

There was a meeting to take with House Daikani over a new mine they were proposing in the South. Mikah Radaani had also put a petition with the Master of Tides to schedule a meeting with the Khai Machi to discuss the prospect of resurrecting the summer fair in Amnat-Tan. And there was the letter to the Dai-kvo to compose, and a ceremony at the temple at moonrise at which his presence was required, and so on through the day and into the night. Otah listened patiently to the list of duties and obligations and tried not to feel haunted by the thought that sending the guard away had been the wrong thing to do.

EIAH TOOK a bite of the almond cake, wiping honey from her mouth with the back of her hand, and Maati was amazed again by how tall she'd grown. He still thought of her as hardly standing high as his knees, and here she was—thin as a stick and awkward, but tall as her mother. She'd even taken to wearing a woman's jewelry—necklace of gold and silver, armbands of lacework silver and gems, and rings on half her fingers. She still looked like a girl playing dress-up in her mother's things, but even that would pass soon.

"And how did *he* die?" she asked.

"I never said he did," Maati said.

Eiah's lips bent in a frown. Her dark eyes narrowed.

"You don't tell stories where they live, Uncle Maati. You like the dead ones."

Maati chuckled. It was a fair enough criticism, and her exasperation was as amusing as her interest. Since she'd been old enough to read, Eiah had haunted the library of Machi, poking here and there, reading and being frustrated. And now that she'd reached her fourteenth summer, the time had come for her to turn to matters of court. She was the only daughter of the Khai Machi, and as such, a rare chance for a marriage alliance. She would be the most valued property in the city, and worse for her and her parents, she was more than clever enough to know it. Her time in the library had taken on a tone of defiance, but it was never leveled at Maati, so it never bothered him. In fact, he found it rather delightful.

"Well," he said, settling his paunch more comfortably in the library's deep silk-covered chair, "as it happens, his binding did fail. It was tragic. He started screaming, and didn't stop for hours. He stopped when he died, of course, and when they examined him afterwards, they found slivers of glass all through his blood."

"They cut him open?"

"Of course," Maati said.

"That's disgusting," she said. Then a moment later, "If someone died here, could I help do it?"

"No one's likely to try a binding here, Eiah-kya. Only poets who've trained for years with the Dai-kvo are allowed to make the attempt, and even then they're under strict supervision.

Holding the andat is dangerous work, and not just if it fails."

"They should let girls do it too," she said. "I want to go to the school and train to be a poet."

"But then you wouldn't be your father's daughter anymore. If the Dai-kvo didn't choose you, you'd be one of the branded, and they'd turn you out into the world to make whatever way you could without anyone to help you."

"That's not true. Father was at the school, and he didn't have to take the brand. If the Dai-kvo didn't pick me, I wouldn't take it either. I'd just come back here and live alone like you do."

"But then wouldn't you and Danat have to fight?"

"No," Eiah said, taking a pose appropriate to a tutor offering correction. "Girls can't be Khai, so Danat wouldn't have to fight me for the chair."

"But if you're going to have women be poets, why not Khaiem too?"

"Because who'd want to be Khai?" she asked and took another piece of cake from the tray on the table between them.

The library stretched out around them—chamber after chamber of scrolls and books and codices that were Maati's private domain. The air was rich with the scent of old leather and dust and the pungent herbs he used to keep the mice and insects away. Baarath, the chief librarian and Maati's best friend here in the far, cold North, had kept it before him. Often when Maati arrived in the morning or remained long after dark, puzzling over some piece of ancient text or obscure reference, he would look up, half-wondering where the annoying, fat, boisterous, petty little man had gotten to, and then he would remember.

The fever had taken dozens of people that year. Winter always changed the city, the cold driving them deep into the tunnels and hidden chambers below Machi. For months they lived by firelight and in darkness. By midwinter, the air itself could seem thick and stifling. And illnesses spread easily in the dark and close, and Baraath had grown ill and died, one man among many. Now he was only memory and ash. Maati was the master of the library, appointed by his old friend and enemy and companion Otah Machi. The Khai Machi, husband of Kiyan, and father to this almost-woman Eiah who shared his almond cakes, and to her brother Danat. And, perhaps, to one other.

"Maati-kya? Are you okay?"

"I was just wondering how your brother was," he said.

"Better. He's hardly coughing at all anymore. Everyone's saying he has weak lungs, but I was just as sick when I was young, and I'm just fine."

"People tell stories," Maati said. "It keeps them amused, I suppose."

"What would happen if Danat died?"

"Your father would be expected to take a new, younger wife and produce a son to take his place. More than one, if he could. That's part of why the utkhaiem are so worried about Danat. If he died and no brothers were forthcoming, it would be bad for the city. All the most powerful houses would start fighting over who would be the new Khai. People would probably be killed."

"Well, Danat won't die," Eiah said. "So it doesn't matter. Did you know him?"

"Who?"

"My real uncle. Danat. The one Danat's named for?"

"No," Maati said. "Not really. I met him once."

"Did you like him?"

Maati tried to remember what it had been like, all those years ago. The Dai-kvo had summoned him. That had been the old Dai-kvo—Tahi-kvo. He'd never met the new one. Tahi-kvo had brought him to meet the two men, and set him the task that had ended with Otah on the chair and himself living in the court of Machi. It had been a different lifetime.

"I don't recall liking him or disliking him," Maati said. "He was just a man I'd met."

Eiah sighed impatiently.

"Tell me about another one," she said.

"Well. There was a poet in the First Empire before people understood that andat were harder and harder to capture each time they escaped. He tried to bind Softness with the same binding another poet had used a generation before. Of course it didn't work."

"Because a new binding has to be different," Eiah said.

"But *he* didn't know that."

"What happened to him?"

"His joints all froze in place. He was alive, but like a statue. He couldn't move at all."

"How did he eat?"

"He didn't. They tried to give him water by forcing it up his nostrils, and he drowned on it. When they examined his body, all the bones were fused together as if they had never been separate at all. It looked like one single thing."

"That's disgusting," she said. It was something she often said. Maati grinned.

They talked for another half a hand, Maati telling tales of failed bindings, of the prices paid by poets of old who had attempted the greatest trick in the world and fallen short. Eiah listened and passed her own certain judgment. They finished the last of the almond cakes and called a servant girl in to carry the plates away. Eiah left just as the sun peeked out between the low clouds and the high peaks in the west, brightness flaring gold for a long moment before the city fell into its long twilight. Alone again, Maati told himself that the darkness was only about the accidents of sunlight, and not his young friend's absence.

He could still remember the first time he'd seen Eiah. She'd been tiny, a small, curious helplessness in her mother's arms, and he had been deeply in disfavor with the Dai-kvo and sent to Machi in half-exile for treading too near the line between the poets and the politics of the court. The poets were creatures of the Dai-kvo, lent to the Khaiem. The Dai-kvo took no part in the courtly dramas of generational fratricide. The Khaiem supported the Dai-kvo and his village, sent their excess sons to the school from which they might be plucked to take the honor of the brown robes, and saw to the administration of the cities whose names they took as their own. The Khai Machi, the Khai Yalakeht, the Khai Tan-Sadar. All of them had been other men once, before their fathers had died or become too feeble to rule. All of them had killed their own brothers on the way to claiming their positions. All except Otah.

Otah, the exception.

A scratching at the door roused Maati, and he hauled himself from his chair and went forward. The night had nearly fallen, but torches spattered the darkness with circles of light. Even before he reached the door, he heard music coming from one of the pavilions nearby, the young men and women of the utkhaiem boiling up from the winter earth and celebrating nightly, undeterred by chill or rain or heartbreak. And at the door of his library were two familiar figures, and a third that was only expected. Cehmai, poet of Machi, stood with a bottle of wine in each hand, and behind him the hulking, bemused, inhuman andat Stone-Made-Soft raised its wide chin in greeting. The other—a slender young man in the same brown robes that Cehmai and Maati himself wore—spoke to Cehmai. Athai Vauudun, the envoy from the Dai-kvo.

"He is the most arrogant man I have ever met," the envoy said to Cehmai, continuing a previous conversation. "He has no allies, only one son, and no pause at all at the prospect of alienating every other city of the Khaiem. I think he's *proud* to ignore tradition."

"Our guest has met with the Khai," Stone-Made-Soft said, its voice low and rough as a landslide. "They don't appear to have impressed each other favorably."

"Athai-kvo," Cehmai said, gesturing awkwardly with one full bottle. "This it Maati Vaupathai. Maati-kvo, please meet our new friend."

Athai took a pose of greeting, and Maati answered with a welcoming pose less formal than the one he'd been offered.

"Kvo?" Athai said. "I hadn't known you were Cehmai-cha's teacher."

"It's a courtesy he gives me because I'm old," Maati said. "Come in, though. All of you. It's getting cold out."

Maati led the others back through the chambers and corridors of the library. On the way, they traded the kind of simple, common talk that etiquette required—the Dai-kvo was in good health, the school had given a number of promising boys the black robes, there were discussions of a possible new binding in the next years—and Maati played his part. Only Stone-Made-Soft didn't participate, considering as it was the thick stone walls with mild, distant interest. The inner chamber that Maati had prepared for the meeting was dim and windowless, but a fire burned hot behind iron shutters. Books and scrolls lay on a wide, low table. Maati opened the iron shutters, lit a taper from the flames, and set a series of candles and lanterns glowing around the room until they were all bathed in shadowless warm light. The envoy and Cehmai had taken chairs by the fire, and Maati lowered himself to a wide bench.

"My private workroom," Maati said, nodding at the space around them. "I've been promised there's no good way to listen to us in here."

The envoy took a pose that accepted the fact, but glanced uneasily at Stone-Made-Soft.

"I won't tell," the andat said, and grinned, baring its unnaturally regular stone-white teeth. "Promise."

"If I lost control of our friend here, telling what happened in a meeting wouldn't be the trouble we faced," Cehmai said.

The envoy seemed somewhat mollified. He had a small face, Maati thought. But perhaps it was only that Maati had already taken a dislike to the man.

"So Cehmai has been telling me about your project," Athai said, folding his hands in his lap. "A study of the prices meted out by failed bindings, is it?"

"A bit more than that," Maati said. "A mapping, rather, of the form of the binding to the form that its price took. What it was about this man's work that his blood went dry, or that one's that made his lungs fill with worms."

"You might consider not binding us in the first place," Stone-Made-Soft said. "If it's so dangerous as all that."

Maati ignored it. "I thought, you see, that there might be some way to better understand whether a poet's work was likely to fail or succeed if we knew more of how older failures presented themselves. It was an essay Heshai Antaburi wrote examining his own binding of Removing-the-Part-That-Continues that gave me the idea. You see his binding succeeded—he held Seedless for decades—but in having done the thing and then lived with the consequences, he could better see the flaws in his original work. Here . . ."

Maati rose up with a grunt and fished through his papers for a moment until the old, worn leather-bound book came to hand. Its cover was limp from years of reading, the pages growing yellow and smudged. The envoy took it and read a bit by the light of candles.

"But this is too much like his original work," Athai said as he thumbed through the pages. "It could never be used."

"No, of course not," Maati agreed. "But he made the attempt to examine the form of the binding, you see, in hopes that showing the kinds of errors he'd made might help others avoid things that were similar. Heshai-kvo was one of my first teachers."

"He was the one murdered in Saraykeht, ne?" Athai asked, not looking up from the book in his hands.

"Yes," Maati said.

Athai looked up, one hand taking an informal pose asking excuse.

"I didn't mean anything by asking," he said. "I only wanted to place him."

Maati brought himself to smile and nod.

"The reason I wrote to the Dai-kvo," Cehmai said, "was the application Maati-kvo was thinking of."

"Application?"

"It's too early yet to really examine closely," Maati said. He felt himself starting to blush, and his embarrassment at the thought fueled the blood in his face. "It's too early to say whether there's anything in it."

"Tell him," Cehmai said, his voice warm and coaxing. The envoy put Heshai-kvo's book down, his attention entirely on Maati now.

"There are . . . patterns," Maati said. "There seems to be a structure that links the form of the binding to its . . . its worst expression. Its price. The forms only seem random because it's a very complex structure. And I was reading Catji's meditations—the one from the Second Empire, not Catji Sano—and there are some speculations he made about the nature of language and grammar that . . . that seem related."

"He's found a way to shield a poet from paying the price," Cehmai said.

"I don't know that's true," Maati said quickly.

"But *possibly*," Cehmai said.

The envoy and the andat both shifted forward in their seats. The effect was eerie.

"I thought that, if a poet's first attempt at a binding didn't have to be his last—if an imperfect binding didn't mean death . . ."

Maati gestured helplessly at the air. He had spent so many hours thinking about what it could mean, about what it could bring about and bring back. All the andat lost over the course of generations that had been thought beyond recapture might still be bound if only the men binding them could learn from their errors, adjust their work as Heshai had done after the fact. Softness. Water-Moving-Down. Thinking-in-Words. All the spirits cataloged in the histories, the work of poets who had made the Empire great. Perhaps they were not past redemption.

He looked at Athai, but the young man's eyes were unfocused and distant.

"May I see your work, Maati-kvo?" he asked, and the barely suppressed excitement in his voice almost brought Maati to like him for the moment. Together, the three men stepped to Maati's worktable. Three men, and one other that was something else.

2

>+< Liat Chokavi had never seen seawater as green as the
bays near Amnat-Tan. The seafront at Saraykeht had
always taken its color from the sky—gray, blue, white, yellow, crimson, pink. The water in the far North was different
entirely; green as grass and numbing cold. She could no
more see the fish and seafloor here than read pages from a
closed book. These waters kept their secrets.

A low fog lay on the bay; the white and gray towers of the
low town seemed to float upon it. In the far distance, the deep
blue spire of the Khai Amnat-Tan's palace seemed almost to
glow, a lantern like a star fallen to earth. Even the sailors, she
noticed, would pause for a moment at their work and admire
it. It was the great wonder of Amnat-Tan, second only to
the towers of Machi as the signature of the winter cities. It
would take them days more to reach it; the ports and low
towns were a good distance downriver of the city itself.

The wind smelled of smoke now—the scent of the low town
coming across the water, adding to the smells of salt and fish,
crab and unwashed humanity. They would reach port by midday. She turned and went down the steps to their cabin.

Nayiit swung gently in his hammock, his eyes closed,
snoring lightly. Liat sat on the crate that held their belongings and considered her son; the long face, the unkempt hair,
the delicate hands folded on his belly. He had made an attempt at growing a beard in their time in Yalakeht, but it had

come in so poorly he'd shaved it off with a razor and cold seawater. Her heart ached, listening to him sleep. The workings of House Kyaan weren't so complex that it could not run without her immediate presence, but she had never meant to keep Nayiit so long from home and the family he had only recently begun.

The news had reached Saraykeht last summer—almost a year ago now. It had hardly been more than a confluence of rumors—a Galtic ship in Nantani slipping away before its cargo had arrived, a scandal at the Dai-kvo's village, inquiries discreetly made about a poet. And still, as her couriers arrived at the compound, Liat had felt unease growing in her. There were few enough people who knew as she did that the house she ran had been founded to keep watch on the duplicity of the Galts. Fewer still knew of the books she kept, as her mentor Amat Kyaan had before her, tracking the actions and strategies of the Galtic houses among the Khaiem, and it was a secret she meant to keep. So when tales of a missing poet began to dovetail too neatly with stories of Galtic intrigue in Nantani, there was no one whom she trusted the task to more than herself. She had been in Saraykeht for ten years. She decided to leave again the day that Nayiit's son Tai took his first steps.

Looking back, she wondered why it had been so easy for Nayiit to come with her. He and his wife were happy, she'd thought. The baby boy was delightful, and the work of the house engaging. When he had made the offer, she had hidden her pleasure at the thought and made only slight objections. The truth was that the years they had spent on the road when Nayiit had been a child—the time between her break with Maati Vaupathai and her return to the arms of Saraykeht— held a powerful nostalgia for her. Alone in the world with only a son barely halfway to manhood, she had expected struggle and pain and the emptiness that she had always thought must accompany a woman without a man.

The truth had been a surprise. Certainly the emptiness and struggle and pain had attended their travels. She and Nayiit had spent nights huddling under waxed-cloth tarps while chill rain pattered around them. They had eaten cheap food from low-town firekeepers. She had learned again all she'd known as a girl of how to mend a robe or a boot. And she had discovered a competence she had never believed herself to possess. Before that, she had always had a lover by whom to judge herself. With a son, she found herself stronger, smarter, more complete than she had dared pretend.

The journey to Nantani had been a chance for her to relive that, one last time. Her son was a man now, with a child of his own. There wouldn't be many more travels, just the two of them. So she had put aside any doubts, welcomed him, and set off to discover what she could about Riaan Vaudathat, son of a high family of the Nantani utkhaiem and missing poet. She had expected the work to take a season, no more. They would be back in the compound of House Kyaan in time to spend the autumn haggling over contracts and shipping prices.

And now it was spring, and she saw no prospect of sleeping in a bed she might call her own any time soon. Nayiit had not complained when it became clear that their investigation would require a journey to the village of the Dai-kvo. As a woman, Liat was not permitted beyond the low towns approaching it. She would need a man to do her business within the halls of the Dai-kvo's palaces. They had booked passage to Yalakeht, and then upriver. They had arrived at mid-autumn and hardly finished their investigation before Candles Night. So far North, there had been no ship back to Saraykeht, and Liat had taken apartments for them in the narrow, gated streets of Yalakeht for the winter.

In the long, dark hours she had struggled with what she knew, and with the thaw and the first ships taking passages North, she had prepared to travel to Amnat-Tan, and then Cetani. And then, though the prospect made her sick with anxiety, Machi.

A shout rose on the deck above them—a score of men calling out to each other—and the ship lurched and boomed. Nayiit blinked awake, looked over at her, and smiled. He always had had a good smile.

"Have I missed anything?" he asked with a yawn.

"We've reached the low towns outside Amnat-Tan," Liat said. "We'll be docked soon."

Nayiit swung his legs around, planting them on the deck to keep his hammock from rocking. He looked ruefully around the tiny cabin and sighed.

"I'll start packing our things, then," he said.

"Pack them separate," she said. "I'll go the rest of the way myself. I want you back in Saraykeht."

Nayiit took a pose that refused this, and Liat felt her jaw tighten.

"We've had this conversation, Mother. I'm not putting you out to walk the North Road by yourself."

"I'll hire a seat on a caravan," she said. "Spring's just opening, and there are bound to be any number of them going to Cetani and back. It's not such a long journey, really."

"Good. Then it won't take too long for us to get there."

"You're going back," Liat said.

Nayiit sighed and gathered himself visibly.

"Fine," he said. "Make your argument. Convince me."

Liat looked at her hands. It was the same problem she'd fought all through the long winter. Each time she'd come close to speaking the truth, something had held her back. Secrets. It all came back to secrets, and if she spoke her fears to Nayiit, it would mean telling him things that only she knew, things that she had hoped might die with her.

"Is it about my father?" he said, and his voice was so gentle, Liat felt tears gathering in her eyes.

"In a way," she said.

"I know he's at the court of Machi," Nayiit said. "There's no reason for me to fear him, is there? Everything you've said of him—"

"No, Maati would never hurt you. Or me. It's just . . . it was so long ago. And I don't know who he's become since then."

Nayiit leaned forward, taking her hands in his.

"I want to meet him," he said. "Not because of who he was

to you, or who he is now. I want to meet him because he's my father. Ever since Tai came, I've been thinking about it. About what it would be for me to walk away from my boy and not come back. About choosing something else over my family."

"It wasn't like that," Liat said. "Maati and I were . . ."

"I've come this far," he said gently. "You can't send me back now."

"You don't understand," she said.

"You can explain to me while I pack our things."

In the end, of course, he won. She had known he would. Nayiit could be as soft and gentle and implacable as snowfall. He was his father's son.

The calls of gulls grew louder as they neared the shore, the scent of smoke more present. The docks were narrower than the seafront of Saraykeht. A ship that put in here for the winter had to prepare itself to be icebound, immobile. Trade was with the eastern islands and Yalakeht; it was too far from the summer cities or Bakta or Galt for ships to come from those distant ports.

The streets were black cobbles, and ice still haunted the alleys where shadows held the cold. Nayiit carried their crate strapped across his back. The wide leather belt cut into his shoulders, but he didn't complain. He rarely complained about anything, only did what he thought best with a pleasant smile and a calm explanation ready to hand.

Liat stopped at a firekeeper's kiln to ask directions to the compound of House Radaani and was pleased to discover it was nearby. Mother and son, they walked the fog-shrouded streets until they found the wide arches that opened to the courtyard gardens of the Radaani, torches flickering and guttering in the damp air. A boy in sodden robes rushed up and lifted the crate from Nayiit's back to his own. Liat was about to address him when another voice, a woman's voice lovely and low as a singer's, came from the dim.

"Liat-cha, I must assume. I'd sent men to meet you at the docks, but I'm afraid they came too late."

The woman who stepped out from the fog had seen no more than twenty summers. Her robes were white snowfox, eerie in the combination of pale mourning colors and the luxury of the fur. Her hair shone black with cords of silver woven in the braids. She was beautiful, and likely would be for another five summers. Liat could already see the presentiment of jowls at the borders of her jaw.

"Ceinat Radaani," Liat said, taking a pose of gratitude. "I am pleased to meet you in person at last. This is my son, Nayiit."

The Radaani girl adopted a welcoming pose that included them both. Nayiit returned it, and Liat couldn't help noticing the way his eyes lingered on her and hers on him. Liat coughed, bringing their attention back to the moment. The girl took a pose of apology, and turned to lead them into the chambers and corridors of the compound.

In Saraykeht, the architecture tended to be open, encouraging the breezes to flow and cool. Northern buildings were more like great kilns, built to hold heat in their thick stone walls. The ceilings were low and fire grates burned in every room. The Radaani girl led them through a wide entrance chamber and back through a narrow corridor, speaking as she walked.

"My father is in Council with the Khai, but sends his regards and intends to join us as soon as he can return from the city proper. He would very much regret missing the opportunity to meet with the head of our trading partner in the South."

It was bald flattery. Radaani was among the richest houses in the winter cities, and had agreements with dozens of houses, all through the cities of the Khaiem. The whole of House Kyaan would hardly have made up one of the Radaani compounds, and there were four such compounds that Liat knew of. Liat accepted it, though, as if it were true, as if the hospitality extended to her were more than etiquette.

"I look forward to speaking with him," Liat said. "I am most interested in hearing news of the winter cities."

"Oh, there'll be quite a bit to say, I'm sure," the girl laughed. "There always is once winter's ended. I think people save up all the gossip of the winter to haul out in spring."

She opened a pair of wide wooden doors and led them into small, cozy apartments. A fire popped and murmured in the grate, bowls of mulled wine waited steaming on a low wooden table, and archways to either side showed rooms with real beds waiting for them. Liat's body seemed drawn to the bed like a stone rolling downhill. She had not realized how much she loathed shipboard hammocks.

She took a pose of thanks that the girl responded to neatly as the servant boy put the crate down gently by the fire.

"I will let you rest," the girl said. "If you have need of me, any of the servants can find me for you. And I will, of course, send word when my father returns."

"You're very kind," Nayiit said, smiling his disarming smile. "Forgive me, but is there a bathhouse near? I don't think shipboard life has left me entirely prepared for good company."

"Of course," the girl said. "I would be pleased to show you the way."

I'm sure you would, Liat thought. Was I so obvious at her age?

"Mother," Nayiit said, "would you care to . . ."

Liat waved the offer away.

"A basin and a sponge will be enough for me. I have letters to write before dinner. Perhaps, Ceinat-cha, if you would leave word with your couriers that I will have things to send south?"

The girl took an acknowledging pose, then turned to Nayiit with a flutter of a smile and gestured for him to follow her.

"Nayiit," Liat said, and her son paused in the apartment's doorway. "Find out what you can about the situation in Machi. I'd like to know what we're walking into."

Nayiit smiled, nodded, and vanished. The servant boy also left, promising the basin and sponge shortly. Liat sighed and sat down, stretching her feet out toward the burning logs. The wine tasted good, though slightly overspiced to her taste.

Machi. She was going to Machi. She let her mind turn the fact over again, as if it were a puzzle she had nearly solved. She was going to present her discoveries and her fears to the man she'd once called a lover, back when he'd been a seafront laborer and called himself Itani. Now he was the Khai Machi. And Maati, with whom she had betrayed him. The idea tightened her throat every time she thought of it.

Maati. Nayiit was going to see Maati, perhaps to confront him, perhaps to seek the sort of advice that a son can ask only of a father. Something, perhaps, that touched on the finer points of going to foreign bathhouses with young women in snowfox robes. Liat sighed.

Nayiit had been thinking about what it would be to walk away from his wife, the son he'd brought to the world. He'd said as much, and more than once. She had thought it was a question based in anger—an accusation against Maati. It only now occurred to her that perhaps there was also longing in it, and she thought to wonder how complex her quiet, pleasant son's heart might be.

BALASAR LEANED over the balcony and looked down at the courtyard below. A crowd had gathered, talking animatedly with the brown-skinned, almond-eyed curiosity he had spirited from across the sea. They peppered him with questions— why was he called a poet when he didn't write poems, what did he think of Acton, how had he learned to speak Galtic so well. Their eyes were bright and the conversation as lively as water dropped on a hot skillet. For his part, Riaan Vaudathat drank it all in, answering everything in the slushy singsong accent of the Khaiem. When the people laughed, he joined in as if they were not laughing at him. Perhaps he truly didn't know they were.

Riaan glanced up and saw him, raising his hands in a pose that Balasar recognized as a form of greeting, though he couldn't have said which of the half-thousand possible nuances it held. He only waved in return and stepped away from the edge of the balcony.

"It's like I've taught a dog to wear clothes and talk," Balasar said, lowering himself onto a bench beside Eustin.

"Yes, sir."

"They don't understand."

"You can't expect them to, sir. They're simple folk, most of 'em. Never been as far as Eddensea. They've been hearing about the Khaiem and the poets and the andat all their lives, but they've never seen 'em. Now they have the chance."

"Well, it'll help my popularity at the games," Balasar said, his voice more bitter than he'd intended.

"They don't know the things we do, sir. You can't expect them to think like us."

"And the High Council? Can I expect it of them? Or are they in chambers talking about the funny brown man who dresses like a girl?"

Eustin looked down, silent for long enough that Balasar began to regret his tone.

"All fairness, sir," Eustin said, "the robes do look like a girl's."

It was six years now since he and Eustin and Coal had returned to the hereditary estate outside Kirinton, half a year since they had recruited the fallen poet of Nantani, and three weeks since Balasar had received the expected summons. He'd come to Acton with his best men, the books, the poet, the plans. The High Council had heard him out—the dangers of the andat, the need to end the supremacy of the Khaiem. That part had gone quite well. No one seriously disputed that the Khaiem were the single greatest threat to Galt. It was only when he began to reveal his plans and how far he had already gone that the audience began to turn sour on him.

Since then, the Council had met without him. They might have been debating the plan he had laid out before them, or they might have moved to other business, leaving him to soak in his own sweat. He and Eustin and the poet Riaan had lived in the apartments assigned to them. Balasar had spent his days sitting outside the Council's halls and meeting chambers, and his nights walking the starlit streets, restless as a ghost. Each hour that passed was wasted. Every night was one less that he would have in the autumn when the end of his army was racing against the snow and cold of the Khaiate North. If the Council's intention had been to set him on edge, they had done their work.

A flock of birds, black as crows but thinner, burst from the walnut trees beyond the courtyard, whirled overhead, and settled back where they had come from. Balasar wove his fingers together on one knee.

"What do we do if they don't move forward?" Eustin asked quietly.

"Convince them."

"And if they can't be convinced?"

"Convince them anyway," Balasar said.

Eustin nodded. Balasar appreciated that the man didn't press the issue. Eustin had known him long enough to understand that bloody-mindedness was how Balasar moved through the world. From the beginning, he'd been cursed by a small stature, a shorter reach than his brothers or the boys with whom he'd trained. He'd gotten used to working himself harder, training while other boys slept and drank and whored. Where he couldn't make himself bigger or stronger, he instead became fast and smart and uncompromising.

When he became a man of arms in the service of Galt, he had been the smallest in his cohort. And in time, they had named him general. If the High Council needed to be convinced, then he would by God convince them.

A polite cough came from the archways behind them, and Balasar turned. A secretary of the Council stood in the shade of the wide colonnade. As Balasar and Eustin rose, he bowed slightly at the waist.

"General Gice," the secretary said. "The Lord Convocate requests your presence."

"Good," Balasar said, then turned to Eustin and spoke

quickly and low. "Stay here and keep an eye on our friend. If this goes poorly, we may need to make good time out of Acton."

Eustin nodded, his face as calm and impassive as if Balasar asked him to turn against the High Council half the days of any week. Balasar tugged his vest and sleeves into place, nodded to the secretary, and allowed himself to be led into the shadows of government.

The path beneath the colonnade led into a maze of hallways as old as Galt itself. The air seemed ancient, thick and dusty and close with the breath of men generations dead. The secretary led Balasar up a stone stairway worn treacherously smooth by a river of footsteps to a wide door of dark and carved wood. Balasar scratched on it, and a booming voice called him in.

The meeting room was wide and long, with a glassed-in terrace that looked out over the city and shelves lining the walls with books and rolled maps. Low leather couches squatted by an iron fireplace, a low rosewood table between them with dried fruits and glass flutes ready for wine. And standing at the terrace's center looking out over the city, the Lord Convocate, a great gray bear of a man.

Balasar closed the door behind him and walked over to the man's side. Acton spilled out before them—smoke and grime, broad avenues where steam wagons chuffed their slow way through the city taking on passengers for a half-copper a ride laced with lanes so narrow a man's shoulders could touch the walls on either side. For a moment, Balasar recalled the ruins in the desert, placing the memory over the view before him. Reminding himself again of the stakes he played for.

"I've been riding herd on the Council since you gave your report. They aren't happy," the Lord Convocate said. "The High Council doesn't look favorably on men of . . . what should I call it? Profound initiative? None of them had any idea you'd gone so far. Not even your father. It was impolitic."

"I'm not a man of politics."

The Lord Convocate laughed.

"You've led an army on campaign," he said. "If you didn't understand something of how to manage men, you'd be feeding some Westland tree by now."

Balasar shrugged. It wasn't what he'd meant to do; it was the moment to come across as controlled, loyal, reliable as stone, and here he was shrugging like a petulant schoolboy. He forced himself to smile.

"I suppose you're right," he said.

"But you know they would have refused you."

"*Know* is a strong word. Suspected."

"Feared?"

"Perhaps."

"Fourteen cities in a single season. It can't be done, Balasar. Uther Redcape couldn't have done it."

"Uther was fighting in Eddensea," Balasar said. "They have walls around cities in Eddensea. They have armies. The Khaiem haven't got anything but the andat."

"The andat suffice."

"Only if they have them."

"Ah. Yes. That's the center of the question, isn't it? Your grand plan to do away with all the andat at a single blow. I have to confess, I don't think I quite follow how you expect this to work. You have one of these poets here, ready to work with us. Wouldn't it be better to capture one of these andat for ourselves?"

"We will be. Freedom-From-Bondage should be one of the simplest andat to capture. It's never been done, so there's no worry about coming too near what's been tried before. The binding has been discussed literally for centuries. I've found books of commentary and analysis dating back to the First Empire . . ."

"All of it exploring exactly why it can't be done, yes?" The Lord Convocate's voice had gone as gentle and sympathetic as that of a medic trying to lead a man to realize his own dementia. It was a ploy. The old man wanted to see whether Balasar would lose his temper, so instead he smiled.

"That depends on what you mean by impossible."

The Lord Convocate nodded and stepped to the windows, his hands clasped behind his back. Balasar waited for three breaths, four. The impulse to shake the old man, to shout that every day was precious and the price of failure horrible beyond contemplation, rose in him and fell. This was the battle now, and as important as any of those to come.

"So," the Lord Convocate said, turning. "Explain to me how *cannot* means *can*."

Balasar gestured toward the couches. They sat, leather creaking beneath them.

"The andat are ideas translated into forms that include volition," Balasar said. "A poet who's bound something like, for example, Wood-Upon-Water gains control over the expression of that thought in the world. He could raise a sunken vessel up or sink all the ships on the sea with a thought, if he wished it. The time required to create the binding is measured in years. If it succeeds, the poet's life work is to hold the thing here in the world and train someone to take it from him when he grows old or infirm."

"You're telling me what I know," the old man said, but Balasar raised a hand, stopping him.

"I'm telling you what *they* mean when they say impossible. They mean that Freedom-From-Bondage can't be *held*. There is no way to control something that is the essential nature and definition of the uncontrolled. But they make no distinction between being invoked and being maintained."

The Lord Convocate frowned and rubbed his fingertips together.

"We can bind it, sir. Riaan isn't the talent of the ages, but Freedom-From-Bondage should be easy compared with the normal run. The whole binding's nearly done already—only a little tailoring to make it fit our man's mind in particular."

"That comes back to the issue," the Lord Convocate said. "What happens when this impossible binding works?"

"As soon as it is bound it is freed." Balasar clapped his palms together. "That fast."

"And the advantage of that?" the Lord Convocate said,

though Balasar could see the old man had already traced out the implications.

"Done well, with the right grammar, the right nuances, it will unbind every andat there is when it goes. All of this was in my report to the High Council."

The Lord Convocate nodded as he plucked a circle of dried apple from the bowl between them. When he spoke again, however, it was as if Balasar's objection had never occurred.

"Assuming it works, that you can take the andat from the field of play, what's to stop the Khaiem from having their poets make another andat and loose it on Galt?"

"Swords," Balasar said. "As you said, fourteen cities in a single season. None of them will have enough time. I have men in every city of the Khaiem, ready to meet us with knowledge of the defenses and strengths we face. There are agreements with mercenary companies to support our men. Four well-equipped, well-supported forces, each taking unfortified, poorly armed cities. But we have to start moving men now. This is going to take time, and I don't want to be caught in the North waiting to see which comes first, the thaw or some overly clever poet in Cetani or Machi managing to bind something new. We have to move quickly—kill the poets, take the libraries—"

"After which we can go about making andat of our own at our leisure," the Lord Convocate said. His voice was thoughtful, and still Balasar sensed a trap. He wondered how much the man had guessed of his own plans and intentions for the future of the andat.

"If that's what the High Council chooses to do," Balasar said, sitting back. "All of this, of course, assuming I'm given permission to move forward."

"Ah," the Lord Convocate said, lacing his hands over his belly. "Yes. That will need an answer. Permission of the Council. A thousand things could go wrong. And if you fail—"

"The stakes are no lower if we sit on our hands. And we could wait forever and never see a better chance," Balasar said. "You'll forgive my saying it, sir, but you haven't said no."

"No," he said, slowly. "No, I haven't."

"Then I have the command, sir?"

After a moment, the Lord Convocate nodded.

3

>+< "What's the matter?" Kiyan asked. She was already dressed in the silk shift that she slept in, her hair tied back from her thin foxlike face. It occurred to Otah for the first time just how long ago the sun had set. He sat on the bed at her side and let himself feel the aches in his back and knees.

"Sitting too long," he said. "I don't know why doing nothing should hurt as badly as hauling crates."

Kiyan put a hand against his back, her fingers tracing his spine through the fine-spun wool of his robes.

"For one thing, you haven't hauled a crate for your living in thirty summers."

"Twenty-five," he said, leaning back into the soft pressure of her hands. "Twenty-six now."

"For another, you've hardly done nothing. As I recall, you were awake before the sun rose."

Otah considered the sleeping chamber—the domed ceiling worked in silver, the wood and bone inlay of the floor and walls, the rich gold netting that draped the bed, the still, somber flame of the lantern. The east wall was stone—pink granite thin as eggshell that glowed when the sun struck it. He couldn't recall how long it had been since he'd woken to see that light. Last summer, perhaps, when the nights were shorter. He closed his eyes and lay back into the soft, enfolding bed. His weight pressed out the scent of crushed rose petals. Eyes closed, he felt Kiyan shift, the familiar warmth and weight of her body resting against him. She kissed his temple.

"Our friend from the Dai-kvo will finally leave soon. A message came recalling him," Otah said. "That was a bright moment. Though the gods only know what kept him here so long. Sinja's likely halfway to the Westlands by now."

"The envoy stayed for Maati's work," Kiyan said. "Apparently he hardly left the library these last weeks. Eiah's been keeping me informed."

"Well, the gods and Eiah, then," Otah said.

"I'm worried about her. She's brooding about something. Can you speak with her?"

Dread touched Otah's belly, and a moment's resentment. It had been such a long day, and here waiting for him like a stalking cat was another problem, another need he was expected to meet. The thought must have expressed itself in his body, because Kiyan sighed and rolled just slightly away.

"You think it's wrong of me," Kiyan said.

"Not wrong," Otah said. "Unnecessary isn't wrong."

"I know. At her age, you were living on the streets in the summer cities, stealing pigeons off firekeeper's kilns and sleeping in alleys. And you came through just fine."

"Oh," Otah said. "Have I told that story already?"

"Once or twice," she said, laughing gently. "It's just that she seems so distant. I think there's something bothering her that she won't say. And then I wonder whether it's only that she won't say it to me."

"And why would she talk to me if she won't she talk to you?"

When he felt Kiyan shrug, Otah opened his eyes and rolled to his side. There were tears shining in his lover's eyes, but her expression was more amused than sorrowful. He touched her cheek with his fingertips, and she kissed his palm absently.

"I don't know. Because you're her father, and I'm only her mother? It was just . . . a hope. The problem is that she's half a woman," Kiyan said. "When the sun's up, I know that. I remember when I was that age. My father had me running half of his wayhouse, or that's how it felt back then. Up before the clients, cooking sausages and barley. Cleaning the rooms during the day. He and Old Mani would take care of the evenings, though. They wanted to sell as much wine as they could, but they didn't want a girl my age around drunken travelers. I thought they were being so unfair."

Kiyan pursed her lips.

"But maybe *I've* told *that* story already," she said.

"Once or twice," Otah agreed.

"There was a time I didn't worry about the whole world and everything in it, you know. I remember that there was. It doesn't make sense to me. One bad season, an illness, a fire—anything, really, and I could have lost the wayhouse. But now here I am, highest of the Khaiem, a whole city that will bend itself in half to hand me whatever it thinks I want, and the world seems more fragile."

"We got old," Otah said. "It's always the ones who've seen the most who think the world's on the edge of collapse, isn't it? And we've seen more than most."

Kiyan shook her head.

"It's more than that. Losing a wayhouse would have made the world harder for me and Old Mani. There are more people than I can count here in the city, and all the low towns. And you carry them. It makes it matter more."

"I sit through days of ceremony and let myself be hectored over the things I don't do the way other people prefer," Otah said. "I'm not sure that anything I've done here has actually made any difference at all. If they stuffed a robe with cotton and posed the sleeves . . ."

"You care about them," Kiyan said.

"I don't," he said. "I care about you and Eiah and Danat. And Maati. I know that I'm supposed to care about everyone and everything in Machi, but love, I'm only a man. They can tell me I gave up my own name when I took the chair, but really the Khai Machi is only what I do. I wouldn't keep the work if I could find a way out."

Kiyan embraced him with one arm. Her hair was fragrant with lavender oil.

"You're sweet," she said.

"Am I? I'll try to confess my incompetence and selfishness more often."

"As long as it includes me," she said. "Now go let those poor men change your clothes and get back to beds of their own."

The servants had become accustomed to the Khai's preference for brief ablutions. Otah knew that his own father had managed somehow to enjoy the ceremony of being dressed and bathed by others. But his father had been raised to take the chair, had followed the traditions and forms of etiquette, and had never, that Otah knew of, stepped outside the role he'd been born to. Otah himself had been turned out, and the years he had spent being a simple, free man, reliant upon himself had ruined him for the fawning of the court. He endured the daily frivolity of having foods brought to him, his hands cleaned for him, his hair combed on his behalf. He allowed the body servants to pull off his formal robes and swathe him in a sleeping shift, and when he returned to his bed, Kiyan's breath was already deep, slow, and heavy. He slipped in beside her, pulling the blankets up over himself, and closed his eyes at last.

Sleep, however, did not come. His body ached, his eyes were tired, but it seemed that the moment he laid his head back, Otah's mind woke. He listened to the sounds of the palace in night: the almost silent wind through a distant window, the deep and subtle ticking of cooling stone, the breath of the woman at his side. Beyond the doors to the apartments, someone coughed—one of the servants set to watch over the Khai Machi in case there was anything he should desire in the night. Otah tried not to move.

He hadn't asked Kiyan about Danat's health. He'd meant to. But surely if there had been anything concerning, she would have brought it up to him. And regardless, he could ask her in the morning. Perhaps he would cancel the audiences before midday and go speak with Danat's physicians. And speak to Eiah. He hadn't said he would do that, but Kiyan had asked, and it wasn't as if being present in his own daughter's life should be an imposition. He wondered what it would have been to have a dozen wives, whether he would have felt the need to attend to all of their children as he did to the two he had now, how he would have stood watching his boys grow up when he knew he would have to send them away or else watch them slaughter one another over which of them would take his own place here on this soft, sleepless bed and fear in turn for his own sons.

The night candle ate through its marks as he listened to the internal voice nattering in his mind, gnawing at half a thousand worries both justified and inane. The trade agreements with Udun weren't in place yet. Perhaps something really was the matter with Eiah. He didn't know how long stone buildings stood; nothing stands forever, so it only made sense that someday the palaces would fall. And the towers. The towers reached so high it seemed that low clouds would touch them; what would he do if they fell? But the night was passing and he had to sleep. If he didn't the morning would be worse. He should talk with Maati, find out how things had gone between him and the Dai-kvo's envoy. Perhaps a dinner.

And on, and on, and on. When he gave up, slipping from the bed softly to let Kiyan, at least, sleep, the night candle was past its three-quarter mark. Otah walked to the apartment's main doors on bare, chilled feet and found his keeper in the hall outside dozing. He was a young man, likely the son of some favored servant or slave of Otah's own father, given the honor of sitting alone in the darkness, bored and cold. Otah considered the boy's soft face, as peaceful in sleep as a corpse's, and walked silently past him and into the dim hallways of the palace.

His night walks had been growing more frequent in recent months. Sometimes twice in a week, Otah found himself wandering in the darkness, sleep a stranger to him. He avoided the places where he might encounter another person, jealously keeping the time to himself. Tonight, he took a lantern and walked down the long stairways to the ground, and then on down, to the tunnels and underground streets into which the city retreated in the deep, bone-breaking cold of winter. With spring come, Otah found the palace beneath the palace empty and silent. The smell of old torches, long gone dark, still lingered in the air, and Otah imagined the corridors and galleries of the city descending forever into the earth. Dark archways and domed sleeping chambers cut from stone that had never seen daylight, narrow stairways leading endlessly down like a thing from a children's song.

He didn't consider where he intended to go until he reached his father's crypt and found himself unsurprised to be there. The dark stone seemed to wrap itself in shadows, words of ancient language cut deep into the walls. An ornate pedestal held the pale urn, a dead flower. And beneath it, three small boxes—the remains of Biitrah, Danat, Kaiin. Otah's brothers, dead in the struggle to become the new Khai Machi. Lives cut short for the honor of having a pedestal of their own someday, deep in the darkness.

Otah sat on the bare floor, the lantern at his side, and contemplated the man he'd never known or loved whose place he had taken. Here was how his own end would look. An urn, a tomb, high honors and reverence for bones and ashes. And between the chill floor and the pale urn, perhaps another thirty summers. Perhaps forty. Years of ceremony and negotiation, late nights and early mornings and little else.

But when the time came, at least his crypt would be only his own. Danat, brotherless, wouldn't be called upon to kill or die in the succession. There would be no second sons left to kill the other for the black chair. It seemed a thin solace, having given so much of himself to achieve something that a merchant's son could have had for free.

It would have been easier if he'd never been anything but this. A man born into the Khaiem who had never stepped outside wouldn't carry the memories of fishing in the eastern islands, of eating at the wayhouses outside Yalakeht, of being free. If he could have forgotten it all, becoming the man he was supposed to be might have been easier. Instead he was driven to follow his own judgment, raise a militia, take only one wife, raise only one son. That his experience told him that he was right didn't make bearing the world's disapproval as easy as he'd hoped.

The lantern flame guttered and spat. Otah shook his head, uncertain now how long he had been lost in his reverie. When he stood, his left leg had gone numb from being pressed too long against the bare stone. He took up the lantern and walked—moving slowly and carefully to protect his numbed foot—back toward the stairways that would return him to the surface and the day. By the time he regained the great halls, feeling had returned. The sky peeked through the windows, a pale gray preparing itself to blue. Voices echoed and the palaces woke, and the grand, stately beast that was the court of Machi stirred and stretched.

His apartments, when he reached them, were a flurry of activity. A knot of servants and members of the utkhaiem gabbled like peahens, Kiyan in their center listening with a seriousness and sympathy that only he knew masked amusement. Her hand was on the shoulder of the body servant whom Otah had passed, the peace of sleep banished and anxiety in its place.

"Gentlemen," Otah said, letting his voice boom, calling their attention to him. "Is there something amiss?"

To a man, they adopted poses of obeisance and welcome. Otah responded automatically now, as he did half a hundred times every day.

"Most High," a thin-voiced man said—his Master of Tides. "We came to prepare you and found your bed empty."

Otah looked at Kiyan, whose single raised brow told them that empty had only meant empty of him, and that she'd have been quite pleased to keep sleeping.

"I was walking," he said.

"We may not have the time to prepare you for the audience with the envoy from Tan-Sadar," the Master of Tides said.

"Put him off," Otah said, walking through the knot of people to the door of his apartments. "Reschedule everything you have for me today."

The Master of Tides gaped like a trout in air. Otah paused, his hands in a query that asked if the words bore repeating. The Master of Tides adopted an acknowledging pose.

"The rest of you," he said, "I would like breakfast served in my apartments here. And send for my children."

"Eiah-cha's tutors . . ." one of the others began, but Otah looked at the man and he seemed to forget what he'd been saying.

"I will be taking the day with my family," Otah said.

"You will start rumors, Most High," another said. "They'll say the boy's cough has grown worse again."

"And I would like black tea with the meal," Otah said. "In fact, bring the tea first. I'll be in by the fire, warming my feet."

He stepped in, and Kiyan followed, closing the door behind her.

"Bad night?" she asked.

"Sleepless," he said as he sat by the fire grate. "That's all."

Kiyan kissed the top of his head where she assured him that the hair was not thinning, and stepped out of the room. He heard the soft rustle of cloth against stone and Kiyan's low, contented humming, and knew she was changing her robes. The warmth of the fire pressed against the soles of his feet like a comforting hand, and he closed his eyes for a moment.

No building stands forever, he thought. Even palaces fall. Even towers. He wondered what it would have been like to live in a world where Machi didn't exist—who he might have been, what he might have done—and he felt the weight of stone pressing down upon the air he breathed. What would he do if the towers fell? Where would he go, if he could go anywhere?

"Papa-kya!" Danat's bright voice called. "I was in the

Second Palace, and I found a closet where no one had been in ever, and look what I found!"

Otah opened his eyes, and turned to his son and the wood-and-string model he'd discovered. Eiah arrived a hand and a half later, when the thin granite shutters glowed with the sun. For a time, at least, Otah's own father's tomb lay forgotten.

THE PROBLEM with Athai-kvo, Maati decided, was that he was simply an unlikable man. There was no single thing that he did or said, no single habit or effect that made him grate on the nerves of all those around him. Some men were charming, and would be loved however questionable their behavior. And then on the other end of the balance, there was Athai. The weeks he had spent with the man had been bear-able only because of the near-constant stream of praise and admiration given to Maati.

"It will change everything," the envoy said as they sat on the steps of the poet's house—Cehmai's residence. "This is going to begin a new age to rival the Second Empire."

"Because that ended so well," Stone-Made-Soft rumbled, its tone amused as always.

The morning was warm. The sculpted oaks separating the poet's house from the palaces were bright with new leaves. Far above, barely visible through the boughs, the stone towers rose into the sky. Cehmai reached across the envoy to pour more rice wine into Maati's bowl.

"It is early yet to pass judgment," Maati said as he nodded his thanks to Cehmai. "It isn't as though the techniques have been tried."

"But it makes sense," Athai said. "I'm sure it will work."

"If we've overlooked something, the first poet to try this is likely to die badly," Cehmai said. "The Dai-kvo will want a fair amount of study done before he puts a poet's life on the table."

"Next year," Athai said. "I'll wager twenty lengths of sil-ver it will be used in bindings by this time next year."

"Done," the andat said, then turned to Cehmai. "You can back me if I lose."

The poet didn't reply, but Maati saw the amusement at the corners of Cehmai's mouth. It had taken years to understand the ways in which Stone-Made-Soft was an expression of Cehmai, the ways they were a single thing, and the ways they were at war. The small comments the andat made that only Cehmai understood, the unspoken moments of private struggle that sometimes clouded the poet's days. They were like nothing so much as a married couple, long accustomed to each other's ways.

Maati sipped the rice wine. It was infused with peaches, a moment of autumn's harvest in the opening of spring. Athai looked away from the andat's broad face, discomforted.

"You must be ready to return to the Dai-kvo," Cehmai said. "You've been away longer than you'd intended."

Athai waved the concern away, pleased, Maati thought, to speak to the man and forget the andat.

"I wouldn't have traded this away," he said. "Maati-kvo is going to be remembered as the greatest poet of our generation."

"Have some more wine," Maati said, clinking the envoy's bowl with his own, but Cehmai shook his head and gestured toward the wooded path. A slave girl was trotting toward them, her robes billowing behind her. Athai put down his bowl and stood, pulling at his sleeves. Here was the moment they had been awaiting—the call for Athai to join the caravan to the East. Maati sighed with relief. Half a hand, and his library would be his own again. The envoy took a formal pose of farewell that Maati and Cehmai returned.

"I will send word as soon as I can, Maati-kvo," Athai said. "I am honored to have studied with you."

Maati nodded uncomfortably; then, after a moment's awkward silence, Athai turned. Maati watched until the slave girl and poet had both vanished among the trees, then let out a breath. Cehmai chuckled as he put the stopper into the flask of wine.

"Yes, I agree," Cehmai said. "I think the Dai-kvo must have chosen him specifically to annoy the Khai."

"Or he just wanted to be rid of him for a time," Maati said.

"I liked him," Stone-Made-Soft said. "Well, as much as I like anyone."

The three walked together into the poet's house. The rooms within were neatly kept—shelves of books and scrolls, soft couches and a table laid out with the black and white stones on their board. A lemon candle burned at the window, but a fly still buzzed wildly about the corners of the room. It seemed that every winter Maati forgot about the existence of flies, only to rediscover them in spring. He wondered where the insects all went during the vicious cold, and what the signal was for them to return.

"He isn't wrong, you know," Cehmai said. "If you're right, it will be the most important piece of analysis since the fall of the Empire."

"I've likely overlooked something. It isn't as though we haven't seen half a hundred schemes to bring back the glory of the past before now, and there hasn't been one that's done it."

"And I wasn't there to look at the other ideas," Cehmai said. "But since I was here to talk this one over, I'd say this is at least plausible. That's more than most. And the Dai-kvo's likely to think the same."

"He'll probably dismiss it out of hand," Maati said, but he smiled as he spoke.

Cehmai had been the first one he'd shown his theories to, even before he'd known for certain what they were. It had been a curiosity more than anything else. It was only as they'd talked about it that Maati had understood the depths he'd touched upon. And Cehmai had also been the one to encourage bringing the work to the Dai-kvo's attention. All Athai's enthusiasm and hyperbole paled beside a few thoughtful words from Cehmai.

Maati stayed awhile, talking and laughing, comparing impressions of Athai now that he'd left. And then he took his leave, walking slowly enough that he didn't become short of breath. Fourteen, almost fifteen years ago, he'd come to Machi. The black stone roadways, the constant scent of the coal smoke billowing up from the forges, the grandeur of the palaces and the hidden city far beneath his feet had become his home as no other place ever had before. He strode down pathways of crushed marble, under archways that flowed with silken banners. A singing slave called from the gardens, a simple melody of amazing clarity and longing. He turned down a smaller way that would take him to his apartments behind the library.

Maati found himself wondering what he would do if the Dai-kvo truly thought his discovery had merit. It was an odd thought. He had spent so many years now in disgrace, first tainted by the death of his master Heshai, then by his choice to divide his loyalty between his lover and son on the one hand and the Dai-kvo on the other. And then at last his entrance into the politics of the court, wearing the robes of the poet and supporting Otah Machi, his old friend and enemy, to become Khai Machi. It had been simple enough to believe that his promotion to the ranks of the poets had been a mistake. He had, after all, been gifted certain insights by an older boy who had walked away from the school: Otah, before he'd been a laborer or a courier or a Khai. Maati had reconciled himself to a smaller life: the library, the companionship of a few friends and those lovers who would bed a disgraced poet halfway to fat with rich foods and long, inactive hours.

After so many years of failure, the thought that he might shake off that reputation was unreal. It was like a dream from which he could only hope never to wake, too pleasant to trust in.

Eiah was sitting on the steps when he arrived, frowning intently at a moth that had lighted on the back of her hand. Her face was such a clear mix of her parents—Kiyan's high cheeks, Otah's dark eyes and easy smile. Maati took a pose of greeting as he walked up, and when Eiah moved to reply, the moth took wing, chuffing softly through the air and away. In flight, the wings that had been simple brown shone black and orange.

"Athai's gone then?" she asked as Maati unlocked the doors to his apartments.

"He's likely just over the bridge by now."

Maati stepped in, Eiah following him without asking or being asked. It was a wide room, not so grand as the palaces or so comfortable as the poet's house. A librarian's room, ink blocks stacked beside a low desk, chairs with wine-stained cloth on the arms and back, a small bronze brazier dusted with old ash. Maati waved Eiah off as she started to close the door.

"Let the place air out a bit," he said. "It's warm enough for it now. And what's your day been, Eiah-kya?"

"Father," she said. "He was in a mood to have a family, so I had to stay in the palaces all morning. He fell asleep after midday, and Mother said I could leave."

"I'm surprised. I wasn't under the impression Otah slept anymore. He always seems hip-deep in running the city."

Eiah shrugged, neither agreeing nor voicing her denial. She paced the length of the room, squinting out the door at nothing. Maati folded his hands together on his belly, considering her.

"Something's bothering you," he said.

The girl shook her head, but the frown deepened. Maati waited until, with a quick, birdlike motion, Eiah turned to face him. She began to speak, stopped, and gathered herself visibly.

"I want to be married," she said.

Maati blinked, coughed to give himself a moment to think, and leaned forward in his chair. The wood and cloth creaked slightly beneath him. Eiah stood, her arms crossed, her gaze on him in something almost like accusation.

"Who is the boy?" Maati said, regretting the word *boy* as soon as it left his mouth. If they were speaking of marriage, the least he could do was say *man*. But Eiah's impatient snort dismissed the question.

"I don't know," she said. "Whoever."

"Anyone would do?"

"Not just anyone. I don't want to be tied to some low town firekeeper. I want someone good. And I should be able to. Father doesn't have any other daughters, and I know people have talked with him. But nothing ever happens. How long am I supposed to wait?"

Maati rubbed a palm across his cheeks. This was hardly a conversation he'd imagined himself having. He turned through half a hundred things he might say, approaches he might take, and felt a blush rising in his cheeks.

"You're young, Eiah-kya. I mean . . . I suppose it's natural enough for a young woman to . . . be interested in men. Your body is changing, and if I recall the age, there are certain feelings that it's . . ."

Eiah looked at him as if he'd coughed up a rat.

"Or perhaps I've misunderstood the issue," he said.

"It's not that," she said. "I've kissed lots of boys."

The blush wasn't growing less, but Maati resolved to ignore it.

"Ah," he said. "Well, then. If it's that you want apartments of your own, something outside the women's quarters, you could always—"

"Talit Radaani's being married to the third son of the Khai Pathai," Eiah said, and then a heartbeat later, "She's half a year younger than I am."

It was like feeling a puzzle box click open in his fingers. He understood precisely what was happening, what it meant and didn't mean. He rubbed his palms against his knees and sighed.

"And she gloats about that, I'd bet," he said. Eiah swiped at her betraying eyes with the back of a hand. "After all, she's younger and lower in the courts. She must think that she's got proof that she's terribly special."

Eiah shrugged.

"Or that you aren't," Maati continued, keeping his voice gentle to lessen the sting of the words. "That's what she thinks, isn't it?"

"I don't know what she thinks."

"Well, then tell me what you think."

"I don't know why he can't find me a husband. It isn't as if I'd have to leave. There's marriages that go on for years before anyone does anything. But it's understood. It's arranged. I don't see why he can't do that much for me."

"Have you asked him?"

"He should know this," Eiah snapped, pacing between the open door and the fire grate. "He's the Khai Machi. He isn't stupid."

"He also isn't . . ." Maati said and then bit down on the words *a child*. The woman Eiah thought she was would never stand for the name. "He isn't fourteen summers old. It's not so hard for men like me and your father to forget what it was like to be young. And I'm sure he doesn't want to see you married yet, or even promised. You're his daughter, and . . . it's hard, Eiah-kya. It's hard losing your child."

She stopped, her brow furrowed. In the trees just outside his door, a bird sang shrill and high and took flight. Maati could hear the fluttering of its wings.

"It's not losing me," she said, but her voice was less certain than it had been. "I don't die."

"No. You don't, but you'll likely leave to be in your husband's city. There's couriers to carry messages back and forth, but once you've left, it's not likely you'll return in Otah's life, or Kiyan's. Or mine. It's not death, but it is still loss, dear. And we've all lost so much already, it's hard to look forward to another."

"You could come with me," Eiah said. "My husband would take you in. He wouldn't be worth marrying if he wouldn't, so you could come with me."

Maati allowed himself to chuckle as he rose from his seat.

"It's too big a world to plan for all that just yet," he said, mussing Eiah's hair as he had when she'd been younger. "When we come nearer, we'll see where things stand. I may not be staying here at all, depending on what the Dai-kvo thinks. I might be able to go back to his village and use his libraries."

"Could I go there with you?"

"No, Eiah-kya. Women aren't allowed in the village. I know, I know. It isn't fair. But it isn't happening today, so why don't we walk to the kitchens and see if we can't talk them out of some sugar bread."

They left his door open, leaving the spring air and sunlight to freshen the apartments. The path to the kitchens led them through great, arching halls and across pavilions being prepared for a night's dancing; great silken banners celebrated the warmth and light. In the gardens, men and women lay back, eyes closed, faces to the sky like flowers. Outside the palaces, Maati knew, the city was still alive with commerce—the forges and metalworkers toiling through the night, as they always did, preparing to ship the works of Machi. There was bronze, iron, silver and gold, and steel. And the hand-shaped stonework that could be created only here, under the inhuman power of Stone-Made-Soft. None of that work was apparent in the palaces. The utkhaiem seemed carefree as cats. Maati wondered again how much of that was the studied casualness of court life and how much was simple sloth.

At the kitchens, it was simple enough for the Khai's daughter and his permanent guest to get thick slices of sugar bread wrapped in stiff cotton cloth and a stone flask of cold tea. He told Eiah all of what had happened with Athai since she'd last come to the library, and about the Dai-kvo, and the andat, and the world as Maati had known it in the years before he'd come to Machi. It was a pleasure to spend the time with the girl, flattering that she enjoyed his own company enough to seek him out, and perhaps just the slightest bit gratifying that she would speak to him of things that Otah-kvo never heard from her.

They parted company as the quick spring sun came within a hand's width of the western mountains. Maati stopped at a fountain, washing his fingers in the cool waters, and considered the evening that lay ahead. He'd heard that one of the winter choirs was performing at a teahouse not far from the palaces—the long, dark season's work brought out at last to the light. The thought tempted, but perhaps not more than a book, a flask of wine, and a bed with thick wool blankets.

He was so wrapped up by the petty choice of pleasures that he didn't notice that the lanterns had been lit in his apartments or that a woman was sitting on his couch until she spoke.

4

"Maati," Liat said, and the man startled like a rabbit. For a long moment, his face was a blank confusion as he struggled to make sense of what he saw. Slowly, she watched him recognize her.

In all fairness, she might not have known him either, had she not sought him out. Time had changed him: thickened his body and thinned his hair. Even his face had changed shape, the smooth chin and jaw giving way to jowls, the eyes going narrower and darker. The lines around his mouth spoke of sadness and isolation. And anger, she thought.

She had known when she arrived that she'd found the right apartments. It hadn't been difficult to get directions to Machi's extra poet, and the door had been open. She'd scratched at the doorframe, called out his name, and when she'd stepped in, it was the scent that had been familiar. Certainly there had been other things—the way the scrolls were laid out, the ink stains on the arms of the chairs—that gave evidence to Maati's presence. The faintest hint, a wisp of musk slight as pale smoke, was the thing that had brought back the flood of memory. For a powerful moment, she saw again the small house she'd lived in after she and Maati had left Saraykeht; the yellow walls and rough, wooden floor, the dog who had lived in the street and only ever been half tamed by her of-ferings of sausage ends from the kitchen window, the gray spiders that had built their webs in the corners. The particular scent of her old lover's body brought back those rooms. She knew him better by that than to see him again in the flesh.

But perhaps that wasn't true. When he blinked fast and uncertainly, when his head leaned just slightly forward and a smile just began to bloom on his lips, she could see him there, beneath that flesh. The man she had known and loved. The man she'd left behind.

"Liat?" he said. "You . . . you're here?"

She took a pose of affirmation, surprised to find her hands trembling. Maati stepped forward slowly, as if afraid a sudden movement might startle her into flight. Liat swallowed to loosen the knot in her throat and smiled.

"I would have written to warn you I was coming," she said, "but by the time I knew I was, I'd have raced the letter. I'm . . . I'm sorry if . . ."

But he touched her arm, his fingers on the cloth just above her elbow. His eyes were wide and amazed. As if it were natural, as if it had been a week or a day and not a third of their lives, Liat put her arms around him and felt him enclose her. She had told herself that she would hold back, be careful. She was the head of House Kyaan, a woman of business and politics. She knew how to be hardhearted and cool. There was no reason to think that she would be safe here in the farthest city from her home and facing again the two lovers of her childhood. The years had worked changes on them all, and she had parted with neither of them on good terms.

And yet the tears in her eyes were simple and sincere and as much joy as sorrow, and the touch of Maati's body against her own—strange and familiar both—wasn't awkward or unwelcome. She kissed his cheek and drew back enough to see his still wonder-filled face.

"Well," she said at last. "It's been a while. It's good to see you again, Maati-kya. I wasn't sure it would be, but it is."

"I thought I'd never see you again," he said. "I thought, after all this time . . . My letters . . ."

"I got them, yes. And it's not as if court gossip didn't tell everyone in the world where you were. The last succession of Machi was the favorite scandal of the season. I even saw an epic made from it. The boy who took your part didn't look a thing like you," she said, and then, in a lower voice, "I meant to write back to you, even if it was only to tell you that I'd heard. That I knew. But somehow I never managed. I regret that. I've always regretted that. It only seemed so . . . complex."

"I thought perhaps . . . I don't know. I don't know what I thought."

She stood silently in his arms the space of another breath, part of her wishing that this moment might suffice; that the relief she felt at Maati's simple, unconsidered acceptance might stand in for all that she had still to do. He sensed the change in her thoughts and stepped back, his hands moving restlessly. She smoothed her hair, suddenly aware of the streaks of gray at her temple.

"Can I get something for you?" Maati said. "It's simple enough to call a servant in from the palaces. Or I have some distilled wine here."

"Wine will do," she said, and sat.

He went to a low cabinet beside the fire grate, sliding the wooden panel back and taking out two small porcelain bowls and a stoppered bottle as he spoke.

"I've had company recently. He's only just left. I don't usually live in this disorder."

"I'm not sure I believe that," she said, wryly. Maati chuckled and shrugged.

"Oh, I don't clean it myself. It would be a hundred times worse than this. Otah-kvo's been very kind in loaning me servants. He has more than he has places for."

The name was like a cold breath, but Liat only smiled and accepted the bowl that Maati held out to her. She sipped the wine—strong, peppery, and warm in her throat—to give herself a moment. She wasn't ready yet for the pleasure to end.

"The world's changed on us," she said. It was a platitude, but Maati seemed to take some deeper meaning from it.

"It has," he said. "And it'll keep on changing, I think. When I was a boy, I never imagined myself here, and I can't say for certain what I'll be doing when next summer comes. The new Dai-kvo . . ."

He shook his head slowly and sipped his wine for what Liat guessed was much the same reason she had. The silence between them grew. Maati cleared his throat.

"How is Nayiit?" he asked, careful, Liat noticed, to use the boy's name. Not *our son,* but Nayiit.

She told him about the work of House Kyaan, and Nayiit's role as an overseer. The stories of how he had made the transition from the child of the head of the house to an overseer in his own right. His courtship, his marriage, the child. Maati closed the door, lit a fire in the grate, and listened.

It was odd that of all the subjects she had to bring to the table, Nayiit should be the easiest. And Maati listened to it all, laughing or rapt, delighted and also sorrowful, longing to have been part of something that was already gone. Her words were like rain in a desert; he absorbed them, cherished them. She found herself searching for more—anecdotes of Nayiit and his friends, his early lovers, the city, anything. She searched for them and offered them up, part apology, part sacrifice. The candles had grown visibly shorter before he asked whether Nayiit had stayed in Saraykeht, and Liat reluctantly shook her head.

"I've left him at the wayhouse," she said. "I wasn't certain how this would go, between us. I didn't want him to be here if it was bad."

Maati's hands started to move toward some pose—a denial, perhaps—then faltered. His eyes locked on hers. There were decades in them. She felt tears welling up.

"I'm sorry," she said. "If that's worth anything, I am sorry, Maati-kya."

"For what?" he asked, and his tone said that he could imagine a number of answers.

"That you weren't a part of his life until now."

"It was my choice as much as yours. And it will be good to see him again."

He heaved a sigh and pressed the stopper back into the bottle's neck. The sun was long gone, and a cold breeze, thick with the perfume of night-flowering gardens, raised bumps on her arms. Only the air. Not dread.

"You haven't asked me why I've come," she said.

He chuckled and leaned back against his couch. His cheeks were ruddy from the candlelight and wine. His eyes seemed to glitter.

"I was pretending it was for me. Mending old wounds, making peace," Maati said. The anger she'd seen was there now, swimming beneath the pleasant, joking surface. She wondered if she'd waited too long to come to the issue. She should have asked before she'd told him Nayiit was in the city, before the sour memories came back.

Maati took a pose of query, inviting her to share her true agenda.

"I need your help," Liat said. "I need an audience with the Khai."

"You want to talk to Otah-kvo? You don't need my help for that. You could just—"

"I need you to help me convince him. To argue my case with me. We have to convince him to intercede with the Dai-kvo."

Maati's eyes narrowed, and his head tilted like that of a man considering a puzzle. Liat felt herself starting to blush. She'd had too much of the wine, and her control wasn't all it should be.

"Intercede with the Dai-kvo?" he said.

"I've been following the world. And the Galts. It was what Amat Kyaan built the house to do. I have decades of books and ledgers. I've made note of every contract they've made in the summer cities. I know every ship that sails past, what her captain's name is, and half the time, what cargo she carries. I *know*, Maati. I've seen them scheming. I've even blocked them a time or two."

"They had hands in the succession here too. They were backing the woman, Otah-kvo's sister. Anything you want to say about Galt, he'll half-believe before he's heard it. But how is the Dai-kvo part of it?"

"They won't do it without the Dai-kvo," Liat said. "He has to say it's the right thing, or they won't do it."

"Who won't do what?" Maati said, impatience growing in his voice.

"The poets," Liat said. "They have to kill the Galts. And they have to do it now."

OTAH PRESENTED the meeting as a luncheon, a social gathering of old friends. He chose a balcony high in the palace looking out over the wide air to the south. The city lay below them, streets paved in black stone, tile and metal roofs pointing sharply at the sky. The towers rose above, only sun and clouds hanging higher. The wind was thick with the green, permeating scent of spring and the darker, acrid forge smoke. Between them, the low stone table was covered with plates—bread and cheese and salt olives, honeyed almonds and lemon trout and a sweetbread topped with sliced oranges. The gods alone knew where the kitchen had found a fresh orange.

Yet of all those present none of them ate.

Maati had made the introductions. Liat and Nayiit and Otah and Kiyan. The young man, Liat's son, had taken all the appropriate poses, said all the right phrases, and then taken position standing behind his mother like a bodyguard. Maati leaned against the stone banister, the sky at his back. Otah—formal, uneased, and feeling more the Khai Machi than ever under the anxious gaze of woman who had been his lover in his youth—took a pose of query, and Liat shared the news that changed the world forever: the Galts had a poet of their own.

"His name is Riaan Vaudathat," Liat said. "He was the fourth son of a high family in the courts of Nantani. His father sent him to the school when he was five."

"This was well after our time," Maati said to Otah. "Neither of us would have known him. Not from there."

"He was accepted by the Dai-kvo and taken to the village to be trained," Liat said. "That was eight years ago. He was talented, well liked, and respected. The Dai-kvo chose him to study for the binding of a fresh andat."

Kiyan, sitting at Otah's side, leaned forward in a pose of query. "Don't all the poets train to hold andat?"

"We all try our hands at preparing a binding," Maati said. "We all study enough to know how it works and what it is. But only a few apply the knowledge. If the Dai-kvo thinks you have the temperament to take on one that's already bound, he'll send you there to study and prepare yourself to take over control when the poet grows too old. If you're bright and talented, he'll set you to working through a fresh binding. It can take years to be ready. Your work is read by other poets and the Dai-kvo, and attacked, and torn apart and redone perhaps a dozen times. Perhaps more."

"Because of the consequences of failing?" Kiyan asked. Maati nodded.

"Riaan was one of the best," Liat said. "And then three years ago, he was sent back to Nantani. To his family. Fallen from favor. No one knew why, he just appeared one day with a letter for his father, and after that he was living in apartments in the Vaudathat holdings. It was a small scandal. And it wasn't the last of them. Riaan was sending letters every week back to the Dai-kvo. Asking to be taken back, everyone supposed. He drank too much, and sometimes fought in the streets. By the end, he was practically living in the comfort houses by the seafront. The story was that he'd bet he could bed every whore in the city in a summer. His family never spoke of it, but they lost standing in the court. There were rumors of father and son fighting, not just arguing, but taking up arms.

"And then, one night, he disappeared. Vanished. His family said that he'd been summoned on secret business. The Dai-kvo had a mission for him, and he'd gone the same day the letter had come. But there wasn't a courier who'd admit to carrying any letter like it."

"They might not have said it," Otah said. "They call it the gentleman's trade for a reason."

"We thought of that," Nayiit replied. He had a strong voice; not loud, but powerful. "Later, when we went to the Dai-kvo, I took a list of the couriers who'd come to Nantani in the right weeks. None of them had been to the Dai-kvo's village at the right time. The Dai-kvo wouldn't speak to me. But of the men who would, none believed that Riaan had been sent for."

Otah could still think of several objections to that, but he held them back, gesturing instead for Liat to go on.

"No one connected the disappearance with a Galtic merchant ship that left that night with half her cargo still waiting to be loaded," Liat said. "Except me, and I wouldn't have if I hadn't made it my business to track all things Galtic."

"You think he was on that ship?" Otah said.

"I'm certain of it."

"Why?" he asked.

"The wealth of coincidences," Liat said. "The captain—Arnau Fentin—was the second brother of a family on the Galtic High Council. A servant in the Vaudathat household saw Riaan's father burning papers. Letters, he said. And in a foreign script."

"Any trade cipher could look like a foreign script," Otah said, but Liat wouldn't be stopped.

"The ship had been bound for Chaburi-Tan and then Bakta. But it headed west instead—back to Galt."

"Or Eddensea, or Eymond."

"Otah-kya," Kiyan said, her voice gentle, "let her finish."

He saw Liat's gaze flicker toward her, and her hands take a pose of thanks. He leaned back, his palms flat on his thighs, and silently nodded for Liat to continue.

"There were stories of Riaan having met a new woman in the weeks before he left. That was what his family thought, at least. He'd spent several evenings every week at a comfort house whose back wall was shared with the compound of House Fentin. The captain's family. I have statements that confirm all of this."

"I went to the comfort house myself," Nayiit said. "I asked after the lady Riaan had described. There wasn't anyone like her."

"It was a clumsy lie," Liat said. "All of it from beginning to end. And, Itani, it's the *Galts*."

Whether she had used his old, assumed name in error or as a ploy to make him recall the days of his youth, the effect was the same. Otah drew a deep breath, and felt a sick weight descend to his belly as he exhaled. He had spent so many years wary of the schemes of Galt that her evidence, thin as it was, almost had the power to convince him. He felt the gazes of the others upon him. Maati leaned forward in his seat, fingers knotted together in his lap. Kiyan's rueful half-smile was sympathetic and considering both. The silence stretched.

"Is there any reason to think he would have . . . done this?" Otah asked. "The poet. Why would he agree to this?"

Liat turned and nodded to her son. The man licked his lips before he spoke.

"I went to the Dai-kvo's village," Nayiit said. "My mother, of course, couldn't. There were stories that Riaan had suffered a fever the winter before he was sent away. A serious one. Apparently he came close to death. Afterward, his skin peeled like he'd been too long in the sun. They say it changed him. He became more prone to anger. He wouldn't think before he acted or spoke. The Dai-kvo sat with him for weeks, training him like he was fresh from the school. It did no good. Riaan wasn't the man he'd been when the Dai-kvo accepted him. So . . ."

"So the Dai-kvo sent him away in disgrace for something that wasn't his fault," Otah said.

"No, not at first," Nayiit said. "The Dai-kvo only told him that he wasn't to continue with his binding. That it was too great a risk. They say Riaan took it poorly. There were fights and drunken rants. One man said Riaan snuck a woman into the village to share his bed, but I never heard anyone confirm that. Whatever the details, the Dai-kvo lost patience. He sent him away."

"You learned quite a lot," Otah said. "I'd have thought the poets would be closer with their disgraces."

"Once Riaan left, it wasn't their disgrace. It was his," Nayiit said. "And they knew I had come from Nantani. I traded stories for stories. It wasn't hard."

"The Dai-kvo wouldn't meet with us," Liat said. "I sent five petitions, and for two of them his secretaries didn't even bother to send refusals. It's why we came here."

"Because you wanted me to make this argument? I'm not in the Dai-kvo's best graces myself just now. He seems to think I blame the Galts when I cough," Otah said. "Maati might be the better man to make the case."

Maati took a pose that disagreed.

"I would hardly be considered disinterested," Maati said. His words were calm and controlled despite their depth. "I may have done some interesting work, but no one will have forgotten that I defied the last Dai-kvo by not abandoning these precise two people."

The rest of the thought hung in the air, just beyond speech. *She abandoned me.* It was true enough. Liat had taken the child and made her own way in the world. She had never answered Maati's letters until now, when she had need of him. There was something almost like shame in Liat's downcast eyes. Nayiit shifted his weight, as if to interpose himself between the two of them—between his mother and the man who had wanted badly to be his father and had been denied.

"We could also ask Cehmai," Kiyan said. "He's a poet of enough prestige and ability to hold Stone-Made-Soft, and his reputation hasn't been compromised."

"That might be wise," Otah said, grabbing for the chance to take the conversation away from the complexities of the past. "But let's go over the evidence you have, Liat-cha. All of it. From the start."

It took the better part of the day. Otah listened to the full story; he read the statements of the missing poet's slaves and servants, the contracts broken by the fleeing Galtic trade ship, the logs of couriers whose whereabouts Nayiit had compiled. Whatever objections he raised, Liat countered. He could see the fatigue in her face and hear the impatience in her voice. This matter was important to her. Important enough to bring her here. That she had come was proof enough of her conviction, if not of the truth of her claim. The girl he had known had been clever enough, competent enough, and still had been used as a stone in other people's games. Perhaps he was harsh in still thinking of her in that light. The years had changed him. They certainly could have changed her as well.

And, as the sun shifted slowly toward the western peaks, Otah found his heart growing heavy. The case she made was not complete, but it was evocative as a monster tale told to children. Galt might well have taken in this mad poet. There was no way to know what they might do with him, or what he might do with their help. The histories of the Empire murmured in the back of Otah's mind: wars fought with the power of gods, the nature of space itself broken, and the greatest empire the world had ever known laid waste. And yes, if all Liat suspected proved true, it might happen again.

But if they acted on their fears, if the Dai-kvo mandated the use of the andat to remove the possibility of a Galtic poet, thousands would die who knew nothing of the plots that had brought down their doom. Children not old enough to speak, men and women who led simple, honest lives. Galt would be made a wasteland to rival the ruins of the Empire. Otah wondered how certain they would all have to be in order to take that step. How certain or else how frightened.

"Let me sit with this," he said at last, nodding to Liat and her son. "I'll have apartments cleared for you. You'll stay here at the palaces."

"There may not be much time," Maati said softly.

"I know it," Otah said. "Tomorrow I'll decide what to do. If Cehmai's the right bearer, we can do this all again with him in the room. And then . . . and then we'll see what shape the world's taken and do whatever needs doing."

Liat took a pose of gratitude, and a heartbeat later Nayiit mirrored her. Otah waved the gestures away. He was too tired for ceremony. Too troubled.

When Maati and the two visitors had left, Otah rose and stood beside Kiyan at the railing, looking out over the city as it fell into its early, sudden twilight. Plumes of smoke rose from among the green copper roofs of the forges. The great stone towers thrust toward the sky as if they supported the deepening blue. Kiyan tossed an almond out into the wide air, and a black-winged bird swooped down to catch it before it reached the distant ground. Otah touched her shoulder; she turned to him smiling as if half-surprised to find him there.

"How are you, love?" he asked.

"I should be the one asking," she said. "Those two . . . that's more than one lifetime's trouble they're carrying."

"I know it. And Maati's still in love with her."

"With both of them," Kiyan said. "One way and another, with both of them."

Otah took a pose that agreed with her.

"You know her well enough," Kiyan said. "Does she love him, do you think?"

"She did once," Otah said. "But now? It's too many years. We've all become other people."

The breeze smelled of smoke and distant rain. The first chill of evening raised gooseflesh on Kiyan's arm. He wanted to turn her toward him, to taste her mouth and lose himself for a while in simple pleasure. He wanted badly to forget the world. As if hearing his thought, she smiled, but he didn't touch her again and she didn't move nearer to him.

"What are you going to do?" she asked.

"Tell Cehmai, send out couriers west to see what we can divine about the situation in Galt, appeal to the Dai-kvo. What else can I do? A mad poet, prone to fits of temper and working for the Galtic High Council? There's not a story worse than that."

"Will the Dai-kvo do what she asks, do you think?"

"I don't know," Otah said. "He'll know this Riaan better

than any of us. If he's certain that the man's not capable of a proper binding, perhaps we'll let him try and pay the price of it. One simple death is the best we can hope for, sometimes. If it saves the world."

"And if the Dai-kvo isn't sure?"

"Then he'll spin a coin or throw tiles or whatever it is he does to make a decision, and we'll do that and hope it was right."

Kiyan nodded, crossing her arms and leaning forward, gazing out into the distance as if by considering carefully, she could see Galt from here. Otah's belly growled, but he ignored it.

"He'll destroy them, won't he?" she asked. "The Dai-kvo will use the andat against the Galts."

"Likely."

"Good," Kiyan said with a certainty that surprised him. "If it's going to happen, let it happen there. At least Eiah and Danat are safe from it."

Otah swallowed. He wanted to rise to the defense of the innocent in Galt, wanted to say the sort of high-minded words that he'd held as comfort many years ago when he had been moved to kill in the name of mercy. But the years had taken that man. The years he had lived, and the dark, liquid eyes of his children. If black chaos was to be loosed, he had to side with Kiyan. Better that it was loosed elsewhere. Better a thousand thousand Galtic children die than one of his own. It was what his heart said, but it made him feel lessened and sad.

"And the other problem?" Kiyan asked. Her voice was low, but there was a hardness to it almost like anger. Otah took a querying pose. Kiyan turned to him. He hadn't expected to see fear in her eyes, and the surprise of it filled him with dread as deep as any he had suffered.

"What is it?" he asked.

She looked at him, part in surprise, part accusation.

"Nayiit," she said. "No one would think that man was Maati's child. Not for a heartbeat. You have two sons, Otah-kya."

5

>+< Balasar was quickly coming to resent the late-spring storms of the Westlands. Each morning seemed to promise a bright day in which his masters of supply could make their inventories, his captains could train their men. Before midday, great white clouds would hulk up in the south and advance upon him. The middle afternoon had been roaring rain and vicious lightning for the past six days. The training fields were churned mud, the wood for the steam wagons was soaked, and the men were beginning to mirror Balasar's own impatience.

They had been guests of the Warden of Aren for two weeks now, the troops in their tents outside the city walls, Balasar and his captains sleeping in the high keep. The Warden was an old man, fat and boisterous, who understood as well as Balasar the dangers of an army grown restless, even an army still only half assembled. The Warden put a pleasant face on things—he'd agreed to allow a Galtic army on his lands, after all. There was little enough to do now besides be pleasant and hope they'd go away again.

He had even been so kind as to offer Balasar the use of his library. It was a small room overlooking a courtyard, less grand than Balasar's own home in Galt, less than the smallest apartments of the least of the Khaiate nobility. But it was serviceable, and it had the effect each man desired. Balasar had a place to brood, and the Westlanders had a convenient way to keep clear of him.

The afternoon rains pecked at the windows. The pot of black tea had grown tepid and bitter, ignored on a corner of the wide, oaken table. Balasar looked again at the maps. Nantani would be the first, and the easiest. The western forces would be undivided—five full legions with support of the mercenaries hired with the High Council's gold and promises of plunder. The city wouldn't stand for a morning. Then one legion would turn North, going overland to Pathai while two others took the mercenaries to Shosheyn-Tan, Lachi, and Saraykeht. That left him two legions to go upriver to Udun, Utani, and Tan-Sadar, less whatever men he left behind to occupy the conquered. Eight of the cities. Over half, but the least important.

Coal and his men were already in place, waiting in the low towns and smugglers' camps outside Chaburi-Tan. When the andat failed, they would sack the city, and take ships North to Yalakeht. The pieces for steam-driven boats were already in the warehouses of the Galtic tradesmen, ready to be pegged onto rafts and sped upriver to the village of the Dai-kvo. And then there was only the race to the North to put Amnat-Tan, Cetani, and Machi to the torch before winter came.

Balasar wished again that he had been able to lead the force in Chaburi-Tan. The fate of the world would rest on that sprint to the libraries and catacombs of the poets. If only he had had time to sail out there . . . but days were precious, and Coal had been preparing his men all the time Balasar had played politics in Acton. It was better this way. And still . . .

He traced a finger across the western plains—Pathai to Utani. He wished he knew better how the roads were. The school for the young poets wasn't far from Pathai. That wouldn't be a pleasant duty either. And he couldn't trust the slaughter of children to mercenaries, not with the stakes so high. This wasn't a war that had room for moments of compassion.

A soft knock came at the door, and Eustin stepped in. He wore the deep blue and red of a captain's uniform. Balasar acknowledged him with a nod.

"Has the third legion arrived, then?" Balasar asked.

"No, sir," Eustin said. "We've had a runner from them. They'll be here by the week's end, sir."

"Too long."

"Yes, sir. But there's another problem."

Balasar rose, hands clasped behind him. He could feel his mind straining back toward the plans and maps almost as if it were a physical force, but he believed that battles were won or lost long before they were fought. If Eustin had thought something worth interrupting him, it would likely need his whole attention.

"Go ahead," he said.

"The poet. He's refusing to pay for his whores again, sir. Been saying the honor of being with him should be enough. One of the girls took offense and poured a cup of hot tea in his lap. Scalded his little poet like a boiled sausage."

Balasar didn't smile, nor did Eustin. The moment between them was enough.

"Will he be able to ride?" Balasar asked.

"Given a few days, sir, he'll be fine. But he's demanding the girl be killed. Half the houses in the city have threatened to raise their rates, and they're talking to their local clients too. I've had two letters today that didn't quite say the grain would cost more than expected."

Balasar felt a brief flush of anger.

"They're aware that the majority of the Galtic armies are either in the ward now or will be here shortly?"

"Yes, sir. And they've not said it's final that they'll stick it to us for more silver. But they're proud folks. It's just a whore he wants killed, but she's a Westlands whore, if you see what I mean. She's one of their own."

This was a mess. He didn't want to start the campaign by fighting the Ward of Aren. He didn't yet have all his men assembled. Balasar looked out the windows, casting his gaze over the courtyard below without truly seeing it.

"I suppose I'd best speak with him, then," Balasar said.

"He's in his rooms, sir. Should I bring him here?"

"No," Balasar said. "I'll face the beast in its lair."

"Yessir."

The central city of Aren was a squat affair. Thick stone walls covered with mud and washed white were the order of the day. The constant wars of the Westlands and the occasional attack by Galt had kept the ward cropped low as a rabbit-haunted garden. The highest houses rose no more than four stories above ground, and the streets, even near the palaces of the Warden, smelled of sewage and old food. Balasar reached the building where he and his captains were housed, shook the rain from his cloak, and gestured for Eustin to wait for him. He took the stairs three at a time up to the anteroom of the poet's apartments. The men guarding the door bowed as he entered, then stood aside as he announced himself.

Riaan sat on a low couch, his robes propped up above his lap like a tent, the hem rising halfway up his shins. The awareness of his indignity shone in the poet's face—lips pressed thin, jaw set forward. Even as Balasar made his half-bow, he could tell the man had been working himself into a rage. If any of his captains had acted this way, Balasar would have assigned them to patrolling on horseback until the wounds had healed. Idiocy should carry a price. Instead he lowered himself to a couch across from the poet and spoke gently.

"I heard about your misfortune," Balasar said in the tongue of the Khaiate cities. "I wanted to come and offer my sympathies. Is there anything I can do to be of service?"

"You could bring me the slack-cunt's heart," the poet spat. "I should have cut her down where she stood. She should be drowned in her own shit for this!"

The poet gestured toward his own crotch, demonstrating the depth of his hurt. Balasar didn't smile. With all the gravity he could manage, he nodded.

"It will cause problems if I have her killed," Balasar said. "The local men are uneasy already. I could have her whipped—"

"No! She must *die*!"

"If there was some other way that honor could be served . . ."

Riaan leaned back, his gaze cold. This, Balasar thought, was the man on whom the hopes of the world rested. A man who had leapt at the chance to turn against his own people, who had eaten the interest and novelty of the people of Acton like it was honey bread, who vented his rage on whores and servants. Balasar had never seen a tool less likely. And yet, the poet was what he needed, and the stakes could not have been higher. He sighed.

"I will see to it," Balasar said. "And permit me to send you my own personal physician. I would not have a man of your importance suffer, Most High."

"This should never have happened," Riaan said. "You will do better in the future."

"Indeed," Balasar agreed, then rose, taking what he hoped was an appropriate pose for an honored if somewhat junior man taking leave of someone above his station. He must have come near the mark, because the poet took a pose of dismissal. Balasar bowed and left. He walked back down the steps more slowly, weighing his options. He found Eustin in a common room with three of his other captains. He knew that the poet's injury had been the topic of their conversation. The sudden quiet when he entered and the merriment in their eyes were evidence enough. He greeted each man by name and gestured for Eustin to follow him back out to the street.

"Any luck, sir?"

"No," Balasar said. "He's still talking himself into a tantrum. But I had to try. I'll need Carlsin sent to him with some ointment for the burn. And he'll need to wear good robes. If he shows up in his usual rags, the man will never believe he's my physician."

"I'll see he's told, sir."

They reached the gray-cobbled street, and Balasar turned back toward the Warden's palaces and the little library with all his maps and plans. Eustin kept pace at his side. In the far distance, there was a rumble of thunder. Balasar cursed, and Eustin agreed.

"And the girl, sir?" Eustin asked.

Balasar nodded and blew out his breath.

"Tell all the comfort houses to give Riaan whatever he asks, and send the bills to me. I'll see them fairly paid. Warn them that I'll be keeping account, though. I'm not opening the coffers to every tiles player and alley worker in the West-lands."

"We have enough silver then, sir?"

"We'll have more when we've reached Nantani," Balasar said. "If the men are a little hungry before then, that might even serve us."

A gust of wind brought the harsh blast of rain and a salting of tiny hailstones. Other than raising his voice slightly, Balasar ignored it.

"And the girl herself will have to die," he said. "Tell her employer I'll pay the house fair price for the lost income."

Eustin was silent. Balasar looked at him, and the man's face was dark. The general felt his mouth curled in a deep frown.

"Say it," Balasar said.

"I think you're wrong, sir."

Balasar took Eustin's elbow and angled off from the street under a covered stone archway. A girl stood there, a cart of green winter apples at her feet, looking out at the gray-white rain and the foul, brown brook at the edge of the street. Balasar scooped up two of the apples and tossed the girl a wide copper coin before finding a low bench and nodding for Eustin to sit.

He handed his captain one of the apples and said, "Make your case."

Eustin shrugged, bit the apple, and chewed thoughtfully for a long moment. A glance at the apple seller, and then he spoke, his voice so low it was nearly inaudible over the clatter of the storm.

"First off, we haven't got so much gold we can afford to spend all of it here. Having the men hungry, well, that's one thing. But five legions is a lot of men. And there's no cause for this, not really. Any of the other men did the thing, you'd take it out of their skins. And they know it."

"I half think you're sweet on the girl," Balasar said.

"I've got a certain respect for her," Eustin said with a grin, but then sobered. "The thing is, you're not treating him like he was long-term, if you see. The story for the High Council is that once we've settled the Khaiem out, our man Riaan's to hook these andat to our yoke. Tell the Lord Convocate otherwise, and it would be someone else leading this. But if that's true, Riaan's going to be around for the rest of your life and mine, and a damned important man at that. All apologies, but you're dancing to his tune like you're hoping he'll kiss you."

Balasar tossed the apple from hand to hand and waited for the flush of anger to recede.

"I need the man," Balasar said. "If I have to bow and scrape for a time—"

"That's just it, though. *For a time*. None of the men are used to seeing you drink piss and smile. They're waiting to see you crack, to see you put him in his place. It keeps not happening, and they're wondering why. Wondering how you can stand the idea of a life licking that little prick's boot. Time will come they'll understand you *aren't* thinking of him in the long term."

Balasar needed a moment to think that through. He bit the apple; it was tart and chalky and squeaked against his teeth. He tossed the rest of it out into the street where the rain took it rolling downhill, white flesh and green skin in the dark water.

"Do you think Riaan suspects?" Balasar asked at length.

Eustin snorted. "He can't believe the tide would go out so long as he was on the beach. The waves all love him too much to leave. But the men, sir. They'll figure you're planning to kill him. And if they do, they may slip."

Balasar nodded. Eustin was right. He was acting differently

than he would have had Riaan been a problem with a future.
It hadn't been difficult to let the Councilmen in Acton blind
themselves to the poet's character. Visions of godlike power,
of magic bent to the High Council's will, were enough to let
them overlook the dangers. The captains, the men who spoke
with Riaan, would be more likely to understand why he wasn't
to be trusted. They might well see what Balasar had seen
from the beginning, even before he had made the doomed
journey into the desert: that the andat were a dangerous tool,
best discarded the moment the need had passed.

But, and here was the trouble, not a moment before that. If
the poet failed him, everything was lost. He weighed the
risks for a long moment before Eustin spoke again.

"Let me send the girl away, sir. I'll give her enough silver
to take herself out into the farmland for half a year, and tell
her that if we see her in the city, I'll have her head on a pike
for true. I'll send the poet a pig heart, say we cut it out of her.
The man that runs the comfort house'll know. I'll tell the
men it was your idea."

"It's a gamble," Balasar said.

"It's all a gamble, sir," Eustin said, and then, "Besides. He
really did earn it."

To the east, lightning flashed, and before the thunder
reached them, Balasar nodded his assent. Eustin took his
leave, stalking out into the downpour to make this one more
tiny adjustment to the monumental plan Balasar had devised
and directed. At the end of the pathway, the apple-selling girl
sensed some slackening, pulled a hood up over her fair hair,
and darted out into the city. For a time, Balasar sat quietly,
feeling the weariness in his flesh that came from tension
without release. He let his gaze soften, the white walls of the
city fading, losing their separate natures, becoming different
shades of nothing, like the shadows of hills covered by snow.

He wondered what Little Ott would have made of all this:
the campaign, the poet, the wheels within wheels that he'd
put in motion. If it came together as he planned, Balasar
would save the world from another war like the one that had

toppled the Old Empire. If it failed, he might start one. And whatever happened, he had sacrificed Bes, Laran, Kellem, Little Ott. Men who had loved him were dead and would never return. Men alive now who trusted him might well die. His nation, everyone he'd known or cared for—his father growing bent with age, the girl he'd lost his heart to when he was a boy shaking the petals off spring cherry trees, Eustin, Coal—they might all be slaughtered if he once judged poorly. It was something he tried not to consider, afraid the weight of it might crush him. And yet in these still moments, it found him. The dread and the awe at what he had begun. And with it the certainty that he was right.

He imagined Bes standing in the street before him, wide face split in the knowing grin that he would never see again outside memory. Balasar lifted a hand in greeting, and the image bowed to him and faded. They would have understood. All the men whose blood he'd spilled for this would have understood. Or if they didn't, they'd have done it all the same. It was what they meant by faith.

When at last he returned to the library, one of his other captains—a lanky man named Orem Cot—was pacing the length of the room, literally wringing his hands in agitation or excitement. Balasar closed the door behind him with a thump as the captain bowed.

"Sir," he said. "There's a man come wanting to speak with you. I thought I'd best bring him to you myself."

"What's his business?" Balasar asked.

"Mercenary captain, sir. Brought his men down from Annaster."

"I don't need more forces."

"You'll want to talk with this one all the same, sir. His company? They're from the Khaiem. Says they got turned out by the Khai Machi and they've been traveling ever since."

"He's been in the winter cities?"

"For *years,* sir."

"You were right to bring him. Show the man in," Balasar

said, then stopped the captain as he headed to the door. "What's his name?"

"Captain Ajutani, sir. Sinja Ajutani."

IT HAD become clear to Sinja shortly after his arrival in Aren that he had misjudged the situation.

The company, such as it was, had passed through the mountains that divided the Westlands from the lands that, while not directly controlled, had associated themselves with Machi and Pathai weeks before. The men were young and excited to be on the march, so Sinja had pushed them. By the time they'd reached Annaster, they were tired enough to complain, but there was still a light in their eyes. They'd escaped the smothering, peaceful blankets of the Khaiem; they were in the realm where violence was met with violence, and not by the uncanny powers of the poets and their andat. They had come to the place where they could prove themselves on the bodies of their enemies.

Besides Sinja, only a dozen or so of the higher ranks had ever been in battle. For the rest, this was like walking into a children's tale. Sinja hadn't tried to explain. Perhaps they'd be able to find glory in the soul-crushing boredom of a siege; perhaps they'd face their first battles and discover that they loved violence. More likely, he'd be sending half of them home to their mothers by midsummer, and that would have been fine. He was here as much to stretch his legs as to keep his master and friend the Khai Machi out of trouble with the Dai-kvo.

He hadn't expected to walk into the largest massing of military force in memory.

Galt was in the southern wards, and it was there in force. All through the Westlands, Wardens had forgotten their squabbles. Every gaze was cast south. The common wisdom was that Galt had finally decided to end its generations-long games of raid and abandon. It had come to take control of the whole of the Westlands from the southern coast up to

Eddensea. There were even those who wondered whether it was going to be a good season for Eddensea.

Sinja had done what he did best—listened. The stories he heard were, of course, overblown. Men and women throughout the Westlands were in different stages of panic. Someone had seen a thousand ships off the coast. There had been agreements signed with Aren, but all the other Wardens and all their children were to be slaughtered to assure that no one would have claim to rule once the Galts had come through. There were even a few optimists who thought that Balasar Gice—the general at the head of this largest of all gathered armies—wasn't looking to the Westlands, but gathering his forces to take control of Galt itself. He could overthrow the High Council and install himself as autocrat.

What it all came to was this: Any mercenary company working for anyone besides Galt was likely to be on the losing side of the fight. The collected Wardens were putting out calls for free companies and garrison forces, preparing themselves as best they could. The fees that Sinja was offered would have been handsome for a band of veterans and siege captains, much less for a few hundred foreign sell-swords one step up from thugs. And so Sinja had considered the money, considered the offers and the stories and his own best instincts, then quietly packed up his men and headed south to Aren to sell their services at a fourth of the price, but to the winners.

The men had grumbled. Wide, square Westland coins had been dancing in their minds. Morale had started to fail. So Sinja had paused in the Ward of Castin, made contact with a free company who'd taken contract there, and challenged their veterans to a day of games. Once Sinja's men had understood and accepted his point, they bound their ribs and continued to the south. No one had questioned his judgment again.

Aren was one of the wards farthest to the south. Low hills covered with rich green grasses, towns of stone buildings with thatched roofs, elk and deer so wise to the ways of men that the bowmen he sent ahead to forage never caught one of them. Wherever they went, Sinja saw the signs of an army having passed—ruined crops, abandoned campsites with the ashes of a half hundred fires churned into the mud. But even with this, he had been shocked when they topped one of the many hills and caught first sight of the city of Aren.

No city under siege had ever seen so many troops at its wall. Tents and low pavilions were laid out around it on all sides, dark oiled cloth shining in row after row after row. The smoke of cook fires left a low haze through the valley that even the rain could not wholly dispel, the strange bulbous steam wagons the Galts used to move supplies and leave their men unburdened seemed as numerous as horses in the fields, and the squirming, streaming activity of men moving through each of the opened gates made the city seem like a dead sparrow overrun by ants.

His men set camp at a polite distance from the existing companies while Sinja dared the city itself. He entered the gates at midday. It wasn't more than three hands later he was being escorted through the halls of the Warden's palace to the library and the general himself. He'd surrendered his blades and the garrote he kept at his waist before being permitted to speak with the great man. Either Balasar Gice felt this unprecedented mass of men was too little for whatever task lay ahead of him and was grabbing at every spare sword and dagger in the world, or else Sinja was, for reasons that passed imagining, of particular interest to him.

Either way, Sinja disliked it.

Balasar Gice turned out to be a smallish man, mouse-brown hair running to white at the temples. He wore the gray tunic of command that Sinja had seen before when he'd been in the field as a young man fighting against the Galts or else with them. He might have been anyone, to look at him. A farmer or a merchant seaman or a seafront customs agent.

"Bad weather for traveling," the general said, amiably, as if they were simply two men who'd met at a wayhouse. He spoke the Khaiate tongue clearly, his accent flavoring the words rather than obscuring them.

"It's always wet in the South this time of year," Sinja agreed in Galtic. "Not always so cold, but that's why the gods made wool. That or as a joke against sheep."

The general smiled, either at the words or the language they were in, Sinja wasn't certain. Sinja kept his expression pleasant and empty. They both knew he was here to sell the use of his men, but only the general knew why the meeting was here and not with some low captain. Sinja opted to wait and see what came of it. Balasar Gice seemed to read his intention; he nodded and walked to a side table, where he poured them both clear wine from a cut-glass carafe. No, not wine. Water.

"I hear the Khai Machi turned you out," the general said in Galtic as he passed a cup to Sinja. That wasn't true. Sinja had told the captain that they were out from Machi, but perhaps there had been some misunderstanding. Sinja shrugged. It was too early in the game to correct anyone's misconceptions.

"It's his right," he said. "Some of the men were causing trouble. Too long in a quiet place. I'm sure you understand."

Balasar chuckled. It was a warm sound, and Sinja found himself liking the man. Balasar nodded to a couch beside the brazier. Sinja made a small bow and sat, the general leaning casually against the table.

"You left on good terms?"

"We didn't turn back and burn the city," Sinja said, "if that's what you mean."

"Do you owe the Khai Machi loyalty? Or are you a free company?"

The truth was that any silver he took would find its way back to Otah Machi's coffers. The company was no more free than the Galtic armies outside the city. And yet there was something in the general's voice when he asked the question, something in his eyes.

"We're mercenaries. We follow whoever pays us," Sinja said.

"And if someone should offer to pay you more? No offense,

but the one thing you can say of loyalty for hire is that it's for hire."

"We'll finish out a contract," Sinja said. "I've been through enough to know what happens to a company with a reputation for switching sides mid-battle. But I won't lie, the boys I have are green, most of them. They haven't seen many campaigns."

It was a softening of *these poor bastards hardly know which end's the sharp one* but the meaning was much the same. The general waved the concern aside, which was fascinating. Balasar Gice wasn't interested in their field prowess. Which meant he either wanted them to lead the charges and soak up a few enemy spears and arrows—hardly a role that asked the general's presence at the negotiation—or there was something more, something that Sinja was still missing.

"How many of them speak Galt?"

"A third," Sinja said, inventing the number on the spot.

"I may have use for them. How loyal are they to you?"

"How loyal do they need to be?"

The general smiled. There was a touch of sorrow in his eyes and a long, thoughtful pause. Sinja felt a decision being made, though he couldn't say what the issue was.

"Enough to go against their own kind. Not in the field, but I'll want them as translators and agents. And whatever you can tell me of the winter cities. I'll want that as well."

Sinja smiled knowingly to cover his racing mind. Gice wasn't taking his army North. He was going east, into the cities of the Khaiem, with something close to every able-bodied man in Galt behind him. Sinja chuckled to hide a rush of fear.

"They'll follow you any place you care to go, so long as they're on the winning side," Sinja said. "Are you sure that's going to be you?"

"Yes," the general said, and the bare confidence in his voice was more persuasive than any reasoned argument he might have given. If the man had been trying to convince himself, he would have had a speech ready—why this insanity would work, how the army could overpower the andat, something. But Balasar was certain. The general sipped his water, waiting the space of five long breaths together. Then he spoke again. "You're thinking something?"

"You're not stupid," Sinja said. "So you're either barking mad, or you know something I don't. No one can take on the Khaiem."

"You mean no one can face the andat."

"Yes," Sinja agreed. "That's what I mean."

"I can."

"Forgive me if I keep my doubts about me," Sinja said.

The general nodded, considered Sinja for a long moment, then gestured toward the table. Sinja put down his bowl and stepped over as the general unrolled a long cloth scroll with a map of the cities of the Khaiem on it. Sinja stepped back from it as if there were an asp on it.

"General," he said, "if you're about to tell me your plans for this campaign, I think we might be ahead of where we should be."

Balasar put a hand on Sinja's arm. The Galt's gaze was firm and steady, his voice low and strangely intimate. Sinja saw how a personality like his own could command an army or a nation. Possibly, he thought, a world.

"Captain Ajutani, I don't share these plans with every mercenary captain who walks through my door. I don't trust them. I don't show them to my own captains, barring the ones in my small Council. The others I expect to trust me. But we're men of the world, you and I. You have something I think I could use."

"And you have nothing to lose by telling me," Sinja said, slowly. "Because I'm not leaving this building, am I?"

"Not even to go speak to your men," the general said. "You're here as my ally or my prisoner."

Sinja shook his head.

"That's a brave thing to say, General. It's only the two of us in here."

"If you attacked me, I'd kill you where you stood," Balasar

said in the same tone of voice he'd used before, and Sinja believed him. Balasar smiled gently and nudged him forward, toward the table.

"Let me show you why ally would be the better choice."

Still, Sinja held back.

"I'm not an idiot," he said. "If you tell me you plan to take over the Khaiem by flying through the sky on winged dogs, I'll still clap you on the back and swear I'm your ally."

"Of course you will. You'll say you're my dearest friend and solidly behind me. I'll thank you and distrust you and keep you unarmed and under guard. We'll each avoid turning our backs on the other. I think we can take that all as given," Balasar said with a dismissive wave. "I don't care what you say or do, Captain. I care what you *think*."

Sinja felt a genuine smile blooming on his lips. When he laughed, Balasar laughed with him.

"Well," Sinja said. "As long as we're agreed on all that. Go ahead. Convince me that you're going to prevail against the poets."

They talked for what seemed like the better part of the evening. Outside, the storm slackened, the clouds broke. By the time a servant boy came to light the lanterns, a moon so full it seemed too heavy to rise glowed in the indigo sky. Gnats and midges buzzed through the open windows, ignored by both men as they discussed Balasar's intentions and strategies. The general was open and forthcoming and honest, and with every unfolding scheme, Sinja understood that his life was worth whatever Balasar Gice said it was worth. It was up to him to convince the general that letting him live after he'd heard all this wouldn't be a mistake. It was a clever tactic, all the more so because once Sinja understood the trick, it lost none of its power.

Afterward, armsmen escorted him to a small, well-appointed bedchamber with windows too narrow to crawl out and a bar on the outside of the door. Sinja lay in the bed, listening to the nearly inaudible hiss and tick of the candle flame. His body felt poorly attached, likely to slip free of his mind at any moment. Light-headed, he washed his face in cold water, cracked his knuckles, anything to bring his mind to something real and immediate. Something the Galtic general had not just torn away.

It was as if he had fallen into a nightmare, or woken to something worse than one. He felt as if he'd just watched a man he knew well die by violence. The Galt's plan would end the world he had known. If it worked. And in his bones, he knew it would.

The hours passed, the night seeming to stretch on without end. Sinja paced his room or sat or lay sleepless on the bed, remembering the illness he had felt after his first battle. This was the same disease, back again. But the more he thought about it, the more his mind tracked across the maps he and the general had considered, the more his conviction grew.

The turncoat poet and the army were only a part of it—in some ways the least. It was the general's audacity and certainty and caution. It was the force of his personality. Sinja had seen commanders and wardens and kings, and he could tell the sort that fated themselves to lose. Balasar Gice was going to win.

And so, Sinja supposed with a sense of genuine regret, the right thing was to work for him.

6

>+< The poet's house was warm, the scent of trees thick in the air. The false dawn, prolonged by the mountains to the east, had just come, the sun making its way above the peaks to bathe the world in light. Through the opened door, Maati could hear the songs of birds deep in the yearly quest to draw mates to their nests. The dances and parties of the utkhaiem were much the same—who had the loveliest plumage, the more enticing song. There were fewer differences between men and birds than men liked to confess.

He sat on a couch, watching Cehmai at one side of the small table and Stone-Made-Soft at the other. Between them was the game board with its worn lines and stones. The game had been central to the binding Manat Doru had performed generations ago that first brought Stone-Made-Soft into existence, and as part of the legacy he bore, Cehmai had to play the game again—white stones moving forward against the black—as a reaffirmation of his control over the spirit. Fortunately, Manat Doru had also made Stone-Made-Soft a terrible player. Cehmai tapped his fingertips against the wood and shifted a black stone in the center of the board toward the left. Stone-Made-Soft frowned, its wide face twisted in concentration.

"No word yet," Cehmai said. "It's early days, though."

"What do you think he'll do?" Maati asked.

"I'm trying to think, please," the andat rumbled. They ignored it.

Cehmai leaned back in his seat. The years had treated him kindly. The fresh-faced, talented young man Maati had met when he first came to Machi was still there. If there was the first dusting of gray in the boy's hair, if the lines at the corners of his mouth were deeper now, and less prone to vanish when he relaxed, it did nothing to take away from the easy smile or the deep, grounded sense of self that Cehmai had always had. And even the respect he had for Maati—no longer a dread-touched awe, but still profound in its way—had never failed with familiarity.

"I'm afraid he'll do the thing," Cehmai said. "I suppose I'm also afraid that he won't. There's not a good solution."

"He could take a middle course," Maati said. "Demand that the Galts hand back Riaan on the threat of taking action. If the Dai-kvo tells them that he knows, it might be enough."

The andat lifted a thick-fingered hand, gently touched a white stone, and slid it forward with a hiss. Cehmai glanced over, considered, and pushed the black stone he'd moved before back into the space it had come from. The andat coughed in frustration and set its head on balled fists, staring at the board.

"It's odd," Cehmai said. "There was a time when I was at the school—before I'd even taken the black robes, so early on. There was a pigeon that had taken up residence in my cohort's rooms. Nasty thing. It would flap around through the air and drop feathers and shit on us all, and every time we waved it outside, it would come back. Then one day, one of the boys got lucky. He threw a boot at the poor thing and broke its wing. Well, we knew we were going to have to kill it. Even though it had been nothing but annoyance and filth, it was hard to break its neck."

"Were you the one that did it?" Maati asked.

Cehmai took a pose of acknowledgment.

"It felt like this," the younger poet said. "I won't enjoy this, if it's what we do."

The andat looked up from the board.

"Has it ever struck you people how arrogant you are?" it

asked, huge hands taking an attitude of query that bordered on accusation. "You're talking of slaughtering a nation. Thousands of innocent people destroyed, lands made barren, mountains leveled and the sea pulled up over them like a blanket. And you're feeling sorry for yourself that you had to wring a bird's neck as a boy? How can anyone have feelings that delicate and that numbed both at the same time?"

"It's your move," Cehmai said.

Stone-Made-Soft sighed theatrically—it had no need for breath, so every sigh it made was a comment—and turned back toward the game. It was essentially over. The andat had lost again as it always did, but they played to the last move, finishing the ritual humiliation once again.

"We're off to the North," Cehmai said as he put the stones back into their trays. "There's a new vein the Radaani want to explore, but I'm not convinced it's possible. Their engineers are swearing that the structure won't collapse, but those mountains are getting near lacework."

"Eight generations is a long time," Maati agreed. "Even without help, the mines would have become a maze by now."

"I fear the day an earthquake comes," Cehmai said as he stood and stretched. "One shake, and half these mountains will fold up flat, I'd swear it."

"Then I suppose we'd have to spend months digging up the bodies," Maati said.

"Not really," the andat said. Its voice was placid again, now that the game was ended. "If we make it soft enough, the bodies will float up through it. If stone is water, almost anything floats. We could have a whole field of stone flat as a lake, with mine dogs and men popping up out of it like bubbles."

"What a pleasant thought," Cehmai said, gently sarcastic. "And here I was wondering why we weren't invited to more dinners. And you, Maati-kvo? What's your day?"

"More work in the library," Maati said. "I want the place in order. If the Dai-kvo calls for me . . ."

"He will," Cehmai said. "You can count on that."

"If he does, I want the place left in order. A sane order that someone else could make sense of. Baarath had the thing put together like a puzzle. Took me three years just to make sense of it, and even then some of it I just went through book by book and made my own classifications."

"Well, he had a different opinion than yours," Cehmai said. "He wanted the library to be a place to bury secrets, not display them. It was how he made himself feel as if he mattered. I don't suppose I can blame him too much for that."

"I suppose not," Maati agreed.

The three of them walked along the wooded path that led to the palaces of the Khai. The stone towers of Machi rose high above the city, bright with the light of morning, and the smoke of the forges plumed up from the metalworkers' district in the south. Maati kept company with Cehmai and Stone-Made-Soft as far as the compound of House Radaani, where a litter and donkeys were waiting. They took poses of farewell, even the andat, and Maati sat on the steps of the compound to watch them lumber away to the North.

In the days since he, Otah, and Liat had broken the news to Cehmai, Maati had found himself less and less able to do his work. The familiar stacks and shelves and galleries of the library were uncomforting. The songs of the singing slaves in the gardens seemed to pull at him when he caught a phrase of their melodies. He found himself seeking out food when he wasn't hungry, wine when he had no thirst. He walked the streets of the city and the paths of the palaces more than he had in living memory, and even when his knees ached, he found himself unconsciously rising to pace the rooms of his apartments. Restless. He had become restless.

In part it was the knowledge that Liat and Nayiit were in the city, in the palaces even. At any time, he could seek them out, invite them to eat with him or talk with him. Nayiit, whom he had not known since the boy was shorter than little Danat was now. Liat, whose breath and body he had once said he would never be whole without. They were here at last.

In part it was the anticipation of a courier from the Dai-kvo, whether about his own work or Liat's case against the Galts. And of the two, he found the Galtic issue the lesser. Liat's argument was enough to convince him that they did have a rogue poet, but the chances that he would bind a new andat seemed remote. There in the middle of Galt without references, without the Dai-kvo or his fellow poets to work through the fine points of the binding, the most likely thing was that the man would try, fail, and die badly. It was a problem that would solve itself. And if the Dai-kvo took Liat's view and turned the andat loose against Galt, the chances of tragedy coming to the cities of the Khaiem was even less.

No, his unease came more from the prospect of his own success. He had lived so long as a failure that the prospect of success disturbed him. He knew that his heart should have been singing. He should have been drunk with pride.

And yet he found himself waking in the night, knotted with anger. In the darkness of his room, he would wake with the night candle over half burned, and stare at the netting above his bed as it shifted in barely felt drafts. The targets of his rage seemed to shift; one night he might wake with a list of the wrongs done him by Liat, the next with the conviction that he had suffered insult at the hands of Otah or the Dai-kvo. With the coming of dawn, the fit would pass, insubstantial as a dream, the complaints that had haunted him in darkness thin as cheesecloth in the light.

And still, he was restless.

He made his way slowly through the palaces and out to the city itself. The black-cobbled streets were alive with people. Carts of vegetables and early berries wound from the low towns toward the markets in the center of the city. Lambs on rough hemp leads trotted in ignorance toward the butchers' stalls. And wherever he went, a path was made for him, people took poses of respect and welcome and he returned them by habit. He paused at a cart and bought a meal of hot peppered beef and sweet onions wrapped in waxed paper. The young man running the cart refused to accept his lengths of copper. Another small amenity granted to the other poet of

Machi. Maati took a pose of thanks as best he could with one hand full of the food.

The towers of Machi seemed to touch the lowest clouds. It had been years since Maati had gone up one of the great towers. He remembered the platform swaying, its great arm-thick chains clanking against the stones as he rose. That far above the city, he had felt he was looking out from a mountain peak—the valley spread below so vast he'd imagined he could almost see the ocean. Not remotely truth, but what it felt like all the same. Looking at the towers now, he remembered what Cehmai had said. If there were an earthquake, the towers would certainly fall. For an instant, he imagined the stones pattering down in a deadly rain, the long, slumped piles of rubble that would lie where they fell. The corpses of giants.

He shook himself, pushing the darkness away, and turned back toward the palaces. He wondered, as he trundled toward the library, where Nayiit was today. He had seen the boy—a man old enough to have a child of his own, and still in Maati's mind a boy—several times since his arrival. Dinners, dances, formal meetings. They had not yet had a conversation as father and son. Maati wondered whether he wanted them to, or if the reminder of what might have been would be too uncomfortable for them both. Perhaps he could track the boy down, show him through the city for a day. Or through the tunnels. There were a few teahouses still in business down in their winter quarters. That was the sort of thing only a local would know. Maybe the boy would be interested. . . .

He paused as he rounded the slow curving path toward the library. Two forms were sitting on its wide stone steps, but neither of them was Nayiit. The older, rounder woman wore robes of seafoam green embroidered with yellow. Liat's hair was still as dark as when she'd been a girl sitting beside him on a cart leaving Saraykeht behind them. Her head still took the same just-off angle when she was speaking to someone to whom she was trying especially to be kind.

The younger looked thin and coltish beside her. Her robes were deep blue shot with white, and Eiah had her hair up, held in place with thick silvered pins that glittered even from here. She was the first to catch sight of him, and her thin arm rose, waving him nearer. He was too thick about the belly these days to trot or he would have.

"We've been waiting for you," Eiah said as he drew near. Her tone was accusing. Liat glanced up at him, amused.

"I was seeing Cehmai off on his journey," Maati said. "He's going to the Radaani mines in the North. A new vein, I think. But I did take the longer way back. If I'd known you were waiting, I'd have been here sooner."

Eiah considered this, and then without word or gesture visibly accepted the apology.

"We've been talking about marriage," Liat said.

"Did you know that Liat-cha never got married to anyone? Nayiit's her son. She had a baby, but she's never been wed?"

"Well, the two things aren't perfectly related, you know," Maati began, but Eiah rolled her eyes and took a pose that unasked the question.

"Eiah-cha and I were going to the high gardens. I've packed some bread and cheese. We thought you might care to join us?"

"You've already eaten," Eiah said, pointing to the waxed paper in his hand.

"This?" Maati said. "No, I was feeding this to the pigeons. Wait a moment, I'll get a jug of wine and some bowls. . . ."

"I'm old enough to drink wine," Eiah said.

"Three bowls, then," Maati said. "Just give me a moment."

He walked back to his apartments, feeling something very much like relief. The afternoon trapped with old scrolls and codices, books and frail maps was banished. He was saved from it. He threw the waxed paper with the remaining onions into a corner where the servants would clean it, took a thick earthenware jug of wine off his shelves, and dropped three small wine bowls into his sleeve. On his way back out to the steps, where he was certain no one could see him, he trotted.

* * *

DANAT'S COUGH had returned.

Otah had filled his day playing Khai Machi. He had reviewed the preparations for the Grand Audience he was already past due holding. There was an angry letter from the Khai Tan-Sadar asking for an explanation of Otah's decision not to take his youngest daughter as one of his wives that he responded to with as much aplomb as he could muster. His Master of Stone—responsible for keeping the books of the city—had discovered that two of the forms from which silver lengths were struck had been tampered with and reported the progress of his investigation into the matter. The widow of Adaiit Kamau demanded an audience, insisting again that her husband had been murdered and demanding justice in his name. The priests asked for money for the temple and the procession of the beasts. A young playwright, son of Oiad How of House How, had composed an epic in the honor to the Khai Machi, and asked permission to perform it. Permission and funding. The representative of the tinsmiths petitioned for a just distribution of coal, as the ironworkers had been taking more than their share. The ironworkers' explaining that they worked iron, not—sneering and smiling as if Otah would understand—*tin*. And on and on and on until Otah was more than half tempted to grab a passing servant, put him on the black lacquer chair, and let the city take its chances. And at the end, with all the weight of the city and the impending death of Galt besides, the thing that he could not face was that Danat's cough had returned.

The nursery glowed by the light of the candles. Kiyan sat on the raised bed, talking softly to their son. Great iron statues of strange, imagined beasts had been kept in the fire grates all day and pulled out when night fell, and as he quietly walked forward, Otah could feel the heat radiating from them. The physician's assistant—a young man with a serious expression—took a respectful pose and walked quietly from the room, leaving the family alone.

Otah stepped up to the bedside. Danat's eyes, half closed in drowse, shifted toward him and a smile touched Otah's mouth.

"I got sick again, Papa-kya," he said. His voice was rough and low; the familiar sign of a hard day.

"Don't talk, sweet," Kiyan said, smoothing Danat's forehead with the tips of her fingers. "You'll start it again."

"Yes," Otah said, sitting across from his wife, taking his son's hand. "I heard. But you've been sick before, and you've gotten better. You'll get better again. It's good for boys to be a bit ill when they're young. It gets all the hardest parts out of the way early. Then they can be strong old men."

"Tell me a story?" Danat asked.

Otah took a breath, his mind grasping for a children's story. He tried to recall being in this room himself or one like it. He had been, when he'd been Danat's age. Someone had held him when he'd been ill, had told him stories to distract him. But everything in his life before he'd been disowned and sent to the school existed in the blur of half-memory and dream.

"Papa-kya's tired, sweet," Kiyan said. "Let Mama tell you about . . ."

"No!" Danat cried, his face pulling in—mouth tight, brows thunderously low. "I want Papa-kya—"

"It's all right," Otah said. "I'm not so tired I can't tell my own boy a story."

Kiyan smiled at him, her eyes amused and apologetic both. *I tried to spare you.*

"Once, back before the Empire, when the world was very new," Otah said, then paused. "There, ah. There was a goat."

The goat—whose name was coincidentally also Danat—went on to meet a variety of magical creatures and have long, circuitous conversations to no apparent point or end until Otah saw his son's eyes shut and his breath grow deep and steady. Kiyan rose and silently snuffed all but the night candle. The room filled with the scent of spent wicks. Otah let go of his son's hand and quietly pulled the netting closed.

In the near-darkness, Danat's eyelids seemed darker, smudged with kohl. His skin was smooth and brown as eggshell. Kiyan touched Otah's shoulder and motioned with her gaze to the door. He laced his fingers in hers and together they walked to the hallway.

The physician's assistant sat on a low stool, a bowl of rice and fish in his hands.

"I will be here for the night, Most High," the assistant said as Otah paused before him. "My teacher expects that the boy will sleep soundly, but if he wakes, I will be here."

Otah took a pose expressing gratitude. It was a humbling thing for a Khai to do before a servant, even one as skilled as this. The physician's assistant bowed deeply in response. The walk to their own rooms was a short one—down one hallway, up a wide flight of stairs worked in marble and silver, and then the gauntlet of their own servants. The evening's meal was set out for them—quail glazed with pork fat and honey, pale bread with herbed butter, fresh trout, iced apples. More food than any two people could eat.

"It isn't in his chest," Kiyan said as she lifted the trout's pale flesh from delicate, translucent bones. "His color is always good. His lips never blue at all. The physician didn't hear any water when he breathes, and he can blow up a pig's bladder as well as I could."

"And all that's good?" Otah said. "He can't run across a room without coughing until his head aches."

"All that's better than the alternative," Kiyan said. "They don't know what it is. They give him teas that make him sleep, and hope that his body's wise enough to mend itself."

"This has been going on too long. It's been almost a year since he was really well."

"I know it," Kiyan said, and the weariness in her voice checked Otah's frustration. "Really, love, I'm quite clear."

"I'm sorry, Kiyan-kya," he said. "It's just . . ."

He shook his head.

"Hard feeling powerless?" she said gently. Otah nodded. Kiyan sighed softly, a sympathy for his pain. Then, "A *goat*?"

"It was what came to mind."

After the meal, after their hands had been washed for them in silver bowls, after Otah had suffered yet another change of robes, Kiyan kissed him and retreated to her rooms. Otah stepped down from his palace, instructed the retinue of servants that he wished to be left alone, and made his way west, toward the library. The sun had long since slipped behind the mountains, but the sky remained a bright gray, the clouds touched with rose and gold. Spring would soon give way to summer, the long, bright days and brief nights. Still, it was not so early in the season that lanterns didn't glow from the windows that he passed. Stars glittered in the east as the night rose. The library itself was dark, but candles burned in Maati's apartments, and Otah made his way down the path.

Voices came to him, raised in laughter. A man's and a woman's, and both familiar as memory. They sat on chairs set close together. In the yellow candlelight, Maati's cheeks looked rosy. Liat's hair had escaped its bun, locks of it tumbling across her brow, down the curve of her neck. The air smelled of mulling spices and wine, and Eiah lay on a couch, one long, thin arm cast over her eyes. Liat's eyes went wide when she caught sight of him, and Maati turned toward the door to see what had startled her.

"Otah-kvo!" he said, waving him forward. "Come in. Come in. It's my fault. I've kept your daughter too long. I should have sent her home sooner. I wasn't thinking."

"Not at all," Otah said, stepping in. "I've come for your help actually."

Maati took a pose of query. His hands were not perfectly steady, and Liat stifled a giggle. Both of them were more than a little drunk. A bowl of warmed wine sat on the edge of the brazier, a silver serving cup hooked to the rim. Otah glanced at it, and Maati waved him on. There were no bowls, so Otah drank from the serving cup.

"What can I do, Most High?" Maati asked with a grin that was for the most part friendly.

"I need a book. Something with children's stories in it. Fables, or light epics. History, if it's well enough written. Danat's asking me to tell stories, and I don't really know any."

Liat chuckled and shook her head, but Maati nodded in understanding. Otah sat beside his sleeping daughter while Maati considered. The wine was rich and deep, and the spices alone made Otah's head swim a little.

"What about the one from the Dancer's Court?" Liat said. "The one with the stories about the half-Bakta boy who intrigued for the Emperor."

Maati pursed his lips.

"They're a bit bloody, some of them," he said.

"Danat's a boy. He'll love them. Besides, you read them to Nayiit without any lasting damage," Liat said. "Those and the green book. The one that was all political allegories where people turned into light or sank into the ground."

"The Silk Hunter's Dreams," Maati said. "That's a thought. I have a copy of that one too, where I can put my hand on it. Only, Otah-kvo, don't tell him the one with the crocodile. Nayiit-kya wouldn't sleep for days after I told him that one."

"I'll trust you," Otah said.

"Wait," Maati said, and with a grunt he pulled himself to standing. "You two stay here. I'll be back with it in three heartbeats."

An uncomfortable silence fell on Otah and Liat. Otah turned to consider Eiah's sleeping face. Liat shifted in her chair.

"She's a lovely girl," Liat said softly. "We spent the day together, the three of us, and I was sure she'd wear us thin by the end of it. Still, we're the ones that lasted longest, eh?"

"She doesn't have a head for wine yet," Otah said.

"We didn't give her wine," Liat said, then chuckled. "Well, not much anyway."

"If the worst she does is sneak away to drink with the pair of you, I'll be the luckiest man alive," Otah said. As if hearing him, Eiah sighed in her sleep and shifted away, pressing her face to the cushions.

"She looks like her mother," Liat said. "Her face is that same shape. The eyes are your color, though. She'll be stunning when she's older. She'll break hearts. But I suppose they all do. Ours if no one else's."

Otah looked up. Liat's expression had darkened, the shadows of lanternlight gathering on the curves of her face. It had been another lifetime, it seemed, when Otah had first known her. Only four years older than Eiah was now. And he'd been younger than Nayiit. Babies, it seemed. Too young to know what they were doing, or how precarious the world truly was. It hadn't seemed that way at the time, though. Otah remembered it all with a terrible clarity.

"You're thinking of Saraykeht," she said.

"Was it that obvious?"

"Yes," Liat said. "How much have you told them? About what happened?"

"Kiyan knows everything. A few others."

"They know how Seedless was freed? And Heshai-kvo, how he was killed?"

For a sick moment, Otah was back in the filthy room, in the stink of mud and raw sewage from the alley. He remembered the ache in his arms. He remembered the struggle as the old poet fought for air with the cord biting into his throat. It had seemed the right thing, then. Even to Heshai. The andat, Seedless, had come to Otah with the plan. Aid in Heshai-kvo's suicide—for in many ways that was what it had been—and Liat would be saved. Maati would be saved. A thousand Galtic babies would stay safely in their mother's wombs, the power of the andat never turned against them.

Otah wondered when things had changed. When he had stopped being someone who would kill a good man to protect the innocent, and become willing to let a nation die if it meant protecting his own. Likely it had been the moment he'd first seen Eiah squirming on Kiyan's breast.

"Do you know?" Otah asked. "How it happened, I mean."

"Only guesses," Liat said. "If you wanted to tell me . . ."

"Thank you," Otah said with a sigh, "but maybe it's best to

leave that buried. It's all finished now, and there's no undo-ing any of it."

"Perhaps you're right."

"We will need to talk about Nayiit," Otah said. "Not now. Not with . . ." He nodded to the sleeping girl.

"I understand," Liat said and brushed her hair back from her eyes. "I don't mean any harm, 'Tani. I wouldn't hurt you or your family. I didn't come here . . . I wouldn't have come here if I hadn't had to."

The door swung open, a gust of cool air coming from it, and Maati stood triumphantly in the frame. He held a small book bound in blue silk as if it were a trophy of war.

"Got the bastard!" he said, and walked over to Otah, pre-senting it over one arm like a sword. "For you, Most High, and your son."

Over Maati's shoulder, Otah could see Liat look away. Otah only took the book, adopted a pose of thanks, and turned to gently shake Eiah's shoulder. She grunted, her brow furrow-ing.

"It's time to come home, Eiah-kya," Otah said. "Come along."

"'M'wake," Eiah protested, but slowly. Rubbing her eyes with the back of one hand, she rose.

They said their good nights, and Otah led his daughter out, closing the door to Maati's apartments behind them. The night had grown cool, and the stars had occupied the sky like a conquering army. Otah laid his arm across Eiah's shoulder, hers under it, around his ribs. She leaned into him as they walked. Night-blooming flowers scented the air, soft as rain. They were just coming in sight of the entrance of the First Palace when Eiah spoke, her voice still abstracted with sleep.

"Nayiit-cha's yours, isn't he, Papa-kya?"

LIAT WOKE in dim moonlight; the night candle had gone out or else they hadn't bothered to light it. She couldn't recall which. Beside her, Maati mumbled something in his sleep, as he always had. Liat smiled at the dim profile on the pillow beside her. He looked younger in sleep, the lines at his mouth softened, the storm at his brow calmed. She resisted the urge to caress his cheek, afraid to wake him. She had taken lovers in the years since she'd returned to Saraykeht. A half-dozen or so, each a man whose company she had enjoyed, and all of whom she could remember fondly.

She thought, sometimes, that she'd reversed the way women were intended to love. Butterfly flirtations, flitting from one man to another, taking none seriously, were best kept by the young. Had she taken her casual lovers as a girl, they would have been exciting and new, and she would have known too little to notice that they were empty. Instead, Liat had lost her heart twice before she'd seen twenty summers, and if those loves were gone—even this one, sleeping now at her side—the memory of them was there. Once, she had told herself the world was nothing if she didn't have a man who loved her. A man of importance and beauty, a man whom she might, through her gentle guidance, save.

She had been another woman, then. And who, she wondered, had she become now?

She rose quietly, parting the netting, and stepped out onto the cool floor. She found her outer robe and wrapped it around herself. Her inner robes and her sandals she could reclaim tomorrow. Now she wanted her own bed, and pillows less thick with memories.

She slipped out the door, pulling it closed behind her. So far North and without an ocean to hold the warmth of the day, Machi's nights were cold, even now with spring at its height. Gooseflesh rose on her legs and arms, her belly and breasts, as she trotted along the wide, darkened paths to the apartments that Itani or Otah or the Khai Machi had given to her and her son.

More than a week had passed since he had come to Maati's apartments, gathering up a children's book and a daughter halfway to womanhood and leaving behind a lasting unease. Liat had not spoken with him since, but the dread of the coming conversation weighed heavy. As Nayiit had grown, she'd seen nothing in him but himself. Even when people swore that the boy had her eyes, her mouth, her way of sighing, she'd never seen it. Perhaps when there was no space between a mother and her child, the sameness becomes invisible. Perhaps it merely seemed normal. She would have admitted that her son looked something like his father. It was only in seeing them together, seeing the simple, powerful knowing in Otah's wife's expression, that Liat understood the depth of her error in letting Nayiit come.

And with that came her understanding of how it could not be undone. Her first impulse had been to send him away at once, to hide him again the way a child caught with a forbidden sweet might stuff it away into a sleeve as if unseen now might somehow mean never seen at all. Only the years of running her house had counseled her otherwise. The situation was what it was. Attempting any subterfuge would only make the Khai wary, and his unease might mean Nayiit's death. As long as her son lived, he posed a threat to Danat, and she knew enough to understand that a babe held from its first breath meant something that a man full-grown never could. If Otah were forced to choose, Liat had no illusions what that choice would be.

And so she prepared herself, prepared her arguments and her negotiating strategies, and told herself it would end well. They were all together, allies against the Galts. There would be no need. She told herself there would be no need.

At her apartments, no candles were lit, but a fire burned in the grate: old pine, rich with sap that popped and hissed and filled the air with its scent. When she entered, her son looked up from the flames and took a pose of welcome, gesturing to a divan beside him. Liat hesitated, surprised by a sudden embarrassment, then gathered her sense of humor and sat beside him. He smelled of wine and smoke, and his robes hung as loose on him as her own did on her.

"You've been to the teahouses," Liat said, trying to keep any note of disapproval from her voice.

"You've been with my father," he replied.

"I've been with Maati," Liat said as if it were an agreement and not a correction.

Nayiit leaned forward and took up a length of iron, prodding the burning logs. Sparks rose and vanished like fireflies.

"I haven't been able to see him," Nayiit said. "We've been here weeks now, and he hasn't come to speak with me. And every time I go to the library he's gone or he's with you. I think you're trying to keep us from each other."

Liat raised her eyebrows and ran her tongue across the inside of her teeth, weighing the coppery taste that sprang to her mouth, thinking what it meant. She coughed.

"You aren't wrong," she said at last. "I'm not ready for it. Maati's not who he was back then."

"So instead of letting us face each other and see what it is we see, you've decided to start up an affair with him and take all his time and attention?" There was no rancor in his voice, only sadness and amusement. "It doesn't seem the path of wisdom, Mother."

"Well, not when you say it that way," Liat said. "I was thinking of it as coming to know him again before the conflict began. I did love him, you know."

"And now?"

"And still. I still love him, in my fashion," Liat said, her voice rueful. "I know I'm not what he wants. I'm not the person he wants me to be, and I doubt I ever have been, truly. But we enjoy each other. There are things we can say to each other that no one else would understand. They weren't there, and we were. And he's such a little boy. He's carried so much and been so disappointed, and there's still the possibility in him of this . . . *joy*. I can't explain it."

"If I ask you as a favor, will you let me know him as well? We may not actually fight like pit dogs if you let us in the same room together. And if there's conflict at all, it's between us. Not you."

Liat opened her mouth, closed it, shook her head. She sighed.

"Of course," she said. "Of course, I'm sorry. I've been an old hen, and I'm sorry for it, but . . . I know it's not a trade. We aren't negotiating, not really. But Nayiit-kya, you can't say you haven't been with a woman since we've come here. You didn't choose to go south, even when I asked you to. Sweet, is it so bad at home?"

"Bad?" he said, speaking slowly. As if tasting the word. "I don't know. No. Not bad. Only not good. And yes, I know I haven't been keeping to my own bed. Do you think my darling wife has been keeping to hers?"

Liat's mind turned, searching for words, making sense as best she could of what he had asked and what he had meant by it. It was true enough that Tai had come into the world at an odd time, but he was a first child, and wombs weren't made to be certain. She rushed through her memory, looking for signs she might have missed, suggestions back in their lives in Saraykeht that would have pointed at some venomous question, and slowly she began, if not to understand, then at least to guess.

"You think he isn't yours," she said. "You think Tai is another man's child."

"Nothing like that," Nayiit said. "It's only that you can make a child from love or from anger. Or inattention. Or only from not knowing what better to do. A baby isn't proof of anything between the father and mother beyond a few moments' pressure."

"It isn't the child's fault."

"No, I suppose not," Nayiit said.

"This is why you came, then? To Nantani, and then up here? To be away from them?"

"I came because I wanted to. Because it was the world, and when was I going to see it again? Because you wanted someone to carry your bags and wave off dogs. It was only partly that I couldn't stay. And then when you were going to see him, Maati-cha . . . How could I not come along for that too? The chance to see my father again. I remember him, you know? I do, from when I was small, I remember a day we were all in a small hut. There was an iron stove, and it was raining, and you were singing while he bathed me. I don't know when that was, I can't put a time on it. But I remember his face."

"You would have known him, if you'd seen him in passing. You'd have known who he was."

Nayiit took a pose of affirmation. He pursed his lips and chuckled ruefully.

"I don't know what it is to be a father. I'm only working from—"

"Nayiit-kya?" came a voice from the shadows behind them. A soft, feminine voice. "Is everything well?"

She stepped toward the light. A young woman, twenty summers, perhaps as many as twenty-two. She wore bedding tied around her waist, her breasts bare, her hair still wild from the pillows.

"Jaaya-cha, this is my mother. Mother, Jaaya Biavu."

The girl blanched, then flushed. She took a pose of welcome, not bothering to cover herself, but her gaze was on Nayiit. It spoke of both humiliation and contempt. Nayiit didn't look at her. The woman turned and stalked away.

"That wasn't kind," Liat said.

"Very little of what she and I do involves kindness," he said. "I don't expect I'll see her again. By which I mean, I don't suppose she'll see me."

"Is she politically connected? If her family is utkhaiem . . ."

"I don't think she is," Nayiit said, his face in his hands. It was hard to be sure in the firelight, but she thought the tips of his ears were blushing. "I suppose I should have asked."

He struggled for a moment, trying to speak and failing. His brow furrowed and Liat had to resist the urge to reach over and smooth it with her thumb, the way she had when he'd been a babe.

"I'm sorry," he said. "You know that I'm sorry."

"For what?" she asked, her voice low and stern. As if there were any number of things for which he might be.

"For not being a better man," he said.

The fire popped, as if in comment. Liat took her son's hand, and for a long moment, they were silent. Then:

"I don't care what you do with your marriage, Nayiit-kya. If you don't love her, end it. Or if you don't trust her. As you see fit. People come together and they part. It's what we do. But the boy. You can't leave the boy. That isn't fair."

"It's what Maati-cha did to us."

"No," Liat said, giving his hand the smallest pressure, and then releasing it. "We left him."

Nayiit turned to her slowly, his hands folding into a pose that asked confirmation. It was as if the words were too dangerous to speak.

"I left him," Liat said. "I took you when you were still a babe, and I was the one to leave him."

She saw a moment's shock in his expression, gone as fast as it had come. His face went grave, his hands as still as stones. As still as a man bending his will to keep them still.

"Why?" he asked. His voice was low and thready.

"Oh, love. It was so long ago. I was someone else, then," she said, and knew as she said it that it wasn't enough. "I did because he was only half there. And because I couldn't see to all of his needs and all of yours and have no one there to look after me."

"It was better without him?"

"I thought it would be. I thought I was cutting my losses. And then, later, when I wasn't so certain anymore, I convinced myself it had been the right thing, just so I could tell myself I hadn't been wrong."

He was shaken, though he tried to cover it. She knew him too well to be fooled.

"He wasn't there, Nayiit. But he never left you."

And part of me never left him, she thought. What would the world have been if I had chosen otherwise? Where would we all be now if that part of him and of me had been enough? Still in that little hut in the low town near the Dai-kvo? Would they all have lived together in the library these past years as Maati had?

Those other, ghostlike people made a pretty dream, but then there would have been no one to hear of the Galts and the missing poet, no one to travel to Nantani. And little Tai would not have been born, and she would never have seen Amat Kyaan again. Someone else would have been with the old woman when she died—someone else or no one. And Liat would never have taken House Kyaan, would never have proven herself competent to the world and to her own satisfaction.

It was too much. The changes, the differences were too great to think of as good or as bad. The world they had now was too much itself, good and evil too tightly woven to wish for some other path. And still it would be wrong to say she found herself without regrets.

"Maati loves you," she said, softly. "You should see him. I won't interfere again. But first, you should go tend to your guest. Smooth things over."

Nayiit nodded, and then a moment later, he smiled. It was the same charming smile she'd known when she was a girl and it had been on different lips. Nayiit would charm the girl, say something sweet and funny, and the pain would be forgotten for a time. He was his father's son. Son of the Khai Machi. Eldest son, and doomed to the fratricidal struggle of succession that stained every city in each generation. She wondered how far Otah would go to avoid that, to keep his boy safe from her schemes. That conversation had to come, and soon. Perhaps it would be best if she took it to the Khai herself, if she stopped waiting for him to find a right moment.

Nayiit took a querying pose, and Liat shook herself. She waved his concern away.

"I'm tired," she said. "I've come all this way back to have my own bed to myself, and I'm still not in it. I'm too old to sleep in a lover's arms. They twitch and snore and keep me awake all night."

"They do, don't they?" Nayiit said. "Does it get better, do you think? With enough time, would you be so accustomed to it, you'd sleep through?"

"I don't know," Liat said. "I've never made the attempt."

"Like mother, like son, I suppose," Nayiit said as he rose. He bent and kissed the crown of her head before he retreated back into the shadows.

Like mother, like son.

Liat pulled her robe tighter and sat near the fire, as if touched by a sudden chill.

7

>+<   The jeweler was a small man, squat but broad. To his credit, he seemed truly ill at ease. It took courage, Otah thought as he listened, to bring a matter such as this before a Khai. He wondered how many others had seen something of the sort and looked away. Any merchant has to expect some losses from theft. And after all, she was the daughter of the Khai. . . .

When it was over—and it seemed to take half a day, though it couldn't have lasted more than half a hand—Otah thanked the man, ordered that payment be made to him, and waited calm and emotionless until the servants and court followers had gone. Only the body servants remained, half a dozen men and women of the utkhaiem who dedicated their lives to bringing him a cracker if he felt like one, or a cup of limed water.

"Find Eiah and take her to the blue chamber. Bring her under guard if you have to."

"Under guard?" the eldest of the servants said.

"No, don't. Just bring her. See that she gets there."

"Most High," the man said, taking a pose that accepted the command. Otah rose and walked out of the room without replying. He stalked the halls of the palace, ignoring the Master of Tides and his ineffectual flapping papers, ignoring the poses of obeisance and respect turned to him wherever he went, looking only for Kiyan. The rest of these people were unimportant.

He found her in the great kitchens, standing beside the chief cook with a dead chicken in her hands. The cook, a woman of not less than sixty summers who had served Otah's father and grandfather, met his eyes and went pale. He wondered belatedly how many times the previous Khaiem of Machi had visited their kitchens, great or low.

"What's happened?" Kiyan asked instead of a greeting.

"Not here," Otah said. His wife nodded, passed the bird's carcass back to the cook, and followed Otah to their rooms. As calmly as he could, Otah related the audience. Eiah and two of her friends—Talit Radaani and Shoyen Pak—had visited a jeweler's shop in the goldsmiths' quarter. Eiah had stolen a brooch of emerald and pearl. The jeweler and his boy had seen it, had come to the court asking for payment.

"He was quite polite about the whole thing," Otah said. "He cast it as a mistake. Eiah-cha, in her girlish flights of attention, forgot to arrange for payment. He was sorry to bother me with it, but he hadn't been sure who I would prefer such issues be taken to and on and on and on. Gods!"

"How much was it?" Kiyan asked.

"Three lengths of gold," Otah said. "Not that it matters. I've got the whole city to put on for taxes and half a thousand bits of jewelry in boxes that no one's worn in lifetimes. It's . . . She's a thief! She's going through the city, taking whatever catches her eye and . . ."

Otah ran out of words and had to make do with a rough, frustrated grunt. He threw himself down on a couch, shaking his head.

"It's my fault," he said. "I've been too busy with the court. I haven't been a decent father to her. All the time she's spent with the daughters of the utkhaiem, playing idiot court games about who has the prettiest dress or the most servants—"

"Or the highest marriage," Kiyan said.

Otah put his hand over his eyes. That was more than he could think about just now. How to correct his daughter, how to show her what she'd done wasn't right, how to try to be a father to her; yes, that he could sit with. That it was too late, that she was already old enough to be another man's wife; that was too much to bear.

"It's a problem, love, yes," Kiyan said. "But sweet. She's fourteen summers old. She stole a pretty thing to see if she could. It's not actually unusual. I was a year older than her when my father caught me sneaking apples off the back of a farmer's cart."

"And did he marry you off to the farmer in punishment?"

"I'm sorry I brought up the marriage. I only meant that Eiah's world's no simpler than ours. It only seems that way from here. To her, it's just as confused and difficult as anything you deal with. She's only half a girl, and not quite half a woman."

Kiyan frowned. Her eyes were rueful and resigned, and she stretched her arms until the elbows cracked.

"My father made me apologize to the farmer and work for the man until I'd earned back twice the cost of what I'd taken. I don't know that's much guidance for us, though. I don't think any of these girls could do work worth three lengths of gold."

"So what do we do?"

"It doesn't matter, love. As long as she's clear that what she did didn't end the way she'd hoped, we'll have come as close as we can. I'd say restrict her from seeing Talit Radaani for a week's time, but that hardly seems equal to the stakes."

"She could assist the physicians," Otah said. "Carry out the night pans, wash dressings for the hurt. A week of that to pay back the city for what it bought her."

Kiyan chuckled.

"So long as she doesn't start enjoying it. She plays at being repulsed by blood because it's expected of her. I think at heart, there's nothing she'd like more than to cut a body apart and see how it's built. She'd have made a fine physician if she'd been born a bit lower."

They talked a bit longer, and Otah felt his rage and uncertainty fade. Kiyan's quiet, sane, thoughtful voice was the most soothing thing he knew. She was right. It wasn't strange, it wasn't a sign that Eiah would grow up to be her aunt Idaan, scheming and killing and lying for the pleasure of it. It was a girl of fourteen summers seeing how far she could go, and the answer was not so far as this. Otah kissed Kiyan before they left, his lips on her cheek. She smiled. There were crow's-feet at the corners of her eyes now. White strands had shot her hair since she'd been young, but there were more now. Her eyes still glittered as they had when he'd met her in Udun when she'd been the keep of a wayhouse and he had been a courier. She seemed to sense his thoughts, and put her hand to his cheek.

"Shall we go be the troll-like, unfair, unfeeling, stupid, venal dispensers of unjust punishment?" she asked.

The blue chamber was wide and round, a table of white marble dominating it like a sheet of ice floating in a far northern sea. The windows looked out on the gardens through walls so thick that sparrows and grackles perched in the sills and pecked at the carved meshwork of the inner shutters. Eiah had been pacing, but stopped when they came in. She looked from one to the other, trying for an innocence of expression that she couldn't quite reach.

"Come, sit," Kiyan said, gesturing to the table. Eiah came forward as if against her will and sat in one of the carved wooden chairs. Her gaze darted between the two of them, her chin already beginning to slide forward.

"I understand you took something from a jeweler. A brooch," Otah said. "Is that true?"

"Who told you that?" Eiah asked.

"Is it true?" Otah repeated, and his daughter looked down. When she frowned, the same small vertical line appeared between her brows that would sometimes show Kiyan's distress. Otah felt the passing urge to soothe her fears, but this wasn't the moment for comfort. He scowled until she looked up, then down again, and nodded. Kiyan sighed.

"Who told you?" Eiah asked again. "It was Shoyen, wasn't it? She's jealous because Talit and I were—"

"You told us, just now," Otah said. "That's all that matters."

Eiah's lips closed hard. Kiyan took a turn, telling Eiah that she'd done wrong, and they all knew it. Even she had to know that simply taking things wasn't right. They had paid her debt, but now she would have to make it good herself. They had decided that she would work with the physicians for a week, and if she didn't go, the physicians had instructions to send for . . .

"I'm not going to," Eiah said. "It's not fair. Talit Radaani sneaks things out of her father's warehouse all the time and no one ever makes her do anything for it."

"I can see that changes," Otah said.

"Don't!" Eiah barked. The birds startled away; a flutter of wings that sounded like panic. "Don't you dare! Talit will hate me forever if she thinks I'm making her . . . Papa-kya! Please, don't do that."

"It might be wise," Kiyan said. "All three girls were party to it."

"You can't! You can't do that to me!" Eiah's eyes were wild. She pushed back the chair as she stood. "I'll tell them Nayiit's your son! I'll tell!"

Otah felt the air go out of the room. Eiah's eyes went wide, aware that she had just done something worse than stealing a bauble, but unsure what it was. Only Kiyan seemed composed and calm. She smiled dangerously.

"Sit down, love," she said. "Please. Sit."

Eiah sat. Otah clasped his hands hard enough the knuckles ached, but there weren't words for the mix of guilt and shame and anger and sorrow. His heart was too many things at once. Kiyan didn't look at him when she spoke; her gaze was on Eiah.

"You will never repeat what you've just said to anyone. Nayiit-cha is Liat's son by Maati. Because if he isn't, if he's the thing you just said, then he will have to kill Danat or

Danat will have to kill him. And when that happens, the blood will be on your hands, because you could have prevented it and chose not to. Don't speak. I'm not finished. If any of the houses of the utkhaiem thought Danat was not the one and only man who could take his father's place, some of them would start thinking of killing him themselves in expectation of Nayiit-cha favoring them once he became Khai Machi. I can't protect him from everyone in this city, any more than I can protect him from air or his own body. You have done a wrong thing, stealing. And if you truly mean to hold your brother's life hostage to keep from being chastised for it, I would like to know that now."

Eiah wept silently, shocked by the cold fire in Kiyan's voice. Otah felt as if he'd been slapped as well. As if he ought somehow to have known, all those years ago, in that distant city, that the consequences of taking to his lover's bed would come back again to threaten everything he held dear. His daughter took a pose that begged her mother's forgiveness.

"I won't, Mama-kya. I won't say anything. Not ever."

"You'll apologize to the man you stole from and you will go in the morning to the physician's house and do whatever they ask of you. I will decide what to do about Talit and Shoyen."

"Yes, Mama-kya."

"You can leave now," Kiyan said and looked away. Eiah rose, silent except for the rough breath of tears, and left the room. The door closed behind her.

"I'm sorry—"

"Don't," Kiyan said. "Not now. I can't . . . I don't want to hear it just now."

Otah rose and walked to the window. The sun was high, but the towers cast shadows across the city all the same, like trees above children. Far to the west, clouds were gathering over the mountains, towering white thunderheads with bases dark as a bruise. There would be a storm later. It would come. One of the sparrows returned, considered Otah once with each eye, and then flew away again.

"What would you ask me to do?" Otah said. His voice was placid. No one would have known from the words how much pain lay behind them. No one except Kiyan. "I can't unmake him. Should I have him killed?"

"How did Eiah know?" Kiyan asked.

"She saw. Or she guessed. She knew the way that you did."

"No one told her? Maati or Liat or Nayiit. None of them told her?"

"No."

"You're sure?"

"I am."

"Because if they did, if they're spreading it through the city that you have—"

"They aren't. I was there when she realized it. Only me. No one else."

Kiyan took a long, low, shuddering breath. If it had been otherwise—if someone had told Eiah as part of a plan to spread word of Nayiit's parentage—Kiyan would have asked him to have the boy killed. He wondered what he would have done. He wondered how he would have refused her.

"They'll leave the city as soon as we have word from the Dai-kvo," Otah said. "Either they'll go back to Saraykeht or they'll go to the Dai-kvo's village. Either way, they'll be gone from here."

"And if they come back?"

"They won't. I'll see to it. They won't hurt Danat, love. He's safe."

"He's ill. He's still coughing," Kiyan said. That was it too, of course. Seasons had come and gone, and Danat was still haunted by illness. It was natural for them—Kiyan and himself both—to bend themselves double to protect him from the dangers that they could, especially since there were so many so close over which they were powerless.

It was part of why Otah had postponed for so long the conversation he was doomed to have with Liat Chokavi. But it was only part. Kiyan's chair scraped against the floor as she rose. Otah put his hand out to her, and she took it, stepping in close to him, her arms around him. He kissed her temple.

"Promise me this all ends well," she said. "Just tell me that."

"It will be fine," he said. "Nothing's going to hurt our boy."

They stood silently for a time, looking at each other, and then out at the city. The plumes of smoke rising from the forges, the black-cobbled streets and gray slanted roofs. The sun slipped behind the clouds or else the clouds rose to block the light. The knock that interrupted them was sharp and urgent.

"Most High?" a man's voice said. "Most High, forgive me, but the poets wish to speak with you. Maati-cha says the issue is urgent."

Kiyan walked with him, her hand in his, as they went to the Council chamber where Maati waited. His face was flushed, his mouth set in a deep scowl. A packet of paper fluttered in his hand, the edges rough where he'd ripped them rather than take the labor of unsewing the sheets. Cehmai and Stone-Made-Soft were also there, the poet pacing restlessly, the andat smiling its placid, inhuman smile at each of them in turn.

"News from the Dai-kvo?" Otah asked.

"No, the couriers we sent west," Cehmai said.

Maati tossed the pages to the table as he spoke. "The Galts have fielded an army."

THE THIRD legion arrived on a bright morning, the sun shining on the polished metal and oiled leather of their armor as if they'd been expecting a victory parade instead of the start of a war. Balasar watched from the walls of the city as they arrived and made camp. The sight was so welcome, even the smell of a hundred and a half camp latrines couldn't undermine his pleasure.

They were later even than they'd expected, and with stories and excuses to explain the delay. Balasar, leaning against the map table, listened and kept his expression calm as the officers apprised him of the legion's state—the men, the food, the horses, the steam wagons, the armor, the arms. Mentally, he put the information into the vast map that was the campaign, but even as he did, he felt the wolfish grin coming to his lips. These were the last of his forces to come into place. The hour was almost upon him. The war was about to begin.

He listened as patiently as he could, gave his orders on the disposition of their men and matériel, and told them not to get comfortable. When they were gone, Eustin came in alone, the same excitement that Balasar felt showing on his face.

"What's next, sir? The poet?"

"The poet," Balasar said, leading the way out the door.

They found Riaan in the Warden's private courtyard. He was sitting in the wide shade of a catalpa tree heavy with wide, white blooms and wide leaves the same green as the poet's robes. He'd had someone bring out a wide divan for him to lounge on. Across a small table, the Khaiate mercenary captain was perched on a stool. Both men were frowning at a handful of stones laid out in a short arc. The captain rose when he caught sight of them. The poet only glanced up, annoyed. Balasar took a pose of greeting, and the poet replied with something ornate that he couldn't entirely make sense of. The glitter in the captain's eyes suggested that the complexity was intentional and not entirely complimentary. Balasar put the insult, whatever it was, aside. There was no call to catalog more reasons to kill the man.

"Sinja-cha," Balasar said. "I need to speak with the great poet in private."

"Of course," the captain said, then turning to Riaan with a formal pose, "We can finish the game later if you like."

Riaan nodded and waved, the movement half permission for Sinja to go, half shooing him away. The amusement in the captain's eyes didn't seem to lessen. Eustin escorted the man away, and when they were alone, Balasar took the vacated stool.

"My men are in place," he said. "The time's come."

He kept his gaze on the poet, looking for reluctance or

unease in his eyes. But Riaan smiled slowly, like a man who had heard that his dearest enemy had died, and laced his fingers together on his belly. Balasar had half-expected the poet to repent, to change his mind when faced with the prospect of the deed itself. There was nothing of that.

"Tomorrow morning," Riaan said. "I will need a servant to attend me today and through the night. At first light tomorrow, I will prove that the Dai-kvo was a fool to send me away. And then I shall march to my father's house with your army behind me like a flood."

Balasar grinned. He had never seen a man so shortsighted, vain, and petty, and he'd spent three seasons in Acton with his father and the High Council. As far as the poet was concerned, none of this was for anything more important than the greater glory of Riaan Vaudathat.

"How can we serve you in this?" Balasar asked.

"Everything is already prepared. I must only begin my meditations."

It sounded like dismissal to Balasar. He rose, bowing to the poet.

"I will send my most trusted servant," he said. "Should anything more arise, only send word, and I will see it done."

Riaan smiled condescendingly and nodded his head. But as Balasar was just leaving the garden, the poet called his name. A cloud had come over the man, some ghost of uncertainty that had not risen from the prospect of binding.

"Your men," the poet said. "They have been instructed that my family is not to be touched, yes?"

"Of course," Balasar said.

"And the library. The city is, of course, yours to do with as you see fit, but without the libraries of the Khaiem, binding a second andat will be much more difficult. They aren't to be entered by any man but me."

"Of course," Balasar said again, and the poet took a pose accepting his assurances. The concern didn't leave Riaan's brow, though. So perhaps the man wasn't quite as dim as he seemed. Balasar told himself, as he strode back through the covered pathways to his own rooms, that he would have to be more careful with him in the future. Not that there was much future for him. Win or lose, Riaan was a dead man.

The day seemed more real than the ones that had come before it: the sunlight clearer, the air more alive with the scents of flowers and sewage and grass. The stones of the walls seemed more interesting, the subtle differences in color and texture clear where previous days had made them only a field of gray. Even Balasar's body hummed with energy. It was like being a boy again, and diving into the lake from the highest cliff—the one all the other boys feared to jump from. It was dread and joy and the sense of no longer being able to take his decision back. It was what Balasar lived for. He knew already that he would not sleep.

Eustin was waiting for him in the entrance hall.

"There's someone wants a word with you, sir."

Balasar paused.

"The Khaiate captain. He wanted to speak about fallback plans for his men."

Eustin nodded to a side room. There was distrust in his expression, and Balasar waited a long moment for him to speak. Eustin added nothing. Balasar went to the wide, dark oaken door, knocked once, and went in. It was a preparation room for servants—muddy boots cast beside benches and waiting to be scraped clean, cloaks of all weights and colors hung from pegs. It smelled of wet dog, though there was no animal present. The captain sat on a stool tilted back against the wall, cleaning his nails with a knife.

"Captain Ajutani," Balasar said.

The stool came down, and the captain rose, sheathing his blade and bowing in the same motion.

"I appreciate the time, General," he said. "I know you've a great deal on your mind just now."

"I'm always available," Balasar said. "Though the surroundings are . . ."

"Yes. Your man Eustin seemed to think it more appropriate for me to wait here. I'm not sure he likes me." The captain was more amused than offended, so Balasar also smiled and shrugged.

"Your men are in place?" he asked.

"Yes, yes. Broken into groups of three or four, each assigned to one of your sergeants. Except for myself, of course."

"Of course."

"Only I wanted to ask something of you, General. A favor of sorts."

Balasar crossed his arms and nodded for the man to continue.

"If it fails—if our friend Riaan doesn't do his magic trick well enough—don't kill them. My boys. Don't have them killed."

"Why would I do that?" Balasar asked.

"Because it's the right thing," Sinja said. The amusement was gone from the man's eyes. He was in earnest now. "I'm not an idiot, General. If it happens that the binding fails, you'll be standing here in Aren with an army the size of a modest city. People have already noticed it, and the curiosity of the Khaiem is the last thing you'd want. They'd still have their andat, and all you'd have is explanations to give. You'll turn North and make all those stories about conquering the whole of the Westlands to the border with Eddensea true just to make all this—" The captain gestured to the door at Balasar's back. "—seem plausible. All I ask is, let us go with you. If it happens that you have to keep to this coast and not the cities of the Khaiem, I'll re-form the group and lead them wherever you like."

"I wouldn't kill them," Balasar said.

"It would be dangerous, letting them go back home. Stories about how they were set to be interpreters and guides? Not one of them knows the Westlands except the part we walked through to get here. If the Khaiem are wondering whether you had some other plan to start with . . ."

Sinja raised his hands, palms up as if he were offering Balasar the truth resting there. Balasar stepped close, putting his own hands below the captain's and curling the other man's fingers closed.

"I won't kill them," Balasar said. "They're my men now, and I don't kill my own. You can tell them that if you'd like. And that aside, Riaan isn't going to fail us."

Sinja looked down, his head shifting as if he were weighing something.

"I can be sure," Balasar said, answering the unasked question.

"I've never seen one of these before," Sinja said. "Have you? I mean, I assume there's some ceremony, and he'll do something. If there was an andat beside him at the end, you'd have proof, but this thing you're doing . . . there's nothing to show, is there? So how will you know?"

"It *would* be embarrassing to walk into Nantani and have the andat waiting to greet us," Balasar agreed. "But don't let it concern you. Riaan isn't going to mumble into the air and send us all off to die. I'll be certain of that."

"You have a runner in Nantani? Someone who can bring word when the andat's vanished?"

"Don't concern yourself, Sinja," Balasar said. "Just be ready to move when I say and in the direction I choose."

"Yes, General."

Balasar turned and strode to the door. He could see Eustin standing close, his hand on his sword. It was a reassuring sight.

"Captain Ajutani," Balasar said over his shoulder. "What were you speaking to Riaan about before we came?"

"Himself mostly," the captain said. "Is there another subject he's interested in?"

"He was concerned when I spoke with him. Concerned with things that never seemed to occur to him before. You wouldn't have anything to do with that, would you?"

"No, General," Sinja said. "Wouldn't be any profit in it."

Balasar nodded and resumed the path to his rooms. Eustin fell in beside him.

"I don't like that man," Eustin said under his breath. "I don't trust him."

"I do," Balasar said. "I trust him to be and to have always

been my staunchest supporter just as soon as he's sure we're going to win. He's a mercenary, but he isn't a spy. And his men will be useful."

"Still."

"It will be fine."

Balasar didn't give his uncertainties and fears free rein until he was safely alone in the borrowed library, and then his mind rioted. Perhaps Sinja was right—the poet could fail, the Khaiem could divine his purpose, the destruction he'd dedicated himself to preventing might be brought about by his miscalculation. Everything might still fail. A thousand threats and errors clamored.

He took out his maps again for the thousandth time. Each road was marked on the thin sheepskin. Each bridge and ford. Each city. Fourteen cities in a single season. They would take Nantani and then scatter. The other forces would come in from the sea. It was nearing summer, and he told himself again and again as if hoping to convince himself that after the sun rose tomorrow, it would be a question only of speed.

In the first battle he'd fought, Balasar had been a crossbowman. He and a dozen like him were supposed to loose their bolts into the packed, charging bodies of the warriors of Eymond and then pull back, letting the men with swords and axes and flails—men like his father—move in and take up the melee. He'd hardly been a boy at the time, much less a man. He had done as he was told, as had the others, but once they were safely over the rise of the hill, out of sight of the enemy and the battle, Balasar had been stupid. The grunts and shrieks and noise of bodies in conflict were like a peal of thunder that never faded. The sound called to him. With each shriek from the battle, he imagined that it had been his father. The nightmare images of the violence happening just over the rise chewed at him. He'd had to see it. He had gone back over. It had almost cost him his life.

One of the soldiers of Eymond had spotted him. He'd been a large man, tall as a tree it had seemed at the time. He'd broken away from the fight and rushed up the hill, axe raised and blood on his mind. Balasar remembered the panic when he understood that his own death was rushing up the hill toward him. The wise thing would have been to flee; if he could have gotten back to the other bowmen, they might have killed the soldier. But instead, without thought, he started to bend back the leaves of the crossbow, fumbling the bolt with fingers that had seemed numb as sausages. Though only one of them was running, it had been a race.

When he'd raised the bow and loosed the bolt, the man had been fewer than ten feet from him. He could still feel the thrum of the string and feel the sinking certainty that he had missed, that his life was forfeit. In point of fact, the bolt had sunk so deep into the man it only seemed to have vanished. The breaths between when he'd fired and when the soldier sank to the ground were the longest he had ever known.

And here he was again. Only this time he was the one in motion. The poets of the Khaiem would have a chance to call up another of the andat—and the measure of that hope was his speed in finding them, killing them, and burning their books.

It was a terrible wager, and more than his own life was in the balance. Balasar was not a religious man. Questions of gods and heavens had always seemed too abstract to him. But now, putting aside the maps, the plans, all the work of his life prepared to find its fruition or else its ruin, he walked to the window, watched the full moon rising over this last night of the world as it had been, and put his hand to his heart, praying to all the gods he knew with a single word.

Please.

8

>+< Twilight came after the long sunset, staining red the high clouds in the west. A light wind had come from the North, carrying the chill of mountaintop glaciers with it, though there was little snow left on even the highest peaks that could be seen from the city. It grabbed at the loose shutters, banging them open and closed like an idiot child in love with the noise. Banners rippled and trees nodded like old men. It was as if an errant breath of winter had stolen into the warm nights. Otah sat in his private chambers, still in his formal robes. He felt no drafts, but the candles flickered in sympathy with the wind.

The letters unfolded before him were in a simple cipher. The years he had spent in the gentleman's trade, carrying letters and contracts and information on the long roads between the cities of the Khaiem, returned to him, and he read the enciphered text as easily as if it had been written plainly. It was as Maati and Cehmai had said. The Wards of the Westlands were united in a state of panic. The doom of the world seemed about to fall upon them.

Since the letters had arrived, Otah's world had centered on the news. He had sent another runner to the Dai-kvo with a pouch so heavy with lengths of silver, the man could have bought a fresh horse at every low town he passed through if it would get him there faster. Otah had sat up long nights with Maati and Cehmai, even with Liat and Nayiit. Here was the plan, then. With the threat of an andat of their own, the Galts would roll through the Westlands, perhaps Eddensea as well. In a year, perhaps two, they might own Bakta and Eymond too. The cities of the Khaiem would find themselves cut off from trade, and perhaps the rogue poet would even become a kind of Galtic Dai-kvo in time. The conquest of the Westlands was the first campaign in a new war that might make the destruction of the Old Empire seem minor.

And still, Otah read the letters again, his mind unquiet. There was something there, something more, that he had overlooked. The certainty of the Galts, their willingness to show their power. Whenever they tired of trade or felt themselves losing at the negotiating tables, Galt had been pleased to play raider and pirate. It had been that way for as long as Otah could remember. The Galtic High Council had schemed and conspired. It shouldn't have been odd that, emboldened by success, they would take to the field. And yet . . .

Otah turned the pages with a sound as dry as autumn leaves. They couldn't be attacking the Khaiem; even with an andat in their possession, they would be overwhelmed. The cities might have their rivalries and disputes, but an attack on one would unite them against their common foe. Thirteen cities each with its own poet added to whatever the Dai-kvo held in reserve in his village. At worst, more than a dozen to one, and each of them capable of destruction on a scale almost impossible to imagine. The Galts wouldn't dare attack the Khaiem. It was posturing. Negotiation. It might even be a bluff; the poet might have tried his binding, paid the price of failure, and left the Galts with nothing but bluster to defend themselves.

Otah had heard all these arguments, had made more than one of them himself. And still night found him here, reading the letters and searching for the thoughts behind them. It was like hearing a new voice in a choir. Somewhere, someone new had entered the strategies of the Galts, and these scraps of paper and pale ink were all that Otah had to work out what that might mean.

He could as well have looked for words written in the air.

A scratching came at the door, followed by a servant boy. The boy took a pose of obeisance and Otah replied automatically.

"The woman you sent for, Most High. Liat Chokavi."

"Bring her in. And bring some wine and two bowls, then see we aren't disturbed."

"But, Most High—"

"We'll pour our own wine," Otah snapped, and regretted it instantly as the boy's face went pale. Otah pressed down the impulse to apologize. It was beneath the dignity of the Khai Machi to apologize for rudeness—one of the thousand things he'd learned when he first took his father's chair. One of the thousand missteps he had made. The boy backed out of the room, and Otah turned to the letters, folding them back in their order and slipping them into his sleeve. The boy preceded Liat into the room, a tray with a silver carafe and two hand-molded bowls of granite in his hands. Liat sat on the low divan, her eyes on the floor in something that looked like respect but might only have been fear.

The door closed, and Otah poured a generous portion of wine into each bowl. Liat took the one he proffered.

"It's lovely work," Liat said, considering the stone.

"It's the andat," Otah said. "He turns the quarry rock into something like clay, and the potters shape it. One of the many wonders of Machi. Have you seen the bridge that spans the river? A single stone poured over molds and shaped by hand five generations back. And there's the towers. Really, we're a city of petty miracles."

"You sound bitter," she said, looking up at last. Her eyes were the same tea-and-milk color he remembered. Otah sighed as he sat across from her. Outside, the wind murmured.

"I'm not," he said. "Only tired."

"I knew you wouldn't end as a seafront laborer," she said.

"Yes, well . . ." Otah shook his head and sipped from the bowl. It was strong wine, and it left his mouth feeling clean and his chest warm. "It's time we spoke about Nayiit."

Liat nodded, took a long drink, and held the cup out for more. Otah poured.

"It's all my fault," she said as she sat back. "I should never have brought him here. I never saw it. I never saw you in him. He was always just himself. If I'd known that . . . that he resembled you quite so closely, I wouldn't have."

"Late for that," Otah said.

Liat sighed her agreement and looked up at him. It was hard to believe that they had been lovers once. The girl he had known back then hadn't had gray in her hair, weariness in her eyes. And the boy he'd been was as distant as snow in summer. Yes, two people had kissed once, had touched each other, had created a child who had grown to manhood. And Otah remembered some of those moments now—showering at the barracks while she spoke to him, the ink blocks at the desk in her cell at the compound of House Wilsin, the feel of a young body pressed against his own, when his flesh had also been new and unmarked. If those days long past had been foolish or wrong, the only evidence was the price they both paid now. It hadn't seemed so at the time.

"I've been thinking of it," Liat said. "I haven't told him. I wasn't sure how you wanted to address the problem. But I think the wisest thing to do is to speak with him and with Maati, and then have Nayiit-kya take the brand. I know it's not something done with firstborn sons, but it's still a repudiation of his right to become Khai. It will make it clear to the world that he doesn't have designs on your chair."

"That isn't what I'd choose," Otah said. His words were slow and careful. "I'm afraid my son may die."

She caught her breath. It was hardly there, no more than a tremor in the air she took in, but he heard it.

"Itani," she said, using the name of the boy he'd been in Saraykeht, "please. I'll swear on anything you choose. Nayiit's no threat to Danat. It was only the Galts that brought us here. I'm not looking to put my son in your chair. . . ."

Otah put down his bowl and took a pose that asked for her silence. Her face pale, she went quiet.

"I don't mean that," he said softly. "I mean that I don't . . . Gods. I don't know how to say this. Danat's not well. His lungs are fragile, and the winters here are bad. We lose people to the cold every year. Not just the old or the weak. Young people. Healthy ones. I'm afraid that Danat may die, and there'll be no one to take my place. The city would tear itself apart."

"But . . . you want . . ."

"I haven't done a good job as Khai. I haven't been able to put the houses of the utkhaiem together except in their distrust of me and resentment of Kiyan. There's been twice it came near violence, and I only held the city in place by luck. But keeping Machi safe is my responsibility. I want Nayiit unbranded, in case . . . in case he becomes my successor."

Liat's mouth hung open, her eyes were wide. A stray lock of hair hung down the side of her face, three white hairs dancing in and out among the black. He felt the faint urge—echo of a habit long forgotten—to brush it back.

"There," Otah said and picked up his wine bowl. "There, I've said it."

"I'm sorry," Liat said, and Otah took a pose accepting her sympathy without knowing quite why she was offering it. She looked down at her hands. The silence between them was profound but not uncomfortable; he felt no need to speak, to fill the void with words. Liat drank her wine, Otah his. The wind muttered to itself and to the stones of the city.

"It's not a job I'd want," Liat said. "Khai Machi."

"It's all power and no freedom," Otah said. "If Nayiit were to have it, he'd likely curse my name. There are a thousand different things to attend to, and every one of them as serious as bone to someone. You can't do it all."

"I know how it feels," Liat said. "I only have a trading house to look after, and there's days I wish that it would all go away. Granted, I have men who work the books and the negotiations and appeals before the low judges and the utkhaiem . . ."

"I have all the low judges and the utkhaiem appealing to me," Otah said. "It's never enough."

"There's always the descent into decadence and self-absorption," Liat said, smiling. It was only half a joke. "They say the Khai Chaburi-Tan only gets sober long enough to bed his latest wife."

"Tempting," Otah said, "but somewhere between taking the chair to protect Kiyan and tonight, it became my city. I came from here, and even if I'm not much good at what I do, I'm what they have."

"That makes sense," Liat said.

"Does it? It doesn't to me."

Liat put down her bowl and rose. He thought her gaze spoke of determination and melancholy, but perhaps the latter was only his own. She stepped close and kissed him on the cheek, a firm peck like an aunt greeting a favorite nephew.

"Amat Kyaan would have understood," she said. "I won't tell Nayiit about this. If anyone asks, I'll deny it unless I hear differently from you."

"Thank you, Liat-cha."

She stepped back. Otah felt a terrible weariness bearing him down, but forced a charming smile. She shook her head.

"Thank *you*, Most High."

"I don't think I've done anything worth thanking me."

"You let my son live," Liat said. "That was one of the decisions you had to make, wasn't it?"

She took his silence as an answer, smiled again, and left him alone. Otah poured the last of the wine from carafe to bowl, and then watched the light die in the west as he finished it; watched the stars come out, and the full moon rise. With every day, the light lasted longer. It would not always. High summer would come, and even when the days were at their warmest, when the trees and vines grew heavy with fruit, the nights would already have started their slow expansion. He wondered whether Danat would get to play outside in the autumn, whether the boy would be able to spend a long afternoon lying in the sunlight before the snows came and drove them all down to the tunnels. He was raising a child to live in darkness and planning for his death.

There had been a time Otah had been young and sure

enough of himself to kill. He had taken the life of a good man because they both had known the price that would have to be paid if he lived. He had been able to do that.

But he had seen forty-eight summers now. There were likely fewer seasons before him than there were behind. He'd fathered three children and raised two. He could no longer hold himself apart from the world. It was his to see that the city was a place that Danat and Eiah and children like them could live safe and cared for until they too grew old and uncertain.

He looked at the swirl of red at the bottom of his bowl. Too much wine, and too much memory. It was making him maudlin. He stopped at his private chambers and allowed the servants to switch his robes to something less formal. Kiyan lay on a couch, her eyes closed, her breath deep and regular. Otah didn't wake her, only slid one of the books from his bedside table into the sleeve of his robe and kissed her temple as he left.

The physician's assistant was seated outside Danat's door. The man took a pose of greeting. Otah responded in kind and then nodded to the closed door.

"Is he asleep?" he whispered.

"He's been waiting for you."

Otah slipped into the room. Candles flickered above two great iron statues that flanked the bed—hunting cats with the wings of hawks. Soot darkened their wings from a day spent in the fire grates, and they radiated the warmth that kept the cool night breeze at bay. Danat sat up in his bed, pulling aside the netting.

"Papa-kya!" he said. He didn't cough, didn't sound frail. It was a good day, then. Otah felt a tightness he had not known he carried loosen its grip on his heart. He pulled his robes up around his knees and sat on his son's bed. "Did you bring it?" Danat asked.

Otah drew the book from his sleeve, and the boy's face lit so bright, he might have almost read by him.

"Now, you lie back," Otah said. "I've come to help you sleep, not keep you up all night."

Danat plopped down onto his pillow, looking like the farthest thing from sleep. Otah opened the book, turning through the ancient pages until he found his place.

"In the sixteenth year of the reign of the Emperor Adani Beh, there came to court a boy whose blood was half Bakta, his skin the color of soot, and his mind as clever as any man who has ever lived. . . ."

"THIS IS spring?" Nayiit said as they walked. The wind had blown away even the constant scent of forge smoke, and brought in a mild chill. Mild, at least, to Maati. Nayiit wore woolen robes, thick enough that they had hardly rippled. Maati's own were made for summer, and pressed against him, leaving, he was sure, no doubt as to the shape of his legs and belly. He wished he'd thought to wear something heavier too.

"It's always like this," Maati said. "There's one last death throe, and then the heat will come on. Still nothing like the summer cities, even at its worst. I remember in Saraykeht, I had a trail of sweat down my back for weeks at a time."

"We call that *pleasantly warm,*" Nayiit said, and Maati chuckled.

In truth, the chill, moonless night was hardly anything to him now. For over a decade, he'd lived through the bone-cracking cold of Machi winters. He'd seen snowdrifts so high that even the second-story doors couldn't be opened. He'd been out on days so cold the men coated their faces with thick-rendered fat to keep their skin from freezing. There was no way to describe those brief, bitter days to someone who had never seen them. So instead, he told Nayiit of the life below ground, the tunnels of Machi, the bathhouses hidden deep below the surface, the streets and apartments and warehouses, the glitter of winter dew turning to frost on the stone of the higher passages. He spoke of the choirs who took the long, empty weeks to compose new songs and practice old ones—weeks spent in the flickering, buttery light of oil lamps surrounded by music.

"I'm amazed people don't stay down there," Nayiit said as they turned a corner and left the white and silver paths of the palaces behind for the black-cobbled streets of the city proper. "It sounds like one huge, warm bed."

"It has its pleasures," Maati agreed. "But people get thirsty for sunlight. As soon as they can stand it, people start making treks up to the streets. They'll go up and lie naked on an ice sheet sometimes just to drink in a little more light. And the river freezes, so the children will go skating on it. There's only about seven weeks when no one comes up. Here. This street. There's a sweet wine they serve at this place that's like nothing you've ever tasted."

It was less awkward than he'd expected, spending the evening with Nayiit. The first time the boy had come to the library alone—tentative and uncertain—Maati had been acutely aware of Liat's absence. She had always been there, even in the ancient days before they had parted. Maati knew how to speak with Liat whether she was alone or with their son, and Maati had discovered quickly how much he'd relied upon her to mediate between him and the boy. The silences had been awkward, the conversations forced. Maati had said something of how pleased he was that Nayiit had come to Machi and felt in the end that he'd only managed to embarrass them both.

It was going to the teahouses and bathhouses and epics that let them speak at last. Once there was a bit of shared experience, a toehold, Maati was able to make conversation, and Nayiit was an expert listener to stories. For several nights in a row, Maati found himself telling tales of the Dai-kvo and the school, the history of Machi and the perils he had faced years ago when he'd been sent to hunt Otah-kvo down. In the telling, he discovered that, to his profound surprise, his life had been interesting.

The platform rested at the base of one of the lower towers, chains thick as a man's arm clanking against it and against the stone as they rose up into the sky like smoke. Nayiit paused to stare up at it, and Maati followed his gaze. The looming, inhuman bulk of the tower, and beyond it the full moon hanging like a lantern of rice paper in the black sky.

"Does anyone ever fall from up there?" Nayiit asked.

"Once every year or so," Maati said. "There's winter storage up there, so there are laborers carrying things in the early spring and middle autumn. There are accidents. And the utkhaiem will hold dances at the tops of them sometimes. They say wine gets you drunk faster at the top, but I don't know if that's true. Then sometimes men kill themselves by stepping through the sky doors when the platform's gone down. It would happen more if there were people up there more often. Otah-kvo has a plan for channeling the air from the forges up through the center of one so it would be warm enough to use in the winter, but we've never figured out how to make the change without bringing the whole thing down."

Nayiit shuddered, and Maati was willing to pretend it was the wind. He put his arm on the boy's shoulder and steered him farther down the street to a squat stone building with a copper roof gone as green as trees with time. Inside, the air was warmed by braziers. Two old men were playing tin-and-silver flutes while a young woman kept time on a small drum and sang. Half a hundred bodies were seated at long wooden tables or on benches. The place was rich with the smell of roast lamb even though the windows were unshuttered; it was as if no one in Machi would miss the chance for fresh air. Maati sympathized.

He and Nayiit took a bench in the back, away from singers and song. The serving boy was hardly as old as Eiah, but he knew his trade. It seemed fewer than a dozen heartbeats before he brought them bowls of sweet wine and a large worked-silver bowl filled with tender slivers of green: spring peas fresh from the vines. Maati, hands full, nodded his thanks.

"And you've worked your whole life in House Kyaan, then?" Maati asked. "What does Liat have you doing?"

"Since we've been traveling, I haven't been doing much at all. Before that, I had been working the needle trades," Nayiit said as he tucked one leg up under him. It made him sit taller.

"The spinners, the dyers, the tailors, and the sailmakers and all like that. They aren't as profitable as they were in the days before Seedless was lost, but they still make up a good deal of the business in Saraykeht."

"Habits," Maati said. "The cotton trade's always been in Saraykeht. People don't like change, so it doesn't move away so quickly as it might. Another generation and it'll all be scattered throughout the world."

"Not if I do my work," Nayiit said with a smile that showed he hadn't taken offense.

"Fair point," Maati said. "I only mean that's what you have to work against. It would be easier if there was still an andat in the city that helped with the cotton trade the way Seedless did."

"You knew it, didn't you? Seedless, I mean."

"I was supposed to take him over," Maati said. "The way Cehmai took Stone-Made-Soft from his master, I was to take Seedless from Heshai-kvo. In a way, I was lucky. Seedless was flawed work. Dangerously flawed. Brilliant, don't misunderstand. Heshai-kvo did brilliant work when he bound Seedless, but he made the andat very clever and profoundly involved with destroying the poet. They all want to be free—it's their nature—but Seedless was more than that. He was vicious."

"You sound as though you were fond of it," Nayiit said, only half-teasing.

"We were friendly enough, in our fashion," Maati said. "We wouldn't have been if things had gone by the Dai-kvo's plan. If I'd become the poet of Saraykeht, Seedless would have bent himself to destroying me just the way he had to Heshai-kvo."

"Have you ever tried to bind one of the andat?"

"Once. When Heshai died, I had the mad thought that I could somehow retrieve Seedless. I had Heshai-kvo's notes. Still have them, for that. I even began the ceremonies, but it would never have worked. What I had was too much like what Heshai had done. It would have failed, and I'd have paid its price."

"And then I suppose I would never have been born," Nayiit said.

"You would have," Maati said, solemnly. "Liat-kya didn't know she was carrying you when she stopped me, but she was. I thought about it, afterward. About binding another of the andat, I mean. I even spent part of a winter once doing the basic work for one I called Returning-to-True. I don't know what I would have done with it, precisely. Unbent things, I suppose. I'd have been brilliant repairing axles. But my mind was too fuzzy. There were too many things I meant, and none of them precisely enough."

The musicians ended their song and stood to a roar of approving voices and bowls of wine bought by their admirers. One of the old men walked through the house with a lacquer begging box in his hand. Maati fumbled in his sleeve, came out with two lengths of copper, and tossed them into the box with a satisfying click.

"And then, I also wasn't in the Dai-kvo's best graces," Maati continued. "After Saraykeht . . . Well, I suppose it's poor etiquette to let your master die and the andat escape. I wasn't blamed outright, but it was always hanging there. The memory of it."

"It can't have helped that you brought back a lover and a child," Nayiit said.

"No, it didn't. But I was very young and very full of myself. It's not easy, being told that you are of the handful of men in the world who might be able to control one of the andat. Tends to create a sense of being more than you are. I thought I could do anything. And maybe I could have, but I tried to do *everything,* and that isn't the same." He sighed and ate a pea pod. Its flesh was crisp and sweet and tasted of spring. When he spoke again, he tried to make his voice light and joking. "I didn't wind up doing a particularly good job of either endeavor."

"It seems to me you've done well enough," Nayiit said as he waved at the serving boy for more wine. "You've made yourself a place in the court here, you've been able to study in the libraries here, and from what Mother says, you've found something no one else ever has. That alone is more than most men manage in a lifetime."

"I suppose," Maati said. He wanted to go on, wanted to say that most men had children, raised them up, watched them become women and men. He wanted to tell this charming boy who stood now where Maati himself once had that he regretted that he had not been able to enjoy those simple pleasures. Instead, he took another handful of pea pods. He could tell that Nayiit sensed his reservations, heard the longing in the brevity of his reply. When the boy spoke, his tone was light.

"I've spent all my life—well, since I've been old enough to think of it as really mine and not something Mother's let me borrow—with House Kyaan. Running errands, delivering contracts. That's how I started, at least. Mother always told me I had to do better than the other boys who worked for the house because I was her son, and if people thought I was getting favors because of it, they wouldn't respect her or me. She was right. I can see that. At the time it all seemed monstrously unfair, though."

"Do you like the work?" Maati asked.

The girl with the drum began tapping a low tattoo, her voice droning in a lament. Maati shifted to look at Nayiit. The boy's gaze was fixed on the singer, his expression melancholy. The urge to put his hand to Nayiit's shoulder, to offer some comfort, however powerless, moved through Maati and faded. He sat still and quiet as the chant rose, the anguish in the singer's voice growing until the air of the teahouse hummed with it, and then it faded into despair. The man with the lacquer box came past again, but Maati didn't put in any copper this time.

"You and Mother. You're lovers again?"

"I suppose so," Maati said, surprised to feel a blush in his cheeks. "It happens sometimes."

"What happens when you're called away to the Dai-kvo?"

"Are we walking the same path a second time, you mean? We're waiting to hear two things from the Dai-kvo—whether he thinks my speculations about avoiding the price of a failed binding are worth looking into and whether to act against Galt. Either one puts me someplace away from Liat. But we aren't who we were then. I don't pretend that we can be. And anyway, I have all the habits of being without her. I've missed her for more years than I spent in her company."

I have missed you, he thought but didn't say. I have missed you, and it's too late now for anything more than awkward conversations and late nights getting drunk together. Nothing will ever make that right.

"Do you regret that?" Nayiit asked. "If you could go back and do things again, would you want to love her less? Would you want to have gone to the Dai-kvo and been able to leave that . . . that longing behind you?"

"I don't know what you mean."

Nayiit looked up.

"I would hate her, if I were you. I would think she'd taken my chance to be what I was supposed to be, to do what I could have done. There you were, a poet, and favored enough that you were expected to hold the andat, and because of her you fell into disfavor. Because of her, and because of me." Nayiit's jaw clenched, his eyes only a half shade darker than the pale brown of his mother's staring at something that wasn't there, his attention turned inward. "I don't know how you stand the sight of us."

"It wasn't like that," Maati said. "It was never like that. If it were all mine again, I would have followed her."

The words struck the boy hard. His gaze lost its focus; his mouth tightened like that of a man in pain.

"What is it, Nayiit-kya?"

Nayiit seemed to snap back to the room, an embarrassed grin on his face. He took a pose of apology, but Maati shook his head.

"Something's bothering you," Maati said.

"It's nothing. I've only . . . It's not worth talking about."

"Something's bothering you, son."

He had never said the word aloud. *Son.* Nayiit had never heard it from his lips, not since he'd been too young for it to mean anything. Maati felt his heart leap and race like a startled deer, and he saw the shock on the boy's face. This was the moment, then, that he'd feared and longed for. He waited to hear what Nayiit would say. Maati dreaded the polite deflection, the retreat back into the roles of a pair of strangers in a tearoom, the way a man falling from a cliff might dread the ground.

Nayiit opened his mouth, closed it, and then said, almost too low to hear over the music and the crowd, "I'm trying to choose between what I am and what I want to be. I'm trying to want what I'm supposed to want. And I'm failing."

"I see."

"I want to be a good man, Father. I want to love my wife and my son. I want to *want* them. And I don't. I don't know whether to walk away from them or from myself. I thought you had made that decision, but . . ."

Maati settled back on the bench, put down his bowl still half full of wine, and took Nayiit's hand in his own. Father. Nayiit had said *Father.*

"Tell me," Maati said. "Tell me all of it."

"It would take all night," the boy said with a rueful chuckle. But he didn't pull back his hand.

"Let it," Maati said. "There's nothing more important than this."

BALASAR HADN'T slept. The night had come, a late rain shower filling the air with the scent of water and murmur of distant thunder, and he had lain in his bed, willing himself to a forgetfulness that wouldn't come.

The orders waited in stacks on his desk in the library, commands to be issued to each of his captains, outlining the first stage of his campaign. There were two sets, of course, just as the Khaiate mercenary captain had surmised. Those he'd sealed in green would lead the army to the North, laying waste to the Westlands and sending the thin stream of gold and silver that could be wrung from them back to the coffers of the High Council. Those he'd sealed in red would wheel the army—twenty thousand armsmen, three hundred steam wagons, six thousand horses, and God only knew how many servants and camp followers—to the east and the most glorious act of conquest the world had ever known.

If he succeeded, he would be remembered as the greatest general in history, at least in his audacity. The battles themselves he expected to be simple enough. The Khaiem had no experience in tactics and no armies to protect them. Balasar would be remembered for two things only: the unimaginable wealth he was about to pour into Galt and the ceremony that would come with the dawn. The plot that stripped the andat from the world.

As the dark hours passed, the thought pricked at him. He had put everything in place. The poet, the books that concerned Freedom-From-Bondage, the army, the arms. There was nothing he would ever do that would match this season. Succeed or fail, this was the high-water mark of his life. He imagined himself an old man, sitting at a street café in Kirinton. He wondered what those years would be like, reaching from here to the grave. He wondered what it would be like to have his greatness behind him. He told himself that he would retire. There would be enough wealth to acquire anything he wanted. A reasonable estate of his own, a wife, children; that seemed enough. If he could not regain this season, he could at least not humiliate himself by trying. He thought of the war leaders who haunted the corridors and wineshops of Acton reliving triumphs the world had forgotten. He would not be one of those. He would be the great General who had done his work and then stepped back to let the world he had made safe follow its path.

At heart, he was not a conqueror. Only a man who saw what needed doing, and then did it.

Or else he would fail and he and every Galtic man and woman would be a corpse or a refugee.

He twisted in his sheets. The stars shone where the clouds were thin enough to permit it. Framed in the opened shutters, they glittered. The stars wouldn't care what happened here. And yet by the next time their light silvered these stones, the fate of the world would have turned one way or the other.

Once, he came near to sleep. His eyes grew heavy, his mind began to wander into the half-sense of dreams. And then, irrationally, he became certain that he had mixed one of the orders. The memory, at first vague but clearer as he struggled to capture it, of sealing a packet with red that should have been green swam through his mind. He thought he might have noted at the time that it would need changing. And yet he hadn't done it. The wrong orders would go out. A legion would start to the North while the others moved east. They would lose time finding the error, correcting it. Or the poet would fail, and some stray company of armsmen would find its way to Nantani and reveal him to the Khaiem. Half a thousand stories plagued him, each less likely than the last. His sense of dread grew.

At last, half in distress and half in disgust, he rose, pulled on a heavy cotton shirt and light trousers, and walked barefoot from his room toward the library. He would have to open them all, check them, reseal them, and keep a careful tally so that the crazed monkey that had taken possession of his mind could be calmed. He wondered, as he passed through hallways lit only by his single candle, whether Uther Redcape had ever rechecked his own plans in the dead of night like an old, fearful merchant rattling his own shutters to be sure they were latched. Perhaps these indignities were part of what any man suffered when the weight of so many lives was on his back.

The guards outside his library door stood at attention as he passed them, whatever gossip or complaint they had been using to pass the dark hours of the night forgotten at the first sight of him. Balasar nodded to them gravely before passing through the door. With the stub of his bedside candle, he lit the lanterns in the library until the soft glow filled the air. The orders lay where he had left them. With a sigh, he took out the bricks of colored wax and his private seal. Then he began the long, tedious task of cracking each seal, reviewing his commands, and putting the packets back in order again. The candle stub had fizzled to nothing and the lanterns' oil visibly dropped before he was finished. The memory had been a lie. Everything had been in place. Balasar stood, stretched, and went to the window. When he opened the shutters, the cool breeze felt fresh as a bath. Birds were singing, though there was no light yet in the east. The full moon was near to setting. The dawn was coming. There would be no sleep for him. Not now.

A soft scratch came at the door, and after Balasar called his permission, Eustin entered. There were dark pouches under the man's eyes, but that was the only sign that he had managed no better with his sleep. His uniform was crisp and freshly laundered, the marks of rank on his back and breast, his hair was tied back and fastened with a thick silver ceremonial bead, and there was an energy in all his movements that Balasar understood. Eustin was dressed to witness the change of the world. Balasar was suddenly aware of his rough clothes and bare feet.

"What news?" Balasar said.

"He's been up all through the night, sir. Meditating, reading, preparing. Truth is I don't know that half of what he's done is needed, but he's been doing it all the same."

"Almost none of it's strictly called for," Balasar said. "But if it makes him feel better, let him."

"Yes, sir. I've called for his breakfast. He says that he'll want to wait a half a hand for his food to go down, and then it's time. Says that dawn's a symbolic moment, and that it'll help."

"I suppose I'll be getting prepared, then," Balasar said. "If this isn't a full-dress occasion, I don't know what is."

"I've sent men to wait for the signal. We should know by nightfall."

Balasar nodded. All along the highest hills from Nantani to Aren, bonfires were set. If all worked as they hoped, there would be a signal from the agents he had placed in the city, and they would be lit, each in turn. A thin line of fire would reach from the Khaiem to his own door.

"Have a mug of kafe and some bread sent to my rooms," Balasar said. "I'll meet you before the ceremony."

"Not more than that, sir? The bacon's good here. . . ."

"After," Balasar said. "I'll eat a decent meal after."

The room given them by the Warden had been in its time a warehouse, a meeting hall, and a temple, the last being the most recent. Tapestries of the Four Gods the Warden worshipped had been taken down, rolled up, and stacked in the corner like carpet. The smooth stone walls were marked with symbols, some familiar to Balasar, others obscure. The eastern wall was covered with the flowing script of the fallen Empire, like a page from a book of poetry. A single pillow rested in the center of the room, and beside it a stack of books, two with covers of ruined leather, one whose cover had been ripped from it, and one last closed in bright metal. It had been years since Balasar had carried those books out of the desert wastes. He nodded to them when he saw them, as if they were old friends or perhaps enemies.

Riaan himself was walking around the room with long, slow strides. He breathed in audibly with one step, blew the air out on the next. His face was deeply relaxed; his arms were swinging free at his sides. To look at the two of them, Balasar guessed he would look more like the man about to face death. He took a pose of respect and greeting. The poet came slowly to a halt, and returned the gesture.

"I trust all is well with you," Balasar said in the tongue of the Khaiem.

"I am ready," Riaan said, with a smile that made him seem almost gentle. "I wanted to thank you, Balasar-cha, for this opportunity. These are strange times that men such as you and I should find common cause. The structures of the Dai-kvo have caused good men to suffer for too many generations. I honor you for the role you have played in bringing me here."

Balasar bowed his head. Over the years he had known many men whose minds had been touched by wounds—blows from swords or stones, or fevers like the one that had prompted Riaan's fall from favor. Balasar knew how impulsive and unreliable a man could become after such an injury. But he also knew that with many there was also a candor and honesty, if only because they lacked the ability they had once had to dissemble. Against his own will, he found himself touched by the man's words.

"We all do what fate calls us to," he said. "It's no particular virtue of mine."

The poet smiled because he didn't understand what Balasar meant. And that was just as well. Eustin arrived moments later and made formal greeting to them both.

"There's breakfast waiting for us, when we're done here," Eustin said, and even such mundane words carried a depth.

"Well then," Balasar said, turning to Riaan. The poet nodded and took a pose more complex than Balasar could parse, but that seemed to be a farewell from a superior to someone of a lower class. Then Riaan dropped his pose and walked with a studied grace to the cushion in the room's center. Balasar stood against the back wall and nodded for Eustin to join him. He was careful not to obscure the symbols painted there, though Riaan wasn't looking back toward them.

For what seemed half a day and was likely no more than two dozen breaths together, the poet was silent, and then he began, nearly under his breath, to chant. Balasar knew the basic form of a binding, though the grammars that were used for the deepest work were beyond him. It was thought, really. Like a translation—a thought held that became something like a man as a song in a Westlands tongue might take new words in Galt but hold the same meaning. The chant was a device of memory and focus, and Balasar remained silent.

Slowly, the sound of the poet's voice grew, filling the space with words that seemed on the edge of comprehension. The sound began to echo, as if the room were much larger than the walls that Balasar could see, and something like a wind that somehow did not stir the air began to twist through the space. For a moment, he was in the desert again, feeling the air change, hearing Little Ott's shriek. Balasar put his arm back, palm pressed against the stone wall. He was here, he was in Aren. The chanting grew, and it was as if there were other voices now. Beside him, Eustin had gone pale. Sweat stood on the man's lip.

Under Balasar's fingertips, the wall seemed to shift. The stone hummed, dancing with the words of the chant. The script on the front wall shifted restlessly until Balasar squinted and the letters remained in their places. The air was thick.

"Sir," Eustin whispered, "I think it might be best if we stepped out, left him to—"

"No," Balasar said. "Watch this. It's the last time it's ever going to happen."

Eustin nodded curtly and turned with what seemed physical strain to look ahead. Riaan had risen, standing where the cushion had been, or perhaps he was floating. Or perhaps he was sitting just as he had been. Something had happened to the nature of the space between them. And then, like seven flutes moving from chaos to harmony, the world itself chimed, a note as deep as oceans and pure as dawn. Balasar felt his heart grow light for a moment, a profound joy filling him that had nothing to do with triumph, and there, standing before the seated poet, was a naked man, bald as a baby, with eyes white as salt.

The blast pressed Balasar back against the wall. His ears rang, and Eustin's voice seemed to come from a great distance.

"Riaan, sir!"

Balasar fought to focus his eyes. Riaan was still seated where he had been, but his shoulders were slumped, his head bowed is if in sleep. Balasar walked over to him, the sound of his own footsteps lost in his half-deafened state. It was like floating.

He was breathing. The poet breathed.

"Did it work, sir?" Eustin yelled from half a mile away or else there at his shoulder. "Does that mean it worked?"

9

>+< "What is he to do?" Maati asked and then sipped his tea. It was just slightly overbrewed, a bitter aftertaste haunting the back of his mouth. Or perhaps it was only that he'd drunk too much the night before, sitting up with his son until the full moon set and the eastern sky began to lighten. Maati had seen Nayiit back to the boy's apartments, and then, too tired to sleep, wandered to the poet's house where Cehmai was just risen for breakfast. He'd sent the servants back to the kitchens to bring a second meal, and while they waited, Cehmai shared what he had—thin butter pastry, blackberries still just slightly underripe, overbrewed tea. Everything tasted of early summer. Already the morning had broken the chill of the previous night.

"Really, he's been good to the woman. He's acknowledged the babe, he's married her. But if he doesn't love her, what's he to do? Love's not something you can command."

"Not usually," Stone-Made-Soft said, and smiled wide enough to bare its too-even white marble teeth. It wasn't a human mouth.

"I don't know," Cehmai said, ignoring the andat. "Really, you and I are probably the two worst men in the city to ask about things like that. I've never been in the position to have a wife. All the women I've been with knew that this old bastard came before anything."

Stone-Made-Soft smiled placidly. Maati had the uncomfortable sense that it was accepting a compliment.

"But you can see his dilemma," Maati said.

Outside, beyond the carefully sculpted oaks that kept the poet's house separate from the palaces, the city was in shadow. The sun, hidden behind the mountains to the east, filled the blue dome of air with soft light. The towers stood dark against the daylight, birds wheeling far below their highest reaches.

"I see that he's in a difficult position," Cehmai said. "And I'm in no position to say that good men never lose their hearts to . . . what? Inappropriate women?"

"If you mean the Khai's sister, the term is vicious killers," Stone-Made-Soft said. "But I think we can generalize from there."

"Thank you," Cehmai said. "But you've made the point yourself, Maati. Nayiit's married her. He's acknowledged the child. Doing that binds him to something, doesn't it? He's made an agreement. He's made a kind of promise, or else why say that he's been good to her? If he can put those things aside, then that goodness is just a formality."

Maati sighed. His mind felt thick. Too much wine, too little rest. He was old to be staying up all night; it was a young man's game. And still, he felt it important that Cehmai understand. If he could explain Nayiit to someone else, it would make the night and all their conversations through it real. It would put them into the world in a way that now might only have been a dream. He was silent too long, struggling to put his thoughts in order. Cehmai cleared his throat, shot an uncomfortable glance at Maati, and changed the subject.

"Forgive me, Maati-cha, but I thought there was some question about Nayiit's . . . ah . . . parentage? I know the Khai signed a document denying him, but that was when there was some question about the succession, and I'd always thought he'd done it as a favor. If you see what I . . ."

Maati put down his tea bowl and took a pose that disagreed. "There's more to being a father than a few moments between the sheets," Maati said. "I was there when Nayiit took his first steps. I sang him to sleep as often as I could. I brought food for him. I held him. And tonight, Cehmai. He came to me. He talked to *me*. I don't care whose blood he has, that boy's mine."

"If you say so," Cehmai said, but there was something in his voice, some reservation. Maati felt his face begin to flush. Anger straightened his back. Stone-Made-Soft raised a wide, thick hand, palm out, silencing them both. Its head tilted, as if hearing some distant sound.

Its brow furrowed.

"Well," the andat said. "*That's* interesting."

And then it vanished.

Maati blinked in confusion. A few heartbeats later, Cehmai drew a long, shuddering breath. The poet's face was bloodless.

Maati sat silently as Cehmai stood, hands trembling, and walked back into the dimness of the house, and then out again. Cehmai's gaze darted one direction and another, searching for something. His eyes were so wide, the whites showed all the way around.

"Oh," Cehmai said, and his voice was thin and reedy. "Maati . . . Oh gods. I didn't do anything. I didn't . . . Oh gods. Maati-kvo, he's *gone*."

Maati rose, brushing the crumbs from his robes with a sense of profound unreality. Once before, he had seen the last moments of an andat in the world. It wasn't something he'd expected to suffer again. Cehmai paced the wide porch, his head turning one way and another, directionless as a swath of silk caught in the wind.

"Stay here. I'll get Otah-kvo," Maati said. "He'll know what to do."

THE WALLS of the audience chamber swooped up, graceful as a dove's wing. The high, pale stone looked as soft as fresh butter, seamless where the stones had joined and been smoothed into one piece by the power of the andat. Tiny web-works of stone fanned out from the walls at shoulder height, incense smoke rising from them in soft gray lines. High above, windows had been shaped by hand. Spare and elegant and commanding, it was a place of impossible beauty, and Otah suspected the world would never see another like it.

He sat in the black chair his father had sat in, and his father before him, and on back through the generations to when the Empire had still stood, and the name Khai had meant honored servant. Before him, seated on soft red cushions and intricately woven rugs, were the heads of the highest families of the utkhaiem. Vaunani, Radaani, Kamau, Daikani, Dun, Isadan, and half a dozen others. For each of these, there were ten more families. Twenty more. But these were the highest, the richest, the most powerful men of Machi. And they were the ones who had just suffered the worst loss. Otah waited while his news sank in, watched the blood drain from their faces. Otah kept his visage stern and his posture formal and rigid. His robes were simple, pale, and severe. His first impulse—a ceremonial black shot with red and long, flexible bone sewn in to give it shape—had been too gaudy; he would have seemed to be taking refuge in the cloth. The important things now were that they know he was in control and that they put trust in him. It would be too easy for the city to fall into panic, and here, now, through the force of his own will, he could hold it back. If these men left the room unsure, it would be too late. He could hold a stone, but he couldn't stop a rockslide.

"C-Can we get it back?" Wetai Dun asked, his voice shaking. "There are andat that poets have caught three, four times. Water-Moving-Down was . . ."

Otah took a deep breath. "There is a chance," he said. "It has been done, but it will be harder than it was the first time. The poet who does will have to create a binding sufficiently different from the original. Or it could be that the Dai-kvo will be able to give us an andat that is different, but that still speeds the mining trades."

"How long will it take?" Ashua Radaani asked. The Radaani

were the richest family in the city, with more silver and gold in their coffers than even Otah himself could command.

"We can't know until we hear from the Dai-kvo," Otah said. "I've sent my best courier with enough gold in his sleeve to buy a fresh horse every time he needs one. We will hear back as soon as it is possible to know. Until that happens, we will work as we always have. Stone-Made-Soft made the mines here and in the North the most productive in the world, that's true. But it didn't run the forges. It didn't smelt the ore. The stone potters will have to go back to working clay, that's true, but—"

"How did this happen?" Caiin Dun cried. His voice was as anguished as if he'd lost a son. There was a stirring in the air. Fear. Without thinking, Otah rose, his hands flowing into a pose of censure.

"Dun-cha," he said, his voice cold as stone and harder. "You are not here to shout me down. I have brought you here as a courtesy. Do you understand that?"

The man took an apologetic pose, but Otah pressed.

"I asked whether you understood, not whether you were regretful."

"I understand, Most High," the man muttered.

"The potters will have to work clay until some other accommodation can be made," Otah said. "With proper control, this will be an inconvenience, not a catastrophe. The city is wounded, yes. We all know that, and I won't have that made worse by panic. I expect each of you to stand with your Khai, and make your people know that there is nothing to fear. The contracts directly affected by this loss will be brought to me personally. I will see to it that any losses are recompensed so that no one family or house carries more of this burden than its share. And any contracts not directly affected by the andat's absence are still in force. Do each of you understand that?"

A low chorus of affirmation rose. They sounded as reluctant as boys before a tutor.

"Also I have put armsmen on the bridge. Any house who chooses this time to relocate its wealth to some other city will forfeit their holdings here. Any silver over a hundred lengths that leaves Machi at one time must be allowed by me."

Ashua Radaani took a pose that begged permission to speak. It was proper etiquette, and Otah felt the tightness in his chest release by half a turn. At least they were now respecting forms.

"Most High," Radaani said, "this may not be the best time to put restrictions on trade. Machi will need to keep its ties to the other cities strong if we're to weather this tragedy."

"If the smaller houses see carts of gold rolling away to Cetani and Udun, they'll start talking of how the rats all run when the house catches fire," Otah said. "My house hasn't caught fire."

Radaani pursed his lips, his eyes shifting as if reading some invisible text as he reconsidered some internal plan that Otah had just ruined, but he said nothing more.

"Machi needs your loyalty and your obedience," Otah said. "You are all good men, and the leaders of respected families. Understand that I value each of you, and your efforts to keep the peace in this time will be remembered and honored."

And the first of you to bolt, I will destroy and sow your lands with salt, Otah thought but didn't say. He let his eyes carry that part of the message, and from the unease in the men before him, he knew that they had understood. For over a decade, they had thought themselves ruled by a softhearted man, an upstart put in his father's chair by strange fortune and likely less suited to the role than his lady wife, the innkeep. And as terrible as this day was, Otah found he felt some small joy in suggesting they might have been mistaken.

Once they had been dismissed, Otah waved away his servants and walked to his private apartments. Kiyan came to him, taking his hand in her own. Cehmai sat on the edge of a low couch, his face still empty with shock. He had been weeping openly when Otah left.

"How did it go?" Kiyan asked.

"Well, I think. Strangely, it's much easier than dealing with Eiah."

"You don't love them," Kiyan said.

"Ah, is that the difference?"

A plate of fresh apples stood on a copper table, a short, wicked knife beside it. Otah sliced a bit of the white flesh and chewed thoughtfully.

"They'll still move their wealth away, you know," Kiyan said. "Blocking the bridge won't stop a ferry crossing in the night with its lanterns shuttered or wagons looping up north and crossing the water someplace in the mountains."

"I know it. But if I can keep the thing down to a few ferries and wagons, that will do. I'll also need to send messages to the Khaiem," Otah said. "Cetani and Amnat-Tan to start."

"Better they hear the bad news from you," she agreed. "Should I call for a scribe?"

"No. Just paper and a fresh ink brick. I'll do the thing myself."

"I'm sorry, Most High," Cehmai said again. "I don't know . . . I don't know how it happened. He was there, and then . . . he just wasn't. There wasn't even a struggle. He just . . ."

"It doesn't matter," Otah said. "It's gone, and so it's gone. We'll move forward from that."

"It does matter, though," the poet said, and his voice was a cry of despair. Otah wondered what it would feel like, dedicating a life to one singular thing and then in an instant, losing it. He himself had led a half-dozen lives—laborer, fisherman, midwife's assistant, courier, father, Khai—but Cehmai had never been anything besides a poet. Exalted above all other men, honored, envied. And now, suddenly, he was only a man in a brown robe. Otah put a hand to the man's shoulder, and saw a moment's passing shame in Cehmai's expression. It was, perhaps, too early still for comfort.

A scratch came at the door and a servant boy entered, took a formal pose, and announced the poet Maati Vaupathai and Liat Chokavi. A moment later, Maati rushed in, his cheeks an alarming red, his breath hard, his belly heaving. Liat was no more than a step behind. He could see the alarm in her expression. Kiyan stepped forward and helped Maati to a seat. The two women met each other's gaze, and there was a moment's tension before Otah stepped forward.

"Liat-cha," he said. "Thank you for coming."

"Of course," she said. "I came as soon as Maati asked me. Is something wrong? Have we heard from the Dai-kvo?"

"No," Maati said between gasps. "Not that."

Otah took a questioning pose, and Maati shook his head.

"Didn't say. People around. Would have been heard," Maati said. Then, "Gods, I need to eat less. I'm too fat to run anymore."

Otah took Liat's elbow and guided her to a chair, then sat beside Cehmai. Only Kiyan remained standing.

"Liat-cha, you worked with Amat Kyaan," Otah said. "You've taken over the house she founded. She must have spoken with you about how those first years were. After Heshai-kvo died and Seedless escaped."

"Of course," Liat said.

"I need you to tell us about that," Otah said. "I need to know what she did to keep Saraykeht together. What she tried that worked, what failed. What she wished the Khai Saraykeht had done in response, what she would have preferred he had not. Everything."

Liat's gaze went to Maati and then Cehmai and then back to Otah. There was still a deep confusion in her expression.

"It's happened again," Otah said.

10

>+< Given a half-decent road, the armies of Galt could travel faster than any in the world. It was the steam wagons, Balasar reflected, that made the difference. As long as there was wood or coal to burn and water for the boilers, the carts could keep their pace at a fast walk. In addition to the supplies they carried—food, armor, weapons that the men were then spared—a tenth of the infantry could climb aboard the rough slats, rest themselves, and eat. Rotated properly, his men could spend a full day at fast march, make camp, and be rested enough by morning to do the whole thing again. Balasar sat astride his horse—a nameless mare Eustin had procured for him—and looked back over the valley; the sun dropping at their back stretched their shadows to the east. Hundreds of plumes of dark smoke and pale steam rose from the green silk banners rippling above and beside them. The plain behind him was a single, ordered mass of the army stretching back, it seemed, to the horizon. Boots crushed the grasses, steam wagons consumed the trees, horses tramped the ground to mud. Their passing alone would scar these fields and meadows for a generation.

And the whole of it was his. Balasar's will had gathered it and would direct it, and despite all his late-night sufferings, in this moment he could not imagine failure. Eustin cleared his throat.

"If they had found some andat to do this," Balasar said, "do you know what would have happened?"

"Sir?" Eustin said.

"If the andat had done this—Wagon-That-Pulls-Itself or Horse-Doesn't-Tire, something like that—no one would ever have designed a steam wagon. The merchants would have paid some price to the Khai, the poet would have been set to it, and it would have worked until the poet fell down stairs or failed to pass the andat on."

"Or until we came around," Eustin said, but Balasar wasn't ready to leave his chain of thought for self-congratulations yet.

"And if someone *had* made the thing, had seen a way that any decent smith could do what the Khai charged good silver for, he'd either keep it quiet or find himself facedown in the river," Balasar said and then spat. "It's no way to run a culture."

Eustin's mount whickered and shifted. Balasar sighed and shifted his gaze forward to the rolling hills and grasslands where the first and farthest-flung of Nantani's low towns dotted the landscape. Another day, perhaps two, and he would be there. He was more than half tempted to press on; night marches weren't unheard-of and the anticipation of what lay before them sang to him, the hours pressing at him. But the summer was hardly begun. Better not to suffer surprises too early in the campaign. He moved a practiced gaze over the road ahead, considered the distance between the reddening orb of the sun and the horizon, and made his decision.

"When the first wagon reaches that stand of trees, call the halt," he said. "That will still give the men half a hand to forage before sunset."

"Yes, sir," Eustin said. "And that other matter, sir?"

"After dinner," Balasar said. "You can bring Captain Ajutani to my tent after dinner."

His impulse had been to kill the poet as soon as the signal arrived. The binding had worked, the cities of the Khaiem lay open before him. Riaan had outlived his use.

Eustin had been the one to counsel against it, and Sinja Aju-tani had been the issue. Balasar had known there was something less than trust between the two men; that was to be expected. He hadn't understood how deeply Eustin suspected the Khaiate mercenary. He had tracked the man—his visits to the poet, the organization of his men, how Riaan's unease had seemed to rise after a meeting with Sinja and fall again after he spoke with Balasar. It was nothing like an accusation; even Eustin agreed there wasn't proof of treachery. The mercenary had done nothing to show that he wasn't staying bought. And yet Eustin was more and more certain with each day that Sinja was plotting to steal Riaan back to the Khaiem, to reveal what it was he had done and, just possibly, find a way to undo it.

The problem, Balasar thought, was a simple failure of imag-ination. Eustin had followed Balasar through more than one campaign, had walked through the haunted desert with him, had stood at his side through the long political struggle that had brought this army to this place on this supreme errand. Loyalty was the way Eustin understood the world. The thought of a man who served first one cause and then another made no more sense to him than stone floating on water. Balasar had agreed to his scheme to prove Captain Ajutani's standing, though he himself had little doubt. He took the exercise seri-ously for Eustin's sake if nothing else. Balasar would be ready for them when they came.

His pavilion was in place before the last light of the sun had vanished in the west: couches made from wood and canvas that could be broken down flat and carried on muleback, flat cushions embroidered with the Galtic Tree, a small writing table. A low iron brazier took the edge from the night's chill, and half a hundred lemon candles filled the air with their scent and drove away the midges. He'd had it set on the top of a rise, looking down over the valley where the light of cook fires dot-ted the land like stars in the sky. A firefly had found its way through the gossamer folds of his tent, shining and then van-ishing as it searched for a way out. A thousand of its fellows glittered in the darkness between camps. It was like something from a children's story, where the Good Neighbors had breached the division between the worlds to join his army. He saw the three of them coming toward him, and he knew each long before he could make out their faces.

Eustin's stride was long, low, and deceptively casual. Captain Ajutani moved carefully, each step provisional, the weight always held on his back foot until he chose to shift it. Riaan's was an unbalanced, civilian strut. Balasar rose, opened the flap for them to enter, and rolled down the woven-grass mats to give them a level of visual privacy, false walls that shifted and muttered in the lightest of breezes.

"Thank you all for coming," Balasar said in the tongue of the Khaiem.

Sinja and Riaan took poses, the forms a study in status; Sinja accepted the greeting of a superior, Riaan condescended to acknowledge an honored servant. Eustin only nodded. In the corner of the pavilion, the firefly burst into sudden brilliance and then vanished again. Balasar led the three men to cushions on a wide woven rug, seating himself to face Sinja. When they had all folded their legs beneath them, Balasar leaned forward.

"When I began this campaign," he said, "it was not my intention to continue the rule of the poets and their andat over the rest of humanity. In the course of my political life, I allowed certain people to misunderstand me. But it is not my intention that Riaan-cha should be burdened by another andat. Or that anyone should. Ever."

The poet's jaw dropped. His face went white, and his hands fluttered toward poses they never reached. Sinja only nodded, accepting the new information as if it were news of the weather.

"That leaves me with an unpleasant task," Balasar said, and he drew a blade from his vest. It was a thick-bladed dagger with a grip of worked leather. He tossed it to the floor. The metal glittered in the candlelight. Riaan didn't understand; his confusion was written on his brow and proclaimed by his silence. If he'd understood, Balasar thought, he'd be begging by now.

Sinja glanced at the knife, then up at Balasar and then Eustin. He sighed.

"And you've chosen me to see if I'd do it," the mercenary said with a tone both weary and amused.

"I don't . . ." Riaan said. "You . . . you can't mean that . . . Sinja-kya, you wouldn't—"

The motion was casual and efficient as swatting at a fly. Sinja leaned over, plucked the knife from the rug, and tossed it into the poet's neck. It sounded like a melon being cleaved. The poet rose half to his feet, clawing at the handle already slick with his blood, then slowly folded, lying forward as if asleep or drunk. The scent of blood filled the air. The poet's body twitched, heaved once, and went still.

"Not your best rug, I assume," Sinja said in Galtic.

"Not my best rug," Balasar agreed.

"Will there be anything else, sir?"

"Not now," Balasar said. "Thank you."

The mercenary captain nodded to Balasar, and then to Eustin. His gait as he walked out was the same as when he'd walked in. Balasar stood and stepped back, kicking the old, flat cushion onto the corpse. Eustin also stood, shaking his head.

"Not what you'd expected, then?" Balasar asked,

"He didn't even try to talk you out of it," Eustin said. "I thought he'd at least play you for time. Another day."

"You're convinced, then?"

Eustin hesitated, then stooped to roll the rug over the corpse. Balasar sat at the writing desk, watching as Eustin finished covering the poor, arrogant, pathetic man in his ignominious shroud and called in two soldiers to haul him away. Riaan Vaudathat, the world's last poet if Balasar had his way, would rest in an unmarked grave in this no-man's-land between the Westlands and Nantani. It took more time than throwing him into a ditch, and there were times that Balasar had been tempted. But treating the body with respect said more about the living than the dead, and it was a dignity with only the smallest price. A few men, a little work.

A new rug was brought in, new pillows, and a plate of curried chicken and raisins, a flagon of wine. The servants all left, and Eustin still hadn't spoken.

"When you brought this to me," Balasar said, "you said his hesitation would be proof of his guilt. Now you're thinking his lack of hesitation might be just as damning."

"Seemed like he might be trying to keep the poor bastard from saying something," Eustin said, his gaze cast down. Balasar laughed.

"There's no winning with you. You know that."

"I suppose not, sir."

Balasar took a knife and cut a slice from the chicken. It smelled lovely, sweet and hot and rich. But beneath it and the lemon candles, there was still a whiff of death and human blood. Balasar ate the food anyway. It tasted fine.

"Keep watch on him," Balasar said. "Be polite about it. Nothing obvious. I don't want the men thinking I don't believe in him. If you don't see him plotting against us by the time we reach Nantani, perhaps you'll sleep better."

"Thank you, sir."

"It's nothing. Some chicken?"

Eustin glanced at the plate, and then his eyes flickered toward the tent flap behind him.

"Or," Balasar said, "would you rather go set someone to shadow Captain Ajutani."

"If it's all the same, sir," Eustin said.

Balasar nodded and waved the man away. In the space of two breaths, he was alone. He ate slowly. When the meal was almost done—chicken gone, flagon still over half full—a chorus of crickets suddenly burst out. Balasar listened. The poet was dead.

There was no turning back now. The High Council back in Acton would be desperately angry with him when they heard the news, but there wasn't a great deal they could do to breathe life back into a corpse. And if his work went well, by the time winter silenced these crickets, there would no longer be a man alive in the world who could take Riaan's place. And yet, his night's work was not complete.

He wiped his hands clean, savored a last sip of wine, and took the leather satchel from under his cot. He put the books on his writing table, side by side by side. The ancient pages seemed alive with memory. He still bore the scars on his shoulder from hauling these four books out of the desert. He still felt the ghosts of his men at his back, watching in silence, waiting to see whether their deaths had been noble or foolish. And beyond that—beyond himself and his life and struggles—the worn paper and pale ink knew of ages. The hand that had copied these words had been dust for at least ten generations. The minds that first conceived these words had fallen into forgetfulness long before that. The emperor whose greater glory they had been offered to was forgotten, his palaces ruins. The lush forests and jungles of the Empire were dune-swept. Balasar put his hand on the cool metallic binding of the first of the volumes.

Killing the man was nothing. Killing the books was more difficult. The poet, like any man, was born to die. Moving his transition from flesh to spirit forward by a few decades was hardly worth considering, and Balasar was a soldier and a leader of soldiers. Killing men was his work. It would have been as well to ask a farmer to regret the fate of his wheat. But to take these words which had lasted longer than the civilization that created them, to slaughter history was a task best done by the ignorant. Only a man who did not understand his actions would be callous enough to destroy these without qualm.

And yet what must be done, must be done. And it was time.

Carefully, Balasar laid the books open in the brazier. The pages shifted in the breeze, scratching one on another like dry hands. He ran his fingers along one line, translating as best he could, reading the words for the last time. The lemon candle spilled its wax across his knuckles as he carried it, and the flame leapt to twice its height. He touched the open leaves with the burning wick as a priest might give a blessing, and the books seemed to embrace the fire. He sat, watching the pages blacken and curl, bits of cinder rise and dance in the air. A pale smoke filled the air, and Balasar rose, opening the flap of the pavilion to the wide night air.

The firefly darted past him, glowing. Balasar watched it fly out to freedom and the company of its fellows until it went dark and vanished. The cook fires were fewer, the stars hanging in the sky bright and steady. A strange elation passed through him, as if he had taken off a burden or been freed himself. He grinned like an idiot at the darkness and had to fight himself not to dance a little jig. If he'd been certain that none of his men were near, that no one would see, he would have allowed himself. But he was a commander and not a child. Dignity had its price.

When he returned to the brazier, nothing was left but blackened hinges, split leather, gray ash. Balasar stirred the ruins with a stick, making sure no text had survived, and then, satisfied, turned to his cot. The day before him would be long.

As he lay in the darkness, half asleep, he felt the ghosts again. The men he had left in the desert. The men still alive whom he would leave in the field. Riaan, books cradled in his arms. Balasar's sacrifices filled the pavilion, and their presence and expectation comforted him until a small voice came from the back of his mind.

Kya, it said. *Sinja-kya, he called him. Sinja-cha would have been the proper form, wouldn't it? Kya is used for a lover or a brother. Why would Riaan have thought of Sinja as a brother?*

And then, as if Eustin were seated beside the cot, his voice whispered, *Seemed like he might be trying to keep the poor bastard from saying something.*

LIAT WALKED through darkness between the Khai's palaces and the library where Maati, she hoped, was still awake and waiting for her. She felt like a washrag wrung out, soaked, and wrung out again. It was seven days now since Stone-Made-Soft had escaped, and she'd spent the time either meeting with the Khai Machi or waiting to do so. Long days spent in the gilded halls and corridors of the palaces were, she found, more tiring than travel. Her back ached, her legs were sore, and she couldn't even think what she had done to earn the pain. Sitting shouldn't carry such a price. If she'd lifted something heavy, there would at least be a reason. . . .

The city seemed darker now than when she'd arrived. It might be only her imagination, but there seemed fewer lanterns lit on the paths, fewer torches at the doorways. The windows of the palaces that shone with light seemed dimmed. No slaves sang in the gardens, the members of the utkhaiem that she saw throughout her day all shared a tension that she understood too well.

Candles flickered behind Maati's closed shutters, a thin line of light where the wooden frames had warped over the years. Liat found herself more grateful than she had expected to be as she took the last steps down the path that led to his door.

Maati sat on the low couch, a bowl of wine cradled in his fingers. A bottle less than half full sat on the floor at his feet. He smiled as she let herself in, but she saw at once that something wasn't well. She took a pose of query, and he looked away.

"Maati-kya?"

"I've had a letter from the Dai-kvo," Maati said. "The timing of all this isn't what I'd hoped, you know. I've spent years puttering through the library here, looking for nothing in particular, and only stumbled on my little insight now. Just when the Galts have gotten out of hand. And now Cehmai. And . . . forgive me, love, and you. And our boy."

"I don't understand," Liat said. "The Dai-kvo. What did he say?"

"He said that I should come." Maati sighed. "There's nothing in the letter about the Galts or the missing poet. There's nothing about Stone-Made-Soft, of course. The courier won't be there with that sorry news for days yet. It's only about me. It's the thing I'd always hoped for. It's my absolution, Liat-kya. I have been out of favor since before Nayiit was born. After I took Otah's cause in the succession, they almost forbade me from wearing the robes, you know. The old Dai-kvo made it very clear he didn't consider me a poet."

Liat leaned against the cool stone wall. Her pains were forgotten. She watched Maati raise his brows, shake his head. His lips shifted as if he were having some silent conversation to which she was only half welcome. A familiar heaviness touched her heart.

"You must have hoped for this," she said.

"Dreamed of it, when I dared to. I'm welcomed back with honor and dignity. I'm saved."

"That's a bitter tone for a saved man," she said.

"I've only just met you again. I've only just started to know Nayiit. And Otah-kvo's in need. And the Galts are stirring trouble again. My shining hour has come to call me away from everyone who actually matters."

"You can't refuse the Dai-kvo," Liat said softly. "You have to go."

"Do I?"

The air between them grew still. Half a hundred other conversations echoed in their words. Liat closed her eyes, weariness dragging her like rain-heavy robes.

"It's all happening again, isn't it?" she said. "It's all the things we've suffered before, coming back at once. The Galts. Stone-Made-Soft set free. Cehmai lost and mourning the way Heshai was that summer, after Seedless killed the baby. And then us. You and I."

"You and I, ending again," Maati said. "All of history pressed into one season. It doesn't seem fair."

"How is Cehmai?" she asked, turning the conversation to safer ground, if only for a moment. "Has he been eating?"

"A little. Not enough."

"Does he know yet what happened? How Stone-Made-Soft slipped free?"

"No, but . . . but he suspects. And I do, too."

Liat moved forward, sat beside Maati, took the bowl from his hands and drank the wine. Her throat and chest warmed and relaxed. Maati took a bottle from the floor.

"Not every poet is made for slaughter," Maati said as he tipped rice wine clear as water into the bowl. "There was a part of him that rebelled at the prospect of turning the andat against the Galts. I know he struggled with it, and he and I both believed he'd made his peace with it."

"But now you think not?"

"Now I think perhaps he wasn't as certain as he told himself he was. He may not even have known what he meant to do. It would take so little, in a way. The decision of a moment, and then gone beyond retrieval. If he regretted it in the next breath, it would already be too late. But it can't be a coincidence, the Galts and Stone-Made-Soft."

Liat sipped now, just enough to maintain the warmth in her body but not so much as to make her drunk. Maati drank directly from the bottle, wiping it with his sleeve after.

"There's another explanation," she said. "The Galts could have done it."

"How? They can't unmake a binding."

"They could have bought him."

Maati shook his head, frowning. "Not Cehmai. There's not a man in the world less likely to turn against the Khaiem."

"You're sure of that?"

"Yes. I'm sure," Maati said. "He was happy. He had his life and his place in the world, and he was happy."

"So much the worse for him," Liat said. "At least we don't have that to suffer, eh?"

"And now who sounds bitter?"

Liat chuckled and took a pose accepting the point that was made awkward by the bowl in one hand.

"How are things with Otah-kvo?" Maati asked.

"He's like the wind on legs," Liat said. "He wants to know everything at once, control all of it, and I think he's driving the court half mad. And . . . don't say I said it, but it's almost as if he's enjoying it. Everything's falling apart except him. If simple force of will can hold a city together, I think Machi will be fine."

"It can't, though."

"No," she agreed. "It can't."

The back of Maati's hand brushed against her arm. It was a small, tentative gesture, familiar as breath. It was something he had always done when he was uncertain and in need of comfort. There had been times when she'd found it powerfully annoying and times when she'd found herself doing it too. Now, she shifted the wine bowl to her other hand, and resolutely laced her fingers with his.

"I haven't written back to the Dai-kvo," Maati said. His voice was as low as a confession. "I'm not sure what I should . . . I haven't been back to Saraykeht, you know. I could . . . I mean . . . Gods, I'm saying this badly. If you want it, Liat-kya, I could come back with you. You and Nayiit."

"No," she said. "There isn't room for you. My life there has a certain shape to it, and I don't want you to be a part of it. And Nayiit's a grown man. It's too late to start raising him now. I love you. And Nayiit is better, I think, knowing you than he was before. But you can't come back with us. You aren't welcome."

Maati looked down at his knees. His hand seemed to relax into her palm.

"Thank you," he whispered.

She raised his hand and kissed the wide, soft knuckles. And then his mouth. He touched her neck gently, his hand warm against her skin.

"Put out the candles," she said.

Time had made him a better lover than when they had been young. Time and experience—his and her own both. Sex had been so earnest then; so anxious, and so humorless. She had spent too much time as a girl worried about whether her breasts looked pleasing or if her hips were too thin. In the years she had kept a house with him, Maati had tried to hold in his belly whenever his robes came off. Youth and vanity, and now that they were doomed to sagging flesh and loose skin and short breath, all of it could be forgiven and left behind.

They laughed more now as they shrugged out of their robes and pulled each other down on the wide, soft bed. They paused in their passions to let Maati rest. She knew better now what would bring her the greatest pleasure, and had none of her long-ago qualms about asking for it. And when they were spent, lying wrapped in a soft sheet, Maati's head on her breast, the netting pulled closed around them, the silence was deeper and more intimate than any words they had spoken.

She would miss this. She had known the dangers when she had taken his hand again, when she had kissed him again. She had known there would be a price to pay for it, if only the pain of having had something pleasant and precious and brief. For a moment, her mind shifted to Nayiit and his lovers, and she was touched by sorrow on his behalf. He was too much her son and not enough Otah's. But she didn't want Otah in this room, in this moment, so she put both of these other men out of her mind and concentrated instead on the warmth of her own flesh and Maati's, the slow, regular deepening of his breath and of hers.

Her thoughts wandered, slowing and losing their coherence; turning into something close kin to dream. She had almost slipped into the deep waters of sleep when Maati's sudden spasm brought her back. He was sitting up, panting like a man who'd run a mile. It was too dark to see his face.

She called his name, and a low groan escaped him. He stood and for a moment she was afraid that he would stagger and fall. But she made out his silhouette, a deeper darkness, and he did not sway. She called his name again.

"No," he said, then a pause and, "No no no no no. Oh gods. Gods, no."

Liat rose, but Maati was already walking. She heard him bark his shin against the table in the front room, heard the wine bottle clatter as it fell. She wrapped her sheet around herself and hurried after him just in time to see him lumbering naked out the door and into the night. She followed.

He trotted into the library, his hands moving restlessly. When he lit a candle, she saw his face etched deep with dread. It was as if he was watching someone die that only he could see.

"Maati. Stop this," she said, and the fear in her voice made her realize that she was trembling. "What's the matter? What's happened?"

"I was wrong," he said. "Gods, Cehmai will never forgive me doubting him. He'll never forgive me."

Candle in hand, Maati lumbered into the next room and began frantically looking through scrolls, hands shaking so badly the wax spilled on the floor. Liat gave up hope that he would speak, that he would explain. Instead, she took the candle from his hand and held it for him as he searched. In the third room, he found what he'd been seeking and sank to the floor. Liat came to his side, and read over his shoulder as he unfurled the scroll. The ink was pale, the script the alphabet of the Old Empire. Maati's fingertips traced the words, looking for something, some passage or phrase. Liat found herself holding her breath. And then his hand stopped moving.

The grammar was antiquated and formal, the language almost too old to make sense of. Liat silently struggled to translate the words that had caught Maati short.

The second type is made up of those thoughts impossible to bind by their nature, and no greater knowledge shall ever permit them. Examples of this are Imprecision and Freedom-From-Bondage.

"I know what they've done," he said.

11

>+< Nantani had been one of the first cities built when the Second Empire reached out past its borders to put its mark on the distant lands they now inhabited. The palace of the Khai was topped by a dome the color of jade—a single stone shaped by the will of some long-dead poet. When the sunlight warmed it in just the right way, it would chime, a low voice rolling out wordlessly over the whitewashed walls and blue tile roofs of the city.

Sinja had wintered in Nantani for a few seasons, retreating from the snowbound fields of the Westlands to wait in comfort for the thaw and spend the money he'd earned. He knew the scent of the sea here, the feel of the soft, chalky soil beneath his feet. He knew of an old man who sold garlic sausages from a stall near the temple that were the best he'd had in the world. He knew the sound of the great sun chime. He had not known that the deep, throbbing tone would also come when the palace below it burned.

There were other fires as well: pillars of black, rolling smoke that rose into the air like filthy clouds. The doors he passed as he walked down to the seafront were broken and splintered. The shutters at the windows clacked open and closed in the breeze. Often they passed wide swaths of half-dry blood on the ground or smeared on the rough white walls.

The city had been home to over a hundred thousand people. It had fallen in a morning.

Balasar had sent three forces in through the wide streets to the Khai's palace, the poet's house, the libraries. When those three things were destroyed, the signal went out—brass horns blaring the sack. When the signal reached the remaining forces, it was a storm of chaos. Some men ran for the inner parts of the city, hoping to find richer pickings. Others grabbed the first mercantile house they saw and took whatever was there to find—goods, gold, women. For the time it took the sun to travel the width of a man's hand, Nantani was a scene from the old stories of hell as the soldiery took what they could for themselves.

And then the second call came, and the looting stopped. Those few who were so maddened by greed or lust that they ignored the call were taken to their captains, relieved of what wealth they had grabbed, and then a fifth of them killed as an example to others. This was an army of discipline, and the free-for-all was over. Now the studied, considered dismantling of the city began.

Quarter by quarter, street by street, the armies of Galt stripped the houses and basements, outbuildings and kitchens and coal stores. Sinja's own men led each force, calling out in breaking voices that Nantani had fallen, that her people were permanently indentured to Galt, their belongings forfeit. And all the wealth of the city was stripped down, put on carts and wagons, and pulled to a great pile at the seafront. Some men fought and were killed. Some fled and were hunted down or ignored, at the whim of the soldiers who found them. And the great blackening dome of jade sang out its grief and mourning.

Sinja caught sight of the pavilion erected by the growing pile of treasure. The banners of Galt and Gice hung from the bar that topped the fluttering canvas. Sinja and the soldiers Balasar Gice had sent to collect him strode to it. At the seafront, ships stood ready to receive what had once been Nantani, and was now the fortune of Galt. Balasar stood at a writing desk, consulting with a clerk over a ledger. The general still wore his armor—embroidered silk as thick as three fingers together.

Sinja had seen its like before. Armor that would stop a spear or a sword cut, but weighed likely half as much as the man who wore it. And still when Balasar caught sight of them and walked forward, hand outstretched to Sinja, there was no weariness in him.

"Captain Ajutani," Balasar said, his hand clasping Sinja's, "come sit with me."

Sinja took a pose appropriate for a guard to his commander. It wasn't quite the appropriate thing, but it came near enough for the general to take its sense. Sinja walked behind the man to a low table where a bottle of wine stood open, two perfect porcelain wine bowls glowing white at its side. Balasar waved the attendant away and poured the wine himself. Sinja accepted a bowl and sat across from him.

"It was nicely done," Sinja said, gesturing with his free hand toward the city. "Well-managed and quick."

Balasar looked up, almost as if noticing the streets and warehouses for the first time. Sinja thought a hint of a smile touched the general's lips, but it was gone as soon as it came. The wine was rich and left Sinja's mouth feeling almost clean.

"It was competent," Balasar agreed. "But it can't have been easy. For you and your men."

"I didn't lose one of them," Sinja said. "I don't know that I've ever seen a campaign start where we took a city and didn't lose anyone."

"This is a different sort of war than the usual," Balasar said. And there, in the pale eyes, Sinja saw the ghosts. The general wasn't at ease, however casual he chose to be with his wine. It was an interesting fact, and Sinja put it at the back of his mind. "I wanted to ask after your men."

"Have there been complaints?"

"Not at all. Every report suggests that they did their work admirably. But this wasn't the adventure they expected."

"They expected the women they raped to look less like their sisters, that's truth," Sinja said. "And honestly, I expect we'll lose some. I don't know how it is in Galt, sir, but when I've taken a green company into battle the first time, we always lose some."

"Inexperience," Balasar said, agreeing.

"No, sir. I don't mean the enemy spits a few, though that's usually true as well. I mean there are always a few who came into the work with epics in their heads. Great battles, honor, glory. All that pig shit. Once they see what a battlefield or a sacked town really looks like, they wake up. Half these boys are still licking off the caul. Some of them will think better and sneak off."

"And how do you plan to address the problem?"

"Let them go," Sinja said and shrugged. "We haven't seen a fight yet, but before this is finished, we will. When it happens I'd rather have twenty soldiers than thirty men looking for a reason to retreat."

The general frowned, but he also nodded. At the edge of the pier, half a hundred seagulls took to the air at once, their cries louder than the waves. They wheeled once over the ships and then settled again, just where they had been.

"Unless you have a different opinion, sir," Sinja said.

"Do this," Balasar said, looking up from under his brow. "Go to them. Explain to them that I will never turn against my men. But if they leave me . . . if they leave my service, they aren't my men any longer. And if I find them again, I won't be lenient."

Sinja scratched his chin, the stubble just growing in, and felt a smile growing in his mind.

"I can see that they understand, sir," he said. "And it might stop some of the ones who'd choose to hang up their swords. But if there's someone you feel isn't loyal, one of my men that you think isn't yours, I'd recommend you kill him now. There's no room on a campaign like this for someone who'll take up arms against the man that pays his wage."

Balasar nodded, leaning back in his chair.

"I think we understand each other," he said.

"Let's be certain," Sinja said, and put his hands open and

palms-down on the table between them. "I'm a mercenary, and to judge by that pile of silk and cedar chests you're about to ship back to Galt, you're the man who's got the money to pay my contract. If I've given you reason to think there's more happening than that, I'd rather we cleared it up now."

Balasar chuckled. It was a warm sound. That was good.

"Are you ever subtle?" Balasar asked.

"If I'm paid to be," Sinja said. "I've had a bad experience working for someone who thought I might look better with a knife-shaped hole in my belly, sir, and I'd rather not repeat it. Have I done something to make you question my intentions?"

Balasar considered him. Sinja met his gaze.

"Yes," Balasar said. "You have. But it's nothing I would be comfortable hanging you for. Not yet at least. The poet, when you killed him. He addressed you in the familiar. Sinja-kya."

"Men begging for their lives sometimes develop an inaccurate opinion of how close they are to the men holding the blades," Sinja said, and the general had the good manners to blush. "I understand your position, sir. I've been living under the Khaiem for a long time now. You don't know my history, and if you did, it wouldn't help you. I've broken contracts before, and I won't lie about it. But I would appreciate it if we could treat each other professionally on this."

Balasar sighed.

"You've managed to shame me, Captain Ajutani."

"I won't brag about that if you'll agree to be certain you've a decent cause to kill me before taking action," Sinja said.

"Agreed," Balasar said. "But your men? I meant what I said about them."

"I'll be sure they understand," Sinja said, then swigged down the last of his wine, took a pose appropriate to taking leave of a superior, and walked back into the streets of the fallen city, hoping that it wouldn't be clear from his stride that his knees felt loose. Not that a sane measure of fear could be held against him, but there was pride to consider. And someone was watching him. He could be damned sure of that. So he walked straight and calm through the streets and the smoke and the wailing of the survivors until he reached the camp outside the last trailing building of Nantani. The tents were far from empty—the thugs and free armsmen of Machi didn't all have a stomach for looting Nantani—but he didn't speak to his men until just after nightfall.

They had a fire burning, though the summer night wasn't cold. The light of it made the tents glow gold and red. The men were quiet. The boasting and swaggering that the Galts were doing didn't have a place here. It would have if the burning city had been made from gray Westlands stone. Sinja stood at the front on a plank set up on chairs in a makeshift dais. He wanted them to see him. The scouts he'd sent out to assure that the conversation was private returned and took a confirming pose. If General Gice had set a watch over him, they'd gone to their own camps or else come from within his own company. He'd done what he could about the first, and the second there was no protection for. He raised his hands.

"So most of what we've done since the spring opened has been walk," he said. "Well, we're in summer now, and you've seen what war looks like. It's not the war I expected, that's truth. But it's the one we've got, and you can all thank the gods that we're on the side most likely to win. But don't think that because this went well, this is over with. It's a long walk still ahead of us."

He sighed and shifted his weight, the plank wobbling a little under his feet. A log in the fire popped, firing sparks up into the darkness like an omen.

"There are a few of you right now who are thinking of leaving. Don't . . . Quiet now! All of you! Don't lie to yourselves about it and don't lie to me. This is the first taste of war most of you've seen. And some of you might have had family or friends in Nantani. I did. But here's what I have to say to you: Don't do it. Right now it looks like our friends the Galts can't be stopped. All the gods know there's not a fighting force anywhere in the cities that could face them, that's truth. But there's worse things for an army to face than another army. Look at the size of this force, the simple number of men. It can't carry the food it needs with it. It can't haul that much water. We have to rely on the land we're covering. The low towns, the cities. The game we can hunt, the trees and coal we can feed into those traveling kilns of theirs. The water we can get from the rivers.

"If the cities North of here can organize—if they can burn the food and the trees so we have to spend more of our time finding supplies, if they foul the wells so that we can't move far from the rivers, if they get small, fast bands together to harass our hunting parties and scouts—we could still be in for hell's own fight. We took Nantani by surprise. That won't happen twice. And that's why I need every man among you here, keeping that from happening. And besides that, any of you that leave, the general's going to hunt down like low-town dogs and slit your bellies for you."

Sinja paused, looking out at the earnest, despairing faces of the boys he'd led from Machi. He felt old. He rarely felt old, but now he did.

"Don't be stupid," he said, and got down from the plank.

The men raised a late and halfhearted cheer. Sinja waved it away and headed back to his tent. Overhead, the stars shone where the smoke didn't obscure them. The cooks had made chicken and pepper rice. Stinging flies were out, and, to Sinja's mild disgust, Nantani seemed to be a haven for grass ticks. He spent a quiet, reflective time plucking the insects out of his skin and cracking them with his thumbnails. It was near midnight when he heard the roaring crash, thunder rolling suddenly from the ruined city, and then silence. The dome had fallen, then.

How many of his men would know what the sound had meant, he wondered. And how many would understand that he'd given them all the strategy for slowing the Galts, point by point by point. And how many would have snuck away to the North by morning, thinking they were being clever. But he could tell the general he'd done as he was told, and no man present would be able to say otherwise. So maybe he could lull the general back into trusting him for a while longer at least. And maybe Kiyan's husband would find a good way to make use of the time Sinja won for him.

"Ah, Kiyan-kya," he said to the night and the northern stars, "look what you've done. You've made me into a politician."

"MOST HIGH," Ashua Radaani said, taking a pose that was an apology and a refusal, "this is . . . this is folly. I understand that the poets are concerned, but you have to see that we have *nothing* that supports their suspicion. We're in summer. It's only a few weeks before we have to harvest the spring crops and plant for autumn. The men you're asking for . . . we can't just send away our laborers."

Otah frowned. It was not a response his father would have gotten. The other Khaiem would have raised a hand, made a speech, perhaps only shifted hands into a pose asking for the speaker to repeat himself. The men and horses and wagons of grain and cheese and salt-packed meats would simply have appeared. But not for Otah Machi, the upstart who had not won his chair, who had married a wayhouse keeper and produced only one son and that one sickly. He felt the urgency like a hand pressing at his back, but he forced himself to remain calm. He wouldn't have what he wanted by blustering now. He smiled sweetly at the round, soft man with his glittering rings and calculating eyes.

"Your huntsmen, then," Otah said. "Bring your huntsmen. And come yourself. Ride with me, Ashua-cha, and we'll go see whether there's any truth to this thing. If not, you can bear witness yourself, and reassure the court."

The young man's lips twisted into a half-smile.

"Your offer is kind, Most High," he said. "My huntsmen are yours. I will consult with my overseer. If my house can spare me, I would be honored to ride at your side."

"It would please me, Ashua-cha," Otah said. "I leave in two days, and I look forward to your company."

"I will do all I can."

They finished the audience with the common pleasantries,

and a servant girl showed the man out. Otah called for a bowl of tea and used the time to consider where he stood. If Radaani sent him a dozen huntsmen, that took the total to almost three hundred men. House Siyanti had offered up its couriers to act as scouts. None of the families of the utkhaiem had refused him; Daikani and old Kamau had even given him what he asked. The others dragged their feet, begged his forgiveness, compromised. If Radaani had backed him, the others would have fallen in line.

And if he had thought Radaani was likely to, he'd have met with him first instead of last.

It was the price, he supposed, of having played the game so poorly up to now. Had he been the man they expected him to be all these years—had he embraced the role he'd accepted and fathered a dozen sons on as many wives and assured the ritual bloodbath that marked the change of generations—they would have been more responsive now. But his own actions had called the forms of court into question, and now that he needed the traditions, he half-regretted having spent years defying them.

The tea came in a bowl of worked silver carried on a pillow. The servant, a man perhaps twenty years older than Otah himself with a long, well-kept beard and one clouded eye, presented it to him with a grace born of long practice. This man had done much the same before Otah's father, and perhaps his grandfather. The presentation of this bowl of tea might be the study and center of this man's life. The thought made the tea taste worse, but Otah took as warm a pose of thanks as would be permitted between the Khai Machi and a servant, however faithful.

Otah rose, gesturing to the doorway. One of his half-hundred attendants rushed forward, robes flowing like water over stones.

"I'll see him now," Otah said. "In the gardens. And see we aren't disturbed."

The sky was gray and ivory, the breeze from the south warm

as breath and nearly as gentle. The cherry trees stood green—
the pink of the blossoms gone, the crimson of the fruit not yet
arrived. The thicker blossoms of high summer had begun to
unfurl, rose and iris and sun poppy. The air was thick with the
scent. Otah walked down the path, white gravel fine as salt
crunching like snow under his feet. He found Maati sitting on
the lip of a stone pool, gazing up at the great fountain. Twice
as high as a man, the gods of order stood arrayed in bas-relief
shaped from a single sheet of bronze. The dragons of chaos
lay cowed beneath their greened feet. Water sluiced down the
wall, clear until it touched the brows and exultant, upraised
faces of the gods, and there it splattered white. Otah sat beside
his old friend and considered.

"The dragon's not defeated," Maati said. "Look. You see
the third head from the left? It's about to bite that woman's
calf. And the man on the end? The one who's looking down?
He's lost his balance."

"I hadn't noticed," Otah said.

"You should have another one made with the dragons on
top. Just to remind people that it's never over. Even when you
think it's done, there's something waiting to surprise you."

Otah nodded, dipping his fingers into the dancing ripples
of the pool. Gold and white koi darted toward his fingertips
and then as quickly away.

"I understand if you're angry with me," Otah said. "But I
didn't ask him. Nayiit came to me. He volunteered."

"Yes. Liat told me."

"He's spent half a season in the Dai-kvo's village. He
knows it better than anyone but you or Cehmai."

Maati looked up. There was a darkness in his expression.

"You're right," Maati said. "If this is the Galts and they've
freed the andat, then protecting the Dai-kvo is critical. But it
would be faster to send for him to come to us. We can build
defenses here, train men. Prepare."

"And if the Dai-kvo didn't come?" Otah asked. "How long
has he been mulling over Liat's report that the Galts have a

poet of their own? I've sent word. I've sent messages. The world can't afford to wait and see if the Dai-kvo suddenly becomes decisive."

"And you speak for the world now, do you?" There was acid in Maati's tone, but Otah could hear the fear behind it and the despair. "If you insist on charging out into whatever kind of war you find out there, take one of us with you. We've lived there. We know the village. Cehmai's still young. Or strap me on the back of a horse and pull me there. Leave Nayiit out of this."

"He's a grown man," Otah said. "He's not a child any longer. He has his own mind and his own will. I thought about refusing him, for your sake and for Liat's. But what would that be to him? He's not still wrapped in crib cloths. How would I say that I wanted him safe because his mother would worry for him?"

"And what about his father," Maati said, but it had none of the inflection of a question. "You have an opinion, Most High, on what his father would think."

Otah's belly sank. He dried his hand on his sleeve, only thinking afterward that it was the motion of a commoner—a dockfront laborer or a midwife's assistant or a courier. The Khai Machi should have raised an arm, summoned a servant to dry his fingers for him on a cloth woven for the purpose and burned after one use. His face felt mask-like and hard as plaster. He took a pose that asked clarification.

"Is that the conversation we're having, then?" he asked. "We're talking about fathers?"

"We're talking about sons," Maati said. "We're talking about you scraping up all the disposable men that the utkhaiem can drag out of comfort houses and slap sober enough to ride just so they can appease the irrational whims of the Khai. Taking those men out into the field because you think the armies of Galt are going to slaughter the Dai-kvo is what we're talking about, and about taking Nayiit with you."

"You think I'm wrong?"

"I *know* you're right!" Maati was breathing hard now. His

face was flushed. "I know they're out there, with an army of veterans who are perfectly accustomed to hollowing out their enemies' skulls for wine bowls. And I know you sent Sinja-cha away with all the men we had who were even half trained. If you come across the Galts, you will lose. And if you take Nayiit, he'll die too. He's still a child. He's still figuring out who he is and what he intends and what he means to do in the world. And—"

"Maati. I know it would be safer for me to stay here. For Nayiit to stay here. But it would only be safe for the moment. If we lose the Dai-kvo and all he knows and the libraries he keeps, having one more safe winter in Machi won't mean anything. And we might not even manage the winter."

Maati looked away. Otah bowed his head and pretended not to have seen the tears on his old friend's cheeks.

"I've only just found him again," Maati said, barely audible over the splashing water. "I've only just found him again, and I don't want him taken away."

"I'll keep him safe," Otah said.

Maati reached out his hand, and Otah let him lace his fingers with his own. It wasn't an intimacy that they had often shared, and against his will, Otah found something near to sorrow tightening his chest. He put his free hand to Maati's shoulder. When Maati spoke, his voice was thick and Otah no longer ignored his tears.

"We're his fathers, you and I," Maati said. "So we'll take care of him. Won't we?"

"Of course we will," Otah said.

"You'll see him home safe."

"Of course."

Maati nodded. It was an empty promise, and they both knew it. Otah smoothed a palm over Maati's thinning hair, squeezed his palm one last time, and stood. He was moved to speak, but he couldn't find any words that would say what he meant. Instead he turned and softly walked away. His servants and attendants waited just outside the garden, attentive as puppies whose mother has left them. Otah waved them away, as he always had. And as he might not do again. The Master of Tides brought the ledger that outlined the rest of his day, and the day after, and was suddenly perfectly blank after that. In two days, he would be traveling with what militia he could, and there was no point planning past that. As the man spoke, Otah gently took the book from him, closed it, and handed it back. The Master of Tides went silent, and no one followed Otah when he walked away.

He strode through the palaces, ignoring the poses of obeisance and respect that bloomed wherever he went. He didn't have time for the forms and rituals. He didn't have time to respect the traditions he was about to put his life in danger to protect. He wasn't entirely sure what that said about him. He took the wide, marble stairs two at a time, rising up from the lower palace toward his personal apartments. When he arrived, Kiyan wasn't there. He paced the rooms, plucking at the papers on the wide table he'd had brought for him. Maps and histories and lists of names. Numbers of men and of wagons and routes. It looked like a nest for rats: the piled books, the scattered notes. It was vaguely ridiculous, he thought as he read over the names of the houses and families who had sworn him support. He was no more a general than he was a tinsmith, and still, here he was, the man stuck with the job.

He didn't recall picking up the map. And yet there it was, in his hands. His eyes traced the paths he and his men might take. He and the men Maati had called disposable. It wasn't the first time he'd wished Sinja-cha were still in the city, if only to have the dispassionate eye of a man who had actually fought in the field. Otah was an amateur at war. He had the impression that it was a poor field for amateurs. He traded the map for the lists of men and studied it again as if there were a cipher hidden in it. He didn't notice when Kiyan and Eiah arrived. When he looked up from his papers, they were simply there.

His wife was calm and collected, though he could see the strain in the thinness of her lips and the tightness of her jaw. Her hair was grayer now than the image of her in his mind.

Her face seemed older. For a moment, he was back in the way-house she'd taken over from her father, years ago in Udun. He was in her common room, listening to a flute player fumble through old tunes that everyone knew, and wondering if the lovely fox-faced woman serving the wine had meant to touch his hand when she poured. From such small things are lives constructed. Something of his thought must have shown in his face, because her features softened and something near a blush touched her cheeks as Eiah lowered herself to a couch and collapsed. He noticed that her usual array of rings and jewels were gone; but for the quality of her robe, she could have been a merchant's daughter.

"You look spent, Eiah-kya," Otah said. Then, to Kiyan, "What's she been doing? Carrying stones up the towers? And what's happened to jewelry?"

"Physicians don't wear metalwork," she said, as if he'd asked something profoundly stupid. "Blood gets caught in the settings."

"She's been with them all day," Kiyan said.

"We had a boy come in with a crushed arm," Eiah said, her eyes closed. "It was all bloody and the skin scraped off. It looked like something from a butcher's stall. I could see his knuckle bones. Dorin-cha cleaned it up and wrapped it. We'll know in a couple days whether he'll have to have it off."

"*We'll* know?" Otah asked. "They're having you decide the fate of men's elbows?"

He saw a dark glitter where his daughter's eyes cracked just slightly open. "Dorin-cha will tell me, and then we'll both know."

"She's been quite the asset, they say," Kiyan said. "The matrons keep trying to send her away, and she keeps coming back. They tell her it's unseemly for her to be there, but the physicians seem flattered that she's interested."

"I like it," Eiah said, her voice slurring. "I don't want to stop. I want to help."

"You don't have to stop," Otah said. "I'll see to it."

"Thank you, Papa-kya," Eiah murmured.

"Off to your bed," Kiyan said, gently shaking Eiah's knee. "You're already half-dreaming."

Eiah frowned and grunted, but then came to her feet. She stumbled over to Otah, genuine exhaustion competing with the theatrics of being tired, and threw her arms around his neck. Her hair smelled of the vinegar the physicians used to wash down their slate tables. He put his arms around her. He could feel tears welling up in his eyes. His baby girl, his daughter. He would see her tomorrow, and then he would march out into the gods only knew what.

Tomorrow, he told himself, I will see her again tomorrow. This won't be the last time. Not yet. He kissed her forehead and let her go.

Eiah tottered to her mother for another kiss, another hug, and then they were alone. Kiyan gently plucked the papers from his hands and put them back on the desk.

"I'm not certain that worked as a punishment," Otah said. "We're halfway to raising a physician."

"It lets her feel she's useful," Kiyan said as she pulled him to the couch. He sat at her side. "It's normal for her to want to feel she's in control of something. And she isn't squeamish. I'll hand her that much."

"I hope feeling useful is enough," Otah said. "She's got her own will, and I don't think she'd be past following it over a cliff if it led her there."

He saw Kiyan read his deeper meaning. *I hope we are all still here to worry about it.*

"We do as well by them as we can, love," she said.

"I think about Idaan," Otah said.

Kiyan took his hand.

"Eiah isn't your sister. She isn't going to do the things she did," she said. "And more to the point, you aren't your father."

For a moment, he was consumed by memories: the father he had met only once, the sister who had engineered the old man's murder. Hatred and violence and ambition had destroyed his family once. He supposed it was inevitable that he should fear it happening again. Otah raised Kiyan's hand to his lips, and then sighed.

"I have to go to Danat. I haven't seen him yet. Go with me?"

"He's asleep already, love. We stopped in on our way here. He won't wake before morning. And you'll have to find different stories to read to him next time. Everything you left there, he's read to himself. Our boy's going to grow up a scholar at this rate."

Otah nodded, pushing aside a moment's guilt over the relief he felt. Seeing Danat was one less thing, even if it was more important than most of the others he'd already done. And there would be tomorrow. There would at least be tomorrow.

"How is he?"

"His color is better, but he has less energy. The fever is gone for now, but he still coughs. I don't know. No one does."

"Can he travel?"

Kiyan turned. Her gaze darted across his face as if he were a book that she was trying to read. Her hands took a querying pose.

"I've been thinking," Otah said. "Planning."

"For if you're killed," Kiyan said. Her voice made it plain she'd been thinking of it as well.

"The mines. If I don't come back, I want you to take to the mines in the North. Cehmai will go with you, and he knows them better than anyone. If you can, take the children and as much gold as you can carry and head west. Sinja and the others will be there somewhere, working whatever contract they've taken. They'll protect you."

"You're sending me to *him*?" Kiyan asked softly.

"Only if I don't come back."

"You will."

"Still," Otah said. "If . . ."

"If," Kiyan agreed and took his hand. Then, a long moment later, "We were never lovers, he and I. Not the way . . ."

Otah put a finger to her lips, and she went quiet. There were tears in her eyes, and in his.

"Let's not open that again," he said.

"You could come away too. We could all leave quietly. The four of us and a fast cart."

"And spend our lives on a beach in Bakta," Otah said. "I can't. I have this thing to do. My city."

"I know. But I had to say it, just so I know it was said."

Otah looked down. His hands looked old—the knuckles knobbier than he thought of them, the skin looser. They weren't an old man's hands, but they weren't a young man's any longer. When he spoke, his voice was low and thoughtful.

"It's strange, you know. I've spent years chafing under the weight of being Khai Machi, and now that it's harder than it ever was, now that there's something real to lose, I can't let go of it. There was a man once who told me that if it were a choice between holding a live coal in my bare fist or letting a city of innocent people die, of course I would do my best to stand the pain. That it was what any decent man would do."

"Don't apologize," Kiyan said.

"Was I apologizing?"

"Yes," she said. "You were. You shouldn't. I'm not angry with you, and there's nothing to blame you for. They all think you've changed, you know, but this is who you've always been. You were a poor Khai Machi because it didn't matter until now. I understand; I'm just frightened to death, love. It's nothing you can spare me."

"Maati could be wrong," Otah said. "The Galts may be busy rolling over the Westlands and none of it anything to do with Stone-Made-Soft. I may arrive at the Dai-kvo's village and be laughed at all the way back north."

"He's not wrong."

The great stones of the palaces creaked as they cooled, the summer sun fallen behind the mountains. The scent of incense long since burned and the smoke of snuffed lanterns filled the air like a voice gone silent. Shadows touched the corners of the apartments, deepening the reds of the tapestries and giving the light a feeling of physical presence. Kiyan's hand felt warm and lost in his own.

"I know he's not," Otah said.

He left orders with the servants at his door that unless there was immediate threat to him or his family—fire or sudden illness or an army crossing the river—he was to be left alone for the night. He would speak with no one, he would read no letter or contract, he wished no entertainments. Only a simple meal for him and his wife, and the silence for the two of them to fill as they saw fit.

They told stories—reminiscences of Old Mani and the wayhouse in Udun, the sound of the birds by the river. The time a daughter of one of the high families had snuck into the rooms her lover had taken and had to be smuggled back out. Otah told stories from his time as a courier, traveling the cities on the business of House Siyanti under his false name. They were all stories she'd heard before, of course. She knew all his stories.

They made love seriously and gently and with a profound attention. He savored every touch, every scent and motion. He fought to remember them and her, and he felt Kiyan's will to store the moment away, like food packed away for the long empty months after the last leaf of autumn has fallen. It was, Otah supposed, the kind of sex lovers had on the nights before wars, pleasure and fear and a sorrow that anticipated the losses ahead. And afterward, he lay against her familiar, beloved body and pretended to sleep until, all unaware, the pretense became truth and he dreamed of looking for a white raven that everyone else but him had seen, and of a race through the tunnels beneath Machi that began and ended at his father's ashes. He woke to the cool light of morning and Kiyan's voice.

"Sweet," she said again. Otah blinked and stretched, remembering his body. "Sweet, there's someone come to see you. I think you should speak with him."

Otah sat up and adopted a pose that asked the question, but Kiyan, half smiling, nodded toward the bedchamber's door. Before the servants could come and dress him, Otah pulled on rose-red outer robes over his bare skin and, still tying the stays, walked out to the main rooms. Ashua Radaani sat at the edge of a chair, his hands clasped between his knees. His face was as pale as fresh dough, and the jewels set in his rings and sewn in his robes seemed awkward and lost.

"Ashua-cha," Otah said, and the man was already on his feet, already in a pose of formal greeting. "What's happened?"

"Most High, my brother in Cetani . . . I received a letter from him last night. The Khai Cetani is keeping it quiet, but no one has seen poet or andat in the court in some time."

"Not since the day Stone-Made-Soft escaped," Otah said.

"As nearly as we can reckon it," he agreed.

Otah nodded, but took no formal pose. Kiyan stood in the doorway, her expression half pleasure and half dread.

"May I have the men I asked of you, Ashua-cha?"

"You may have every man in my employ, Most High. And myself as well."

"I will take whoever is ready at dawn tomorrow," Otah said. "I won't wait past that."

Ashua Radaani bowed his way out, and Otah stood watching him leave. That would help, he thought. He'd want the word spread that Radaani was firmly behind him. The other houses and families might then change their opinions of what help could be spared. If he could double the men he'd expected to have . . .

Kiyan's low chuckle startled him. She still stood in the doorway, her arms crossed under her breasts. Her smile was gentle and amazed. Otah raised in hands in query.

"I have just watched the Khai Machi gravely accept the apology and sworn aid of his servant Radaani. A day ago you were an annoyance to that man. Today, you're a hero from an Old Empire epic. I've never seen things change around a man so quickly as they change around you."

"It's only because he's frightened. He'll recover," Otah said. "I'll be an incompetent again when he's safe and the world's back where it was."

"It won't be, love," Kiyan said. "The world's changed, and it's not changing back, whatever we do."

"I know it. But it's easier if I don't think too much about it just yet. When the Dai-kvo's safe, when the Galts are defeated,

I'll think about it all then. Before that, it doesn't help," Otah said as he turned back toward the bed they had shared for years now, and would for one more night at least. Her hand brushed his cheek as he stepped past, and he turned to kiss her fingers. There were no tears in her eyes now, nor in his.

12

> + < "I gave him too much and not enough men to do it,"
Balasar said as they walked through the rows of men
and horses and steam wagons. Eustin shrugged his disagreement.

Around them, the camps were being broken down. Men
loaded rolled canvas tents onto mules and steam wagons. The
washerwomen loaded the pans and stones of their trade into
packs that they carried on bent shoulders. The last of the captured slaves helped to load the last of the ships for the voyage
back to Galt. The gulls whirled and called one to another; the
waves rumbled and slapped the high walls of the seafront; the
world smelled of sea salt and fire. And Balasar's mind was on
the other side of the map, uneased and restless.

"Coal's a good man," Eustin said. "If anyone can do the
thing, it's him."

"Six cities," he said. "I set him six cities. It's too much.
And he's got far fewer men than we do."

"We'll get finished here in time to help him with the last
few," Eustin said. "Besides, one of them's just a glorified village, and Chaburi-Tan was likely burning before we were out
of Aren. So that's only four and a half cities left."

There was something in that. Coal's men had been on the
island and in the city and in ships off the coast, waiting for the
signal that would follow the andat's vanishing. Even now, Coal
and his men—between five thousand and six—were sailing

fast to Yalakeht. A handful more waited there in the warehouses of Galtic traders, preparing for the trip upstream to the village of the Dai-kvo and the libraries at the heart of the Khaiem. The other cities would have their scrolls and codices, but only there, in the palaces carved from the living rock, were the great secrets of the fallen Empire kept. His war turned on that fire and on the deaths of the men who knew what those soon-burned books said.

And he wouldn't be there for it.

"The southern legions are ready, sir," Eustin said. "Eight thousand for Shosheyn-Tan, Lachi, and Saraykeht. My legion's two thousand strong. Should be enough for Pathai and that school out on the plains. That'll leave you a full half of the forces for the river cities. Udun and Utani and Tan-Sadar."

Balasar struggled with the impulse to send more of the men with Eustin. It was the illusion he always suffered when tactics required that he split his forces. He would make do with less in order to keep his best men safe. Pathai was only half the size of Nantani, but Eustin was taking only a tenth of the men. It was unlikely that word had traveled fast enough for the Khai Pathai to hire some fleet-footed mercenary company out of the Westlands, but unlikely wasn't impossible. Two thousand more men might make the difference if something went wrong.

But he had the longest journey ahead of him—Nantani to Udun, and some of it over plains where there were no good roads and the steam wagons would have to be pulled. On rough ground, the boilers were too likely to explode. The journey would take time, and so Udun and Utani and Tan-Sadar would have the longest time to prepare. They would be the hardest to capture or destroy. It was why he had chosen them for himself. Except, of course, for what he had tasked to Coal. Five thousand men to take six cities. Five cities, now. Four and a half.

"We'll get there in time to help him if he needs us, sir," Eustin said, reading his face. "And keep in mind, there's not a fighting force anywhere in the Khaiem. Coal's in more danger of tripping on his spear than of facing an enemy worth sneezing at."

Balasar laughed. Two armsmen busy folding a tent looked up, saw him and Eustin, and grinned.

"It's like me, isn't it?" Balasar said. "Here we have just made the greatest sack of a city in living history, captured enough gold to keep us both fed the best food and housed in the best brothels for the rest of our lives, and I can't bring myself to enjoy a minute of it."

"You do tend to worry most when things are going well, sir."

They reached a place where the mud path split, one way to the west, the other to the north. Balasar put out his hand, and Eustin took it. For a moment, they weren't general and captain. They were friends and conspirators in the plot to save the world. Balasar found his anxiety ebbing, felt the grin on his face and saw it mirrored in his man's.

"Meet me in Tan-Sadar before the leaves turn," Balasar said. "We'll see then whether Coal has use for us or if it's time to go home."

"I'll be there, sir," Eustin said. "Rely on it. And as a favor to me? Keep an eye on Ajutani."

"Both, when I can spare them," Balasar promised. And then they parted. Balasar walked through the thin mud and low grass to the camp at the head of the first legion. His groom stood waiting, a fresh horse munching contentedly at the roadside weeds. A second horse stood beside it, a rider in the saddle looking out bemused at the men and the rolling hills and the horizon beyond.

"Captain Ajutani," Balasar said, and the rider turned and saluted. "You're ready for the march?"

"At your command, General."

Balasar swung himself up onto the horse and accepted the reins from his groom.

"Then let's begin," he said. "We've got a war to finish."

*   *   *

IT HAD taken a few lengths of copper to convince the keepers of the wide platforms to unhook their chains and haul her skyward, but Liat didn't care. The dread in her belly made small considerations like money seem trivial. Money or food or sleep. She stood now at the open sky doors and looked out to the south and east, where the men of Machi made their way through the high green grasses of summer. From this distance, they looked like a single long black mark on the landscape. She could no more make out an individual wagon or rider than she could take to the air and fly. And still she strained her eyes, because one part of that distant mark was her only son.

He had only told her when it was already done. She had been in her apartments—the apartments given her by the man who had once been her lover. She had been thinking of how a merchant or tradesman who took in an old lover so casually would have been the subject of gossip—even a member of the utkhaiem would have had answers to make—but the Khai was above that. She had gone as far as wondering, not for the first time, what Kiyan-cha thought and felt on the matter, when Nayiit had scratched at her door and let himself in.

She knew when she saw his face that something had happened. There was a light in his eyes brighter than candles, but his smile was the too-charming one he always employed when he'd done something he feared she'd fault him for. Her first thought was that he'd offered to marry some local girl. She took a pose that asked the question even before he could speak.

"Sit with me," he said and took her by the hand.

They sat on a low stone bench near the window. The shutters were opened, and the evening breeze had smelled of forge smoke. He kept her hand in his as he spoke.

"I've been to see the Khai," Nayiit said. "You know he believes what Maati-cha . . . what Father said. About the Galts."

"Yes," Liat said. She still hadn't understood what she was seeing. His next words came like a blow.

"He's taking men, all the men he can find. They're going overland to the Dai-kvo. I've asked to go with them, and he's accepted me. He's finding me a sword and something like armor. He says we'll leave before the week's out," he said, then paused. "I'm sorry."

She knew that her grip on his hand had gone hard because he winced, but not because she felt it. This hadn't been their plan. This had never been their plan.

"Why?" she managed, but she already knew.

He was young and he was trapped in a life he more than half regretted. He was finding what it meant to him to be a man. Riding out to war was an adventure, and a statement—oh, by all the gods—it was a statement that he had faith in Maati's guess. It was a way to show that he believed in his father. Nayiit only kissed her hand.

"I know the Dai-kvo's village," he said. "I can ride. I'm at least good enough with a bow to catch rabbits along the way. And someone has to go, Mother. There's no reason that I shouldn't."

You have a wife, she didn't say. You have a child. You have a city to defend, and it's Saraykeht. You'll be killed, and I cannot lose you. The Galts have terrorized every nation in the world that didn't have the andat for protection, and Otah has a few armsmen barely competent to chase down thieves and brawl in the alleys outside comfort houses.

"Are you sure?" she said.

She sat now, looking out over the wide, empty air as the mark grew slowly smaller. As her son left her. Otah had managed more men than she'd imagined he would. At the last moment, the utkhaiem had rallied to him. Three thousand men, the first army fielded in the cities of the Khaiem in generations. Untried, untested. Armed with whatever had come to hand, armored with leather smith's aprons. And her little boy was among them.

She wiped her eyes with the cloth of her sleeve.

"Hurry," she said, pressing the word out to the distant men. Get the Dai-kvo, retrieve the poets and their books, and come back to me. Before they find you, come back to me.

The sun had traveled the width of two hands together be-

fore she stepped out onto the platform and signaled the men
far below her to bring her down. The chains clattered and the
platform lurched, but Liat only held the rail and waited for it
to steady in its descent. She knew she would not fall. That
would have been too easy.

She had done a poor job of telling Maati. Perhaps she'd assumed Nayiit would already have told him. Perhaps she'd
been trying to punish Maati for beginning it all. It had been the
next night, and she had accepted Maati's invitation to dinner
in the high pavilion. Goose in honey lacquer, almonds with cin-
namon and raisin sauce, rice wine. Not far away, a dance had
begun—silk streamers and the glow of torches, the trilling of
pipes and the laughter of girls drunk with flirtation. She remembered it all from the days after Saraykeht had fallen.
There was only so long that the shock of losing the andat
could restrain the festivals of youth.

The young are blind and stupid, she'd said, and their breasts
don't sag. It's the nearest thing they've got to a blessing.

Maati had chuckled and tried to take her hand, but she
couldn't stand the touch. She'd seen the surprise in his expression, and the hurt. That was when she'd told him. She'd said it
lightly, acidly, fueled by her anger and her despair. She had
been too wrapped up in herself to pay attention to Maati's
shock and horror. It was only later, when he'd excused himself
and she was walking alone in the dim paths at the edge of the
dance, that she understood she'd as much as accused him of
sending Nayiit to his death.

She had gone by Maati's apartments that night and again the
next day, but he had gone and no one seemed to know where.
By the time she found him, he had spoken with Otah and
Nayiit. He accepted her apology, he cradled her while they
both confessed their fears, but the damage had been done. He
was as haunted as she was, and there was nothing to be done
about it.

Liat realized she'd almost reached the ground, startled to
have come so far so quickly. Her mind, she supposed, had been
elsewhere.

Machi in the height of summer might almost have been a southern city. The sun made its slow, stately way across the sky. The nights had grown so short, she could fall asleep with a glow still bright over the mountains to the west and wake in daylight, unrested. The streets were full of vendors at their carts selling fresh honey bread almost too hot to eat or sausages with blackened skins or bits of lamb over rice with a red sauce spicy enough to burn her tongue. Merchants passed over the black-cobbled streets, wagon wheels clattering. Beggars sang before their lacquered boxes. Firekeepers tended their kilns and saw to the small business of the tradesmen— accepting taxes, witnessing contracts, and a hundred other small duties. Liat pulled her hands into her sleeves and walked without knowing her destination.

It might only have been her imagination that there were fewer men in the streets. Surely there were still laborers and warehouse guards and smiths at their forges. The force marching to the west could account for no more than one man in fifteen. The sense that Machi had become a city of women and old men and boys could only be her mind playing tricks. And still, there was something hollow about the city. A sense of loss and of uncertainty. The city itself seemed to know that the world had changed, and held its breath in dread anticipation, waiting to see whether this transformed reality had a place for Machi in it.

She found herself back at her apartments—feet sore, back aching—before the sun had touched the peaks to the west. As she approached her door, a young man rose from the step. For a moment, her mind tricked her into thinking Nayiit had returned. But no, this boy was too thin through the shoulders, his hair too long, his robes the black of a palace servant. He took a pose of greeting as she approached, and Liat made a brief response.

"Liat Chokavi?"

"Yes."

"Kiyan Machi, first wife of the Khai Machi, extends her invitation. If you would be so kind, I will take you to her."

"Now?" Liat asked, but of course it was now. She waved away the question even before the servant boy could recover from the surprise of being asked in so sharp a tone. When he turned, spine straight and stiff with indignation, she followed him.

They found Otah's wife standing on a balcony overlooking a great hall. Her robes were delicate pink and yellow, and they suited her skin. Her head was turned down, looking at the wide fountain that took up the hall below, the sprays of water reaching up almost to the high domed ceiling above. The servant boy took a pose of obeisance before her, and she replied with one that both thanked and dismissed him. Her greeting of Liat was only a nod and a smile, and then Kiyan's attention turned back to the fountain.

There were children playing in the pool—splashing one another or running, bandy-legged, through water that reached above their knees and would only have dampened half of Liat's own calves. Some wore robes of cotton that clung to their tiny bodies. Some wore loose canvas trousers like a common laborer's. They were, Liat thought, too young to be utkhaiem yet. They were still children, and free from the bindings that would hold them when there was less fat in their cheeks, less joy in their movement. But that was only sentiment. The children of privilege knew when they were faced with a child of the lower orders. These dancing and shouting in the clean, clear water could dress as they saw fit because they were all of the same ranks. These were the children of the great houses, brought to play with the one boy, there, in the robe. The one deep in disagreement with the petulant-looking girl. The one who had eyes and mouth the same shape as Otah's.

Liat looked up and found Kiyan considering her. The woman's expression was unreadable.

"Thank you for coming," Kiyan said over the sounds of falling water and shrieking children.

"Of course," Liat said. She nodded down at the boy. "That's Danat-cha?"

"Yes. He's having a good day," she said. Then, "Please, come this way."

Liat followed her through a doorway at the balcony's rear and into a small resting room where Kiyan sat on a low couch and motioned Liat to do the same. The sounds of play were muffled enough to speak over, but they weren't absent. Liat found them oddly comforting.

"I heard that Nayiit-cha chose to go with the men," Kiyan said.

"Yes," Liat said, and then stopped, because she didn't know what more there was to say.

"I can't imagine that," Kiyan said. "It's hard enough imagining Otah going, but he's my husband. He's not my son."

"I understand why he went. Nayiit, I mean. But his father asked the Khai to take care of him."

Kiyan looked up, confused for a moment, then nodded.

"Maati, you mean?"

"Of course," Liat said.

"Do we have to keep up that pretense?"

"I think we do, Kiyan-cha."

"I suppose," she said. And then a moment later, "No. You're right. You're quite right. I don't know what I was thinking."

Liat considered Otah's wife—thin face, black hair shot with threads of white, so little paint on her cheeks that Liat could see where the lines that came with age had been etched by pain and laughter. There was an intelligence in her face and, Liat thought, a sorrow. Kiyan took a deep breath and seemed to pull herself back from whatever place her mind had gone. She smiled.

"Otah has left the city with a problem," she said. "With so many men gone, the business of things is bound to suffer. There are crops that need bringing in and others that need planting. Roofs need the tiles repaired before autumn comes. There are still parts of the winter quarters that haven't been cleaned out since we've all resurfaced. And the men who coordinate those things or else who oversee the men who do are all off with Otah playing at war."

"That is a problem," Liat agreed, unsure why Kiyan had brought her here to tell her this.

"I'm calling a Council of wives," Kiyan said. "I think we're referring to it as an afternoon banquet, but I mean it to be more than light gossip and sweet breads. I'm going to take care of Machi until Otah comes back. I'll see to it that we have food and coal to see us through the winter."

If, Kiyan didn't need to say, we all live that long. Liat looked at her hands and pressed the dark thoughts away.

"That seems wise," she said.

"I want you to come to the Council, Liat-cha. I want your help."

Liat looked up. Kiyan's whole attention was on her. It made her feel awkward, but also oddly flattered.

"I don't know what I could do—"

"You're a woman of business. You understand schedules and how to coordinate different teams in different tasks so that the whole of a thing comes together the way it should. I understand that too, but frankly most of these women would be totally lost. They've bent their minds to face paints and robes and trading gossip and bedroom tricks," Kiyan said, and then immediately took a pose that asked forgiveness. "I don't mean to make them sound dim. They aren't. But they're the product of a Khai's court, and the things that matter there aren't things that matter, if you see what I mean?"

"Quite well," Liat said with a chuckle.

Kiyan leaned forward and scooped up Liat's hand as if it were the most natural thing to do.

"You helped Otah when he asked it of you. Will you help me now?"

The assent came as far as Liat's lips and then died there. She saw the distress in Kiyan's eyes, but she couldn't say it.

"Why?" Liat whispered. "Why me? Why, when we are what we are to each other."

"When we're what to each other?"

"Women who've loved the same man," Liat said. "Mothers of . . . of *our* sons. How can you put that aside, even only for a little while?"

Kiyan smiled. It was a hard expression. Determined. She did not let go of Liat's hand, but neither did she hold it captive.

"I want you with me because we can't have other enemies now," she said. "And because you and I aren't so different. And because I think perhaps the distraction is something you need as badly as I do. There's war enough coming. I want there to be peace between us."

"I have a price," Liat said.

Kiyan nodded that she continue.

"When Nayiit comes back, spend time with him. Talk with him. Find out who he is. Know him."

"Because?"

"Because if you're going to have me fall in love with your boy, you owe it to fall a little in love with mine."

Kiyan grinned, tears glistening in her eyes. Her hand squeezed Liat's. Liat closed her grip, fierce as a drowning man holding to a rope. She hadn't understood until this moment how deep her fear ran or the loneliness that even Maati couldn't assuage. She couldn't say whether she had pulled Kiyan to her or if she herself had been pulled, but she found herself sobbing into the other woman's shoulder. Otah's wife wrapped fierce arms around her, embracing her as if she would protect Liat from the world.

"They would never understand this," Liat managed when her breath was her own again.

"They're men," Kiyan said. "They're simpler."

13

>+<   For years, Otah had been a traveler by profession. He had worked the gentleman's trade, traveling as a courier for a merchant house with business in half the cities of the Khaiem. He had spent days on horseback or hunkered down in the backs of wagons or walking. He remembered with fondness the feeling of resting at the end of a day, his limbs warm and weary, sinking into the woolen blanket that only half protected him from the ticks. He remembered looking up at the wide sky with something like contentment. It seemed fourteen years sleeping in the best bed in Machi had made a difference.

"Is there something I can bring you, Most High?" the servant boy asked from the doorway of the tent. Otah pulled open the netting and turned over in his cot, twisting his head to look at him. The boy was perhaps eighteen summers old, long hair pulled back and bound by a length of leather.

"Do I seem like I need something?"

The boy looked down, abashed.

"You were moaning again, Most High."

Otah let himself lie back on the cot. The stretched canvas creaked under him like a ship in a storm. He closed his eyes and cataloged quietly all his reasons for moaning. His back ached like someone had kicked him. His thighs were chafed half raw. They were hardly ten days out from Machi, and it was becoming profoundly clear that he didn't know how to march a military column across the rolling, forested hills that stretched from Machi almost to the mountains north of the Dai-kvo. The great Galtic army that had massed in the South was no doubt well advanced, and the Dai-kvo was in deadly danger, if he hadn't been killed already. Otah closed his eyes. Right now, the throbbing sting of his abused thighs bothered him most.

"Go ask the physicians to send some salve," he said.

"I'll call for the physician."

"No! Just . . . just get some salve and bring it here. I'm not infirm. And I wasn't moaning. It was the cot."

The boy took a pose of acceptance and backed out of the tent, shutting the door behind him. Otah let the netting fall closed again. A tent with a door. Gods.

The first few days hadn't been this bad. The sense of release that came from taking real action at last had almost outweighed the fears that plagued him and the longing for Kiyan at his side, for Eiah and Danat. The northern summer was brief, but the days were long. He rode with the men of the utkhaiem, trotting on their best mounts, while the couriers ranged ahead and the huntsmen foraged. The wide, green world smelled rich with the season. The North Road ran only among the winter cities—Amnat-Tan, Cetani, Machi. There was no good, paved road direct from Machi to the village of the Dai-kvo, but there were trade routes that jumped from low town to low town. Mud furrows worn by carts and hooves and feet. Around them, grasses rose high as the bellies of their horses, singing a dry song like fingertips on skin when the wind stirred the blades. The feeling of the sure-footed animal he rode had been reassuring at first. Solid and strong.

But the joy of action had wearied while the dread grew stronger. The steady movement of the horse had become wearisome. The jokes and songs of the men had lost something of their fire. The epics and romances of the Empire included some passages about the weariness and longing that came of living on campaign, but they spoke of endless seasons and years without the solace of home. Otah and his men hadn't yet traveled two full weeks. They were still well shy of the journey's halfway mark, and already they were losing what cohesion they had.

With every day, most men were afoot while huntsmen and scouts and utkhaiem rode. Horsemen were called to the halt long before the night should have forced them to make camp, for fear that those following on foot would fail to reach the tents before darkness fell. And even so, men continued to straggle in long after the evening meals had been served, leaving them unrested and fed only on scraps when morning came. The army, such as it was, seemed tied to the speed of its slowest members. He needed speed and he needed men at his side, but there was no good way to have both. And the fault, Otah knew, was in himself.

There had to be answers to this and the thousand other problems that came of leading a campaign. The Galts would know. Sinja could have told him, had he been there and not out in some Westlands garrison waiting for a flood of Galts that wasn't coming. They were men that had experience in the field, who had more knowledge of war than the casual study of a few old Empire texts fit in between religious ceremonies and high court bickering.

The scratch came at the door, soft and apologetic. Otah swung his legs off the cot and sat up. He called out his permission as he parted the netting, but the one who came in wasn't the servant boy. It was Nayiit.

He looked tired. His robes had been blue once, but from the hem to the knee they were stained the pale brown of the mud through which they had traveled. Otah considered the weight of their situation—the young man's dual role as Maati's son and his own, the threat he posed to Danat and the promise to Machi, the aid he might be in this present endeavor to prevent harm to the Dai-kvo—and dismissed it all. He was too tired and pained to chew everything a hundred times before he swallowed.

He took a pose of welcome, and Nayiit returned one of greater formality. Otah nodded to a camp chair and Nayiit sat.

"Your attendant wasn't here. I didn't know what the right etiquette was, so I just came through."

"He's running an errand. Once he's back, I can have tea brought," Otah said. "Or wine."

Nayiit took a pose of polite refusal. Otah shrugged it away.

"As you see fit," Otah said. "And what brings you?"

"There's grumbling in the ranks, Most High. Even among some of the utkhaiem."

"There's grumbling in here, for that," Otah said. "There's just no one here to listen to me. Are there any suggestions? Any solutions that the ranks have seen that escaped me? Because, by all the gods that have ever been named, I'm not too proud to hear them."

"They say you're driving them too hard, Most High," Nayiit said. "That the men need a day's rest."

"Rest? Go slower? That's the solution they have to offer? What kind of brilliance is that?"

Nayiit looked up. His face was long, like a Northerner's. Like Otah's. His eyes were Liat's tea-with-milk brown. His expression, however, owed to neither of them. Where Liat would have kept her eyes down or Otah would have made himself charming, Nayiit's face belonged on a man bearing a heavy load. Whatever was in his mind, in this moment it was clear that he would press until the world was the way he wanted it or it crushed him. It was something equal parts weariness and joy, like a man newly acquainted with certainty. Otah found himself curious.

"They aren't wrong, Most High. These men aren't accustomed to living on the road like this. You can't expect the speed of a practiced army from them. And the walkers have been rising early to drill."

"Have they?"

"They have the impression their lives may rest on it. And the lives of their families. And, forgive me Most High, but your life too."

Otah leaned forward, his hands taking a questioning pose.

"They're afraid of failing you," Nayiit said. "It's why no one would come to you and complain. I've been keeping company with a man named Saya. He's a blacksmith. Plow blades, for the most part. His knees are swollen to twice their normal size, and he wakes before dawn to tie on leather and wool and swing sticks with the others. And then he walks until he can't. And then he walks farther."

Nayiit's voice was trembling now, but Otah couldn't say if it was with weariness or fear or anger.

"These aren't soldiers, Most High. And you're pushing them too hard."

"We've been moving for ten days—"

"And we're coming near to halfway to the Dai-kvo's village," Nayiit said. "In *ten days*. And drilling, and sleeping under thin blankets on hard ground. Not couriers and huntsmen, not men who are accustomed to this. Just men. I've spoken to the provisioners. We left Machi three thousand strong. Do you know how many have turned back? How many have deserted you?"

Otah blinked. It wasn't a question he'd ever thought to ask.

"How many?"

"None."

Otah felt something loosen in his chest. A warmth like the first drink of wine spread through him, and he felt tears beginning to well up in his eyes. If he had been less exhausted, it would never have pierced his reserve, and still . . . *none*.

"With every low town we pass, we take on a few more," Nayiit was saying. "They're afraid. The word has gone out that all the andat are gone, that the Galts are going to invade or are invading. It's the thing every man had convinced himself would never happen. I hear the things they say."

"The things they say?"

"That you were the only one who saw the danger. You were training men even before. You were preparing. They say that you've traveled the world when you were a boy, that you understand it better than any other Khai. Some of them are calling you the new Emperor."

"They should stop that," Otah said.

"Most High, they're desperate and afraid, and they want a hero out of the old epics. They need one."

"And you? What do you need?"

"I need Saya to stop walking for a day."

Otah closed his eyes. Perhaps the right thing was to send the experienced men on ahead. They could clear spaces for the camps. Perhaps missing a single day would not be too much. And there was little point in running if it was only to be sure they came to the battle exhausted and ready for slaughter. The Dai-kvo would have gotten his warning by now. The poets might even now be in flight toward Otah and his ragtag army. He took in a deep breath and let it out slowly through his nose. Letting his body collapse with it.

"I'll consider what you've said, Nayiit-cha," Otah said. "It wasn't where my mind had led me, but I can see there's some wisdom in it."

Nayiit took a pose of gratitude as formal as any at court. He looked nearly as spent as Otah felt. Otah raised his hands in a querying pose.

"The utkhaiem didn't feel comfortable bringing these concerns to me," he said. "Why did you?"

"I think, Most High, there's a certain . . . reluctance in the higher ranks to second-guess you again. And the footmen wouldn't think of approaching you. I grew up with stories about you and Maati-cha, so I suppose I can bring myself to think of you as one of my mother's friends. That, and I'm desperately tired. If you had me sent back in disgrace, I could at least get a day's rest."

Otah smiled, and saw his own expression reflected back at him. He had never known this boy, had never lifted him over his head the way he had Danat. He had had no part in teaching Nayiit wisdom or folly. Even now, seeing himself in his eldest son's movements and expressions, he could hardly think of him with the bone-deep protectiveness that shook him when he thought of Eiah and Danat. And yet he was pleased that he had accepted Nayiit's offer to join him in this half-doomed campaign. Otah leaned forward, his hand out. It was the gesture of friendship that one seafront laborer might offer another. Nayiit only looked shocked for a moment, then clasped Otah's hand.

"Whenever they're too nervous to tell me what I'm doing wrong, you come to me, Nayiit-cha. I haven't got many people I can trust to do that, and I've left most of them back in Machi."

"If you'll promise not to have me whipped for impertinence," the boy said.

"I won't have you whipped, and I won't have you sent back."

"Thank you," Nayiit said, and again Otah was moved to see that the gratitude was genuine. After Nayiit had gone, Otah was left with the aches in his body and the unease that came with having a man with a wife and child thank you for leading him toward the real chance of death. The life of the Khai Machi, he thought, afforded very few opportunities to be humbled, but this was one. When the attendant returned, Otah didn't recognize the sound of his scratching until the man's voice came.

"Most High?"

"Yes, come in. And bring that ointment here. No, I can put it on myself. But bring me the captains of the houses. I've decided to take a day to rest and send the scouts ahead."

"Yes, Most High."

"And when you've done with that, there's a man named Saya. He's on foot. A blacksmith from Machi, I think."

"Yes, Most High?"

"Ask him to join me for a bowl of wine. I'd like to meet him."

MAATI WOKE to find Liat already gone. His hand traced the indentation in the mattress at his side where she had slept. The world outside his door was already bright and warm. The birds whose songs had filled the air of spring were busy now teaching their hatchlings to fly. The pale green of new leaves had deepened, the trees as rich with summer as they would ever be. High summer had come. Maati rose from his bed with a grunt and went about his morning ablutions.

The days since the ragged, improvised army of Machi began its march to the east had been busy. The loss of Stone-Made-Soft would have sent the court and the merchant houses scurrying like mice before a flood even if nothing more had happened. Word of the other lost andat and of the massed army of Galt made what in other days would have been a cataclysm seem a side issue. For half a week, it seemed, the city had been paralyzed. Not from fear, but from the simple and profound lack of any ritual or ceremony that answered the situation. Then, first from the merchant houses below and Kiyan-cha's women's banquets above and then seemingly everywhere at once, the utkhaiem had flushed with action. Often disorganized, often at crossed purpose, but determined and intent. Maati's own efforts were no less than any others.

Still, he left it behind him now—the books stacked in distinct piles, scrolls unfurled to particular passages as if waiting for the copyist's attention—and walked instead through the wide, bright paths of the palaces. There were fewer singing slaves, more stretches where the gravel of the path had scattered and not yet been raked back into place, and the men and women of the utkhaiem who he passed seemed to carry themselves with less than their full splendor. It was as if a terrible wind had blown through a garden and disarrayed those blossoms it did not destroy.

The path led into the shade of the false forest that separated the poet's house from the palaces. There were old trees among these, thick trunks speaking of generations of human struggle and triumph and failure since their first tentative seedling leaves had pushed away this soil. Moss clothed the bark and scented the air with green. Birds fluttered over Maati's head, and a squirrel scolded him as he passed. In winter, with these oaks bare, you could see from the porch of the poet's house out almost to the palaces. In summer, the house might have been in a different city. The door of the poet's house was standing open, and Maati didn't bother to scratch or knock.

Cehmai's quarters suffered the same marks as his own—books, scrolls, codices, diagrams all laid out without respect to author or age or type of binding. Cehmai, sitting on the floor with his legs crossed, held a book open in his hand. With the brown robes of a poet loose around his frame, he looked, Maati thought, like a young student puzzling over an obscure translation. Cehmai looked up as Maati's shadow crossed him, and smiled wearily.

"Have you eaten?" Maati asked.

"Some bread. Some cheese," Cehmai said, gesturing to the back of the house with his head. "There's some left, if you'd like it."

It hadn't occurred to Maati just how hungry he was until he took up a corner of the rich, sweet bread. He knew he'd had dinner the night before, but he couldn't recall what it had been or when he'd eaten it. He reached into a shallow ceramic bowl of salted raisins. They tasted rich and full as wine. He took a handful and sat on the chair beside Cehmai to look over the assorted results of their labor.

"What's your thought?" Cehmai said.

"I've found more than I expected to," Maati said. "There was a section in Vautai's *Fourth Meditations* that actually clarified some things I hadn't been certain of. If we were to put together all the scraps and rags from all of the books and histories and scrolls, it might be enough to support binding a fresh andat."

Cehmai sighed and closed the book he'd been holding.

"That's near what I've come to," the younger poet agreed. Then he looked up. "And how long do you think it would take to put those scraps and rags into one coherent form?"

"So that it stood as a single work? I'm likely too old to start it," Maati said. "And without the full record from the Dai-kvo, there would be no way to know whether a binding was dangerously near one that had already been done."

"I hated those," Cehmai said.

"They went back to the beginning of the First Empire," Maati said. "Some of the descriptions are so convoluted it takes reading them six times to understand they're using fifty words to carry the meaning of five. But they are complete, and that's the biggest gap in our resources."

Cehmai got to his feet with a grunt. His hair was disheveled and there were dark smudges under his eyes. Maati imagined he had some to match.

"So to sum up," Cehmai said, "if the Khai fails, we might be able to bind a new andat in a generation or so."

"Unless we're unlucky and use some construct too much like something a minor poet employed twenty generations back. In that case, we attempt the binding, pay the price, and die badly. Except that by then, we'll likely all have been slaughtered by the Galts."

"Well," Cehmai said and rubbed his hands together. "Are there any of those raisins left?"

"A few," Maati said.

Maati could hear the joints in Cehmai's back cracking as he stretched. Maati leaned over and scooped up the fallen book. It wasn't titled, nor was the author named, but the grammar in the first page marked it as Second Empire. Loyan Sho or Kodjan the Lesser. Maati let his gaze flow down the page, seeing the words without taking in their meanings. Behind him, Cehmai ate the raisins, lips smacking until he spoke.

"The second problem is solved if your technique works. It isn't critical that we have all the histories if we can deflect the price of failing. At worst, we'll have lost the time it took to compose the binding."

"Months," Maati said.

"But not death," Cehmai went on. "So there's something to be said for that."

"And the first problem can be skirted by not starting wholly from scratch."

"You've been thinking about this, Maati-kvo."

Cehmai slowly walked back across the floor. His footsteps were soft and deliberate. Outside, a pigeon cooed. Maati let the silence speak for him. When Cehmai returned and sat again, his expression was abstracted and his fingers picked idly at the cloth of his sleeves. Maati knew some part of what haunted the younger man: the danger faced by the city, the likelihood of the Khai Machi retrieving the Dai-kvo, the shapeless and all-pervading fear of the Galtic army that had gathered in the South and might now be almost anywhere. But there was another part to the question, and that Maati could not guess. And so he asked.

"What is it like?"

Cehmai looked up as if he'd half-forgotten Maati was there. His hands flowed into a pose that asked clarification.

"Stone-Made-Soft," Maati said. "What is it like with him gone?"

Cehmai shrugged and turned his head to look out the un-shuttered windows. The trees shifted their leaves and adjusted their branches like men in conversation. The sun hung in the sky, gold in lapis.

"I'd forgotten what it was like to be myself," Cehmai said. His voice was low and thoughtful and melancholy. "Just myself and not him as well. I was so young when I took control of him. It's like having had someone strapped to your back when you were a child and then suddenly lifting off the burden. I feel alone. I feel freed. I'm shamed to have failed, even though I know there was nothing I could have done to keep hold of him. And I regret now all the years I could have sunk Galt into ruins that I didn't."

"But if you could have him back, would you?"

The pause that came before Cehmai's reply meant that no, he would have chosen his freedom. It was the answer Maati had expected, but not the one he was ready to accept.

"The Khai may be able to save the Dai-kvo," Cehmai said. "He may get there before the Galts."

"But if he doesn't?"

"Then I would rather have Stone-Made-Soft back than decorate the end of some Galtic spear," Cehmai said, a grim humor in his voice. "I have some early work. Drafts from when I was first studying him. There are places where the options . . . branched. If we used those as starting points, it would make the binding different from the one I took over, and we still wouldn't have to begin from first principles."

"You have them here?"

"Yes. They're in that basket. There. You should take them back to the library and look them over. If we keep them here I'm too likely to do something unpleasant with them. I was half-tempted to burn them last night."

Maati took the pages—small, neat script on cheap, yellowing parchment—and folded them into his sleeve. The weight of them seemed so slight, and still Maati found himself uncomfortably aware of them and of the return to a kind of waking prison that they meant for Cehmai.

"I'll look them over," Maati said. "Once I have an idea what would be the best support for it, I'll put some reading together. And if things go well, we can present it all to the Dai-kvo when he arrives. Certainly, there's no call to do anything until we know where we stand."

"We can prepare for the worst," Cehmai said. "I'd rather be pleasantly surprised than taken unaware."

The resignation in Cehmai's voice was hard to listen to. Maati coughed, as if the suggestion he wished to make fought against being spoken.

"It might be better . . . I haven't attempted a binding myself. If I were the one . . ."

Cehmai took a pose that was both gratitude and refusal. Maati felt a warm relief at Cehmai's answer and also a twinge of regret.

"He's my burden," Cehmai said. "I gave my word to carry Stone-Made-Soft as long as I could, and I'll do that. I wouldn't want to disappoint the Khai." Then he chuckled. "You know, there have been whole years when I would have meant that as a sarcasm. Disappointing the Khaiem seems to be about half of what we do as poets—no, I can't somehow use the andat to help you win at tiles, or restore your prowess with your wives, or any of the thousand stupid, petty things they ask of us. But these last weeks, I really would do whatever I could, not to disappoint that man. I don't know what's changed."

"Everything," Maati said. "Times like these remake men. They change what we are. Otah's trying to become the man we need him to be."

"I suppose that's true," Cehmai said. "I just don't want this all to be happening, so I forget, somehow, that it is. I keep thinking it's all a sour dream and I'll wake out of it and stumble down to play a game of stones against Stone-Made-Soft. That that will be the worst thing I have to face. And not . . ."

Cehmai gestured, his hands wide, including the house and the palaces and the city and the world.

"And not the end of civilization?" Maati suggested.

"Something like that."

Maati sighed.

"You know," he said, "when we were young, the man who was Dai-kvo then chose Otah to come train as a poet. He refused, but I think he would have been good. He has it in him to do whatever needs doing."

Killing a man, taking a throne, marching an army to its death, Maati thought but did not say. Whatever needs doing.

"I hope the price he pays is smaller than ours," Cehmai said.

"I doubt it will be."

14

⟩+⟨   Balasar had not been raised to put faith in augury. His
father had always said that any god that could create
the world and the stars should be able to put together a few
well-formed sentences if there was something that needed saying; Balasar had accepted this wisdom in the uncritical way of
a boy emulating the man he most admires. And still, the dream
came to him on the night before he had word of the hunting
party.

It was far from the first time he had dreamt of the desert.
He felt again the merciless heat, the pain of the satchel cutting
into his shoulder. The books he had borne then had become
ashes in the dream as they had in life, but the weight was no
less. And behind him were not only Coal and Eustin. All of
them followed him—Bes, Mayarsin, Little Ott, and the others.
The dead followed him, and he knew they were no longer his
allies or his enemies. They came to keep watch over him, to
see what work he wrought with their blood. They were his
judges. As always before, he could not speak. His throat was
knotted. He could not turn to see the dead; he only felt them.

But there seemed more now—not only the men he had left
in the desert, but others as well. Some of them were soldiers,
some of them simple men, all of them padding behind him,
waiting to see him justify their sacrifices and his own pride.
The host behind him had grown.

He woke in his tent, his mouth dry and sticky. Dawn had not yet come. He drank from the water flask by his bed, then pulled on a shirt and simple trousers and went out to relieve himself among the bushes. The army was still asleep or else just beginning to stir. The air was warm and humid so near the river. Balasar breathed deep and slow. He had the sense that the world itself—trees, grasses, moon-silvered clouds—was heavy with anticipation. It would be two weeks before they would come within sight of the river city Udun. By month's end another poet would be dead, another library burned, another city fallen.

Thus far, the campaign had proved as simple as he had hoped, though slower. He had lost almost no men in Nantani. The low towns that his army had come across in their journey to the North had emptied before them; men, women, children, animals—all had scattered before them like autumn leaves before a windstorm. The only miscalculation he had made was in how long to rely on the steam wagons. Two boilers had blown on the rough terrain before Balasar had called to let them cool and be pulled. Five men had died outright, another fifteen had been scalded too badly to continue. Balasar had sent them back to Nantani. There had been less food captured than he had hoped; the residents of the low towns had put anything they thought might be of use to Balasar and his men to fire before they fled. But the land was rich with game fowl and deer, and his supplies were sufficient to reach the next cities.

As dawn touched the eastern skyline, Balasar put on his uniform and walked among the men. The morning's cook fires smoked, filling the air with the scents of burning grass and wood and coal filched from the steam wagons, hot grease and wheat cakes and kafe. Captains and footmen, archers and carters, Balasar greeted them all with a smile and considered them with approving nods or small frowns. When a man lifted half a wheat cake to him, Balasar took it with thanks and squatted down beside the cook to blow it cool and eat it. Every man he met, he had made rich. Every man in the camp would stand before him on the battle lines, and only a few, he hoped, would walk behind him in his dream.

Sinja Ajutani's camp was enfolded within the greater army's but still separate from it, like the Baktan Quarter in Acton. A city within a city, a camp within a camp. The greeting he found here was less warm. The respect he saw in these dark, almond eyes was touched with fear. Perhaps hatred. But no mistake, it was still respect.

Sinja himself was sitting on a fallen log, shirtless, with a bit of silver mirror in one hand and a blade in the other. He looked up as Balasar came close, made his salute, and returned to shaving. Balasar sat beside him.

"We break camp soon," Balasar said. "I'll want ten of your men to ride with the scouting parties today."

"Expecting to find people to question?" Sinja asked. There was no rancor in his voice.

"This close to the river, I can hope so."

"They'll know we're coming. Refugees move faster than armies. The first news of Nantani likely reached them two, maybe three weeks ago."

"Then perhaps they'll send someone here to speak for them," Balasar said. Sinja seemed to consider this as he pressed the blade against his own throat. There were scars on the man's arms and chest—long raised lines of white.

"Would you prefer I ride with the scouts, or stay close to the camp and wait for an emissary?"

"Close to camp," Balasar said. "The men you choose for scouting should speak my language well, though. I don't want to miss anything that would help us do this cleanly."

"Agreed," Sinja said, and put the knife to his own throat again. Before Balasar could go on, he heard his own name called out. A boy no older than fourteen summers wearing the colors of the second legion came barreling into the camp. His face was flushed from running, his breath short. Balasar stood and accepted the boy's salute. In the corner of his eye, he saw Sinja put away knife and mirror and reach for his shirt.

"General Gice, sir," the boy said between gasps. "Captain Tevor sent me. We've lost one of the hunting parties, sir."

"Well, they'll have to catch up with us as best they can," Balasar said. "We don't have time for searching."

"No, sir. They aren't missing, sir. They're killed."

Balasar felt a grotesque recognition. The other men in his dream. This was where they'd come from.

"Show me," he said.

The trap had been sprung in a clearing at the end of a game trail. Crossbow bolts had taken half a dozen of the men. The others were marked with sword and axe blows. Their armor and robes had been stripped from them. Their weapons were gone. Balasar stepped through the low grass cropped by deer and considered each face.

The songs and epics told of warriors dying with lips curled in battle cry, but every dead man Balasar had ever seen looked at peace. However badly they had died, their bodies surrendered at the end, and the calm he saw in those dead eyes seemed to say that their work was done now. Like a man playing at tiles who has turned his mark and now sat back to ask Balasar what he would do to match it.

"Are there no other bodies?" he asked.

Captain Tevor, at his elbow, shook his great woolly head.

"There's signs that our boys did them harm, sir, but they took their dead with them. It wasn't all fast, sir. This one here, there's burn marks on him, and you can see on his wrists where they bound him up. Asked him what he knew, I expect."

Sinja knelt, touching the dead man's wounds as if making sure they were real.

"I have a priest in my company," Captain Tevor said. "One of the archers. I can have him say a few words. We'll bury them here and catch up with the main body tomorrow, sir."

"They're coming with us," Balasar said.

"Sir?"

"Bring a pallet and a horse. I want these bodies pulled

through the camp. I want every man in the army to see them. Then wrap them in shrouds and pack them in ashes. We'll bury them in the ruins of Udun with the Khai's skull to mark their place."

Captain Tevor made his salute, and it wasn't Balasar's imagination that put the tear in the old man's eye. As Tevor barked out the orders to the men who had come with them, Sinja stood and brushed his palms against each other. A smear of old blood darkened the back of the captain's hand. Balasar read the disapproval in the passionless eyes, but neither man spoke.

The effect on the men was unmistakable. The sense of gloating, of leisure, vanished. The tents were pitched, the wagons loaded and ready, the soldiers straining against time itself to close the distance between where they now stood and Udun. Three of his captains asked permission to send out parties. Hunting parties still, but only in part searching for game. Balasar gave each of them his blessing. The dream of the desert didn't return, but he had no doubt that it would.

In the days that followed, he felt keenly the loss of Eustin. Somewhere to the west, Pathai was falling or had fallen. The school with its young poets was burning, or would burn. And through those conflagrations, Eustin rode. Balasar spent his days riding among his men, talking, planning, setting the example he wished them all to follow, and he felt the absence of Eustin's dry pessimism and distrust. The fervor he saw here was a different beast. The men here looked to him as something besides a man. They had never seen him weep over Little Ott's body or call out into the dry, malign desert air for Kellem. To this army, he was General Gice. They might be prepared to kill or die at his word, but they did not know him. It was, he supposed, the difference between faith and loyalty. He found faith isolating. And it was in this sense of being alone among many that the messenger from Sinja Ajutani found him.

The day's travel was done, and they had made good time again. His outriders had made contact with local forces twice—farm boys with rabbit bows and sewn leather armor—and had done well each time. The wells in the low towns had been fouled, but the river ran clean enough. Another two days, three at the most, and they would reach Udun. In the meantime, the sunset was beautiful and birdsong filled the evening air. Balasar rested beneath the wide, thick branches of a cottonwood, flat bread and chicken still hot from the fires on a metal field plate by his side, their scents mixing with those of the rich earth and the river's damp. The man standing before him, hands flat at his sides, looked no more than seventeen summers, but Balasar knew himself a poor judge of ages among these people. He might have been fifteen, he might have been twenty. When he spoke, his Galtic was heavily inflected.

"General Gice," the boy said. "Captain Ajutani would like a word with you, if it is acceptable to your will."

Balasar sat forward.

"He could come himself," Balasar said. "He has before. Why not now?"

The messenger boy's lips went tight, his dark eyes fixed straight ahead. It was anger the boy was controlling.

"Something's happened," Balasar said. "Something's happened to one of yours."

"Sir," the boy said.

Balasar took a regretful look at the chicken, then rose to his feet.

"Take me to Captain Ajutani," Balasar said.

Their path ended at the medical tent. The messenger waited outside when Balasar ducked through the flap and entered. The thick canvas reeked with concentrated vinegar and pine pitch. The medic stood over a low cot where a man lay naked and bloody. One of Sinja's men. The captain himself stood against the tent's center pole, arms folded. Balasar stepped forward, taking in the patient's wounds with a practiced eye. Two parallel cuts on the ribs, shallow but long. Cuts on the hands and arms where the boy had tried to ward off the blades. Skinned knuckles where he'd struck out at someone. Balasar caught the medic's eye and nodded to the man.

"No broken bones, sir," the medic said. "One finger needed

sewing, and there'll be scars, but so long as we keep the wounds from festering, he should be fine."

"What happened?" Balasar asked.

"I found him by the river," Sinja said. "I brought him here."

Balasar heard the coolness in Sinja's voice, judged the tension in his face and shoulders. He steeled himself.

"Come, then," Balasar said as he lifted open the tent's wide flap, "eat with me and you can tell me what happened."

"No need, General. It's a short enough story. Coya here can't speak Galtic. There's been footmen from the fourth legion following him for days now. At first it was just mocking, and I didn't think it worth concern."

"You have names? Proof that they did this?"

"They're bragging about it, sir," Sinja said.

Sinja looked down at the wounded man. The boy looked up at him. The dark eyes were calm, perhaps defiant. Balasar sighed and knelt beside the low cot.

"Coya-cha?" he said in the boy's own language. "I want you to rest. I'll see the men who did this disciplined."

The wounded hands took a pose that declined the offer.

"It isn't a favor to you," Balasar said. "My men don't treat one another this way. As long as you march with me, you are my soldier, whatever tongues you speak. I'll be sure they understand it's my wrath they're feeling, and not yours."

"Your dead men are the problem, sir," Sinja said, switching the conversation back to Galtic.

The medic coughed once, then discreetly stepped to the far side of the tent. Balasar folded his hands and nodded to Sinja that he should continue. The mercenary sucked his teeth and spat.

"Your men are angry. Having those shrouds along is like putting a burr under their saddles. They're calling my men things they didn't when this campaign began. And they act as if it were harmless and in fun, but it isn't."

"I'll see your men aren't attacked again, Sinja. You have my word on it."

"It's not just that, sir. You're sowing anger. Yes, it keeps them traveling faster, and I respect that. But once we reach Udun and Utani, they're going to have their blood up. It's easier for ten thousand soldiers to defeat a hundred thousand tradesmen if the tradesmen don't think defeat means being beaten to death for sport. And a bad sack can burn in resentments that last for lifetimes. All respect, those cities are as good as taken, and we both know it. There's no call to make this worse than it has to be."

"I should be careful?" Balasar said. "Move slowly, and let the cities fall gently?"

"You said before you wanted this done clean."

"Yes. Before. I said that *before*."

"They're going to be your cities," Sinja said doggedly as a man swimming against the tide. "There's more to think about than how to capture them. It's my guess Galt's going to be ruling these places for a long time. The less the people have to forget, the easier that rule's going to be."

"I don't care about holding them," Balasar said. "There are too many to guard, and once the rest of the world scents blood, it's going to be chaos anyway. This war isn't about finding ways for the High Council to appoint more mayors."

"Sir?"

"We are carrying the dead because they are *my* dead." Balasar kept his voice calm, his manner matter-of-fact. The trembling in his hands was too slight to be seen. "And I haven't come to conquer the Khaiem, Captain Ajutani. I've come to destroy them."

THE FIRST refugees appeared when Otah's little army was still three days' march from the village of the Dai-kvo. They were few and scattered in the morning, and then more and larger groups toward the day's end. The stories they told Otah were the same. Ships had come to Yalakeht—warships loaded heavy with Galtic soldiers. Some of the ships were merchant vessels that had been on trade runs to Chaburi-Tan. Others were unfamiliar. The harbor master had tried to refuse them berths, but a force of men had come from the warehouse district and taken control of the seafront. By the time the Khai had gathered a force to drive them back, it was too late. Yalakeht had fallen. Any hope that Otah's army might be on a fool's errand ended with that news.

In the night, more men came, drawn by the light and scent of the army's cook fires. Otah saw that they were welcomed, and the tale grew. Boats had been waiting, half assembled, in the warehouses of Galtic merchants in Yalakeht. Great metal boilers ran paddle wheels, and pushed their wide, shallow boats upriver faster than oxen could pull. Boats loaded with men and steam wagons. The low towns nearest Yalakeht had been overrun. Another force had been following along the shore, hauling food and supplies. The soldiers themselves had sped for the Dai-kvo. Just as Otah had feared they would.

Otah sat in his tent and listened to the cicadas. They sang as if nothing was changing. As if the world was as it had always been. A breeze blew from the south, heavy with the smell of rain though the clouds were still few and distant. Trees nodded their branches to one another. Otah kept his back to the fire and stared out at darkness.

There was no way to know whether the Galtic army had reached the village yet. Perhaps the Dai-kvo was preparing some defense, perhaps the village had been encircled and overrun. From the tales he'd heard, once the Galts and their steam wagons reached the good roads leading from the river to the village itself, they would be able to travel faster than news of them.

It had been almost thirty years ago when Otah had traveled up that river carrying a message from Saraykeht. The memory of it was like something from a dream. There had been an older man—younger, likely, than Otah was now—who had run the boat with his daughter. They had never spoken of the girl's mother, and Otah had never asked. That child daughter would be a woman now, likely with children of her own. Otah wondered what had become of her, wondered whether that half-recalled river girl was among those flying out of the storm into which he was heading, or if she had been in one of the towns that the army had destroyed.

A polite scratch came at the door, his servant announcing himself. Otah called out his permission, and the door opened. He could see the silhouettes of Ashua Radaani and his other captains looming behind the servant boy's formal pose.

"Bring them in," Otah said. "And bring us wine. Wait. Watered wine."

The six men lumbered in. Otah welcomed them all with formal gravity. The fine hunting robes in which they had come out from Machi had been scraped clean of mud. The stubble had been shaved from their chins. From these small signs and from the tightness in their bodies, Otah knew they had all drawn the same conclusions he had. He stood while they folded themselves down to the cushion-strewn floor. Then, silently, Otah sat on his chair, looking down at these grown men, heads of their houses who through the years he had known them had been flushed with pride and self-assurance. The servant boy poured them each a bowl of equal parts wine and fresh water before ghosting silently out the door. Otah took a pose that opened the audience.

"We will be meeting the Galts sometime in the next several days," Otah said. "I can't say where or when, but it will be soon. And when the time comes, we won't have time to plan our strategy. We have to do that now. Tonight. You have all brought your census?"

Each man in turn took a scroll from his sleeve and laid it before him. The number of men, the weapons and armor, the horses and the bows and the numbers of arrows and bolts. The final tally of the strength they had managed. Otah looked down at the scrawled ink and hoped it would be enough.

"Very well," he said. "Let's begin."

None of them had ever been called upon to plan a battle before, but each had an area of expertise. Where one knew of the tactics of hunting, another had had trade relations with the

Wardens of the Westlands enough to speak of their habits and insights. Slowly they made their plans: What to do when the scouts first brought news of the Galts. Who should command the wedges of archers and crossbowmen, who the footmen, who the horsemen. How they should protect their flanks, how to pull back the archers when the time came near for the others to engage. Their fingers sketched lines and movements on the floor, their voices rose, became heated, and grew calm again. The moon had traveled the width of six hands together before Otah declared the work finished. Orders were written, shifting men to different commands, specifying the shouted signals that would coordinate the battle, putting the next few uncertain days into the order they imagined for them. When the captains bowed and took their poses of farewell, the clouds had appeared and the first ticking raindrops were striking the canvas. Otah lay on his cot wrapped in blankets of soft wool, listening to the rain, and running through all that they had said. If it worked as they had planned, perhaps all would be well. In the darkness with his belly full of wine and his mind full of the confident words of his men, he could almost think there was hope.

Dawn was a brightening of clouds, east as gray as west. They struck camp, loaded their wagons, and once again made for the Dai-kvo. The flow of refugees seemed to have stopped. No new faces appeared before them—no horses, no men on foot. Perhaps the rain and mud had stopped them. Perhaps something else. Otah rode near the vanguard, the scouts arriving, riding for a time at his side, and then departing again. It was midmorning and the sun was still hidden behind the low gray ceiling of the world when Nayiit rode up on a thin, skittish horse. Otah motioned him to ride near to his side.

"I'm told I'm to be a messenger," Nayiit said. There was a controlled anger in his voice. "I've drilled with the footmen. I have a sword."

"You have a horse too."

"It was given to me with the news," Nayiit said. "Have I done something to displease you, Most High?"

"Of course not," Otah said. "Why would you think you had?"

"Why am I not permitted to fight?"

Otah leaned back, and his mount, reading the shift of his weight, slowed. His back ached and the raw places on his thighs were only half healed. The rain had soaked his robes, so that even the oiled cloth against his skin felt clammy and cold. The rain that pressed Nayiit's hair close against his neck also tapped against Otah's squinting eyes.

"How are you not permitted to fight?" Otah said.

"The men who are making the charge," Nayiit said. "The men I've been traveling with. That I've trained with. I want to be with them when the time comes."

"And I want you to be with me, and with them," Otah said. "I want you to be the bridge between us."

"I would prefer not to," Nayiit said.

"I understand that. But it's what I've decided."

Nayiit's nostrils flared, and his cheeks pinked. Otah took a pose that thanked the boy and dismissed him. Nayiit wheeled his mount and rode away, kicking up mud as he did. In the distance, the meadows began to rise. They were coming to the Dai-kvo from the north and west, up the long, gentle slope of the mountains rather than the cliffs and crags from which the village was carved. Otah had never come this way before. For all his discomfort and the dread in his belly, this gray-green world was lovely. He tried not to think of Nayiit or of the men whom his boy had asked permission to die with. We are his fathers, Maati had said, and Otah had agreed. He wondered if the others would also see Nayiit's duty as a protection of him. He wondered if they would guess that Danat wasn't his only son. He hoped that they would all live long enough for such problems to matter.

The scout came just before midday. He'd seen a rider in Galtic colors. He'd been seen as well. Otah accepted the information and set the couriers to ride closer and in teams. He felt his belly tighten and wondered how far from its main force the Galts would send their riders. That was the distance between him and his first battle. His first war.

It was near evening when the two armies found each other. The scouts had given warning, and still, as Otah topped the rise, the sight of them was astounding. The army of Galt stood still at the far end of the long, shallow valley, silent as ghosts in the gray rain. Their banners should have been green and gold, but in the wet and with the distance, they seemed merely black. Otah paused, trying to guess how many men faced him. Perhaps half again his own. Perhaps a little less. And they were here, waiting for him. The Dai-kvo's village was behind them.

He wondered if he had come too late. Perhaps the Galts had sacked the village and slaughtered the Dai-kvo. Perhaps they had had word of Otah's coming and bypassed the prize to reach him here, before his men could take cover in the buildings and palaces of mountain. Perhaps the Galts had divided, and the men facing him were what he had spared the Dai-kvo. There was no way to know the situation, and only one course available to him, whatever the truth.

"Call the formation," Otah said, and the shouts and calls flowed out behind him, the slap of leather and metal. The army of Machi took its place—archers and footmen and horsemen. All exhausted by their day's ride, all facing a real enemy for the first time. From across the valley, a sound came, sharp as cracking thunder—thousands of voices raised as one. And then, just as suddenly, silence. Otah ran his hand over the thick leather straps of the reins and forced himself to think.

In the soft quarter of Saraykeht, Otah had seen showfighters pout and preen before the blows came. He had seen them flex their muscles and beat their own faces until there was blood on their lips. It had been a show for the men and women who had come to partake of brutality as entertainment, but it had also been the start of the fight. A display to unnerve the enemy, to sow fear. This was no different. A thousand men who could speak in one voice could fight as one. They were not men, they were a swarm; a single mind with thousands of bodies. *Hear us,* the wordless cry had said, *and die.*

Otah looked at the darkening sky, the misty rain. He thought of all the histories he had read, the accounts of battles lost and won in ancient days before the poets and their andat. Of the struggles in the low cities of the world. He raised his hands, and the messengers, Nayiit among them, came to his side.

"Tell the men to make camp," he said.

The silence was utter.

"Most High?" Nayiit said.

"They won't begin a battle now that they'd have to finish in darkness. This is all show and bluster. Tell the men to set their tents and build what cook fires we can in all this wet. Put them here where those bastards can see the light of them. Tell the men to rest and eat and drink, and we'll set up a pavilion and have songs before we sleep. Let the Galts see how frightened we are."

The messengers took poses that accepted the order and turned their mounts. Otah caught Nayiit's gaze, and the boy hesitated. When the others had gone, Otah spoke again.

"Also find the scouts and have them set a watch. In case I'm wrong."

He saw Nayiit draw breath, but he only took the accepting pose and rode away.

The night was long and unpleasant. The rain had stopped; the clouds thinned and vanished, letting the heat of the ground fly out into the cold, uncaring sky. Otah passed among the fires, accepting the oaths and salutes of his men. He felt his title and dignity on his shoulders like a cloak. He would have liked to smile and be charming, to ease his fears with companionship and wine, just as his men did. It would have been no favor to them, though, so he held back and played the Khai for another night. No attack came, and between the half candle and the three-quarter mark, Otah actually fell asleep. He dreamed of nothing in particular—a bird that flew upside down, a river he recalled from childhood, Danat's voice in an adjacent room singing words Otah could not later recall. He woke in darkness to the scent of frying pork and the sound of voices.

He pulled on his robes and boots and stepped out into the chill of the morning. The cook fires were lit again or had never been put out. And across the valley, the Galt army had lit its own, glittering like orange and yellow stars fallen to earth. His attendant rushed up, blinking sleep from his eyes.

"Most High," the boy said, falling into a pose of abject apology. "I had thought to let you sleep. Your breakfast is nearly ready—"

"Bring it to my tent," Otah said. "I'll be back for it."

He walked to the edge of the camp where the firelight would not spoil his night vision and looked out into the darkness. In the east, the sky had become a paler blackness, the deep gray of charcoal. The stars had not gone out, but they were dimmed. In the trees that lined the valley, birds were beginning their songs. A strange tense peace came over him. His disquiet seemed to fade, and the dawn, gray then cool yellow and rose and serene blue that filled the wide bowl of the sky above him, was beautiful and calm. Whatever happened here in this valley, the sun would rise upon it again tomorrow. The birds would call to one another. Summer would retreat, autumn would come. The lives of men and nations were not the highest stakes to play for. He pulled his hands into his sleeves and turned back to the camp. At his tent, his messengers awaited him, including Nayiit.

"Call the formation," Otah said. "It's time."

The messengers scattered, and it seemed fewer than a dozen breaths before the air was filled with the sounds of metal against metal, shouts and commands as his army pulled itself to the ready.

"Your food, Most High," the attendant said, and Otah waved the man away.

By the time Otah's footmen and horsemen had taken their places between and just behind the wedges of archers, it was bright enough to see the banners and glittering mail of the Galts. Otah's mount seemed to sense the impending violence, dancing uncomfortably as Otah rode back and forth behind his men, watching and waiting and preparing to call out his commands. From across the valley, the shout and silence came again as it had the night before. Then twice more.

"Call the archers to ready!" Otah called out, and like whisperers in court relaying the words to lower men waiting in the halls, his words echoed in a dozen voices. He saw his archers lift their bows and shift in their formations. A long shout, rolling like thunder, came from across the valley. The Galts were moving forward. "Call the march! And be prepared to loose arrows!"

As they had drilled, his men moved forward, archers to the front, footmen between them with their makeshift shields and motley assortment of swords and spears and threshing flails. Horsemen in the colors of the great houses of the utkhaiem trotted at the sides, ready to wheel and protect the flanks. At a walk, three thousand men moved forward across the still-wet grass and patches of ankle-deep mud. And perhaps half again as many Galts came toward them, shouting.

In the old books and histories, the flights of enemy arrows had been compared to smoke rising from a great pyre or clouds blotting out the sun. In fact, when the first volley struck, it was nothing like that. Otah didn't see the arrows and bolts in the air. He saw them begin to appear, heads buried deep in the ground, fletching green and white in the sunlight, like some strange flower that had sprung up from the meadow grass. Then a man screamed, and another.

"Loose arrows!" Otah called. "Give it back to them! Loose arrows!"

Now that he knew to look, he could see the thin, dark shafts. They rose up from the Galtic mass, slowly as if they were floating. His own archers let fly, and it seemed that the arrows should collide in the air, but then slipped past each other, two flocks of birds mingling and parting again. More men screamed.

Otah's horse twitched and sidestepped, nervous with the sounds and the scent of blood. Otah felt his own heart beating fast, sweat on his back and neck though the morning was still cool. His mind spun, judging how many men he was losing with each volley, straining to see how many Galts seemed to fall. They seemed to be getting more volleys off than his men. Perhaps the Galts had more archers than he did. If that was true, the longer he waited for his footmen to engage, the more he would lose. But then perhaps the Galts were simply better practiced at slaughter.

"Call the attack!" Otah yelled. He looked for his messengers, but only two of them were in earshot, and neither was Nayiit. Otah gestured to the nearest of them. "Call the attack!"

The charge was ragged, but it was not hesitant. He could hear it when the footmen got word—a loud whooping yell that seemed to have no particular start nor any end. One man's voice took up where another paused for breath. Otah cantered forward. His horsemen were streaming forward as well now, careful not to outstrip the footmen by too great a distance, and Otah saw the Galtic archers falling back, their own soldiers coming to the fore.

The two sides met with a sound like buildings falling. Shouts and screams mingled, and any nuanced plan was gone. Otah's urge to rush forward was as much the desire to see more clearly what was happening as to defend the men he'd brought. His archers drew and fired sporadically until he called them to stop. There was no way to see who the arrows struck.

The mass of men in the valley writhed. Once a great surge on Otah's left seemed to press into the Galtic ranks, but it was pushed back. He heard drums and trumpet calls. That's a good idea, Otah thought. Drums and trumpets.

The shouting seemed to go on forever. The sun slowly rose in its arc as the men engaged, pulled back, and rushed at one another again. And with every passing breath, Otah saw more of his men fall. More of his men than of the Galts. He forced his mount nearer. He couldn't judge how many he'd lost. The bodies in the mud might have been anyone.

A sudden upsurge in the noise of the battle caught him. His footmen were roaring and surging forward, the center of the enemy's line giving way. "Call them to stand!" Otah shouted, his voice hoarse and fading. "Stand!"

But if they heard the call, the footmen didn't heed it. They pressed forward, into the gap in the Galtic line. A trumpet blared three times, and the signal given, the Galtic horsemen that had held to the rear, left and right both, turned to the center and drove into Otah's men from either side. It had been a trap, and a simple one, and they had stepped in it. Call the retreat, Otah thought wildly, I have to call the retreat. And then from the right, he heard the retreat called.

Someone had panicked; someone had given the order before he could. His horsemen turned, unwilling, it seemed, to leave the footmen behind. A few footmen broke, and then a few more, and then, as if coming loose, Otah's army turned its backs to the Galts and ran. Otah saw some horsemen trying to draw off the pursuing Galts, but most were flying back in retreat themselves. Otah spun his horse and saw, back on the field, the remnants of his wedges of archers fleeing as well.

"No!" he shouted. "Not you! Stop where you are!"

No one heard him. He was a leaf in a storm now, command gone, hope gone, his men being slaughtered like winter pork. Otah dug his heels into his mount's sides, leaned low, and shot off in pursuit of the archers. It was folly riding fast over mud-slick ground, but Otah willed himself forward. The fleeing archers looked back over their shoulders at the sound of his hooves, and had the naïveté to look relieved that it was him. He rode through the nearest wedge, knocking several to the ground, then pulled up before them and pointed back at the men behind them.

"Loose your arrows," Otah croaked. "It's the only chance they have! Loose arrows!"

The archers stood stunned, their wide confused faces made Otah think of sheep confronted by an unexpected cliff. He had brought farmers and smiths onto a battlefield. He had led men who had never known more violence than brawling drunk outside a comfort house to fight soldiers. Otah dropped from his horse, took a bow and quiver from the nearest man, and aimed high. He never saw where his arrow went, but the bowmen at least began to understand. One by one, and then in handfuls, they began to send their arrows and bolts up over the retreating men and into the charging Galts.

"They'll kill us!" a boy shrieked. "There's a thousand of them!"

"Kill the first twenty," Otah said. "Then let the ones still standing argue about who'll lead the next charge."

Behind them, the other fleeing archers had paused. As the first of the fleeing horsemen passed, Otah caught sight of Ashua Radaani and raised his hands in a pose that called the man to a halt. There was blood on Radaani's face and arms, and his eyes were wide with shock. Otah strode to him.

"Go to the other archers. Tell them that once the men have reached us here, they're to start loosing arrows. We'll come back with the men."

"You should come now, Most High," Radaani said. "I can carry you."

"I have a horse," Otah said, though he realized he couldn't say what had become of his mount. "Go. Just go!"

The Galtic charge thinned as they drew into range of the arrows. Otah saw two men fall. And then, almost miraculously, the Galts began to pull back. Otah's footmen came past him, muddy and bleeding and weeping and pale with shock. Some carried wounded men with them. Some, Otah suspected, carried men already dead. The last, or nearly the last, approached, and Otah turned, gesturing to the archers, and they all walked back together. The few Galts that pressed

on were dissuaded by fresh arrows. Ashua had reached the
other wedge. Thank the gods for that, at least.

The army of Machi, three thousand strong that morning,
found itself milling about, confused and without structure as
the evening sun lengthened their shadows. They had fled back
past the northern lip of the valley where they had made camp
the night before onto green grass already tramped flat by their
passage. Some supply wagons and tents and fresh water had
been caught up in the retreat, but more was strewn over the
ground behind them. The wounded were lined up on hillsides
and cared for as best the physicians could. Many of the
wounds were mild, but there were also many who would not
live the night.

The scouts were the first to recover some sense of purpose. The couriers of the trading houses rode back and forth,
reporting the movements of the Galts now that the battle was
finished. They had scoured the field, caring for their own
men and killing the ones Otah had left behind. Then, with
professional efficiency, they had made their camp and prepared their dinner. It was clear that the Galts considered the
conflict ended. They had won. It was over.

As darkness fell, Otah made his way through the camps,
stopped at what cook fires there were. No one greeted him
with violence, but he saw anger in some eyes and sorrow in
others. By far the most common expression was an emptiness
and disbelief. When at last he sat on his cot—set under the
spreading limbs of a shade tree in lieu of his tent—he knew
that however many men he had lost on the battlefield, twice as
many would have deserted by morning. Otah laid an arm over
his eyes, his body heavy with exhaustion, but totally unable
to sleep.

In the long, dreadful march to this battle, not one man had
turned back. At the time, it had warmed Otah's heart. Now he
wanted them all to flee. Go back to their wives and their children and their parents. Go back to where it was safe and forget
this mad attempt to stop the world from crumbling. Except he
couldn't imagine where safety might be. The Dai-kvo would

fall if he hadn't already. The cities of the Khaiem would fall. Machi would fall. For years, he had had the power to command the death of Galt. Stone-Made-Soft could have ruined their cities, sunk their lands below the waves. All of this could have been stopped once, if he had known and had the will. And now it was too late.

"Most High?"

Otah raised his arm, sat up. Nayiit stood in the shadows of the tree. Otah knew him by his silhouette.

"Nayiit-kya," Otah said, realizing it was the first he'd seen Liat's son since the battle. Nayiit hadn't even crossed his mind. He wondered what that said about him. Nothing good. "Are you all right?"

"I'm fine. A little bruised on the arm and shoulder, but . . . but fine."

In the dim, Otah saw that Nayiit held something before him. A greasy scent of roast lamb came to him.

"I can't eat," Otah said as the boy came closer. "Thank you, but . . . give it to the men. Give it to the injured men."

"Your attendant said you didn't eat in the morning either," Nayiit said. "It won't help them if you collapse. It won't bring them back."

Otah felt a surge of cold anger at the words, but bit back his retort. He nodded to the edge of the cot.

"Leave it there," he said.

Nayiit hesitated, but then moved forward and placed the bowl on the cot. He stepped back, but he did not walk away. As Otah's eyes adjusted to the darkness, Nayiit's face took on dim features. Otah wasn't surprised to see that the boy was weeping. Nayiit was older now than Otah had been when he'd fathered him on Liat. Older now than Otah had been when he'd first killed a man with his hands.

"I'm sorry, Most High," Nayiit said.

"So am I," Otah said. The scent of lamb was thick and rich. Enticing and mildly nauseating both.

"It was my fault," Nayiit said, voice thickened by a tight throat. "This, all of this, is my fault."

"No," Otah began. "You can't—"

"I saw them killing each other. I saw how many there were, and I broke," Nayiit said, and his hands took a pose of profound contrition. "I'm the one who called the retreat."

"I know," Otah said.

15

>+< Liat had been nursing her headache since she'd woken that morning; as the day progressed, it had drawn a line from the back of her eyes to her temples that throbbed when she moved too quickly. She had given up shaking her head. Instead, she pressed her fingers into the fine-grained wood of the table and tried to will her frustration into it. Kiyan, seated across from her, was saying something in a reasonable, measured tone that entirely missed her point. Liat took a pose that asked permission to speak, and then didn't wait for Kiyan to answer her.

"It isn't the men," Liat said. "He could have taken twice what he did, and we'd be able to do what's needed. It's that he took all the *horses*."

Kiyan's fox-sharp face tightened. Her dark eyes flickered down toward the maps and diagrams spread out between them. The farmlands and low towns that surrounded Machi were listed with the weight of grain and meat and vegetables that had come from each in the last five years. Liat's small, neat script covered paper after paper, black ink on the butter-yellow pages noting acres to be harvested and plowed, the number of hands and hooves required by each.

The breeze from the unshuttered windows lifted the pages but didn't disarray them, like invisible fingers checking the corners for some particular mark.

"Show me again," Kiyan said, and the weariness in her voice was almost enough to disarm Liat's annoyance. Almost, but not entirely. With a sigh, she stood. The line behind her eyes throbbed.

"This is the number of horses we'd need to plow the eastern farmsteads here and here and here," Liat said, tapping the maps as she did so. "We have half that number. We can get up to nearly the right level if we take the mules from the wheat mills."

Kiyan looked over the numbers, her fingertips touching the sums and moving on. Her gaze was focused, a single vertical line between her brows.

"How short is the second planting now?" Kiyan asked.

"The west and south are nearly complete, but they started late. The eastern farmsteads . . . not more than a quarter."

Kiyan leaned back. Otah's wife looked nearly as worn as Liat felt. The gray in her hair seemed more pronounced, her flesh paler and thinner. Liat found herself wondering if Kiyan had made a practice of painting her face and dyeing her hair that, in the crisis, she had let fall away, or if the task they had set themselves was simply sucking the life out of them both.

"It's too late," Kiyan said. "With the time it would take to get the mules, put them to yoke, and plow the fields, we'd be harvesting snowdrifts."

"Is there something else we could plant?" Liat asked. "Something we have time to grow before winter? Potatoes? Turnips?"

"I don't know," Kiyan said. "How long does it take to grow turnips this far north?"

Liat closed her eyes. Two educated, serious, competent women should be able to run a city. Should be able to shoulder the burden of the world and forget that one stood to lose a husband, the other a son. Should be able to ignore the constant fear that soldiers of a Galtic army might appear any day on the horizon prepared to destroy the city. It should be within their power, and yet they were blocked by idiot questions like whether turnips take longer to grow than potatoes. She took a deep breath and slowly let it out, willing the tension in her jaw to lessen, the pain behind her eyes to recede.

"I'll find out," Liat said. "But will you give the order to the mills? They won't be happy to stop their work."

"I'll give them the option of loaning the Khai their animals or pulling the plows themselves," Kiyan said. "If we have to spend the winter grinding wheat for our bread, it's a small price for not starving."

"It's going to be a thin spring regardless," Liat said.

Kiyan took the papers that Liat had drawn up. She didn't speak, but the set of her mouth agreed.

"We'll do our best," Kiyan said.

The banquet had gone splendidly. The women of the utkhaiem—wives and mothers, daughters and aunts—had heard Kiyan's words and taken to them as if she were a priest before the faithful. Liat had seen the light in their eyes, the sense of hope. For all their fine robes and lives of court scandal and gossip, each of these women was as grateful as Liat had been for the chance of something to do.

The food and fuel, Kiyan had kept for herself. Other people had been tasked with seeing to the wool, to arranging the movement of the summer belongings into the storage of the high towers, the preparation of the lower city—the tunnels below Machi. Liat had volunteered to act as Kiyan's messenger and go-between in the management of the farms and crops, gathering the food that would see them through the winter. Being the lover of a poet—even a poet who had never bound one of the andat—apparently lent her enough status in court to make her interesting. And as the rumors began to spread that Cehmai and Maati were keeping long hours together in the library and the poet's house, that they were preparing a fresh binding, Liat found herself more and more in demand. In recent days it had even begun to interfere with her work.

She had let herself spend time in lush gardens and high-domed dining halls, telling what stories she knew of Maati's work and intentions—what parts of it he'd said would be safe to tell. The women were so hungry for good news, for hope, that Liat couldn't refuse them. After telling the stories often enough, even she began to take hope from them herself. But tea and sweet bread and gossip took time, and they took attention, and she had let it go too far. The second wheat crop would be short, and no amount of pleasant high-city chatter now would fill bellies in the spring. Assuming they lived. If the Galts appeared tomorrow, it would hardly matter what she'd done or failed to do.

"There's going to be enough food," Kiyan said softly. "We may wind up killing more of the livestock and eating the grain ourselves, but even if half the crop failed, we'd have enough to see us through to the early harvest."

"Still," Liat said. "It would have been good to have more."

Kiyan took a pose that both agreed with Liat and dismissed the matter. Liat responded with one appropriate for taking leave of a superior. It was a nuance that seemed to trouble Kiyan, because she leaned forward, her fingertips touching Liat's arm.

"Are you well?" Kiyan asked.

"Fine," Liat said. "It's just my head has been tender. It's often like that when the Khai Saraykeht changes the tax laws again or the cotton crops fail. It fades when the troubles pass."

Kiyan nodded, but didn't pull back her hand.

"Is there anything I can do to help?" Kiyan asked.

"Tell me that Otah's come back with Nayiit, the Galts all conquered and the world back the way it was."

"Yes," Kiyan said. Her eyes lost their focus and her hand slipped back to her side of the table. Liat regretted being so glib, regretted letting the moment's compassion fade. "Yes, it would be pretty to think so."

Liat took her leave. The palaces were alive with servants and slaves, the messengers of the merchant houses and the utkhaiem keeping the life of the court active. Liat walked through the wide halls with their distant tiled ceilings and down staircases of marble wide enough for twenty men to walk abreast. Sweet perfumes filled the air, though their scents brought her no comfort. The world was as bright as it had been before she'd come to Machi, the voices lifted in song as merry and sweet. It was only a trick of her mind that dulled the colors and broke the harmonies. It was only the thought of her boy lying dead in some green and distant field and the dull pain behind her eyes.

When she reached the physicians, she found the man she sought speaking with Eiah. A young man lay naked on the wide slate table beside the pair. His face was pale and damp with sweat; his eyes were closed. His nearer leg was purple with bruises and gashed at the side. The physician—a man no older than Liat, but bald apart from a long gray fringe of hair—was gesturing at the young man's leg, and Eiah was leaning in toward him, as if the words were water she was thirsty for. Liat walked to them softly, partly from the pain in her head, partly from the hope of overhearing their discussion without changing it.

"There's a fever in the flesh," the physician said. "That's to be expected. But the *muscle*."

Eiah considered the leg, more fascinated, Liat noticed, with the raw wounds than with the man's flaccid sex.

"It's stretched," Eiah said. "So there's still a connection to stretch it. He'll be able to walk."

The physician dropped the blanket and tapped the boy's shoulder.

"You hear that, Tamiya? The Khai's daughter says you'll be able to walk again."

The boy's eyes fluttered open, and he managed a thin smile.

"You're correct, Eiah-cha. The tendon's injured, but not snapped. He won't be able to walk for several weeks. The greatest danger now is that the wound where the skin popped open may become septic. We'll have to clean it out and bandage it. But first, perhaps we have a fresh patient?"

Liat found herself disconcerted to move from observer to observed so quickly. The physician's smile was distant and professional as a butcher selling lamb, but Eiah's grin was giddy. Liat took a pose that asked forbearance.

"I didn't mean to intrude," she said. "It's only that my head has been troubling me. It aches badly, and I was wondering whether . . ."

"Come, sit down, Liat-kya," Eiah cried, grabbing Liat's hand and pulling her to a low wooden seat. "Loya-cha can fix *anything*."

"I can't fix everything," the physician said, his smile softening a degree—he was speaking now not only to a patient, but a friend of his eager student and a fellow adult. "But I may be able to ease the worst of it. Tell me when I've touched the places that hurt the worst."

Gently, the man's fingers swept over Liat's face, her temples, touching here and there as gently as a feather against her skin. He seemed pleased and satisfied with her answers; then he took her pulse on both wrists and considered her tongue and eyes.

"Yes, I believe I can be of service, Liat-cha. Eiah, you saw what I did?"

Eiah took a pose of agreement. It was strange to see a girl so young and with such wealth and power look so attentive, to see her care so clearly what a man who was merely an honored servant could teach her. Liat's heart went out to the girl.

"Make your own measures, then," the man said. "I have a powder I'll mix for the patient, and we can discuss what you think while we clean the gravel out of our friend Tamiya."

Eiah's touch was harder, less assured. Where the physician had hardly seemed present, Eiah gave the impression of grabbing for something even when pressing with the tips of her fingers. It was an eagerness Liat herself had felt once, many years ago.

"You seem to be doing very well here," Liat said, her voice gentle.

"I know," the girl said. "Loya-cha's very smart, and he said

246 >+<   DANIEL ABRAHAM

I could keep coming here until Mama-kya or the Khai said different. Can I see your tongue, please?"

Liat let the examination be repeated, then when it was finished said, "You must be pleased to have found something you enjoy doing."

"It's all right," Eiah said. "I'd still rather be married, but this is almost as good. And maybe Papa-kya can find someone to marry me who'll let me take part in the physician's house. I'll probably be married to one of the Khaiem, after all, and Mama-kya's running the whole city now. Everyone says so."

"It may be different later, though," Liat said, trying to imagine a Khai allowing his wife to take a tradesman's work as a hobby.

"There may not be any Khaiem, you mean," Eiah said. "The Galts may kill them all."

"Of course they won't," Liat said, but the girl's eyes met hers and Liat faltered. There was so much of Otah's cool distance in a face that seemed too young to look on the world so dispassionately. She was like her father, prepared to pass judgment on the gods themselves if the situation called her to do it. Comfortable lies had no place with her. Liat looked down. "I don't know," she said. "Perhaps there won't be."

"Here, now," the physician said. "Take this with you, Liatcha. Pour it into a bowl of water and once it's dissolved, drink the whole thing. It will be bitter, so drink it fast. You'll likely want to lie down for a hand or two afterward, to let it work. But it should do what needs doing."

Liat took the paper packet and slipped it into her sleeve before taking a pose of gratitude.

"We should have a lunch in the gardens again," Eiah said. "You and Uncle Maati and me. Loya-cha would come too, except he's a servant."

Liat felt herself blush, but the physician's wry smile told her it was not the first such pronouncement he'd been subjected to.

"Perhaps you should wait for another day," he said. "Liatcha had a headache, remember."

"I know that," Eiah said impatiently. "I meant tomorrow."

"That would be lovely," Liat said. "I'll talk with Maati about it."

"Would you be so good as to get the stiff brushes from the back and wash them for me, Eiah-cha?" the physician said. "Tamiya's anxious to be done with us, I'm sure."

Eiah dropped into a pose of confirmation for less than a breath before darting off to her task. Liat watched the physician, the amusement and fondness in his expression. He shook his head.

"She is a force," he said. "But the powder. I wanted to say, it can be habit-forming. You shouldn't have it more than once in a week. So if the pain returns, we may have to find another approach."

"I'm sure this will be fine," Liat said as she rose. "And . . . thank you. For what you've done with Eiah, I mean."

"She needs it," the man said with a shrug. "Her father's ridden off to die, her mother and her friend the poet are too busy trying to keep us all alive to take time to comfort her. She buries herself in this, and so even if she slows us down, how can I do anything but welcome her?"

Liat felt her heart turn to lead. The physician's smile slipped, and for a moment the dread showed from behind the mask. When he spoke again, it was softly and the words were as gray as stones.

"And, after all, we may need our children to know how to care for the dying before all that's coming is done."

MAATI RUBBED his eyes with the palms of his hands, squinted, blinked. The world was blurry: the long, rich green of the grass on which they lay was like a single sheet of dyed rice paper; the towers of Machi were reduced to dark blurs that the blue of the sky shone through. It was like fog without the grayness. He blinked again, and the world moved nearer to focus.

"How long was I sleeping?" he asked.

"Long enough, sweet," Liat said. "I could have managed

longer, I think. The gods all know we've been restless enough at night."

The sun was near the top of its arc, the remains of breakfast in lacquered boxes with their lids shut, the day half gone. Liat was right, of course. He hadn't been sleeping near enough— late to bed, waking early, and with troubled rest between. He could feel it in his neck and back and see it in the slowness with which his vision cleared.

"Where's Eiah got to?" he asked.

"Back to her place with the physicians, I'd guess. I offered to wake you so that she could say her good-byes, but she thought it would be better if you slept." Liat smiled. "She said it would be restorative. Can you imagine her using that kind of language a season ago? She already sounds like a physician's apprentice."

Maati grinned. He'd resisted the idea of this little outing at first, but Cehmai had joined Eiah's cause. A half-day's effort by a rested man might do better for them than the whole day by someone drunk with exhaustion and despair. And even now the library seemed to call to him—the scrolls he had already read, the codices laid out and put away and pulled out to look over again, the wax tablets with their notes cut into them and smoothed clear again. And in the end, he had never been able to refuse Eiah. Her good opinion was too precious and too fickle.

Liat slid her hand around his arm and leaned against him. She smelled of grass and cherry paste on apples and musk. He turned without thinking and kissed the crown of her head as if it were something he had always done. As if there had not been a lifetime between the days when they had first been lovers and now.

"How badly is it going?" she asked.

"Not well. We have a start, but Cehmai's notes are only beginnings. And they were done by a student. I'm sure they all seemed terribly deep and insightful when he was still fresh from the school. But there's less there than I'd hoped. And . . ."

"And?"

Maati sighed. The towers were visible now. The blades of grass stood out one from another.

"He's not a great inventor," Maati said. "He never was. It's part of why he was chosen to take over an andat that had already been captured instead of binding something new. And I'm no better."

"You were chosen for the same thing."

"Cehmai's clever. I'm clever too, if it comes to that, but we're the second pressing. There's no one we can talk with who's seen a binding through from first principles to a completion. We need someone whose mind's sharper than ours."

There were birds wheeling about the towers—tiny specks of black and gray and white wheeling though the air as if a single mind drove them. Maati pretended he could hear their calls.

"Perhaps you could train someone. There's a whole city to choose from."

"There isn't time," Maati said. He wanted to say that even if there were, he wouldn't. The andat were too powerful, too dangerous to be given to anyone whose heart wasn't strong or whose conscience couldn't be trusted. That was the lesson, after all, that had driven his own life and Cehmai's and the Dai-kvo himself. It was what elevated each of the poets from boy children cast out by their parents to the most honored men in the world. And yet, if there were someone bright enough to hand the power to, he suspected he would. If it brought the army back from the field and put the world back the way it had been, the risk would be worth it.

"Maybe one of the other poets will come," Liat said, but her voice had gone thin and weary.

"You don't have hope for the Dai-kvo?"

Liat smiled.

"Hope? Yes, I have hope. Just not faith. The Galts know what's in play. If we don't recapture the andat, the cities will all fall. If we do, we'll destroy Galt and everyone in her. They'll be as ruthless as we will."

"And Otah-kvo? Nayiit?"

Liat's gaze met his, and he nodded. The knot in her chest, he was certain, was much like his own.

"They'll be fine," Liat said, her tone asking for her own belief in the words as much as his. "It's always the footmen who die in battles, isn't it? The generals all live. And he'll keep Nayiit safe. He said he would."

"They might not even see battle. If they arrive before the Galts and come back quickly enough, we might not lose a single man."

"And the moon may come down and get itself trapped in a teabowl," Liat said. "But it would be nice, wouldn't it? For us, I mean. Not so much for the Galts."

"You care what happens to them?"

"Is that wrong?" Liat asked.

"You're the one who came to Otah-kvo asking that they all be killed."

"I suppose I did, didn't I? I don't know what's changed. Something to do with having my boy out there, I suppose. Slaughtering a nation isn't so much to think about. It's when I start *feeling* that it all goes confused. I wonder why we do it. I wonder why they do. Do you think if we gave them our gold and our silver and swore we would never bind a fresh andat . . . do you think they'd let our children live?"

It took a few breaths to realize that Liat was actually waiting for his answer, and several more before he knew what he believed.

"No," Maati said. "I don't think they would."

"Neither do I. But it would be good, wouldn't it? A world where it wasn't a choice of our children or theirs."

"It would be better than this one."

As if by common consent, they changed the subject, talking of food and the change of seasons, Eiah's new half-apprenticeship with the physicians and the small doings of the women of the utkhaiem now that their men had gone. It was only reluctantly that Maati rose. The sun was two and a half hands past where it had been when he woke, the shadows growing oblong. They walked back to the library, hand in hand at first, and then only walking beside each other. Maati felt his heart growing heavier as they came down the familiar paths, paving stones turning to sand turning to crushed white gravel bright as snow.

"You could come in," Maati said when they reached the wide front doors.

In answer, she kissed him lightly on the mouth, gave his hand a gentle squeeze, and turned away. Maati sighed and turned to lumber up the steps. Inside, Cehmai was sitting on a low couch, three scrolls spread out before him.

"I think I've found something," Cehmai said. "There's reference in Manat-kvo's notes to a grammatic schema called threefold significance. If we have something that talks about that, perhaps we can find a way to shift the binding from one kind of significance to another."

"We don't," Maati said. "And if I recall correctly, the three significators all require unity. There's not a way to pick between them."

"Well. Then we're still stuck."

"Yes."

Cehmai stood and stretched, the popping of his spine audible from across the wide room.

"We need someone who knows this better than we do," Maati said as he lowered himself onto a carved wooden chair. "We need the Dai-kvo."

"We don't have him."

"I know it."

"So we have to keep trying," Cehmai said. "The better prepared we are when the Dai-kvo comes, the better he'll be able to guide us."

"And if he never comes?"

"He will," Cehmai said. "He has to."

16

>+< "Yes," Nayiit said. "That's him."

Otah's mount whickered beneath him as he looked up at the Dai-kvo's body. It had been tied to a stake at the entrance to his high offices; the man had been dead for days. The brown-robed corpses of the poets lay at his feet, stacked like cordwood.

They had taken it all for granted. The andat, the poets, the continuity of one generation following upon another as they always had. It grew more difficult, yes. An andat would escape and for a time the city it had left would suffer, yes. They had not conceived that everything might end. Otah looked at the slaughtered poets, and he saw the world he had known.

The morning after the battle had been tense. He had risen before dawn and paced through the camps. Several of the scouts had vanished, and at first there was no way to know whether they had been captured by the Galts or killed or if they had simply taken their horses, set their eyes on the horizon, and fled. It was only when the reports began to filter back that the shape of things came clear.

The Galts had fallen back, their steam wagons and horses making a fast march to the east, toward the village of the Dai-kvo. There was no pursuit, no rush to find the survivors of that bloody field and finish the work they'd begun. Otah's army had been broken easily, and the Galts' contempt for them was evident in the decision that they were not worth taking the time to kill.

It was humiliating, and still Otah had found himself relieved. More of his men would die today, but only from wounds they already bore. They had given Otah a moment to rest and consider and see how deep the damage had gone.

Four hundred of his men lay dead in the mud and grass beside perhaps a third as many Galts, perhaps less. Another half thousand were wounded or missing. A few hours had cost him a third of what he had, and more than that. The men who had survived the retreat were different from the ones he had spoken to at their cook fires before the fight. These men seemed stunned, lost, and emptied. The makeshift spears and armor that had once seemed to speak of strength and resourcefulness now seemed painfully naïve. They had come to battle armed like children and they had been killed by men. Otah found himself giving thanks to any gods that would listen for all the ones who had lived.

The scouting party left two days later. It was made of twenty horsemen and as many on foot, Otah himself at the lead. Nayiit asked permission to come, and Otah had granted it. It might not have been keeping the boy safe the way he'd promised Maati, but as long as Nayiit blamed himself for the carnage and defeat, it was better that he be away from the wounded and the dying. The rest of the army would stay behind in the camp, tend to the men who could be helped, ease the passing of those past hope, and, Otah guessed, slip away one by one or else in groups. He couldn't think they would follow him into battle again.

The smaller group moved faster, and the path the Galts had left was clear as a new-built road. Churned grass, broken saplings, the damage done by thousands of disciplined feet. The wounded earth was as wide as ten men across—never more, never less. The precision was eerie. It was two days' travel before Otah saw the smoke.

They reached the village near evening. They found a ruin.

Where glittering windows had been, ragged holes remained. The towers and garrets cut from the stone of the mountain were soot-stained and broken. The air smelled of burned flesh and smoke and the copper scent of spilled blood. Otah rode slowly, the clack of his mount's hooves on pavement giving order to the idiot, tuneless wind chimes. The air felt thick against his face, and the place where his heart had once been seemed to gape empty. His hands didn't tremble, he did not weep. His mind simply took in the details—a corpse in the street wearing brown robes made black with blood, a Galtic steam wagon with the wide metalwork on the back twisted open by some terrible force, a firekeeper's kiln overturned and ashen, an arrow splintered against stone—and then forgot them. It was unreal.

Behind him, the others followed in silence. They made their way to the grand office at the height of the village. The great hall, open to the west, caught the light of the setting sun. The white stone of the walls glowed, light where it had escaped the worst damage and a deeper, darker gold where smoke had marked it.

And in the entrance of the hall, the Dai-kvo was tied to a stake. The hopes of the Khaiem lying dead at his feet.

I could have stopped this, Otah thought. The Galts live because I spared them at Saraykeht. This is *my* fault.

He turned to Nayiit.

"Have him cut down," he said. "We can have them buried or burned. Anything but this."

Behind the gruesome sight squatted the remains of a great pyre. Logs as tall as a standing man had been hauled here and set to hold the flames, and had burned nearly through. The spines of ancient books lay stripped in the ashes of their pages and curled from the heat. Shredded ribbons that had held the codices closed shifted in the breeze. Otah touched his palm to the neck of his horse as if to steady it more than himself, then dismounted.

Smoke still rose from the fire, thin gray reeking clouds. He paced the length and breadth of the pyre. Here and there, embers still glowed. He saw more than one bone laid bare and black. Men had died here. Poets and books. Knowledge that could never be replaced. He leaned against the rough bark of a half-burned tree. There had been no battle here. This had been slaughter.

"Most High?"

Ashua Radaani was at his side. Might have been at his side for some time, for all Otah could say. The man's face was drawn, his eyes flat.

"We've taken down the Dai-kvo," he said.

"Five groups of four men," Otah said. "If you can find any lanterns still intact, use them. If not, we'll make torches from something. I can't say how deep into the mountain these hallways go, but we'll walk through the whole thing if we have to."

Radaani glanced over his shoulder at the red and swollen sun that was just now touching the horizon. The others were silhouetted against it, standing in a clot at the mouth of the hall. Radaani turned back and took a pose that suggested an alternative.

"Perhaps we might wait until morning—"

"What if there's a man still alive in there," Otah said. "Will he be alive when the sun's back? If darkness is what we have to work in, we'll work in darkness. Anyone who survived this, I want him. And books. Anything. If it's written, bring it to me. Bring it here."

Radaani hesitated, then fell into a pose of acceptance. Otah put his hand on the man's shoulder.

We've failed, he thought. Of course we failed. We never had a chance.

They didn't make camp, didn't cook food. The horses, nervous from the scent of death all around them, were taken back from the village. Nayiit and his blacksmith friend Saya gleaned lanterns and torches from the wreckage. The long, terrible night began. In the flickering light, the back halls and grand, destroyed chambers danced like things from children's stories of the deepest hells. Otah and the three men with him—Nayiit, Radaani, and a thin-faced boy whose name escaped him—called out into the darkness that they were friends. That help had arrived. Their voices grew hoarse, and only echoes answered them.

They found the dead. In the beds, in the stripped libraries, in the kitchens and alleyways, and floating facedown in the wide wooden tubs of the bathhouse. No man had been spared. There had been no survivors. Twice Otah thought he saw a flicker of recognition in Nayiit's eyes when they found a man lying pale and bloodless, eyes closed as if in sleep. In a meeting chamber near what Otah guessed had been the Dai-kvo's private apartments, Otah found the corpse of Athai-kvo, the messenger who had come in the long-forgotten spring to warn him against training men to fight. His eyes had been gouged away. Otah found himself too numb to react. Another detail to come into his mind and leave it again. As the night's chill stole into him, Otah's fingers began to ache, his shoulders and neck growing tight as if the pain could take the place of warmth.

They fell into their rhythm of walking and shouting and not being answered until time lost its meaning. They might have been working for half a hand, they might have been working for a sunless week, and so the dawn surprised him.

One of the other searching parties had quit earlier. Someone had found a firekeeper's kiln and stoked it, and the rich smell of cracked wheat and flaxseed and fresh honey cut through the smoke and death like a sung melody above a street fight. Otah sat on an abandoned cart and cradled a bowl of the sweet gruel in his hands, the heat from the bowl soothing his palms and fingers. He didn't remember the last time he'd eaten, and though he was bone-weary, he could not bring himself to think of sleep. He feared his dreams.

Nayiit walked to him carrying a similar bowl and sat at his side. He looked older. The horrors of the past days had etched lines at the corners of his mouth. Exhaustion had blackened his eyes. Exhaustion and guilt.

"There's no one, is there?" Nayiit said.

"No. They're gone."

Nayiit nodded and looked down to the neat, carefully fitted bricks that made the road. No blade of grass pressed its way through those stony joints. It struck Otah as strangely obscene that a place of such carnage and destruction should have such well-maintained paving stones. It would be better when tree roots had lifted a few of them. Something so ruined should be a ruin. A few years, perhaps. A few years, and this would all be a wild garden dedicated to the dead. The place would be haunted, but at least it would be green.

"There weren't any children. Or women," Nayiit said. "That's something."

"There were in Yalakeht," Otah said.

"I suppose there were. And Saraykeht too."

It took a moment to realize what Nayiit meant. It was so simple to forget that the boy had a wife. Had a child. Or once had, depending on how badly things had gone in the summer cities. Otah felt himself blush.

"I'm sorry. That wasn't . . . Forgive my saying that."

"It's true, though. It won't change if we're more polite talking about it."

"No. No, it won't."

They were silent for a long moment. Off to their left, three of the others were laying out blankets, unwilling, it seemed, to seek shelter in the halls of the dead. Farther on, Saya the blacksmith was looking over the Galtic steam wagon with what appeared to be a professional interest. High in the robin's-egg sky, a double vee of cranes flew southward, calling to one another in high, nasal voices. Otah took two cupped fingers and lifted a mouthful of the wheat gruel to his lips. It tasted wonderful—sweet and rich and warm—and yet he didn't enjoy it so much as recognize that he should. His limbs felt heavy and awkward as wood. When Nayiit spoke, his voice was low and shaky.

"I know that I won't ever be able to make good for this. If I hadn't called the retreat—"

"This isn't your fault," Otah said. "It's the Dai-kvo's."

Nayiit reared back, his mouth making a small "o." His

hands fumbled toward a pose of query, but the porcelain bowl defeated him. Otah took his meaning anyway.

"Not just this one. The last Dai-kvo. Tahi, his name was. And the one before that. All of them. This is their fault. We trusted everything in the andat. Our power, our wealth, the safety of our children. Everything. We built on sand. We were stupid."

"But it worked for so long."

"It worked until it didn't," Otah said. The response came from the back of his mind, as if it had always been there, only waiting for the time to speak. "It was always certain to fail sometime. Now, or ten generations from now. What difference does it make? If we'd been able to postpone the crisis until my children had to face it, or my grandchildren, or your grandchildren—how would that have been better than us facing it now? The andat have always been an unreliable tool, and poets have always been men with all the vanity and frailty and weakness that men are born with. The Empire fell, and we built ourselves in its image and so now we've fallen too. There's no honor in a lesson half-learned."

"Too bad you hadn't said that to the Dai-kvo."

"I did. To all three of them, one way and another. They didn't take it to heart. And I . . . I didn't stay to press the point."

"Then we'll have to learn the lesson now," Nayiit said. It sounded like an attempt at resolution, perhaps even bravery. It sounded hollow as a drum.

"Someone will," Otah said. "Someone will learn by our example. And maybe the Galts burned all the books that would have let them teach more poets of their own. Perhaps they're already safe from our mistakes."

"That would be ironic. To come all this way and destroy the thing that you'd come for."

"Or wise. It might be wise." Otah sighed and took another mouthful of the wheat. "The Galts are likely almost to Tan-Sadar by now. As long as they're heading south, we may be able to reach Machi again before they do. There's no fighting them, I think we've discovered that, but we might be able to flee. Get people to Eddensea and the Westlands before the passes all close. It's probably too late to take a fast cart for Bakta."

Nayiit shook his head.

"They aren't going south."

Otah took another mouthful. The food seemed to be seeping into his blood; he felt only half-dead with exhaustion. Then, a breath or two later, Nayiit's words found their meaning, and he frowned, put down his bowl, and took a questioning pose. Nayiit nodded down toward the low towns at the base of the mountain village.

"I was talking with one of the footmen. The Galts came up the river from Yalakeht, and they left heading north on the road to Amnat-Tan. They're likely only a day or so ahead of us. It doesn't seem like they're interested in Tan-Sadar."

"Why not?" Otah said, more than half to himself. "It's the nearest city."

"Marshes," a low voice said from behind them. The blacksmith, Saya, had come up behind them. "There's decent roads between here and Amnat-Tan. And then the North Road between all the winter cities. Tan-Sadar's close, Most High. But there's two different rivers find their start in the marshes between here and there, and if their wagons are like the one they've left down there, they'll need roads." The thick arms folded into a pose appropriate for an apprentice to his master. "Come and see yourself, if you'd care to."

The steam wagon was wider than a cart, its bed made of hard, oiled wood at the front, and sheeted with copper at the back. A coal furnace twice the size of a firekeeper's kiln stood around a steel boiling tank. Saya pointed out how the force of the steam drove the wheels, and how it might be controlled to turn slowly and with great force or else more swiftly. Otah remembered a model he'd seen as a boy in Saraykeht. An army of teapots, the Khai Saraykeht had called them. The world had always told them how it would be, how things would fall apart. They had all been deaf.

"It's heavy, though," Saya said. "And there's housings there at the front where you could yoke a team of oxen, but I wouldn't want to pull it through soft land."

"Why would they ever pull it?" Nayiit asked. "Why put all this into making it go on fire and then use oxen?"

"They might run out of coal," Otah said.

"They might," Saya agreed. "But more likely, they don't want to rattle it badly. All this was a rounded chamber like an egg. Built to hold the pressure in. You can see how they leaved the seams. Something cracked that egg, and that's why this is all scrap now. Anyone who was nearby when it happened . . . well. Anything strong enough to make a wagon this heavy move in the first place, and then load it with men or supplies, and *then* keep it going fast enough to be worth doing . . . it'd be a lot to let loose at once."

"How?" Otah said. "How did they break it?"

Saya shrugged.

"Lucky shot with a hard crossbow, maybe. Or the heat came too high. I don't know how gentle these things are. Looking at this one, though, I'd like a nice smooth meadow or a well-made road. Nothing too rutted."

"I can't believe they'd put men on this," Nayiit said. "A wagon that could kill everyone on it if it hits a bad bump? Why would anyone ever do that?"

"Because the gain is worth the price," Otah said. "They think the men they lose from it are a good sacrifice for the power they get."

Otah touched the twisted metal. The egg chamber had burst open like a flower bud blooming. The petals were bright and sharp and too thick for Otah to bend bare-handed. His mind felt perfectly awake, and his head felt full. It was as if he were thinking without yet knowing what he was thinking of. He squatted and looked at the wide, blackened door of the coal furnace.

"This is made of iron," Otah said.

"Yes, Most High," Saya agreed.

"But it doesn't melt. So however hot this runs, it can't be

hotter than an ironworking forge, ne? How do they measure that, would you guess?"

Saya shrugged again.

"They're likely using soft coal, Most High. Use coal out of a Galt mine, it won't matter how much they put in it, it'll only come so hot. Forging iron needs hard coal. It's why the Galts buy their steel from Eddensea."

"And how long would it take them to reach Amnat-Tan if they were using these?"

"I've no way to know, Most High," Saya said taking a pose of apology. "I've never seen one working."

Otah nodded to himself. His head almost ached, but he could feel himself putting one thing with another like seeing fish moving below glass-clear ice.

"Otah-cha?" Nayiit said. "What is it?"

Otah looked up, and was surprised to find himself grinning.

"Tell the men to rest until midday. We'll start back to the main force after that."

Nayiit took an accepting pose. But as they walked away, Otah saw him exchange confused glances with the blacksmith. Back at their little camp, Ashua Radaani was organizing a pile of books. He took a pose of greeting, but his expression was grim. Otah stood beside him, hands pulled into the sleeves of his robes, and considered the volumes.

"This is everything," Radaani said. "Fourteen books out of the greatest library in the world."

Otah glanced at the mouth of the high offices. He tried to guess how much knowledge had been lost there, vanished from the world and never to been found again. Nayiit put a thick, dirty hand reverently on the stack before him.

"I can only read half of them," Radaani said. "The others are too old, I think. One or two from the First Empire."

"We'll take them to Maati and Cehmai," Otah said. "Maybe they'll be of use."

"We're going back to Machi?" Radaani said.

"Those who'd like to, yes. The rest will come with me to Cetani. I'm going to meet with the Khai Cetani. We'll have to hurry, though. The Galts will be taking the long way, and sacking Amnat-Tan while they're at it. I hope that will give us the time we need."

"You have a plan, Most High?" Radaani sounded dubious.

"Not yet," Otah said. "But when I do, it'll be better than my last one. I don't expect many men to follow me. A few will suffice. If they're loyal."

"We could make for Tan-Sadar," Radaani said. "If it's allies we need, they're closer."

"We don't, or at least not as badly as we need rough roads and an early winter."

Radaani didn't show any sign of understanding the comment, he only took a pose of acceptance.

"That does sounds more like Cetani, Most High. I'll have the men ready to go at midday."

Otah took a pose that acknowledged Radaani's words and walked back to the cart where Saya had found him. The wheat gruel had gone cold and sticky but it was still as sweet. In his mind, he was already on his way to Cetani. The road between Cetani and Machi wasn't one he had traveled often; he had kept to the South in the years he had been a courier, and the Khaiem had always been reluctant to meet one another, preferring to send envoys and girl children to wed. Nonetheless, he had traveled it. He was still trying to recall the details when Nayiit interrupted him.

"What are we going to do in Cetani, Most High?"

The boy's face was sharp and focused. Eager. Otah saw something of what he had been at that age. He knew the answer to Nayiit's question as soon as it was spoken, but still it took him a moment to bring himself to say it.

"You aren't coming, Nayiit-cha. I need you to see those books back to Maati."

"Anyone can do that," Nayiit said. "I'll be of use to you. I've been through Cetani. I was there just weeks ago, when we were coming to Machi. I can—"

"You can't," Otah said, and took the boy's hand. His son's hand. "You called a retreat when no one had given the order.

In the Old Empire, I'd have had to see you killed for that. I can't have you come now."

The surprise on Nayiit's face was heartbreaking.

"You said it wasn't my fault," he said.

"And it isn't. I would have called the retreat myself if you hadn't. What happened to our men, what happened here, to the Dai-kvo . . . none of that's yours to carry. If you'd done differently, it would have changed nothing. But there will be a next time, and I can't have someone calling commands who might do what you've done."

Nayiit stepped back, just out of his reach. Ah, Maati, Otah thought, what kind of son have we made, you and I?

"It won't," Nayiit said. "It won't happen again."

"I know. I know it won't," Otah said, making his tone gentle to soften hard words. "Because you're going back to Machi."

UDUN WAS a river city. It was a city of bridges, and a city of birds. Sinja had lived there briefly while recovering from a dagger wound in his thigh. He remembered the songs of the jays and the finches, the sound of the river. He remembered Kiyan's stories of growing up a wayhouse keeper's daughter— the beggars on the riverside quays who drew pictures with chalks to cover the gray stone or played the small reed flutes that never seemed to be popular anywhere else; the canals that carried as much traffic as the streets. The palaces of the Khai Udun spanned the river itself, sinking great stone stanchions down into the river like the widest bridge in the world. As a girl, Kiyan had heard stories about the ghouls that lived in the darkness under those great palaces. She had gone there in boats with her cohort in the dark of night, the way that Sinja himself had dared burial mounds at midnight with his brothers. She had kissed her first lover in the twilight beneath a bridge just north of here. He had spent so little time in Udun, and yet he felt he knew it so well.

The wayhouse where Sinja housed his men was south of the palaces. Its walls were stone and mud and thick as the length of his arm. The shutters were a green so dark they seemed almost black. It hadn't been built to fit as many men as Sinja commanded, but the standards of a soldier were lower than those of a normal traveler. And the standards of a soldier as likely to be mistaken for the enemy by his alleged fellows as killed by the defending armsmen were lower still. The great common room was covered from one wall to the other with thin cotton bedrolls. The upper rooms, intended for four men or fewer, housed eight or ten. There had been a few men who had ventured as far as the stables, but Sinja had called them back inside. There was a madness on Balasar Gice's men, and he didn't intend to have his own fall to it.

In the small walled garden at the back, Sinja sat on a camp stool and drank a bowl of mint tea brewed with fresh-plucked leaves. Thyme and basil grew around him, and a small black-leaf maple gave shade. Smoke rose into the sky, dark and solid as the towers of Machi. The birds were silent or fled. The scouts he'd sent out, their uniforms clearly the colors of Galt, reported that the rivers and canals had all turned red from the blood and the fish were dying of it. Sinja wasn't sure he believed that, but it seemed to catch the flavor of the day. Certainly he wasn't going to go out and look for himself.

An ancient man, spine bent and mouth innocent of anything resembling teeth, poked his head out the wide oaken doors at the end of the garden. The red-rimmed eyes seemed uncertain. The old hands shook so badly Sinja could see the trembling from where he sat. War is no place for the old, Sinja thought. It's meant for young men who can't yet distinguish between excitement and fear. Men who haven't yet grown a conscience.

"Mani-cha," Sinja called to the wayhouse keeper. "Is there something I can do for you?"

"There's a man come for you, Sinja-cha. Say's he's the . . . ah . . . the general."

"Bring him here," Sinja said.

The wayhouse keeper took a pose of acknowledgment,

smiled an uncertain smile, and wavered half in, half out of the doorframe.

"You'll be fine, Mani-cha. You've my protection. He's not going to have you hanged, I promise. But you might bring him a bowl of tea."

Old Mani blinked and nodded his apology before ducking back into the house. The protection wasn't a promise he could keep. He hadn't asked General Gice's permission before he'd extended it. And still, he thought the old man's chances were good.

Balasar stepped into the garden as if he knew it, as if he owned it. It wasn't arrogance. That was what made the man so odd. The general's expression was drawn and thoughtful; that at least was a good sign. Sinja put his bowl of tea on the dusty red brick pathway, stood, and made his salute. Balasar returned it, but his gaze seemed caught by the shifting branches of the maple tree.

"All's well, I hope, sir," Sinja said.

"Well enough," Balasar said. "Well enough for a bad day, anyway. And here? Have your men been . . . Have you lost anyone?"

"I can account for all of them. I can have them ready to go out in half a hand, if you think they're needed, sir."

Balasar shifted, looking straight into Sinja's eyes as if seeing him clearly for the first time.

"No," Balasar said. "No, it won't be called for. What resistance there still is can't last long."

Sinja nodded. Of course not. Udun had numbers and knowledge, but they weren't fighters. The raids had continued for the whole trek upriver. Hunting parties had been harassed, wells fouled, the low towns the army had passed through stripped bare of anything that might have been of use to them. And the bodies of the soldiers slain in the raids were wrapped in shrouds and ashes to join the train. Balasar Gice had left Nantani with ten thousand men, and with all the gods watching him, he'd reached Udun with the full ten thousand, no matter if a few dozen needed carrying. Sinja tried to keep the disapproval from his face, but the general saw it there anyway, frowned, and looked away.

"What's the matter with that tree?" Balasar asked.

Sinja considered the maple. It was small—hardly taller than two men's height—and artfully cut to give shade without obstructing the view of the sky.

"Nothing, sir," he said. "It looks fine."

"The leaves are black."

"They're supposed to be," Sinja said. "If you look close, you can see it's really a very deep green, but they call it black-leaf all the same. When autumn comes, it turns a brilliant red. It's lovely, especially if the leaves haven't let go when the first snow comes."

"I'm sorry I won't be here to see it," the general said.

"Well, not the snows," Sinja said, "but you can see on the edges of those lower leaves where the red's starting."

Balasar stepped over and took a low branch in his hand. He bent it to look at the leaves, but he didn't pluck them free. Sinja gave the man credit for that. Most Galts would have ripped the leaves off to look at them. With a sigh, Balasar let the branch swing back to its place.

"Tea?" Old Mani said from the doorway. Balasar looked over his shoulder at the old man and nodded. Sinja motioned the wayhouse keeper close, took the bowl, and sipped from it before passing it on to the general. Old Mani took a pose of thanks and backed out again.

"Tasting my food and drink?" Balasar asked in the tongue of the Khaiem. There was amusement in his tone. "Surely we haven't come to the point I'd expect you to poison me."

"I didn't brew it," Sinja said. "And Old Mani knew a lot of people you killed today."

Balasar took the cup and frowned into it. He was silent for long enough that Sinja began to grow uncomfortable. When he spoke, his tone was almost confessional.

"I've come to tell you that I was wrong," Balasar said. "You were right. I should have listened."

"I'm gratified that you think so. What was I right about?"

"The bodies. The men. I should have buried them where they lay. I should have left them. Now there's vengeance in it, and it's . . ."

He shook his head and sat on the camp stool. Sinja leaned against the stone wall of the garden.

"War's more fun when the enemy doesn't fight back," Sinja said. "There's never been a sack as easy as Nantani. You had to know things would get harder when the Khaiem got themselves organized."

"I did," Balasar said. "But . . . I carry the dead. I can feel them behind me. I know that they died because of my pride."

Balasar sipped at the tea. Far away across the war, a man shouted something, but Sinja couldn't make out the language, much less the words.

"All respect, Balasar-cha. They died because they were fighting in a war," Sinja said. "It's to be expected."

"They died in my war. My men, in my war."

"I see what you mean about pride."

Balasar looked up sharply, his lips thin, his face flushing. Sinja waited, and the general forced a smile. The maple leaves tapped against each other in the shifting breeze.

"I should have kept better discipline," Balasar said. "The men came to Udun for a slaughter. There's no mercy out there today. It's going to take longer to sack the city, it's going to mean more casualties for us, and Utani and Tan-Sadar will know what happened. They'll know it's a fight to the last man."

"As I recall, you came to destroy the Khaiem," Sinja said. "Not to conquer them."

Balasar nodded, accepting the criticism in Sinja's tone as his due. Sinja half-expected to see the general's hands take a pose of contrition, but instead he looked into Sinja's eyes. There was no remorse there, only the hard look of a man who has claimed his own failures and steeled himself to correcting them.

"I can destroy the Khaiem without killing every fruit seller and baker's apprentice along the way," Balasar said. "I need your help to do it."

"You had something in mind."

"I want your men to carry messages to Utani and Tan-Sadar. Not to the Khaiem. The utkhaiem and merchant houses. Men who have power. Tell them that if they stand aside when we come, they won't be harmed. We want the poets, and the books, and the Khaiem."

Sinja shook his head.

"You might as well run a spear through us now," Sinja said. "We're traitors. Yes, I know we're a mercenary company, and we took service and on and on. But every man I have was born in these cities we're sacking. Waving a contract isn't going to excuse them in the eyes of the citizens. Send prisoners instead. Find a dozen men your soldiers haven't quite hacked to death and use them to carry the messages. They'll be more effective than we will anyway."

"You think they can be trusted not to simply flee?"

"Catch a man and his wife. Or a father and child. There have to be a few left out there. Bring me the hostages and I'll keep them safe. When the husbands and fathers come back, you can give them a few lengths of silver and a day's head start. It won't undo what we've done here, but having a few survivors tell tales of your honorable treatment is better than none."

Balasar sipped his tea. The general's brow was furrowed.

"That's wise," he said at last. "We'll do that. I'll have my men bring the hostages to you by nightfall."

"Best not to rape them," Sinja said. "It takes something from the spirit of the thing if they're treated poorly."

"You're the one looking after them."

"And I can control the situation once they're in my care. It's before that I'm worried by."

"I'll see to it. If I give the order, it will be followed. They're my men." He said it as if he were reminding himself of something more than what the words meant.

For a moment, Sinja saw a profound weariness in the Galt's pale face. It struck him for the first time how small Balasar

Gice was. It was only the way he moved through the world that gave the impression of standing half a head above everyone else in the room. The first dusting of gray had touched his temples, but Sinja couldn't say if it was premature or late coming. The breeze stirred, reeking of smoke.

"I can't tell if you hate war or love it," Sinja said.

Balasar looked up as if he'd forgotten Sinja was there. His smile was amused and bitter.

"I see the necessity of it," Balasar said. "And sometimes I forget that the point of war is the peace at the end of it."

"Is it? And here I thought it was gold and women."

"Those can be the same," Balasar said, ignoring the joke. "There are worse things than enough money and someone to spend it on."

"And glory?"

Balasar chuckled as he stood, but there was very little of mirth in the sound. He put down his bowl and his hands took a rough pose of query, as simple as a child's.

"Do you see glory in this, Sinja-cha? I only see a bad job that needs doing and a man so sure of himself, he's spent other people's lives to do it. Hardly sounds glorious."

"That depends," Sinja said, dropping into the language of the Galts. "Does it really need doing?"

"Yes. It does."

Sinja spread his hands, not a formal pose, but only a gesture that completed the argument. For a moment, something like tears seemed to glisten in the general's eyes, and he clapped Sinja on the shoulder. Without thinking, Sinja put his hand to the general's, clasping it hard, as if they were brothers or soldiers of the same cohort. As if their lives were somehow one. Far away, something boomed deep as a drum. Something falling. Udun, falling.

"I'll get you those hostages," Balasar said. "You take care of them for me."

"Sir," Sinja said, and stood braced at attention until the general was gone and he was alone again in the garden. Sinja swallowed twice, loosening the tightness in his throat. The maple swayed, black leaves touched with red.

In a better world, he thought, I'd have followed that man to hell.

Please the gods, let him never reach Machi.

17

>+< The watchmen Kiyan had placed at the tops of the
     towers began ringing their bells just as the sun touched
the top of the mountains to the west. Traffic stopped in the
streets below and in the palace corridors. All eyes looked up,
straining to see the color of the banners draped from the high,
distant windows. Yellow would mean that a Galtic army had
come at last, that their doom had come upon them. Red meant
that the Khai had returned. So far above the city, colors were
difficult to make out. At least to Maati's eyes, the first movement of the great signal cloth was only movement—the banners flew. It was the space of five fast, shaky breaths before he
made out the red. Otah Machi had returned.

A crowd formed at the edge of the city as the first wagons
came over the bridge. The women and children and old men
of Machi come to greet the militia that had gone out to save
the Dai-kvo. The Dai-kvo and the city and the world. Maati
pushed his way in, elbowing people aside and taking more
than one sharp rebuttal in his own ribs. The horses that pulled
the wagons were blown. The men who rode them were gray-
pale in the face and bloodied. The few who still walked,
shambled. A ragged cheer rose from the crowd and then slunk
away. A girl in a gray robe of cheap wool stepped out from the
edge of the crowd, moving toward the soldiers. From where he
stood trapped in the press of bodies, Maati could see the girl's
head as it turned, searching the coming train of men for some

particular man. Even before the first soldier reached her, Maati saw how small the group was, how many men were missing.

"Nayiit!" he shouted, hoping that his boy would hear him. "Nayiit! Over here!"

His voice was drowned. The citizens of Machi surged forward like an attack. Some of the men crossing the bridge drew back from them as if in fear, and then there was only one surging, swirling mass of people. There was no order, no control. One of the first wagons was pushed sideways from the road, the horses whinnying their protest but too tired to bolt. A man younger than Nayiit with a badly cut arm and a bruise on his face stumbled almost into Maati's arms.

"What happened?" Maati demanded of the boy. "Where's the Khai? Have you seen Nayiit Chokavi?" A blank stare was the only reply.

The chaos seemed to go on for a day, though it wasn't really more than half a hand. Then a loud, cursing voice rose over the tumult, clearing the way for the wagons. There were hurt men. Men who had to see physicians. Men who were dying. Men who were dead. The people stood aside and let the wagons pass. The sounds of weeping and hard wheels on paving stones were the only music. Maati felt breathless with dread.

As he pushed back into the city, following in the path the wagons had opened, he heard bits and snatches from the people he passed. The Khai had taken the utkhaiem and ridden for Cetani. The Galts weren't far behind. The Dai-kvo was dead. The village of the Dai-kvo was burned. There had been a blood-soaked farce of a battle. As many men were dead as still standing.

Rumor, Maati told himself. Everything is rumor and speculation until I hear it from Nayiit. Or Otah-kvo. But his chest was tight and his hands balled in fists so tight they ached when, out of breath and ears ringing, he made his way back to the library. A man in a travel-stained robe squatted beside his door, a tarp-covered crate on the ground at his side.

Nayiit. It was Nayiit. Maati found the strength to embrace

his boy, and allowed himself at last to weep. He felt Nayiit's arms around him, felt the boy soften in their shared grief, and then pull away. Maati forced himself to step back. Nayiit's expression was grim.

"Come in," Maati said. "Then tell me."

It was bad. The Galts were not on Machi's door and Otah-kvo lived, but these were the only bright points in Nayiit's long, quiet recitation. They sat in the dimming front room, shutters closed and candles unlit, while Nayiit told the tale. Maati clasped his hands together, squeezing his knuckles until they ached. The Dai-kvo was dead. The men whom Maati had known in the long years he had lived in the village were memories now. He found himself trying to remember their names, their faces. There were fewer fresh to his mind than he would have thought—the firekeeper whose kiln had been at the corner nearest Maati's cell, the old man who'd run the bathhouse, a few others. They were gone, fallen into the forgetfulness of history. The records of their names had been burned.

"We searched. We searched through everything," Nayiit said. "I brought you what we found."

With a thick rustle, he pulled the thick waxed cloth from out of the crate. Two stacks of books lay beneath it, and Maati, squatting on the floor, lifted the ancient texts out one at a time with trembling hands. Fourteen books. The library of the Dai-kvo reduced to fourteen books. He opened them, smelling the smoke in their pages, feeling the terrible lightness of the bindings. There was no unity to them—a sampling of what had happened to be in a dark corner or hidden beneath something unlikely. A history of agriculture before the First Empire. An essay on soft grammars. Jantan Noya's *Fourth Treatise on Form,* which Maati had two copies of among his own books. None of these salvaged volumes outlined the binding of an andat, or the works of ancient poets.

Stone-Made-Soft wouldn't be bound with these. And so Stone-Made-Soft wouldn't be bound, because these were all that remained. Maati felt a cold, deep calm descend upon him. Grunting, he stood up and then began pacing his rooms.

His hands went through the movements of lighting candles and lanterns without his conscious participation. His mind was as clear and sharp as broken ice.

Stone-Made-Soft could not be bound—not without years of work—and so he put aside that hope. If he and Cehmai failed to bind an andat, and quickly, the Galts would destroy them all. Nayiit, Liat, Otah, Eiah. Everyone. So something had to be done. Perhaps they could trick the Galts into believing that an andat had been bound. Perhaps they could delay the armies arrayed against them until the cold shut Machi against invasion. If he could win the long, hard months of winter in which he could scheme . . .

When the answer came to him, it was less like discovering something than remembering it. Not a flash of insight, but a familiar glow. He had, perhaps, known it would come to this.

"I think I know what to do, but we have to find Cehmai," he began, but when he turned to Nayiit, his son was curled on the floor, head pillowed by his arms. His breath was as deep and regular as tides, and his eyes were sunken and hard shut. Weariness had paled the long face, sharpening his cheeks. Maati walked as softly as he could to his bedchamber, pulled a thick blanket from his bed, and brought it to drape over Nayiit. The thick carpets were softer and warmer than a traveler's cot. There was no call to wake him.

What had happened out there—the battle, the search through the village, the trek back to Machi with this thin gift of useless books—would likely have broken most men. It had likely scarred Nayiit. Maati reached to smooth the hair on Nayiit's brow, but held back and smiled.

"All the years I should have done this," he murmured to himself. "Putting my boy to bed."

He softly closed the door to his apartments. The night was deep and dark, stars shining like diamonds on velvet, and a distant, eerie green aurora dancing far to the North. Maati stopped at the library proper, tucked the book he needed into his sleeve, and then—though the urge to find Cehmai instantly was hard to resist—made his way to the palaces, and to the apartments that Otah had given Liat.

A servant girl showed him into the main chamber. The only light was the fire in the grate, the shadows of flame dancing on the walls and across Liat's brow as she stared into them. Her hair was disarrayed, wild as a bird's nest. Her hands were in claws, trembling.

"I haven't . . . I haven't found—"

"He's fine," Maati said. "He's in my apartments, asleep."

Liat's cry startled him. She didn't walk to him so much as flow through the air, and her arms were around Maati's shoulders, embracing him. And then she stepped back and struck his shoulder hard enough to sting.

"How long has he been there?"

"Since the army came back," Maati said, rubbing his bruised flesh. "He brought books that they salvaged from the Dai-kvo. I was looking them over when—"

"And you didn't send me a runner? There are no servants in the city who you could have told to come to me? I've been sitting here chewing my own heart raw, afraid he was dead, afraid he was still out with Otah chasing the Galts, and he was at your apartments talking about *books*?"

"He's fine," Maati said. "I put a blanket over him and came to you. But he'll need food. Soup. Some wine. I thought you could take it to him."

Liat wiped away a tear with the back of her hand.

"He's all right?" she asked. Her voice had gone small.

"He's exhausted and hungry. But it's nothing a few days' rest won't heal."

"And . . . his heart? You talked with him. Is he . . . ?"

"I don't know, sweet. I'm not his mother. Take him soup. Talk with him. You'll know him better than I can."

Liat nodded. There were tears on her cheeks, but Maati knew it was only the fear working its way through. Seeing their boy would help more than anything else.

"Where are you going?" she asked.

"The poet's house."

The night air was chill, both numbing his skin and making him more acutely aware of it. Summer was failing, autumn clearing its throat. The few men and women Maati passed seemed to haunt the palaces, more spirit than flesh. They took poses of deference to him, more formal or less depending upon their stations, but the stunned expressions spoke of a single thought. The news from the broken army had spread, and everyone knew that the Dai-kvo was gone, the Galts triumphant. With even the last glow of twilight long vanished, the paths were dimmer than usual, lanterns unlit, torches burned to coal. The great halls and palaces loomed, the glimmering from behind closed shutters the only sign that they had not been abandoned. Twists of dry herbs tied with mourning cloth hung from the trees as offering to the gods. The red banner that had announced the army's arrival still hung from the high tower, grayed by the darkness. Colorless.

Maati passed through the empty gardens, and found himself smiling. He felt separate from the city around him, untouched by its despair. Perhaps even invigorated by it. There was nothing the citizens of Machi could do, no path for them to take that might somehow make things right. That was his alone. He would save the city, if it were to be saved, and if Machi fell, it would find Maati working to the end. It was that hope and the clarity of the path that lay before him that made his steps lighter and kept his blood warm.

He wondered if this strange elation was something like what Otah had felt, all those years he had lived under his false name. Perhaps holding himself at a distance from the world was how Otah had learned his confidence.

But no. That thought was an illusion. However much this felt like joy, Maati's rational mind knew it was only fear in brighter robes.

The door of the poet's house stood open. The candlelight from within glowed gold. Maati hauled himself up the stairs and through the doorway without scratching or calling out to announce his presence. The air within smelled of distilled wine and a deep earthy incense of the sort priests burned in the temples. He found Cehmai at the back of the house, eyes bloodshot and wine bowl cupped in his hands. He sat cross-legged on the floor contemplating a linked sigil of order and chaos—mother-of-pearl inlay in a panel of dark-stained rosewood. He glanced up at Maati and made an awkward attempt at some pose Maati could only guess at.

"You've found religion?" Maati asked.

"Chaos comes out of order," Cehmai said. "I can't think of a better time to contemplate the fact. And gods are all we have left now, aren't they?"

Maati reached out, brushing the panel with his fingers before tipping it backward. It slapped the floor with a sound like a book dropped from a table. Cehmai blinked, half shocked, half amused. Before he could speak, Maati fished in his sleeve, brought out the small brown volume, its leather covers worn soft as cloth by the years, and dropped it into Cehmai's lap. He didn't wait for Cehmai to pick it up before he strode back into the front room, closed the door, and dropped two fresh lumps of coal onto the fire in the grate. He found a pan, a flask of fresh water, and a brick of pressed tea leaves. That was good. They'd want that before the night was out. He also found the spent incense—ashes lighter than fresh snow on a black stone burner. He dumped them outside.

A high slate table held their notes. Thoughts and diagrams charting the new and doomed binding of Stone-Made-Soft. Maati scooped up the pages of cramped writing and put them outside as well, with the ashes. Then he carefully smoothed the writing from the wax tablets until they were smooth again, pristine. He took up the bronze-tipped stylus and scored two long vertical lines in the wax, dividing it into three equal columns. Cehmai walked into the room, his head bent over the open book. He was already more than halfway through it.

"You aren't the only one who was ever chosen to bind one of the andat," Maati said. "I even began the binding once, a long time ago. Liat-cha talked me out of trying. She was right. It would have killed me."

"You mean this?" Cehmai said. "You're going to bind Seedless?"

"It was what the Dai-kvo chose me for. Heshai wrote his binding, and his analysis of its flaws. It's too close to the original. I know that. But with the changes we'll need to make in order to include my scheme for avoiding the price of a failed binding and your fresh perspective, we can find another way."

In the first column of the wax tablet, Maati wrote *Seedless*.

"Forgive me, Maati-kvo, but will this really help? Stone-Made-Soft could have dropped their army half into the ground. Water-Moving-Down might have flooded them. But Seedless? Removing-the-Part-That-Continues doesn't have much power to stop an army."

"I can offer to kill all their crops," Maati said, writing *Heshai-kvo* at the top of the second column. "I can threaten to make every cow and pig and lamb barren. I can make every Galtic woman who's bearing a child lose it. Faced with that, they'll turn back."

His stylus paused over the head of the third column, and then he wrote his own name. He and Cehmai could outline the major points here; they could add and remove aspects of Heshai's first vision, interpret the corrections the old poet would have made, had he been given the chance. They could remake the binding, because the binding was already half-remade. If there was time. If they could find a way. If they were clever enough to save the world from the armies of Galt.

"And if they don't turn back?" Cehmai said.

"Then we'll all die. Their cities *and* ours. Check to see if that tea's ready to brew up, will you? I need your help with this, and it will go better if you're sober."

THE SCULPTURE garden of Cetani was the wonder of the city. Two bronze men in the dress of the Emperor's guard stood at the entrances at its northwest end, staring to the south and east, as if still looking to the Empire they had failed to protect. In their great, inhuman shadows, the finest work of the cities of the Khaiem had been gathered over the span of generations. There were hundreds of them, each astounding in its own fashion, under the wide branches of ash and oak with leaves the color of gold. The dragons of Chaos writhed along one long wall, their scales shining with red lacquer and worked silver, chips of lapis and enamel white as milk. In a shadowed niche, Shian Sho, last of the Emperors, sat worked in white marble on a high dais, his head sunk despairingly in his hands. It was a piece done after the Empire's fall. If the Emperor had seen himself shown with such little dignity, the sculptor would have been lucky to have a fast death. But the drape of the final Emperor's robes made the stone seem supple as linen, and the despair and thoughtfulness of the dead man's expression spoke of a time nine generations past when the world had torn itself apart. The sculptor who had found Shian Sho in this stone had lived through that time and had put the burden of his heart into this monument; this empty sepulcher for his age. Otah suspected that no man since then had looked upon it and understood. Not until now.

The Khai Cetani stood at the foot of a life-size bronze of a robed woman with eagle's wings rising wide-spread from her shoulders. He was younger than Otah by perhaps five years, gray only beginning to appear in his night-black hair. His gaze flickered over Otah, giving no sign of the thoughts behind his eyes. Otah felt a moment's self-consciousness at his travel-worn robes and incipient, moth-eaten beard. He took a pose of greeting appropriate for two people of equal status and saw the Khai Cetani hesitate for a moment before returning it. It was likely it was the first time in years anyone had approached him with so little reverence.

"My counselors have told me of your suggestion, my good friend Machi," the Khai Cetani said. "I must say I was . . . surprised. You can't truly expect us to abandon Cetani without a fight."

"You'll lose," Otah said.

"We are a city of fifty thousand people. These invaders of yours are at most five."

"They're soldiers. They know what they're doing. You might slow them, but you won't stop them."

The Khai Cetani sat, crossing his legs. His smile was almost a sneer.

"You think because you failed, no one else can succeed?"

"I think if we had a season, perhaps two, to build an army, we might withstand them. Hire mercenaries to train the men, drill them, build walls around at least the inner reaches of the cities, and we might stand a chance. As it is, we don't. I've seen what they did to the village of the Dai-kvo. I've had reports from Yalakeht. Amnat-Tan will fall if it hasn't already. They will come here next. You have fifty thousand, including the infirm and the aged and children too young to hold a sword. You don't have weapons enough or armor or experience. My proposal is our best hope."

It was an argument he had wrestled with through many of the long nights of his journey to the North. Force of arms would not stop the Galts. Slowing them, letting the winter come and protect them for the long, dark months in which no attacking force would survive the fields of ice and brutally cold nights, winning time for the poets to work a little miracle, bind one of the andat and save them all—it was a thin hope but it was the best they had. And slowly, during the days swaying on horseback and nights sitting by smoldering braziers, Otah had found the plan that he believed would win him this respite. Now if the Khai Cetani would simply see the need of it.

"If you bring your people to Machi, we will have twice as many people who can take the field against the Galts. And if you will do what I've suggested with the coal and food, the Galts will be much worse for the travel than we will be."

"And Cetani will fall without resistance. We will roll over like a soft quarter whore," the Khai Cetani said. "It's simple enough for you to sacrifice my city, isn't it?"

"None of this is easy. But simple? Yes, it's simple. Bring your people to Machi. Bring all the food you can carry and burn what you can't. Mix hard coal in with the soft, so that what we leave behind for the Galts will burn too hot in their steam wagons, and give me the loan of five hundred of your best men. I'll give you a winter and the library of Machi. Between your poet and the two at my court—"

"I have no poet."

Otah took a pose of query.

"He died half a month ago, trying to regain his andat," the Khai Cetani said. "His skin went black as a new bruise and his bones all shattered. I have no poet. All I have is a city, and I won't give it away for nothing!"

The Khai Cetani's words ended in a shout. His face was red with fury. And with fear. There was no more that Otah could say now that would sway him, but years in the gentleman's trade had taught Otah something about negotiations that the Khaiem had never known. He nodded and took a pose that formally withdrew him from the conversation.

"You and your men will stay here," the Khai Cetani said, continuing to speak despite Otah's gesture. "We will make our stand here, at Cetani. We will not fall."

"You will," Otah said. "And my men will leave in the morning, with me."

The Khai Cetani was breathing fast, as if he had run a race. Otah took a pose of farewell, then turned and strode from the garden. To the east, clouds darkened the horizon. The scent of coming rain touched the air. Otah's armsmen and servants fell in with him. The eyes of Cetani's utkhaiem were on the little procession as Otah walked to the apartments granted him by the Khai. He was a curiosity—one of the Khaiem walking with the swagger of a man who'd sat too long on a horse, his retinue looking more like a mercenary captain's crew than courtiers. And Otah suspected that martial air, however undeserved, would serve him. He scowled the way he imagined Sinja might have in his place.

Ashua Radaani was sitting at the fire grate deep in conversation with Saya the blacksmith when Otah entered the wide hall that served as the center of the visitors' palace. Battle and loss and the common enemy of Galt had mixed with the shared recognition of competence to make the two men something like friends. They stood and took poses of respect and welcome that Otah waved away. He sat on a low cushion by the fire and sent his servant boy to find them tea and something to eat.

"It didn't go well, I take it," Radaani said.

"It didn't go well and it didn't go badly," Otah said. "He's smart enough to be frightened. That's good. I was afraid he'd be certain of himself. But his poet's dead. Tried to recapture his andat and paid its price."

Radaani sighed.

"Did he agree to your plan, Most High?" Saya asked.

"No," Otah said. "He's determined that Cetani not fall without a fight. I've told him we're leaving with him or without him. How was your hunting, Ashua-cha?"

Radaani leaned forward. His features were thinner than they had been in Machi, and the ring he turned on his finger wasn't so snug as it had once been.

"The court's frightened," he said. "There are a few people who came here from Yalakeht, and the stories . . . well, either they've grown in the telling, or it wasn't pretty there. And the couriers from Amnat-Tan haven't come the last two days."

"That's bad," Otah said. "Will we have time, do you think?"

"I don't know," Ashua said. He seemed to search for more words, but in the end only shook his head.

"Get the men ready," Otah said. "We'll give Cetani tomorrow to join us. After that, we'll head home. With enough time, we might be able to tear up some sections of the road behind us. Slow down the Galts, even if we can't do all we hoped against them."

"What about the books?" Saya asked. "If their poet's dead, it isn't as if they'll have need of them. Perhaps ours would make something of them."

"I can ask," Otah said. "With luck, we'll have the books and the people and the food stores."

"But the Khai refused you, Most High," Saya said.

Otah smiled and shook his head. Only now that he found himself a moment to rest did the weariness drag at him. He tried to think how many days he'd been riding from first light to last. A lifetime, it felt like. He remembered the man who'd left Machi to save the Dai-kvo, but it no longer felt like something he'd done himself. He was changing. His heart still ached at the thought of Kiyan and Eiah and Danat. His apprehension at the struggle still before him was no less. And still, he was not the man he had once been, and to his surprise and unease, the man he was becoming seemed quite natural.

"Most High?" Saya repeated.

"Walking away from a negotiation isn't the same as ending it," Otah said. "Cetani's proud and he's lost, but he's not a fool. He wants to do what we're asking of him. He just hasn't found the way to say yes."

"You sound sure of that," Saya said.

Otah chose his words carefully.

"If someone had come to me after that battle and said that they knew what to do, that they would take the responsibility, I would have given it to them. And that's just what I've offered him," Otah said. "The Khai Cetani will call for me. Tonight."

He was wrong. The Khai Cetani didn't send for him until the next morning.

The man's eyes were bloodshot, his face slack from worry and exhaustion. Otah doubted the Khai Cetani had slept since they had spoken, and perhaps not for days before that. Through the wide, unshuttered windows, the morning was cold and gray, low clouds seeming to bring the sky no higher than a sparrow might fly. Otah sat on the divan set for him—rich velvet cloth studded with tiny pearls and silver thread, but smelling of dust and age. The most powerful man in Cetani sat across from him on an identical seat. That alone was a concession, and Otah noted it without giving sign one way or the other.

The Khai Cetani motioned the servants to leave them. From the hesitation and surprised glances, Otah took it that he'd rarely done so before. Some men, he supposed, were more comfortable with the constant attention.

"Convince me," the Khai Cetani said when the doors were pulled closed and they were alone.

Otah took a pose of query.

"That you're right," the Khai said. "Convince me that you're right."

There was a hunger in the request, almost a need. Otah took a deep breath and let it out slowly. The fire in the grate popped and shifted while he gathered his thoughts. He had turned his plans over in his mind since he'd left the ruin of the Dai-kvo's village. He'd honed them and tested them and stayed up late into the night despairing at their improbability only to wake in the morning convinced once more. The simplest answer was the best here, and he knew that, but still it was a struggle to find the words that made his mind clear.

"On the field, we can't match them," he said. "If we stay here and face them, we'll lose outright. There's nothing that can keep Cetani from falling to them. But they have two weaknesses. First, the steam wagons. They let them move faster than any group their size should be able to, but they're dangerous. It's a price they're prepared to pay, but they have underestimated the risks. If we start by breaking those—"

"The coal?"

Otah took a confirming pose.

"They aren't built for forge coal," he said. "And the men we're facing? They're soldiers, not smiths and ironmongers. There's no reason for them to look too closely at what they raid out of your stocks. Especially when they're pushing to get to Machi before the winter comes. If we leave them mixed coal, it'll burn too hot. The seams of their metalwork will soften, if the grates don't simply melt out from underneath."

"And so they have to come on foot or by horse?"

Otah remembered the twisted metal from the Dai-kvo's village and allowed himself a smile.

"When those wagons break, it's more than only stopping. They'll lose men just from that, and if we play it well, we can use the confusion to make things worse for them. And there's the other thing. They know we're going to lose. They have the strength, and we're unprepared. The only time we've faced them head-on, we were slaughtered. They know that we can't effectively fight them."

"That's a weakness?" the Khai Cetani asked.

"Yes. It keeps them from paying attention. To them, it's already over. Everything's certain but the details. That something else might happen isn't likely to occur to them. Why should it?"

The Khai Cetani looked into the fire. The flames seemed to glitter in his dark eyes. When he spoke, his voice was grim.

"They've made all the same mistakes we did."

Otah considered that for a moment before nodding.

"The Galts understand war," he said. "They're the best teachers I have. And so I'll do to them what they did to us."

"And to do that, you would have me—Khai of my own city—abandon Cetani to follow *your* lead?"

"Yes," Otah said.

The Khai sat in silence for a long time, then rose. The rustle of his robes as he walked to the window was the only sound. Otah waited as the man looked out over the city. Over Cetani, the city for which this man had killed his brothers, for which he had given up his name. Otah felt the tension in his own back and neck. He was asking this man to abandon everything, to walk away from the only role he had played in his life. Cetani would fall. It would be sacked. Even if everything went perfectly, there might be nothing to rebuild. And what would a Khai be if there was no city left him?

Many years before, Otah had asked another man to do the right thing, even though it would cost him his honor and prestige and the only place he had in the world. Heshai-kvo had refused, and he had died for the decision.

"Most High," Otah began, but the Khai Cetani held up a hand to stop him without even so much as looking back. Otah could see it in the man's shoulders in the moment the decision was made; they lifted as if a burden had been taken from him.

18

>+< Even the winter she had passed in Yalakeht had not
prepared Liat for the fickleness of seasons in the North.
Each day now was noticeably shorter than the one before, and
even when the afternoons were warm, the sun pressing down
benignly on her face, the nights were suddenly bitter. In the
gardens, the leaves all lost their green at once, as if by con-
spiracy. It was unlike the near-imperceptible changes in the
summer cities. In Saraykeht, autumn was a slow, lingering
thing; the warmth of the world made a long good-bye. Things
came faster here, and Liat found the pace disturbing. She was
a woman of the South, and abrupt change uneased her.

For instance, she thought as she sipped smoky tea in her
apartments, she still imagined herself a businesswoman of
Saraykeht. Had anyone asked of her work, she would have
spoken of the combing rooms, the warehouses. Had anyone
asked of her home, she would have described the seafront of
Saraykeht, the scent of the ocean, the babble of a hundred lan-
guages. She would have pictured the brick-built house she'd
taken over when Amat Kyaan had died, and the little bedroom
with its window half-choked with vines. She hadn't seen that
city in over a year, and wouldn't go back now before the
spring at best.

At best.

At worst, Saraykeht itself might be gone. Or she might not
live to see summer again.

The city in which she now passed her days was suffering from change as well. Small shrines with images of the vanished andat had begun to appear in the niches between buildings, as if a few flowers and candles could coax them back. The temples had been filled every day by men and women who might not have sat before a priest in years. The beggars singing with boxes at their feet all chose songs about redemption and the return of things lost.

She sipped her tea. It was no longer hot enough to scald her lips, but it felt good drinking it. It warmed her throat like wine, only without the easing in her muscles or the softness in her mind. The morning before her was full—coordinating the movement of food and fuel into the tunnels below Machi, the raising of stores into the high towers where they would wait out the cold of winter. There wasn't time for dark thoughts. And yet the darkness came whether she courted it or not.

She looked up at the sound of the door. Nayiit stepped in. The nights were not so long or so cold as to keep him in his rooms. Liat put down her bowl.

"Good morning, Mother," he said as he sat on a cushion beside the fire. "You're up early."

"Not particularly," Liat said.

"No?" Nayiit said, and then smiled the disarming, rueful smile that would always and forever mark him as the son of Otah Machi. "No, I suppose not. May I?"

Liat gestured her permission, and Nayiit poured himself a bowl of the tea. He looked tired, and it was more than a night spent in teahouses and the baths. Something had changed while he'd been gone. She had thought at first that it was only exhaustion. When she'd found him asleep on Maati's floor, he had been half-dead from his time on the road and visibly thinner. But since then he'd rested and eaten, and still there was something behind his eyes. An echo of her own bleak thoughts, perhaps.

"I failed him," Nayiit said. Liat blinked and sat back in her chair. Nayiit tilted his head. "It's what you were wondering, ne? What's been eating the boy? Why can't he sleep anymore?

I failed the Khai. I had his good opinion. There was a time that he valued my counsel and listened to me, even when I had unpleasant things to say. And then I failed him. And he sent me away."

"You didn't fail—"

"I did. Mother, I love you, and I know that you'd move the stars for me if you could, but I failed. Your son can fail," Nayiit said. He put down his bowl with a sharp click, and Liat wondered if perhaps he was still just a bit tipsy from his night's revelry. Drink sometimes made her maudlin too. "I'm not a good man, Mother. I'm not. I have left my wife and my child. I have slept with half the women I've met since we left home. I lost the Khai's trust—"

"Nayiit—"

"I killed those men."

His face was still as stone, but a tear crept from the corner of his eye. Liat slid down from her seat to kneel on the floor beside him. She put her hand on his, but Nayiit didn't move.

"I called the retreat," he said. "I saw them fighting, and the Galts were everywhere. They were all around us. All I could think was that they needed to get away. I was calling signals. I knew how to call the retreat, and I did it. And they died. Every man that fell because we ran is someone I killed. And he knew it. The Khai. He knew it, and it's why he sent me back here."

"That battle was doomed from the start," Liat said. "They outnumbered you; they were veterans. Your men were exhausted laborers and huntsmen. If what happened out there is anyone's fault, it's Otah's."

"You don't understand," he said. His voice wasn't angry, only tired. "I want to be a good man. And I'm not. For a time, I thought I was. I thought I *could* be. I was wrong."

Liat felt a thickness at the back of her throat. She forced a smile, half-rose, and kissed him on the top of his head, where the bones hadn't yet grown closed the first time she'd held him.

"Then do better," she said. "As long as you're alive, the next thing you do can be a good one, ne? Besides which, of course you're a good man. Only good men worry about whether they're bad."

Nayiit chuckled. The darkness slid back to the place it had been. Not gone, but hidden.

"And what do bad men worry about?" he asked.

Liat shrugged and started to answer him, but the bells began to ring. It took half a breath for Liat to recall what the deep chiming alarm meant. She didn't remember going to the window; she couldn't say how Nayiit had come to be at her side. She squinted against the blue-yellow light of morning, trying to make out the banners hanging from the towers high above.

"Is it red or yellow?" Liat asked.

"Gods," Nayiit said. "Look at that."

His gaze was nearer the ground. Liat looked to the south. The low cloud of dust seemed to cover half the horizon. Otah's remaining men couldn't have done that. It wasn't him. The Galts had come to Machi. Liat stepped back from the window, her hands gripping the folds of her robe just over her heart.

"We have to get Kiyan-cha," she said. "We have to get Kiyan-cha and the children. And Maati. We have to get them out before—"

"Red," Nayiit said.

Liat shook her head, uncertain for a moment what he meant. Nayiit pointed to the high dark tower and spoke over the still-ringing bells.

"The banner's red," he said. "It's not the Galts. It's the Khai."

Only it wasn't. The couriers reached Kiyan just before Liat did, so when she entered Kiyan-cha's meeting rooms, she found Otah's wife with a thick letter—seams ripped, seal broken—lying abandoned in her lap and an expression equal parts disbelief and outrage on her pale face.

"He's an idiot," Kiyan said. "He's a self-aggrandizing, half-blind idiot who can't think two thoughts in a straight line."

Liat took a pose that asked the question.

"My husband," Kiyan said, color coming at last to her cheeks. "He's sent us another whole *city*."

Cetani, nearest neighbor of Machi, had emptied itself. The couriers had arrived just before the fastest carts. The dust that Liat had mistaken for an army was only the first wave of tens of thousands of men and women—their stores of grains, their chickens and ducks and goats, whatever small precious things they could not bring themselves to leave behind. Otah's letter explained that they were in need of shelter, that Machi should do its best for them. The tone of the words was apologetic, but only for someone who knew the man well. Only to women like themselves. Kiyan held Liat's arm as if for support as they walked together to the bridge outside the city where they awaited her.

The man who stood at the middle point in the bridge wore an elegant robe—black silk shot with yellow—that was only slightly disarrayed by his travels. Servants and armsmen of Machi parted for Kiyan, allowing her passage onto the bridge's western end. Liat tried to disengage, but Kiyan's grip didn't lessen, and so they walked out together. On seeing them, the man took a pose of greeting appropriate for a man of lower rank to the wife of a more prestigious man. This was not the Khai Cetani, then, but some member of the Cetani utkhaiem.

"I have been sent to speak to the first wife of the Khai Machi," he said.

"I am the Khai's only wife," Kiyan said.

He took this odd information in stride, turning his attention wholly to Kiyan. Liat felt awkward and out of place, and oddly quite protective of the woman at her side.

"Kiyan-cha," the man said. "I am Kamath Vauamnat, voice of House Vauamnat. The Khai Cetani has sent us here at your husband's invitation. The army of Galt is still some days behind us, but it is coming. Our city . . ."

Something changed in the courtier's face. It was unlike anything Liat had seen before, except perhaps an actor who in the midst of declaiming some epic has forgotten the words. The mask and distance of etiquette failed, and the words he spoke became genuine.

"Our city's gone. We have what we're carrying. We need your help."

Only Liat was near enough to Kiyan to hear the tiny sigh that escaped before she spoke.

"How could I refuse you?" she said. "I am utterly unprepared, but if you will bring your people across the bridge and make them ready, I will find them places here."

The man took a pose of gratitude, and Kiyan turned back, Liat still at her side, and walked back to the bank where her people waited.

"We'll need something like shelter for these people," Kiyan said, under her breath. "Someplace we can keep them out of the rain until we can find . . . someplace."

"They won't all fit," Liat said. "We can put them in the tunnels, but then there's no place for all of us to go when winter comes. There's too many of them, and they can't have carried enough food to see them through until spring. And we're stretched thin as it is."

"We'll stretch thinner," Kiyan said.

The rest of the day was a single long emergency, events and needs and decisions coming in waves and overlapping each other like the scales of a snake. Liat found herself at the large and growing camp that was forming as the refugees of Cetani reached the bridge. Thankfully, the bridge was only the width of eight men walking abreast, and it kept the flow of humanity and cattle and carts to a speed that was almost manageable. Liat only had to school herself not to look across the water to the larger, shapeless mass of people still waiting to cross. Liat motioned them to different places, the ones too frail or ill to survive another night in the open, the ones robust enough that they might be put to work. There were old men, children, babes hanging in their mothers' exhausted arms.

Liat felt as if she were being asked to engineer a new city of tents and cook fires. They came in the hundreds. In the thousands. Night had fallen before the last man crossed, and Liat could see fires on the far side, camps made by those who'd given up hope of crossing today. Liat sat on the smooth stone rail at the bridge's end and let the aches in her feet and back and legs complain to her. It had been an excruciating day, and the work was far from ended. But at least the refugees were in tents sent out from Machi, safe from the cold. The food carts of Machi had also come out from the city, making their way through the crowds with garlic sausages and honeyed almonds and bowls of noodles and beef. There were even songs. Over the constant frigid rushing of the water, there was the sound of flutes and drums and voices. The temptation to close her eyes was unbearable, and yet. And yet.

I want to be a good man, he'd said. *And I'm not.*

With a sigh she began the long trek back to the city, to the palaces, to Kiyan and Maati and the bathhouses and her bed. The city, as she passed through its streets, was alive. The refugees of Cetani had not all waited in the camp. Or perhaps Kiyan had meant to start bringing them into the city. Whatever the intention had been, they had come, and Machi had poured itself out to make them welcome, to offer them food and wine and comfort, to pull news and gossip from them. The sun was gone, and the darkness was cold, and yet the city was full as a street fair. And as chaotic.

She found Kiyan in the palaces looking as exhausted as she herself felt. Otah's wife waved her near to the long, broad table. Wives of the utkhaiem were consulting one another, writing figures on paper, issuing orders to wide-eyed servants. It was like the middle of a trading company at the height of the cotton harvest, and Liat found it strangely comforting.

"It can be done," Kiyan said. "It won't be pleasant, but it can be done. I've had word from the Poinyat that we can use their mines, and I'm expecting the Daikani any time now."

"The mines?" Liat said. The exhaustion made her slow to understand.

"We'll have to put people in them. They're deep enough to stay warm. It's like living in the tunnels under the city, only rougher. The ones in the plain will even have their own water. There's food and sewage to worry about, but I've sent Jaini Radaani to speak with the engineers, and if she can't convince them to find a solution, I'll be quite surprised."

"That's good," Liat said. "Things at the bridge are under control. We've set up a tent for the physicians down there, and there's food enough. There will be more tomorrow, but I think they've all been seen to."

"Gods, Liat-cha. You look like death and you're cold. Let me have someone see you to the baths, get you warm. Have you eaten?"

She hadn't, but she pushed the thought aside.

"I need something from you, Kiyan-cha."

"Ask."

"Nayiit. He needs . . . something. He needs something to do. Something that he can be proud of. He came back from the battle . . ."

"I know," Kiyan said. "I know what happened there. It was in Otah's letter."

"He needs to help," Liat said, surprised at the pleading tone of her own voice. She hadn't known she felt so desperate for him. "He needs to *matter.*"

Kiyan nodded slowly, then leaned close and kissed Liat's cheek. The woman's lips felt almost hot against Liat's chilled skin.

"I understand, Liat-kya," she said. "Go and rest. I'll see to it. I promise you."

Weeping with fatigue, Liat found her way to her apartments, to her bedchamber, to her bed. Her belly ached with hunger, but she only drank the full carafe of water the servants had left at her bedside. By the time her body learned that it had been tricked, she would already be asleep. She closed her eyes for a moment before pulling off her robes and woke, still dressed, in the morning. The light sifted through the shutters, pressing in at the seams. The night candle was a lump of spent wax, and the air didn't smell of the dying wick.

There was something, though. Pork. Bread. Liat sat up, her head light.

She stripped off yesterday's robes, sticky with sleep sweat, and pulled on a simple sitting robe of thick gray wool. When she stepped out to the main rooms, Kiyan was still arranging the meal on its table.

Thick slices of pink-white meat, bread so fresh it still steamed, trout baked with lemon and salt, poached pears on a silver plate. And a teapot that smelled of white tea and honey. Liat's stomach woke with a sharp pang.

"They told me you hadn't eaten last night," she said. "Either of you. I thought I might bring along something to keep you breathing."

"Kiyan-cha . . ." Liat began, then broke off and simply took a pose of gratitude. Kiyan smiled. She was a beautiful woman, and age was treating her gently. The intelligence in her eyes was matched by the humor. Otah was lucky, Liat thought, to have her.

"It's a trick, really," Kiyan said. "I've come pretending to be a servant girl, when I actually want to speak with Nayiit. If he's awake."

"I am."

His voice came from the shadows of his bedchambers. Nayiit stepped out. His hair pointed in a hundred directions. His eyes were red and puffy. A thin sprinkling of stubble cast a shadow on his jaw. Kiyan took a pose of greeting. He returned it.

"How can I be of service, Kiyan-cha?" he asked. Liat could tell from the too-precise diction that he'd spent his night drinking. He closed his bedroom doors behind him as he stepped in, and Liat more than half thought it was to protect the privacy of whatever woman was sleeping in his bed. Something passed across Kiyan's sharp features; it might have been compassion or sorrow, understanding or recognition. Liat couldn't say, and it was gone almost as soon as it came.

"That's the question, Nayiit-cha. I have something to ask of you. It may come to nothing, and if you should have to act upon my request, I'm afraid I won't be in a position to repay you."

Nayiit came forward slowly and sat at the table. Kiyan filled a plate for him as she spoke, casual as if she were a wayhouse keeper, and he a simple guest.

"You've heard the gossip from Cetani, I assume," she said.

"They've fled before the Galts. The Khai—both of them—are in the rear. To protect the people if the Galts come from behind."

"Yes," Kiyan said. "It's actually more complex than that. Otah has invented a scheme. If it works, he may win us a few months. Perhaps through the winter. If not, I think we can assume the Galts will be here shortly after the last of our cousins from Cetani have arrived."

It was a casual way to express the raw fear that every one of them might die violently before the first frost came. Our lives are measured in days now, Liat thought. But Kiyan had not paused to let the thought grow.

"There is an old mine a day's ride to the north of Machi. It was dug when the first Khai Machi set up residence here. It's been tapped out for generations, but the tunnels are still there. I've been quietly moving supplies to it. A bit of food. Blankets. Coal. A few boxes of gold and jewels. Enough for a few people to survive a winter and still have enough to slip across the passes and into the Westlands when spring came."

Nayiit took a pose that accepted all she said. Kiyan smiled and leaned forward to touch Nayiit's hands with her own. She seemed at ease except for the tears that had gathered in her eyes.

"If the Galts come," she said, "will you take Eiah and Danat there? Will you . . ."

Kiyan stopped, her smile crumbling. She visibly gathered herself. A long, slow breath. And even still, when she spoke, it was hardly more than a whisper.

"If they come, will you protect my children?"

You brilliant, vicious snake, Liat thought. You glorious bitch. You'd ask him to love your son. You'd make caring for

Danat the proof that my boy's a decent man. And you're doing it because I *asked* you to.

It's perfect.

"I would be honored," Nayiit said. The sound of his voice and the awestruck expression in his eyes were all that Liat needed to see how well Kiyan had chosen.

"Thank you, Nayiit-kya," Kiyan said. She looked over to Liat, and her eyes were guarded. They both knew what had happened here. Liat carefully took a pose of thanks, unsure as she did what precisely she meant by it.

THE LIBRARY of Cetani was much smaller than Machi's. Perhaps a third as many books and codices, not more than half as many scrolls. They arrived on Maati's doorway in sacks and baskets, crates and wooden boxes. A letter accompanied them, hardly more than a terse note with Otah's seal on it, telling him that there was no living poet to ask what texts would be of use, that as a result he'd sent everything, and expressing hope that these might help. There was no mention of the Galts or the Dai-kvo or the dead. Otah seemed to assume that Maati would understand how dire the situation was, how much depended on him and on Cehmai.

He was right. Maati understood.

He'd left Cehmai in the library, looking over their new acquisitions, while he sat in the main room of his apartments, marking out grammars and forms. How Heshai had bound Seedless, what he would have done differently in retrospect, and the variations that Maati could make—different words and structures, images and metaphors that would serve the same purpose without coming too near the original. His knuckles ached, and his mind felt woolly. It was hard to say how far into the work they'd come. Perhaps as much as a third. Perhaps less. The hardest part would come at the end; once the binding was mapped out and drafted, there was the careful process of going through, image by image, and checking to see that there were no ambiguities, no unintended meanings, no contradictions where the power of the andat might loop back upon itself and break his hold and himself.

Outside, the wind was blowing cold as it had since the middle morning. The city of tents that had sprung up at Machi's feet would be an unpleasant place tonight. Liat had been entirely absent these last four days, helping to find Cetani a place within Machi. It was just as well, he supposed. If she were here, he'd only want to talk with her. Speak with her. He'd want to hold her. Enough time for those little pleasures when Seedless was bound and the world was set right. Whatever that meant anymore.

The scratch at his door was an annoyance and a relief both. He called out his permission, and the door swung open. Nayiit ducked into the room, an apologetic smile on his face. Behind him, a small figure waddled—Danat wrapped in robes and cloaks until he seemed almost as wide as tall. Maati rose, his back and knees protesting from having been too long in one position.

"I'm sorry, Father," Nayiit said. "I told Danat-cha that you might be busy. . . ."

"Nothing that can't wait a hand or two," Maati said, waving them in. "It might be best, really, if I step away from it all. After a while, it all starts looking the same."

Nayiit chuckled and took a pose that expressed his sympathy. Danat, red-cheeked, shifted his gaze shyly from one man to the other. Maati nodded a question to Nayiit.

"Danat wanted to ask you something," Nayiit said, and squatted down so that his eyes were on a level with the child's. His smile was gentle, encouraging. A favorite uncle helping his nephew over some simple childhood fear. Maati felt the sudden powerful regret that he had never met Nayiit's wife, never seen his child. "Go ahead, Danat-kya. We came so that you could ask, and Maati-cha's here. Do it like we practiced."

Danat turned to Maati, blushing furiously, and took a pose of respect made awkward by the thickness of cloth around his small arms; then he began pulling books out from beneath his robes and placing them one by one in a neat pile before Maati. When the last of them had appeared, Danat shot a glance at Nayiit who answered with an approving pose.

"Excuse me, Maati-cha," Danat said, his face screwed into a knot of concentration, his words choppy from being rehearsed. "Papa-kya's still not back. And I've finished all these. I wondered . . ."

The words fell to a mumble. Maati smiled and shook his head.

"You'll have to speak louder," Nayiit said. "He can't hear you."

"I wondered if you had any others I could read," the boy said, staring at his own feet as if he'd asked for the moon on a ribbon and feared to be mocked for it.

Behind him, where the boy couldn't see, Nayiit grinned. This is who he would be, Maati thought. This is the kind of father my boy would be.

"Well," he said aloud. "We might be able to find something. Come with me."

He led them out and along the gravel path to the library's entrance. The air had a bite to it. He could feel the color coming to his own cheeks. When he'd been young, a child-poet younger than Nayiit, he'd spent his terrible winter in Saraykeht with Seedless and Otah and Liat. In the summer cities, this chill would have been the depth of winter. In the North, it was only the first breath of autumn.

Cehmai looked up when they came in, a scroll case of shattered silk in his hand. A smear of dust marked his cheek like ashes. Boxes and crates lay about the main room, stacked man-high. One of the couches was piled with scrolls that hadn't been looked over, two others with the ones that had. The air was thick with the smells of dust and parchment and old binder's paste. Danat stood in the doorway, his eyes wide, his mouth open. Nayiit stepped around him and drew the boy in, sliding the doors closed behind them. Cehmai nodded his question.

"Danat was asking if we had any other books," Maati said.

"You have *all* of them," the boy said, awe in his voice.

Maati chuckled, and then felt the mirth and simple pleasure fade. The shelves and crates, boxes and piled volumes surrounded them.

"Yes," he said. "Yes, we have all of them."

19

>+<   "How many do we have?" Otah asked.

     The bows had been made for killing bears. Each one stood taller than a man, the bow itself made of ash and horn, the drawstring of wire. It took a man sitting down and using both legs to draw it back. The arrows were blackened oak shafts as long as short spears. The tips—usually a wide, crossed head like twined knives—had been replaced by hard steel points made to punch through metal. The chief huntsman of the Khai Cetani nudged one with his toe, spat, and looked out through the trees toward the road below them.

    "Two dozen," he said. His voice had a Western drawl. "Sixty shafts, more or less."

    "More or less?" the Khai Cetani demanded.

    "We're fashioning more, Most High," the huntsman said.

    "How many men do we have who can use them?" Otah asked. "It won't matter if we have a thousand bows if there's only five men who can aim them."

    "Bear hunters are rare," the huntsman said. "There aren't any old ones."

    "How many?"

    "Eight who are good. Twice that who know how the bow works. With practice . . ."

    The Khai Cetani frowned deeply, and turned to Otah. Otah chewed at the inside of his lip and looked down and to the east. The trees here were thick, unlike the plains nearer to the newly abandoned city where the need for lumber had created new-made meadows. The leaves were red and gold, bright as fire. The days were still warm enough at their height, but the nights were cold and getting colder. Soon it would be freezing before morning, and soon after that—a week, ten days—it wouldn't be thawing by midday.

"We have two and a half thousand men," Otah said. "And you're telling me only eight can work these things?"

"They're not good for much apart from hunting big animals that need killing fast. And there aren't many who care to do that, if they can help it," the huntsman said. "Why learn something with no use?"

Otah squatted and took one of the bows in his hand. It was heavier than it looked. It would be able to throw the bolts hard. Otah wondered how close they could afford to get to the road. Too far back, and the trees would offer as much protection to the Galts as cover for Otah's men. Too close, and they'd be seen before the time came. It wouldn't take much skill to hit the belly of a steam wagon if you were near enough. He tossed the bow from hand to hand as he weighed the risks.

"Go ask for volunteers," Otah said. "Ask on both sides of the road. Anyone who says they're willing, test them. Take the twenty best."

"A man who doesn't know what he's doing with this can scrape the meat off his legs," the huntsman said.

Otah stopped tossing the bow and turned to consider the man. The huntsman blushed, realizing what he had just said and to whom. He took a pose of obeisance and backed away from the two Khaiem, folding himself in among the trees and vanishing. The Khai Cetani sighed and took a pose of apology.

"He's a good enough man," he said, "but he forgets his place."

"He isn't wrong," Otah said. "If this were a better time to have our orders questioned, I'd have listened to him. But then, if it were a better time, we wouldn't be out here."

The last of the men and women fleeing Cetani had passed them five days before, carts and wagons and sacks slung over hunched backs. For five days, the combined forces of Cetani and Machi had haunted these woods, sharpening their weapons and planning the attack. And growing bored and hungry and cold. Two nights ago, Otah had ordered an end to all fires. The smoke would give them away, and the prospect of a half-sleeping man dropping a stray ember on the forest floor was too likely. The men grumbled, but enough of them saw the sense of it that the edict hadn't been ignored. Not yet.

It wouldn't be many more days, though. If the Galts didn't come, the men would grow restive and careless, and when the time came, it would be the battle before the Dai-kvo again, only this time, the Galts would march into Machi. The bodies left in the streets wouldn't be of poets. They would be the families of every man in the hidden clumps that dotted the hills. Their mothers, fathers, lovers, children. Everyone they knew. Everyone that remained. That was good for another day. Perhaps two.

"You're thinking of the frost," the Khai Cetani said. "You're worried that it's going to come and drop our screen of leaves before the Galts do."

Otah smiled.

"No, actually, I'd been worrying about other things entirely. Thank you for distracting me."

The Khai Cetani actually chuckled.

"I'll go and speak with my leaders," he said, clapping Otah on the shoulder. "Keep their spirits up."

"I'll do the same," Otah said. "It's coming. They'll be here soon."

The camps had been divided. Groups of men no larger than twenty. Only one stayed close to the road on either side. The others fanned out to the west. When the Galts appeared at the edge of the last cleared forest, runners would come from the watch camps, and the men would make their way to the road. Trees already had been felled at four places along the path—two before they reached the forest, another halfway to the hill on which Otah now stood, and the last where the road turned a little to the south and then west again toward Machi.

The first time they were forced to stop, they would expect the attack. By the fourth, Otah hoped they would only think it another delay. The mixed coal would have their steam wagons running hotter than they intended. The bear-hunting bows would prick the steel chambers. In the chaos, the armies would appear, falling on the Galts' long vulnerable flanks. If it all went well. If the plan worked. If not, then the gods alone knew how the fight would end.

Night fell cold. The wide cloudless sky seemed to pull the warmth of the day and land up into it, and Otah, most honored and powerful man in his city, wrapped an extra cloak around himself and settled down against a tree, Ashua Radaani snoring gently at his side. He had expected his dreams to be troubled, but instead he found himself ice fishing, and the fish he saw moving below the ice were also Kiyan and his children, playing with him, tugging at the line and then darting away. A trout that was also Kiyan in a silver-blue robe leapt from the water—with the logic of dreams frozen and yet unfrozen—and splashed back down to Otah's delight when a rough hand shook him awake. Dawn was threatening, gray and rose in the east, and Saya the blacksmith towered over him, cheeks so red they seemed dark in the dim light, nose running, and a grin showing his teeth.

"They've come, Most High."

Otah leapt up, his back and hip aching from the cold night and the unforgiving ground. To the east, smoke rose in a wall. Coal smoke from the Galtic wagons strung along the road from Cetani like beads on a string. It was earlier in the day than he'd expected them, and as he pulled on his makeshift armor of boiled leather and metal scale, his mind leapt ahead, guessing at what tactical advantages the Galtic captain intended by arriving with the dawn.

None, of course. They had no way to know Otah's men were there. And still, Otah considered how the light would strike the road, the trees, what it would make visible and what it would hide. He could no more stop his mind than call down the stars.

The sun found the highest reaches of the smoke first, where it had diffused almost to nothing. Closer to the ground, the smoke was already visibly nearer. The Galts had passed the third log barrier while the runners had come to him. The fourth lay in wait where Otah could see it. The innocent forest was alive with his men, or so he hoped. From his place at the ridge of the low hill, he saw only the dozen nearest, crouched behind trees and stones. Otah heard something—the clank of metal or the sound of a raised voice. He willed them to be silent, fear and anger at the sound almost enough to make his teeth ache until he heard it again and realized it was the first of the Galts.

The bear hunter appeared at his side. He held three of the spearlike bolts and the great bow. Saya the blacksmith scampered up with another, its steel heads only just fastened to it. Men appeared on the road below them.

"The horn. Where's the horn?" Otah said, a sudden fear arcing through him. If he had learned the lesson of drums and horns from the Galts only to misplace the signal at the critical moment . . . But the brass horn was at his hip, where it had been since they'd set their trap. He took the cold metal in his hands, brushing dirt from the mouthpiece.

"They look a bit rough around the edges, eh?" Saya whispered, pointing at the road with his chin. "Amnat-Tan must have done them some hurt."

Otah looked at the Galtic soldiers. There were perhaps a hundred that he could see on this small curve of road. He tried to recall what the men he had faced outside the Dai-kvo's village had looked like; how they had walked, how they had held themselves. He couldn't. The memory was only of the battle, and of his men, dying. Saya took a pose of farewell and slunk away, down toward the trees where the battle would soon begin.

The first of the steam wagons came into sight. He could hear it clacking like a loom. The wide belly at its back glowed gold in the rising sun. It was piled with sacks and boxes. Tents, perhaps, or food. Coal for the furnaces. The packs that soldiers would have worn on their shoulders. The wreckage he had seen at the Dai-kvo's village had let him understand what these things were, but seeing one move—wheels turning at the speed of a team at fast trot, and yet without a horse near—was no less strange than his dreams. For a moment, he felt something like awe at the mind who had conceived it. The first of the soldiers below him saw the fallen log and called out—a long musical note that might have been a word or only a signal. The sound of the steam wagon changed, and it slowed, jittered once, and came to a halt. The long call came again and again as it receded down the road like whisperers at court passing the words of the Khai to distant galleries. The Galts came together, conferring. At Otah's side, the bear hunter sat back, bracing the curve of the bow against the soles of his feet. He took one of the bolts, steadying it between his fists as, two-handed, he drew back the wire. The bow creaked.

"Wait," Otah said.

A man came forward, past the steam wagon. He wore a gray tunic marked with the Galtic Tree. His hair was dark as Otah's own, his skin dark and leathern. The crowd of men at the fallen trees turned to face him, their bodies taking attitudes of respect. Otah felt something shift in his belly.

"Him," Otah said.

"Most High?" the huntsman said, strain in his voice.

"Can you hit the man in gray from here?"

The huntsman strained his neck, turned his body and his bow.

"Hard. Shot," he grunted.

"Can you do it?"

The huntsman was silent for half a breath.

"Yes," he said.

"Then do. Do it now."

The wire made a low thrum and the huntsman did something fast with his ankles that caught the bow before it could fall. He was already bending back again when the huge arrow struck. It took the gray man in the side, just below his ribs, and he collapsed without crying out. Otah fumbled with his horn, raising it to his lips. The note he blew filled his ears, so that he only knew the Galts below him were calling out to each other by the movement of their jaws and their drawn swords and axes.

The second bolt flew at the steam wagon as the soldiers fell back. It struck the belly of the steam wagon with a low clank and fell useless to the ground. A horn answering Otah's own called, and something terrible and sudden and louder than anything Otah had ever heard before drowned it out. A great cloud gouted up into the sky from perhaps three hundred yards back in the Galtic column, and then the huntsman at his side loosed the third bolt, and Otah was deafened.

The cloud of steam and smoke boiled up toward him, and Otah found himself coughing in the thick, hot air. The huntsman loosed one last bolt into the murk, stood, drew two daggers, and bounded down toward the road. Otah stepped forward. He was aware of sounds, though they were muffled by the ringing in his ears—screams, a trumpet blast, a distant report as another steam wagon met its end. The road came clear to him slowly as the mist thinned. The cart had tipped on its side, spilling its cargo and its men. Perhaps a dozen men lay on the sodden ground, their flesh seared red as a boiled lobster. Many still stood to fight, but they seemed half-stunned, and his own men were cutting them down with a savage glee. The furnace had cracked open, strewing burning coal across the paving stones. The leaves on the nearest trees, damp from the steam, seemed brighter and more vibrant than before. Two more steam wagons burst, the sound like doubled thunder. Otah cried out, rallying his men to his side, as he moved down to the road and the battle.

The first skirmish, here at the head of the column, was the critical one. The way forward had to be blocked. If they could push the Galts back here, they could drive them into their own men, confuse their formations, keep their balance off. Or so they'd planned, so he hoped. And as he came down the hill, it seemed possible. The Galts were wide-eyed with surprise, confused, afraid. Otah shouted and waved an axe, but there was no one there to threaten with it. It had already happened. The Galts were pulling back.

A bodyguard formed around him as he walked down the road, soldiers falling in around him and marching back toward Cetani, cutting down Galts as they went. In the distance, a horn sounded the call for horsemen to attack. Small formations of Galts—two or three score at most—held the road's center, confused, surrounded, and unable to retreat. A few ran to the trees for cover, only to find the forest alive with enemy blades. The rest fell to arrows and stones. Some engineer had made sense of Otah's trick, and great white plumes of steam rose into the sky as the wagons spent their pressure. The air reeked of blood and hot metal and smoke; it tasted rank. Twice, a wave of Galts swung toward Otah and his steadily increasing guard, only to be thrown back. The Galt army was in disarray, surrounded, confused. Horsemen in the colors of the high families of Machi and Cetani raised their swords in salute when they saw Otah.

He walked over the dead and the dying, past steam wagons that had burst open or been spared, horses that lay dead or flailed and screamed as they died. The sun was almost at the top of its arc, the whole morning gone, when Otah reached the last of the wagons, his bodyguard now nearly the size of his entire force. They had followed him, pinching down on the Galts as he'd moved forward. The plains before them stretched out to Machi, stands of Galtic archers holding positions to cover the retreat. Otah raised his horn to his lips and called the halt. Others horns called the acknowledgment. The battle was ended. The Galts had come this far and would come no farther. Otah felt himself sag.

From the south, he saw a movement among the men like wind stirring tall grass. The Khai Cetani came barreling forward, a wide grin on his face, blood soaking the ornate silk sleeves of his robes. Otah found himself grinning back. He took a pose of congratulations, but the Khai Cetani whooped and wrapped his arms around Otah's waist, lifting him like Otah was a child in his father's arms.

"You've done it!" the Khai Cetani shouted. "You've beaten the bastards!"

We have, Otah tried to say, but he was being lifted upon the shoulders of his men. A roar passed through the assembled men—a thousand throats opening as one. Otah let himself smile, let the relief wash over him. The Galtic army was broken. They would not reach Machi before winter came. He had done it.

They carried him back and forth before the men, the shouts and salutes following him like a windstorm. As he came back to the main road, he was amazed to see the Khai Cetani—all decorum and rank forgotten—dancing arm in arm with common laborers and huntsmen. The Khai Cetani caught sight of him, raised a blade in salute, and called out words that Otah couldn't hear. The men around him abandoned their dance, and drew their own blades, taking up the call, and Otah felt his throat close as he understood the words, as he heard them repeated, moving out through the men like a ripple in a pond.

To the Emperor.

BALASAR STOOD in the great square of Tan-Sadar. The sky was white and chill, and the trees that stood in the eastern corners were nearly bare of leaves. A good day, Balasar thought, for endings. The representatives of the utkhaiem stood beneath square-framed colonnades, staring out at him and his company two hundred strong and in their most imposing array of arms and armor and at the Khai Tan-Sadar, bound and kneeling on the brickwork at Balasar's feet. The poet of the city had burned to death among his books on the day Balasar had entered the city, but the disposition of the Khai was less important. A few days waiting in the public jail where men and women passing by could see him languishing posed no particular threat to the world, and the campaign that was now behind him had left Balasar tired.

"Do you have anything you want to say?" Balasar asked in the Khai's own language.

He was a younger man than Balasar had expected. Perhaps no more than thirty summers. It seemed young to have the responsibility of a city upon him or to be slaughtered in front of the nobles who had betrayed him to a conqueror. The Khai shook his head once, a curt and elegant motion.

"If you swear to serve the High Council of Galt, I'll cut your bonds and we can both walk out of here," Balasar said. "I'll have to keep you prisoner, of course. I can't leave you free to gather up an army. But there are worse things than living under guard."

The Khai almost smiled.

"There are also worse things than dying," he said.

Balasar sighed. It was a shame. But the man had made his decision. Balasar raised his hand, and the drums and trumpets called out. The execution proceeded. When the soldier held up the Khai's head for the crowd to see, a shudder seemed to run through them, but the faces that Balasar saw looking out at him seemed bright and excited.

They know they won't die, he thought. If I'm not killing them, it all becomes another court spectacle. They'll be talking about it in their bathhouses and winter gardens, vying for money and power now that the city's fallen. Half of them will be wearing tunics with the Galtic Tree on it come spring.

He looked down at the body of the man he'd had killed and briefly felt the impulse to put Tan-Sadar to the torch. Instead, he turned and walked away, going back to the palaces he had taken for himself and for his men.

Eight thousand remained to him. Several hundred had been lost in battle or to the raids that had slowed his travel since Nantani. The rest he had left in conquered Utani. There was little enough left of Udun that he hadn't bothered leaving men to occupy the city. There was no call to leave people there to guard ashes.

Utani had offered only token resistance and been for the most part spared. Tan-Sadar had very nearly set the musicians to playing and lined the roads with dancing girls. That wasn't true, but as Balasar stalked back through the great vaulted hall of the Khai's palace, his steps echoing off the blue and gold tilework high above him, his disgust with the place made it seem that way. They hadn't fought, and while that might have been wise, it wasn't something to celebrate. The only ones who had spines had been the poet and the Khai. Well, and the Khai's wives and children, whom he'd had killed. So perhaps he wasn't really in the best position to speak about what was honorable and noble after all.

"Darkness has come on as usual, sir?"

Balasar looked up. Eustin stood in salute at the foot of a wide flight of stairs. His tunic was stained, his chin unshaven, and even from five paces away, he stank of horses. Balasar restrained himself from rushing over and embracing the man.

"The darkness?" Balasar asked through his grin.

"Always happens at the end of a campaign, sir. You fall into a black mood for a few weeks. Happened in Eddensea and after the siege at Malsam. All respect, sir, it's like watching my sister after she's birthed a babe."

Balasar laughed. It felt good to laugh, and to smile, and to be reminded that the foul mood that had come on him was something he often suffered. In truth, he had forgotten. He took Eustin's hand in his own.

"Good to have you back," Balasar said. "I didn't know you'd returned."

"I would have sent a runner to pass the news, but it seemed faster if I came myself."

"Come up," Balasar said. "Tell me what's happened."

"It might be best if I saw a bathhouse, sir. . . ."

"Later," Balasar said. "If you can stand the reek, I can. And besides, you deserve some discomfort after that birthing comment. Come up, and I'll have them send us wine and food."

"Yes, sir," Eustin said.

They sat on couches while pine logs burned in the grate, sap hissing and popping and sending up sparks. True to his word, Balasar sent for rice wine infused with cherries and the stiff salty brown cheese that was a local delicacy of Tan-Sadar.

Eustin recounted his season—the attack on Pathai, his decision to split the force before moving on to the poet's school. Pathai hadn't been as large or as wealthy as a port city like Nantani, but it was near the Westlands. Moving what wealth it had back to Galt would be simpler than the other inland cities.

"And the school?" Balasar said, and a cloud passed over Eustin's face.

"They were younger than I'd thought. It wasn't the sort of thing they sing about. Unless they're singing laments. Then, maybe."

"It was necessary."

"I know, sir. That's why we did it."

Balasar poured him another cup of the wine, and then one for himself, and they drank in silence together before Eustin went on with his report. The men they'd sent to take the southern cities had managed quite well, apart from an incident with poisoned grain in Lachi and a fire at the warehouses of Saraykeht. That matched with what Balasar himself had heard. All the poets had been found, all the books had been burned. No Khai had lived or left heir.

In return, Balasar shared what news he had from the North. Tan-Sadar, the nearest city to the Dai-kvo, had known about the destruction of the village for weeks before Balasar's prisoner-envoys had arrived. The story was also widely known of the battle; one of the Khaiem in the winter cities had fielded an army of sorts. The estimates of the dead went from several hundred to thousands. Few, if any, had been Coal's. The retelling of that tale as much as the sacking of Udun had broken the back of Utani and Tan-Sadar.

A letter in Coal's short, understated style had come south after Amnat-Tan had fallen. Another courier was due any day bringing the news of Cetani and Machi. But if Coal had kept to the pace he'd intended, those cities were also fallen.

"It'll be good to know for certain, though," Eustin said.

"I trust him," Balasar said.

"Didn't mean anything else, sir."

"No. Of course not. You're right. It will be good to know

it's done." Balasar took a bite of the brown cheese and stared at the dancing flames where the wood glowed and blackened and fell to ash. "You'll put your men in Utani?"

"Or send some downriver. Depends how much food there is. There's more than a few who'd be willing to make a winter crossing if it meant getting home to start spending their shares."

"We have made a large number of very rich soldiers," Balasar said.

"They'll be poor again in a season or two, but the dice stands in Kirinton will still be singing our praises when our grandsons are old," Eustin said, then paused. "What about our local man?"

"Captain Ajutani? He's here, in the city. Wintering here with the rest of us. He's done quite well for himself. And for us. He's given me some very good advice."

Eustin grunted and shook his head.

"Still don't trust him, sir."

"He's more or less out of opportunities to betray us," Balasar said, and Eustin spat into the fire by way of reply.

Over the next days, the army shifted slowly from the rigorous discipline of the road to the bawdy, long, low riot that comes with wintering in a captured city. The locals—tradesmen and laborers and utkhaiem alike—seemed stunned by the change. They were polite and accommodating because Balasar's men were armed and practiced and thousands strong, but as Balasar walked down the long, winding red brick streets, he had the feeling that Tan-Sadar was hoping to wake from this nightmare and find the world once again as it had been. A hard, bitter wind came from the north, and behind it, the season's first thin, tentative snow.

He found his mind turning back to the west and home. The darkness Eustin had seen in him grew with the prospect of returning. The years he had spent gathering the threads of his campaign had come to their end; that it was ending in triumph only partly forgave that it was ending. He found himself wondering who he would be now that he was no longer the man driven to destroy the andat. In the mornings, he imagined himself living on his hereditary estate near Kirinton, perhaps taking a wife. Perhaps teaching in one of the military academies. All his old dreams revisited. As the sun peaked low in the sky and scuttled toward the horizon, the fantasy darkened too. He would be a racing dog with nothing left to chase. And worst, in the dark of the nights, he tried to sleep, his mind pricked by another day gone by without word from the North and the sick fear that despite all their successes, something had gone wrong.

And then, on a cold, clear morning, the courier from Coal arrived. Only it wasn't from Coal. Not really. Because Coal was dead, and Balasar had another ghost at his heels.

"They came without warning," Balasar said. "They were hiding in the trees, like street bandits. He was the first to fall."

"I'm sorry to hear it," Sinja said. "It was a dishonorable attack. Not that the honorable one did them much good from what I've heard."

Eustin's face might have been carved from stone.

"You have a point to make, Captain?" Balasar asked.

"Only that he did make an honest man's try on the field outside the Dai-kvo's village, and he failed. There's only so much you can count against him that he tried a different tack."

He killed my men, Balasar wanted to say. Wanted to shout. He killed *Coal*.

Instead, he paced the length of the wide parlor, staring at the maps he'd unrolled after he'd unsewn the letter from the remnants of the northern force. The oil lamps hung from their chains, adding a thick buttery light to the thin gray sunlight that filtered in from the windows. Cetani was occupied, but the library was emptied, Khai and poet missing along with the full population of the city. Machi remained. The last of the poets, the last of the books, the last of the Khaiem. His fingertips traced the route that would take him there.

"It's no use, General," Sinja said. "You can't put an army in the field this late in the season. It's too cold. One half-decent storm will freeze them to death."

"It's still autumn," Eustin said. "Winter's not come quite yet."

"It's a northern autumn," Sinja said. "You're thinking it's like Eddensea, but I'll tell you it's not. There's no ocean nearby to hold the heat in. General, Machi isn't going anywhere between now and the first thaw. The Dai-kvo's meat on a stick. Your man burned his books. They have the same chance of binding a fresh andat before spring that I have of growing wings and flying. And you have every chance of killing more of your men than have died since we left the Westlands if you go out there now."

"You've always given me good advice, Captain Ajutani," Balasar said. "I appreciate your wisdom on this."

"I wouldn't call it wisdom particularly," Sinja said. "Just a common interest in not turning into ice sculpture in a bean field somewhere between here and there."

"Thank you," Balasar said, his tone making it clear that the meeting had ended. Sinja saluted Balasar, nodded to Eustin, and made his way out. The door closed with a click. Eustin coughed.

"Do you think he's lying?" Balasar said. "He'd been living in Machi. If there were a place he didn't want captured, it would be there."

Eustin frowned, arms folded across his chest. He looked older, Balasar thought. The grief of losing Coal was heavy on his shoulders too. In a sense, they were the last. There were other men who had taken part in the campaign, but only the two of them had been there from the beginning. Only they had been to the desert. And so there was no one else who could have this conversation and truly understand it.

"He's not lying," Eustin said. His voice was thick. Balasar could hear how much it had cost him to agree with Sinja. "Everything I've heard says the cold up there is deadly. It's not a pleasant day out now, and the season's milder here."

"And Machi's army?"

Eustin shrugged.

"It wasn't an honorable fight," he said. "If we empty Utani

and Tan-Sadar, we've got something near three times the men Coal had at the end."

It would take them weeks to reach Machi, even if they started now. A bad storm would be worse than a battle. Tan-Sadar, on the other hand, was a safe place to winter, and when the spring came, they could overwhelm Machi in safety. They could revenge Coal a thousand times over. There was no army that could come to Machi's aid. Meaningful defenses for the city couldn't be built in that time.

Snow was the only armor the enemy had, and the turning seasons would be enough to remove it. Every strategist in Galt would counsel that he wait, plan, prepare, rest. But there were poets in Machi, and all the world to lose if he failed.

He looked up from the maps. His gaze met Eustin's, and they stood together in silence, the only two men in the world who would look at these facts, these odds, these stakes, and have no need to debate them.

"I'll break it to the men," Eustin said.

20

>+< "'And quietly, one foot sliding behind the other, for the parapet was too narrow to walk along, the half-Bakta boy went from his own prison chamber around to the bars of the Empress's cell.'" Otah paused, letting the half-Bakta boy hang in the air outside the prison tower. And this time Danat failed to object. His eyes were closed, his breathing heavy and regular. Otah sat for a moment, watching his boy sleep, then closed the book, tucked it in its place by the door, and put out the lantern. Danat murmured and snuggled more deeply into his blankets as Otah carefully opened the door and stepped out into the tunnel.

The physician set to watch over Danat took a pose of obeisance to Otah, and Otah replied with one of thanks before walking to the north, and to the broad spiral stairway that led up to the higher chambers of the underground palace or else down to Otah's own rooms and the women's quarters. Small brass lanterns filled the air with their warmth and the scent of oil. The walls were lighter than sandstone and shone brighter than the flames seemed to warrant. At the stairway, he hesitated.

Above him, Machi was beginning its descent into the other city, washing down into the rooms and corridors reserved for the deep, long winter that was almost upon them. The bath-houses far above had emptied their pipes, shunting the water from their kilns down to lower pools. The towers were being filled with goods of summer, the great platforms crawling up their tracks in the unforgiving stone, and then down again. In the wide, vaulted corridors that would become the main roads and public squares of the winter, beggars sang and food carts filled the air with rich, warm scents: beef soup and peppered pork, fish on hot rice, almond milk and honey cakes. The men and women pulling the carts would be calling, luring the curious and the hungry and the almost-hungry.

Only, of course, they wouldn't be there this winter. Food was no longer an item available for trade. It was being rationed out by the utkhaiem and by the exquisite mechanisms that Kiyan had put in place. The men and women of Cetani had been housed there or in the mines along the plain even before Otah and his army had returned with the news that the Galts had been turned back. Now, with the quarters being shared, there were two and sometimes three families sharing the space meant for one.

There was a part of him that wanted badly to take the stairs leading up, to go out of the palaces, and into the webwork of passages and tunnels one layered upon another that were his city. He knew it was an illusion to think that seeing things would improve them, make them easier to control and make right. But it was a powerful illusion.

He sighed and took the descending stairs. The women's quarters—designed to accommodate a Khai's dozen or more wives—had been changed over to smaller, more private rooms by the addition of a few planks of wood and tapestries taken from the palaces above. The utkhaiem of Cetani—husbands and wives together—found some accommodations there. It had seemed an obvious choice, and Kiyan had never particularly made use of her rooms there. And still it seemed odd to have people so close. Late in the night, he could sometimes hear the voices of people passing by.

The great blue and gold doors to his private apartments stood closed, two guards on either side. Otah noticed as he accepted their salutes how quickly he had come to think of these men as guards where before they had only been servants. Their duties were no different, their robes just the same. It wasn't the world that had changed. It was him.

He found Kiyan sitting at a low table, combing her hair with a wide-toothed comb. Wordless, he took it from her, sitting beside and behind her, and did the little task himself. Her hair was coarser than it had been once, and so shot with white that it seemed almost as much silver as black. He saw the subtle curve in the shape of her cheek as she smiled.

"I heard the Khai Cetani speaking today," she said.

"Really?"

"He was in one of the teahouses. And, honestly, not one of the best ones."

"I won't ask what you were doing in a third-rate tea house," Otah said, and Kiyan chuckled.

"Nothing more scandalous than listening to the Khai," she said. "But that might be enough. He thinks quite highly of you."

"Oh gods," Otah said. "Did the term come up again?"

"Yes, the word *emperor* figured highly in the conversation. He seems to think the sun shines brighter when you tell it to."

"He seems to forget that first battle where I got everyone killed. And that I didn't manage to keep the Dai-kvo from being slaughtered."

"He doesn't forget. But he does say you were the only man who tried to stop the Galts, who banded cities together instead of letting them fall one at a time, and in the end the only man who put them to flight."

"He should stop that," Otah said, and sighed. "He seemed so reasonable when I first met him. Who'd have guessed he was so easily wooed."

"He may not be wrong, you know. We'll need to do something when this is over. An emperor or a way to choose new families to act as Khaiem. A Dai-kvo. That would have to be Maati or Cehmai, wouldn't it?"

It was how all the conversations went now—how to rebuild, how to remake. The polite fiction that the poets were sure to succeed was the tissue that seemed to hold people together, and Otah couldn't bring himself to break it now.

"I suppose so," Otah said. "It'll be a life's work, though. Perhaps more. It was getting hard enough finding andat that could still be bound before this. We've lost so much now, going back will be harder than it was at the first. If we have a new Dai-kvo, he won't have time for anything more than that."

"An emperor, then. One man protecting all the cities. With the poets answering to him. Even just one poet with one andat would be enough. It would protect us."

"I recommend someone else do it. I've decided on a beach hut on Bakta," Otah said, trying to make it a joke. He saw Kiyan's expression. "It's too far ahead to think about now, love. Let it pass, and we'll solve it later if it still needs solving."

Kiyan turned and took his hand. The days since he'd come home hadn't allowed them time together, not as they had had before the war. First, when he and his men had marched across the bridge to trumpets and drums and dancing, it had been a mad festival. They had come out to meet him. He had embraced her, and Eiah, and little Danat whom he had danced around until they were both dizzy. Otah had found himself whirled from one pavilion to the next, balancing the giddy joy of survival with the surprisingly complex work of taking an army—even one as improvised and unformed as his own—apart. And afterward, he'd discovered that Kiyan was still as much in demand now tending the things she'd set in motion as when he had been gone.

Men and women of all classes seemed to have need of her time and attention, coordinating the stores of food and the arrangements of the refugees and the movements of goods and trade that had once been the business of the merchant houses, and had become the work of a few coordinating minds. Kiyan had become the hand that moved Machi, that pushed it into line, that tucked its children into warm beds and kept it from eating all the best food and leaving nothing for tomorrow. It consumed her days.

And the utkhaiem and the high trading families had all

wanted a moment of his day, to congratulate or express thanks or wheedle some favor in light of the changed circumstances of the world. To be here, in the warm light of candles, Kiyan's hand in his, her gaze on him, seemed like a dream badly wished for. And yet, now that he had it, he found himself troubled and unable to relax. She squeezed his hand.

"How bad was it?" she asked, and he knew what she meant. The battles. The Dai-kvo. The war.

Otah began to say something witty, something glib. The words got lost on the way to his lips. For long moment, silence was all he could manage.

"It was terrible," he said. "There were so many of them."

"The Galts?"

"The dead. Theirs. Ours. I've never seen anything like it, Kiyan-kya. I've read the histories and I've heard the epics sung, and it's not the same. They were young. And . . . and they looked like they were sleeping. However badly they'd died, in the end, I kept thinking they'd wake up and speak or call for help or scream. I think about all the men I led out there. The ones who would have lived if we hadn't done this."

"We didn't choose this, love. The Galts haven't given anyone much choice. The men who went with you would have died out there in the field, or here when the city fell. Would one have been better?"

"I suppose not. The other ways it could have gone might be just as bad, but the way it *did* happen, they died from following me. From doing what I asked."

To his surprise, Kiyan chuckled low and mirthless.

"That's why he calls you Emperor, isn't it," Kiyan said, and Otah took a pose of query. "The Khai Cetani. It's from gratitude. If you're the leader of the age, then it stops being his burden. Everything you're suffering, you've saved him."

Otah looked at his hands, rubbing his palms together with a long, dry sound. His throat felt tight, and something deep in his chest ached with the suspicion that she was right. When he had asked the man to abandon his city and take the role of follower, he had also been asking for the right to choose whatever happened after. And the responsibility for it. For a moment, he was on the chill, gray field of the dead, and walking the cold, lifeless ruin where poets had once conspired to bind thoughts themselves. He remembered the Dai-kvo's dead eyes, looking at nothing. The bodies, the Galts' and his own both, and the voices calling him Emperor.

"I'm sorry," Kiyan said, and he could tell from her voice that she knew how inadequate the words were. He pulled his mind back to his soft-lit room, the scent of the candles, the touch of this long-beloved hand.

"They've lived with it," he said. "Galt and Eddensea and the Westlands. It's always been like this for them. War and battle. We'll learn."

"I don't think I'm looking forward to that."

Otah raised her hand to his lips. Gently, she caressed his cheek. He drew her close, folding his arms around her, feeling the warmth of her body against him, smelling the familiar scent of her hair, and willing the moment to not end. If only the future could never come.

Kiyan sensed it in the tension of his spine, the fierceness of his embrace. Something. She did not speak, but only breathed, softening against him with every exhalation, and in time he felt himself beginning to relax with her. One of the lanterns, burning the last of its oil, dimmed, spat, and went out. The smoke touched the air with a smell of endings.

"I missed you," she said. "Every night, I went to bed thinking you might not come back. I kept telling the children over and over that things would be fine, that you'd be home soon. And I was sick. I was sick with it."

"I'm sorry."

"Don't. Don't apologize. Don't be sorry. Just know it. Just know we wanted you back. Not the Khai and not the emperor. *You.* Remember that you are a good man and I love you."

He raised her chin and kissed her, wondering how she knew so well the way to fill him with joy without asking him to abandon his sorrow.

"It's Maati's now," Otah whispered. "If he can bind Seedless before the spring thaw, this will all be over."

He felt an odd relaxation in her body, as if by saying the thing, he'd freed her from some secret effort she'd been making.

"And if he can't?" she asked. "If it's all going to fall apart anyway, can we run? You and me and the children? If I take them and go, are you going to come with us, or stay here and fight?"

He kissed her again. She rested her hands against his shoulders, leaning into him. Otah didn't answer, and he knew from the sound of her breath that she understood.

"IF WE take the nuance of movement-away in *nurat* and the symbol set you worked up for the senses of continuance," Maati said, "I think then we'll have something we can work with."

Cehmai's eyes were bloodshot, his hair wild from another long evening of combing frustrated fingers through it. Around them, the lamplight shone on a bedlam of paper. The library would have seemed a rat's nest to any but the two of them: books laid open; scrolls unfurled and weighted by other scrolls which were themselves unfurled; loose pages of a dozen codices stacked together. The mass of information and inference, grammar and poetry and history would have been overwhelming, Maati thought, to anyone who didn't know how profoundly little it was. Cehmai ran his fingertips down the notes Maati had made and shook his head.

"It's still the same," he said. "*Nurat* is modified by the fourth case of *adat,* and then it's exactly the same logical structure as the one Heshai used."

"No, it isn't," Maati said, slapping the table with an open palm. "It's *different.*"

Cehmai took a long, slow breath, raising his hands palms-out. It wasn't a formal gesture, but Maati understood it all the same. They were both worn raw. He sat back in his chair, feeling the knots in his back and neck. The brazier in the corner made the wide room smell warm without seeming to actually heat it.

"Look," Maati said. "Let's put it aside for the day. We need to move the library underground soon anyway. It's going to be too cold up here to do more than watch our fingers turn blue."

Cehmai nodded, then looked around at the disarray. Maati could read the despair in his face.

"I'll put it back together," Maati said. "Then a dozen slaves with strong backs, and I'll put it all together in the winter quarters in two days' time."

"I should move the poet's house down too," Cehmai said. "I feel like I haven't been there in weeks."

"I'm sorry."

"Don't be. The place seems too big without Stone-Made-Soft anyway. Too quiet. It reminds me of . . . well, of everything."

Maati rose, his knees aching. His feet tingled with the pins and needles that long motionlessness brought him these days. He clapped his hand on Cehmai's shoulder.

"Meet me in three days," he said. "I'll have the books in order. We'll start again fresh."

Cehmai took a pose of agreement, but he looked exhausted. Worn thin. The younger poet began snuffing the lanterns as Maati walked back toward his apartments, placing his feet carefully until normal feeling returned to them. Stepping the wrong way and breaking his ankle would be just the thing to make the winter even more miserable than it already promised to be.

The rooms in which he spent his summers were already bare. The fire grate was empty of everything but old soot. The tapestries were gone, the couches, the tables, the cabinets. Everything had been moved to the lower city. Winter ate the middle of things in the North. The snows would come soon, blocking the doors and windows. The second-story snow doors would open out for anyone who needed to travel into the world. Below, in the warmth of the ground, all the citizens of Machi, and now of Cetani too, would huddle and talk and fight and sing and play at tiles and stones until winter lost its grip and the snows turned to meltwater and washed the black-cobbled streets. Only the metalworkers remained at the ground level, the green copper roofs of the forges free of snow and ice, the plumes of coal smoke rising almost as high as the towers all through the winter.

At least all through *this* winter. This one last winter before the Galts came and butchered them all.

If only there was some other way to phrase the idea of *removing*. Seedless's true name would have been better translated as Removing-the-Part-That-Continues. Continuity was a fairly simple problem. The old grammars had several ways to conceptualize continuance. It was *removal . . .*

Maati reached the thin red doorway at the back of the rooms, and started down the stairs. It was dark as night. Darker. He would need to talk with the palace servant masters about seeing that lanterns were lit here. With as many people as there were filling every available niche in the tunnels and, from what he heard, the mines as well, it seemed unlikely that no one could be spared to be sure there was a little light on his path.

Or they might be rationing lamp oil already. There was a depressing thought.

He descended, one hand on the smooth, cool stone of the wall to keep him steady. He moved slowly because going quickly would get him winded, and it was dark enough that he wanted to stay sure of his footing. His mind was only half concerned with walking anyway. Cehmai was right. The logical structure was the same whether he used *nurat* or something else. So that was another dead end.

Removal.

It was a concept of relative motion. Taking something enclosed and producing a distance between it and its—now previous—enclosure. Plucking out a seed, or a baby. A gemstone from its setting. A man from his bed or his home. Removing. Heshai's work in framing Seedless was so elegant, so simple, that it seemed inevitable. That was the curse of second and third bindings of the same andat. Finding something equally graceful, but utterly different. It made his jaw ache just thinking about it.

He reached the bottom of the stairs and the wide upper chamber of his winter quarters. The night candle burning there was hardly to its first quarter mark, which given the lengthening nights of autumn meant the city beneath him would likely still be awake and active. Rest for him, though. His day had been full already. He took up the candle, passed down a short, close corridor, and reached the second stairway, which led down to the bedchambers.

The air was noticeably warmer here than in the library—in part from the heat of ten thousand people in the earth below him rising up, and in part from its stillness. Servants had prepared his bed with blankets and furs. A light meal of rice and spiced pork in one of the bowls of hand-thick iron that could hold the heat for the better part of a day waited on his writing table. Maati sat, ate slowly, not tasting the food, drinking rice wine as if it were water. Even as he sucked the pepper sauce off the last bit of pork, his feet and fingers were still cold. Removing-the-Chill-From-the-Old-Man's-Flesh. There was an andat.

Maati closed the lid of the great iron bowl, slipped out of his robes, hefted himself into his bed, and willed himself to sleep. For a time, he lay watching the candle burn, smelling the wax as it melted and dripped, and could not get comfortable. He couldn't get the cold out of his toes and knuckles, couldn't make his mind stop moving. He couldn't avoid the growing fear that when he closed his eyes, the nightmares that had begun plaguing him would return.

The images his mind held when his eyes were closed had become more violent, more anxious. Fathers weeping for sons who were also sacks of bloodied grain and dead mice; long, sleepless hours spent searching through bodies in a charnel house hoping to find his child still living and only finding

Otah's children again and again and again; the recurring dream of a tunnel that led down past the city, deeper than the mines, and into the earth until the stone itself grew fleshy and angry and bled. And the cry that woke him—a man's voice shouting from a great distance that demanded to know whose child this was. *Whose child?*

With this mind, Maati thought as he watched the single flame of the night candle, I'm intended to bind an andat. It's like driving nails with rotten meat.

The night candle had burned through three of its smallest marks when he abandoned his bed, pulled on his robes, and left his private chambers for the wide, arched galleries of the tunnels below the palaces. The bathhouses were at least warm. If he wasn't to sleep, he could at least be miserable in comfort.

The public spaces were surprisingly full with men and women in the glorious robes of the utkhaiem. It made sense, he supposed. Cetani had not only brought its merchants and craftsmen. There would be two courts living under the palaces this winter. And so twice the social intrigue. Who precisely was sleeping with whom would be even more complex, and even the threat of their death at the hands of a Galtic army wouldn't stop the courtiers playing for rank.

As he passed, the utkhaiem took poses of respect and welcome, the servants and slaves ones of abasement. Maati repressed a swelling hatred of all of them. It wasn't their fault, after all, that he had to save them. And himself. And Liat and Nayiit and Otah and all the people he had ever known, all the cities he had ever seen. His world, and everything in it.

It was the Galts who deserved his anger. And they would feel it, by all the gods. Failed crops, gelded men, and barren women until they rebuilt everything they'd broken and given back everything they took. If he could only think of a better way to say *removing*.

He brooded his way along the dim galleries and through the great chambers until the air began to thicken with the first presentiment of steam, and the prospect of hot water, and of finally warming his chilled feet, intruded on him.

He found his way into the men's changing rooms, where he shrugged off his robes and boots and let the servant offer him a bowl of clear, cold water to drink before he went into the public baths and sweated it all out again. When he passed through the inner door, Maati shivered at the warmth. Voices filled the dim, gray space—conversations between people made invisible by the steam rising from the water. There had been a time, Maati considered as he stepped gingerly down the submerged stairs and waded toward a low bench, when the idea of strangers wandering naked in the baths—men and women together—had held some erotic frisson. Truth often disappoints.

He lowered himself to the thick, water-logged wood of the bench, the hot water rising past his belly, past his chest, until the small warm waves danced against the hollow of his throat. At last, his feet felt warm, and he leaned back against the warm stone, sighing with a purely physical contentment. He resolved to move down toward the warmer end before he went back to his rooms. If he boiled himself thoroughly enough, he might even carry the heat back to his bed.

Across the bath, hidden in the mist, two men talked of grain supplies and how best to address the problem of rats. Far away toward the hotter end of the bath, someone shouted, and there was a sound of splashing. Children, Maati supposed, and then fell into a long, gnawing plan for how best to move the volumes in the library. His concentration was so profound he didn't notice when the children approached.

"Uncle Maati?"

Eiah was practically at his side, crouched low in the water to preserve her modesty. A gaggle of children of the utkhaiem behind her at what Maati supposed must be a respectful distance. He raised hands from the water and took a pose of greeting, somewhat cramped by being held high enough to be seen.

"I haven't seen you in ages, Eiah-kya," he said. "What's been keeping you?"

The girl shrugged, sending ripples.

"There are a lot of new people from Cetani," she said. "There's a whole other Radaani family here now. And I've been studying with Loya-cha about how to fix broken bones. And . . . and Mama-kya said you were busy and that I shouldn't bother you."

"You should always bother me," Maati said with a grin.

"Is it going well?"

"It's a complicated thing," Maati said. "But it's a long wait until spring. We'll have time."

"Complicated's hard," Eiah said. "Loya-cha says it's always easy to fix things when there's only one thing wrong. It's when there's two or three things at once that it's hardest."

"Smart man, Loya-cha," Maati said.

Eiah shrugged again.

"He's a servant," she said. "If you can't recapture Seedless, we can't beat the Galts can we?"

"Your father did once," Maati said. "He's a very clever man."

"But we might not."

"We might not," Maati allowed.

Eiah nodded to herself, her forehead crinkling as she came to some decision. When she spoke, her voice had a seriousness that seemed out of place from a girl still so young, hardly half-grown.

"If we're all going to die, I wanted you to know that I think you were a very good father to Nayiit-cha."

Maati almost coughed from surprise, and then he understood. She knew. A warm sorrow filled him. She knew that Nayiit was Otah's son. That Maati loved the boy. That it mattered to him deeply that Nayiit love him back. And the worst of it, she knew that he hadn't been a very good father.

"You're kind, love," he said, his voice thick.

She nodded sharply, embarrassed, perhaps, to have completed her task. One of her companions yelped and dropped under the water only to come back up spitting and shaking his head. Eiah turned toward them.

"Leave him be!" Eiah shouted, then turned to Maati with

an apologetic pose. He smiled and waved her away. She went back to her group with the squared shoulders of an overseer facing a recalcitrant band of laborers. Maati let his smile fade.

A good father to Nayiit. And to be told so by Otah's daughter. Perhaps binding the andat wasn't so complex after all. Not when compared with other things. Fathers and sons, lovers and mother and daughters. And the war. Saraykeht and Seedless. All of it touched one edge against another, like tilework. None of it existed alone. And how could anyone expect him to solve the thing when half of everything seemed to be broken, and half of what was broken was still beautiful.

The physician was right. It would be easy to fix one thing, if there were only one thing wrong. But there were so many ways to break something so delicate and so complex. Even the act of making one thing right seemed destined to undo something else. And he was too tired and too confused to say whether one way of being wounded was better than another.

There were so many ways to be wrong.

There were so many ways to break things.

Maati felt the thought fall into place as if it were something physical. It was the moment he was supposed to shout, to stand up and wave his hands about, possessed by insight as if by a demon. But instead, he sat with it quietly, as if it was a gem only he of all mankind had ever seen.

He'd spent too much time with Heshai's binding. Removing-the-Part-That-Continues had been made for the cotton trade—pulling seeds from the fiber and speeding it on its way to the spinners and the weavers and feeding all of the needle trades. But there was no reason for Maati to be restricted by that. He only needed a way to break Galt. To starve them. To see that no other generation of Galtic children ever saw the world.

It wasn't Seedless he needed. It was only Sterile. And there were any number of ways to say that.

He sank lower into the water as the sense of relief and peace consumed him. Destroying-the-Part-That-Continues, he thought as the little waves touched his lips. Shattering-the-Part-That-Continues. Crushing it. Rotting it. Corroding it.

Corrupting it.

In his mind, Galt died. And he, Maati Vaupathai, killed it. What, he asked himself, was victory in a single battle compared with that? Otah had saved the city. Maati saw now how he could save *everything*.

21

>+< Sinja woke, stiff with cold, to the sound of chopping.
Outside the tent, someone with a hand axe was breaking the ice at the top of the barrels. It was still dark, but morning was always dark these days. He kicked off his blankets
and rose. The undyed wool of his inner robes held a bit of the
heat as he pulled on first one outer robe and then another
with a wide leather cloak over the top that creaked when he
fastened the wide bone broochwork.

Outside his tent, the army was already breaking camp.
Columns of smoke and steam rose from the wagons. Horses
snorted, their breath pluming white in the light of a falling
moon. In the southeast, the dawn was still only a lighter shade
of black. Sinja walked to the cook fire and squatted down beside it, a bowl of barley gruel sweetened with wine-packed
prunes in his hands. The heat of it was better than the taste.
Wine could do strange things to prunes.

The army had been marching for two and a half weeks. At
a guess, there were another three before they reached Machi.
If there was no storm, Sinja guessed they would lose a thousand men to frostbite, most of those in the last ten days. He
squinted into the dark, implacable sky and watched the
faintest stars begin to fade. There would still be over nine
thousand men. And every man among them would know that
this battle wasn't for money or glory. Or even for love of the
general. If by some miracle Otah turned the Galts back from

the city, they would die scattered in the frozen plains of the North.

This battle would be the only time in the whole benighted war that the Galts would go in knowing they were fighting for their lives.

"You want more?" the cook asked, and Sinja shook his head. Around him, the members of his personal guard were moving at last. Sinja didn't help them break down the camp. He'd left most of the company behind in Tan-Sadar. They were, after all, on a deadly stupid march that, with luck, would end with them sacking their own homes. It wasn't duty that could be asked of a green recruit of his first campaign. Sinja had taken time handpicking this dozen to accompany him. There wasn't a man among them he liked.

The last tent was folded, poles bound together with their leather thongs, and put on the steam wagon. The fires were all stamped out, and the sun made its tardy appearance. Sinja wrapped the leather cloak closer around his shoulders and sighed. This was a younger man's game. If he'd been as wise as the average rat, he'd be someplace warm and close now, with a good mulled wine and a plate of venison in mint sauce. The call sounded, and he began the walk north. Cold numbed his face and made his ears ache. The air smelled of dust and smoke and horse dung—the miasma of the moving army. Sinja kept his eyes to the horizon, but the only clouds were the high white lace that did little but leach blue from the sky; there was no storm coming today. And still the dusting of snow that had fallen in the last weeks hadn't melted and wouldn't before spring. The world was pale except where a stone or patch of ground stood free of snow. There it was black.

He put one foot in front of the other, his mind growing empty with the rhythm. His muscles slowly warmed. The pain retreated from his ears. With enough effort, the air became almost comfortable. The sun rose quickly behind him, as if in a hurry to finish its day's passage and return the world to darkness.

When he paused to relieve himself on a tree—his piss

steaming in its puddle—he took off the leather cloak. If he got too warm, he'd start to sweat. Soaking through his inner robes was an invitation to death. He wondered how many of Balasar's men knew that. With his sad luck, all of them.

They wouldn't see a low town today. They had overrun one yesterday—the locals surprised to find themselves surrounded by horsemen intent on keeping any word from slipping out to the North. There would be another town in a day or two. If Sinja was lucky, it might mean fresh meat for dinner. The rations set aside by the townsmen to see them through the winter might feed the army for as much as half a day.

They paused at midday, the cooks using the furnaces of the steam wagons to warm the bread and boil water for tea. Sinja wasn't hungry but he ate anyway. The tea was good at least. Overbrewed and bitter, but warm. He sat on the broad back of a steam wagon, and was preparing himself for the second push of the day and estimating how many miles they had covered since morning when the general arrived.

Balasar rode a huge black horse, its tack worked with silver. As small as the man was, he still managed to look like something from a painting.

"Sinja-cha," Balasar Gice said in the tongue of the Khaiem. "I was hoping to find you here."

Sinja took a pose of respect and welcome.

"I'd say winter's come," the general said.

"No, Balasar-cha. If this was real winter, you could tell because we'd all be dead by now."

Balasar's eyes went harder, but his wry smile didn't fade. It wasn't anger that made him what he was. It was determination. Sinja found himself unsurprised. Anger was too weak and uncertain to have seen them all this far.

"I'd have you ride with us," the general said.

"I'm not sure Eustin-cha would enjoy that," Sinja said, then switched to speaking in Galtic. "But if it's what you'd like, sir, I'm pleased to do it."

"You have a horse?"

"Several. I've been having them walked. I've got good enough fighters among my men, but I can't speak all that highly of them as grooms. A horse with a good lather up in this climate and with these boys to care for it is going to be tomorrow night's dinner."

"I have a servant or two I could spare," Balasar said, frowning. Sinja took a pose that both thanked and refused.

"I'd take the loan of one of your horses, if you have one ready to ride. Otherwise, I'll need to get one of mine."

"I'll have one sent," Balasar said. Sinja saluted, and the general made his way back to the main body of the column. Sinja had just washed down the last of the bread with the dregs of his tea when a servant arrived with a saddled brown mare and orders to hand it over to him. Sinja rode slowly past the soldiers, grim-faced and uncomfortable, preparing for their trek or else already marching. Balasar rode just after the vanguard with Eustin and whichever of his captains he chose to speak with. Sinja fell in beside the general and made his salute. Balasar returned it seriously. Eustin only nodded.

"You served the Khai Machi," Balasar said.

"Since before he was the Khai, in fact," Sinja said.

"What can you tell me about him?"

"He has a good wife," Sinja said. Eustin actually smiled at the joke, but Balasar's head tilted a degree.

"Only one wife?" he asked. "That's odd for the Khaiem, isn't it?"

"And only one son. It is odd," Sinja said. "But he's an odd man for a Khai. He spent his boyhood working as a laborer and traveling through the eastern islands and the cities. He didn't kill his family to take the chair. He's been considered something of an embarrassment by the utkhaiem, he's upset the Dai-kvo, and I think he's looked on his position as a burden."

"He's a poor leader then?"

"He's better than they deserve. Most of the Khaiem actually like the job."

Balasar smiled and Eustin frowned. They understood.

"He hasn't posted scouts," Eustin pointed out. "He can't be much of a war leader."

"No one would post scouts this late in the season," Sinja said. "You might as well fault him for not keeping a watch on the moon in case we launched an attack from there."

"And how was it that a son of the Khaiem found himself working as a laborer?" Balasar asked, eager, it seemed, to change the subject.

As he swayed gently on the horse, Sinja told the story of Otah Machi. How he had walked away from the Dai-kvo to take a false name as a petty laborer. The years in Saraykeht, and then in the eastern islands. How he had taken part in the gentleman's trade, met the woman who would be his wife, and then been caught up in a plot for his father's chair. The uncertain first year of his rule. The plague that had struck the winter cities, and how he had struggled with it. The tensions when he had refused marriage to the daughter of the Khai Utani. Reluctantly, Sinja even told of his own small drama, and its resolution. He ended with the formation of the small militia, and its being sent away to the west, and to Balasar's service.

Balasar listened through it all, probing now and again with questions or comments or requests for Sinja to amplify on some point or aspect of the Khai Machi. Behind them, the sun slid down toward the horizon. The air began to cool, and Sinja pulled his leather cloak back over his shoulders. Dark would be upon them soon, and the moon had still not risen. Sinja expected the meeting to come to its close when they stopped to make camp, but Balasar kept him near, pressing for more detail and explanation.

Sinja knew better than to dissemble. He was here because he had played well up to this point, but if his loyalty to the Galts was ever going to break, it would be soon and all three men knew it. If he held back, hesitated, or gave information that seemed intended to mislead, he would fall from Balasar's grace. So he told his story as clearly and truthfully as he could. There wasn't a great deal that was likely to be of use to the general anyway. Sinja had, after all, never seen Otah lead an army. If he'd been asked to guess how such an effort would end, he'd have been proved wrong already.

They ate their evening meal in Balasar's tent of thick hide beside a brazier of glowing coals that made the potato-and-salt-pork soup taste smoky. When at last Sinja found himself without more to say, the questions ended. Balasar sighed deeply.

"He sounds like a good man," he said. "I'm sorry I won't get to meet him."

"I'm sure he'd say the same," Sinja said.

"Will the utkhaiem turn against him? If we make the same offers we made in Utani and Tan-Sadar, can we avoid the fighting?"

"After he beat your men? It's not a wager I'd take."

Balasar's eyes narrowed, and Sinja felt his throat go a bit tighter, half-convinced he'd said something wrong. But Balasar only yawned, and the moment passed.

"How would you expect him to defend his city?" Eustin asked, breaking a stick of bread. "Will he come out to meet us, or hide and make us dig him out?"

"Dig, I'd expect. He knows the streets and the tunnels. He knows his men will break if he puts them in the field. And he'll likely put men in the towers to drop rocks on us as we pass. Taking Machi is going to be unpleasant. Assuming we get there."

"You still have doubts?" Balasar asked.

"I've never had doubts. One bad storm, and we're all dead men. I'm as certain of that as I ever was."

"And you still chose to come with us."

"Yes, sir."

"Why?"

Sinja looked at the burning coals. The deep orange glow and the white dust of ash. Why exactly he had come was a question he'd asked himself more than once since they'd left Tan-Sadar. He could say it was the contract, but that wasn't the truth and all three of them knew it. He flexed his fingers, feeling the ache in his knuckles.

"There's something I want there," he said.

"You'd like to be the new Khai Machi?"

"In a way," Sinja said. "Something I'd ask from you instead of my share of the spoils, at least."

Balasar nodded, already knowing what Sinja was driving toward. "The Lady Kiyan," he said.

"I don't want her raped or killed," Sinja said. "When the city falls, I'd like her handed over to me. I'll see she doesn't do anything stupid or destructive."

"Her husband and children," Eustin said. "We will have to kill them."

"I know it," Sinja said, "but she's not from a high family. She's got no standing aside from her marriage. She won't pose a threat."

"And for her sake, you'd betray the Khai?" Balasar asked.

Sinja smiled. This question, at least, he could answer honestly and without fear.

"For her sake, sir, I'd betray the gods."

Balasar looked at Eustin, his eyebrows rising as if asking an unvoiced question. Eustin considered Sinja for a long moment, then shrugged. Grunting, Balasar shifted and pulled a wooden box from under his cot. He took a stoppered flask from it—good Nantani porcelain—and three small drinking bowls. With growing unease, Sinja waited as Balasar poured out water-clear rice wine in silence, then handed one bowl to Eustin, the next to him.

"I have a favor to ask of you as well," Balasar said.

Sinja drank. The wine was rich and clean and made his chest bloom with warmth, but not so much he lost the tightness in his throat and between his shoulders.

"We can go in," Eustin said. "Waves of us. Small numbers, one after the other, until we've dug out every nook and cranny in the city. But we'll lose men. A lot of them."

"Most," Balasar said. "We'd win. I'm sure of that. But it would take half of my men."

"That's bad," Sinja said. "But there is another plan here, isn't there?"

Balasar nodded.

"We can send a man in who can tell us what the defenses are. Who can send word or sign. If we're lucky, perhaps even a man who can help with planning the defense. And, in return, take the woman he wants."

Sinja felt his mind start to spin. The rice wine made it a bit harder to think, but a bit easier to grin. It was ridiculous, except that it made sense. He should have anticipated this. He should have known.

"You want to send me in? As a spy?"

"Take a couple good horses in the morning, and ride hard for the city," Eustin said. "You'll arrive a few days ahead of us. You were the Khai's advisor before. He'll listen to you, or at least let you listen to him. When the time comes for the attack, you guide us."

The captain made a small gesture with one hand, as if what he'd said was simple. Go into Machi, betray Otah and everyone else he'd known this last decade. If I turn against the general, Sinja thought, it'll be a bad death when these men find me.

"It will be faster this way," Balasar said. "Fewer people will die on both sides. And, because you ask, the woman is yours. Safe and unharmed if I can do it."

"I have your word on that?" Sinja asked.

Balasar took a pose that accepted an oath. It wasn't quite the right vocabulary, but it carried the meaning. Sinja felt unpleasantly like he was looking down over a cliff. His head swam a little, and the tightness in his body fell to knotting his gut. He held out his bowl and Balasar refilled it.

"I'll understand if it's too much," Balasar said, his voice soft. "It will make things easier for both sides and it won't change the way the battle falls, but that doesn't mean it isn't a terrible thing to ask of you. Take a few days to sit with it if you'd like."

"No," Sinja said. "I don't need time. I'll do the thing."

"You're sure?" Eustin asked.

Sinja drained his cup in a gulp. He could feel the flush starting to grow in his neck and cheeks, the nausea starting in his belly and the back of his throat. It was strong wine and a bad night coming.

"It needs doing, and it's the price I asked," Sinja said. "So I'll do it."

CEHMAI SAT forward in his chair. The white marble walls of their workspace glowed with candlelight, but Maati didn't find the brightness reassuring. He was sitting as quietly as he could manage on a red and violet embroidered cushion, waiting. Cehmai lifted one of the wide yellow pages, paused, and turned it over. Maati saw the younger poet's lips moving as he shaped some phrase from the papers. Maati restrained himself from asking which. Interruptions wouldn't make this go any faster.

The simple insight that Eiah had given him that night in the baths had taken the better part of two weeks to work into a draft worthy of consideration. Fitting the grammars so that the nuances of corruption and continuance—destruction and creation, or more precisely the destruction *of* creation—reinforced one another had been tricky. And the extra obstacle of fitting in the structures to protect himself should things go amiss had likely tacked on an extra three or four days to the process.

And still, it had taken him only weeks. Not years, not even months. Weeks. The structure of the binding was laid out now. Corruption-of-the-Generative, called Sterile. The death of the Galt's crops. The gelding of its men. The destruction of its women's wombs. Once he had seen the trick of it, the binding had flowed from his pen.

It had been as if some small voice at the back of his mind was whispering the words, and he'd only had to write them down. Even now, squatting on this damnable cushion, his back aching, his feet cold, waiting for Cehmai to read over the last of the changes, he felt half drunk from the work. He was a poet. All the things that had happened in his life to bring him to this place at this time had built toward these days, and the dry pages that hissed and shushed as Cehmai slid them across each other. Maati bit his lip and did not interrupt.

It seemed like days, but Cehmai came to the final page, fingertips tracing the lines Maati had written there, paused, and set it down with the others. Maati leaned forward, his hands taking a querying pose. Cehmai frowned and gently shook his head.

"No?" Maati asked. Something between rage and dismay shot through his belly, only to vanish when Cehmai spoke.

"It's brilliant," he said. "It's a first draft, but it's a very, very good one. I don't think there are many things we'd have to adjust. A few to make it easier to pass on, perhaps. But we can work with those. No, Maati-kvo, I think this is likely to work. It's just . . ."

"Just?"

Cehmai's frown deepened. His fingertips tapped cautiously on the pages, as if he were testing an iron pot, afraid it would be hot enough to burn. He sighed.

"I've never seen an andat fashioned to be a weapon," he said. "There was a book that the Dai-kvo had that dated from the fall of the Second Empire, but he never let anyone look at it. I don't know."

"There's a war, Cehmai-kya," Maati said. "They killed the Dai-kvo and everyone in the village. The gods only know how many other men they've slaughtered. How many women they're raped. What's on those pages, they've earned."

"I know," Cehmai said. "I do know that. It's just I keep thinking of Stone-Made-Soft. It was capable of terrible things. I can't count the times I had to hold it back from collapsing a mine or a building. It had no respect for the lives of men. But there was no particular malice in it either. This . . . Sterile . . . it seems different."

Maati clamped his jaw. He was tired, that was all. They both were. It was no reason to be annoyed with Cehmai, even if his criticism of the binding was something less than useful. Maati smiled the way he imagined a teacher at the school smiling. Or the Dai-kvo. He took a pose that offered instruction.

"Cutting shears and swords are both sharp. Before the war, you and I and the men like us? We made cutting shears," he said, and gestured to the papers. "That's our first sword. It's only natural that you'd feel uneasy with it; we aren't men of violence. If we were, the Dai-kvo would never have chosen us, would he? But the world's a different place now, and so we have to be willing to do things that we wouldn't have before."

"Then it makes you uneasy too?" Cehmai asked. Maati smiled. It didn't make him uneasy at all, but he could see it was what the man needed to hear.

"Of course it does," he said. "But I can't allow that to stop me. The stakes are too high."

Cehmai seemed to collapse on himself. The dark eyes flickered, searching, Maati thought, for some other path. But in the end, the man only sighed.

"I think you've found the thing, Maati-kvo. There are some passages I'd want to think about. There might be ways we can refine it. But I think we'll be ready to try it well before the thaw."

A tension that Maati hadn't known he was carrying released, and he grinned like a boy. He could imagine himself as the controller of the only andat in the world. He and Cehmai would become the new teachers, and under their protection, they would raise up a new generation of poets to bind more of the andat. The cities would be safe again. Maati could feel it in his bones.

The rest of the meeting went quickly, as if Cehmai wanted to be away from the library as quickly as he could. Maati supposed the prospect of binding Sterile was more disturbing to Cehmai than to him. He hoped, as he walked back up the stairways and corridors to his rooms, that Cehmai would be able to adjust to the new way of things. It couldn't be easy for him. He was at heart a gentle man, and the world was a darker place than it had been.

Maati's mind was still involved in its contemplation of darkness when he stepped into his room. At first, he didn't notice that Liat was there, seated on his bed. She coughed—a wet, close sound close to a sob. He looked up.

"What's the matter, sweet?" he asked, hurrying to her. "What's happened?"

In the steady glow of the lantern, Liat's face seemed veiled by shadows. Her eyes were reddened and swollen, her skin flushed with recent tears. She attempted a smile.

"I need something, Maati-kya. I need you to speak with Nayiit."

"Of course. Of course. What's happened?"

"He's . . ." Liat stopped, took a deep breath, and began again. "He isn't leaving with me. Whatever happens, he's decided to stay here and guard her children."

"What?"

"Kiyan," Liat said. "She set him to watch over Danat and Eiah, and now he's decided to keep to it. To stay in the North and watch over them instead of going home with me. He has a wife and a child, and Otah's family is more important to him than his own. And what if they see that he's . . . what if they see whose blood he is? What if he and Danat have to kill each other?"

Maati sat beside Liat and folded her hand in his. The corners of her mouth twitched down, a mask of sorrow. He kissed her palm.

"He's said this? That he's staying in Machi?"

"He doesn't have to," Liat said. "I've seen the way he looks at them. Whenever I talk about the spring and the South, he smiles that false, charming way he always smiles and changes the subject."

Maati nodded. The lantern flame hissed and shuddered, setting the shadows to sway.

"What is this really?" he asked, gently as he could. Liat pulled back her hand and took a pose that asked clarification. There was anger in her eyes. Maati chewed his lower lip, raised his eyebrows.

"He enjoys a duty that was designed, from what you told

me, to be enjoyable for him. To give him the sense of redeeming himself. He's made friends with Otah's children—"

"His *other* children," Liat said, but Maati had known her too long and too well to let the barb turn him aside.

"And they're very easy to make friends with. Danat and Eiah are charming in their ways. And Nayiit doesn't want to talk about plans he can't really make. About his own child who might already be dead. About a wife he doesn't love and a city that's fallen to the Galts. Why would he want to talk about that? What is there in any of that to cause him anything but pain?"

"You think I'm an idiot," Liat said.

"I think he *hasn't* told you that he's staying. That's something you've decided, and you don't reach conclusions that wild unless there's something more going on," he said. "What it is, sweet?"

Liat's face squeezed tight, her brows and mouth and eyes seeming to pull in together like those of a fighter bracing to take a blow.

"I'm frightened. Is that what you want to hear? All right, then. I'm frightened."

"For him."

"For all of us!" Liat stood and began to pace. "For the people I knew in Saraykeht. For the people I've met here. And the ones I haven't met. Do you know how many people the Galts have killed?"

"No, love."

"No one does. No one knows how bloody this has been. No one knows how much more they'll want before it's over. I knew what the world was when I came here."

"You came here to change the world by slaughtering all of Galt," Maati said.

"Yes, Maati. Yes, so that *this* wouldn't happen. So that *we* wouldn't change!" She was weeping now, though he couldn't hear it in her voice. The tears only ran unnoticed down her cheeks as she moved, restless as a trapped bird. "I don't know the Galts. I don't love them. I don't care if they all die. What's going to happen to *us*? What's going to happen to *him*? What's already happened?"

"It's hard, isn't it? When there's nothing to distract you from it," Maati said. "Harder, I mean. It's not ever easy. You had the organization of the city to keep your mind busy, but that's done, and now there's nothing but the waiting. I've felt it too. If I didn't have the binding to work on, I'd have sunk into it."

Liat stopped. Her hands worried at each other.

"I can't stop thinking about it," she said. "I keep half-expecting that it will all go back to what it was. That we'll go back to Saraykeht and carry on with the business and talk about that terrible year when the Galts came the way we talk about a bad cotton crop."

"It won't, though."

"Then what's going to happen to him?"

"Him? Just Nayiit? He's the only one you wonder that of?"

The tears didn't stop, but a smile as much as sorrow as otherwise touched her.

"He's my son. Who else matters?"

"He's going to be fine," Maati said, and even he heard the conviction in his voice. "The Galts will be turned back, because I will turn them back. Our children won't die. Theirs will. We won't go hungry. They will. Nayiit won't be harmed, and when this is all finished with, he won't stay here with Otah-kvo. He'll go, because he has a child of his own in Saraykeht, and he isn't the kind of man who can walk away from that."

"Isn't he?" Liat asked. Her tone was a plea.

"Either he's Otah's son, and Otah sacrificed his freedom and his dignity to keep Danat and Eiah safe. Or he's mine, and you had to force me away."

"Or he's mine," Liat said. "Then what becomes of him?"

"Then he'll be beautiful and lovely beyond all mortals,

and age gracefully into wisdom. And he'll love his child the way you love him," Maati said. "Silly question."

Liat couldn't help but laugh. Maati rose and took her in his arms. She smelled of tears—wet and salt and flesh. Like blood without the iron. He kissed the crown of her bowed head.

"We'll be fine," he said. "I know what to do. Cehmai's here to help me, and Otah's bought us the time we need. Nothing bad will happen."

"It will," Liat said into his shoulder, and then with something that sounded like hope and surrender, "Only make it happen to someone else."

They stood in silence for a while. Maati felt the warmth of Liat's body against him. They had held each other so many times over the years. In lust and shame, in love and pleasure. In sorrow. Even in anger. He knew the feel of her, the sound of her breath, the way her hand curled round his shoulder. There was no one in the world who he would ever be able to speak with the way he spoke to her. They knew things between them that even Otah could never share—moments in Saraykeht, and after. It wasn't only the great moments—the birth of Nayiit, the death of Heshai, their own last parting; there were also the small ones. The time she'd gotten ill on crab soup and he'd nursed her and cared for the still squalling Nayiit. The flute player with the dancing dog they'd given a length of silver at a firekeeper's kiln in Yalakeht. The way the autumn came to Saraykeht when they were still young.

When she left again, there would be no one to talk to about those things. When she went to the South again and he became the new Dai-kvo, there would be no one to remind him of those moments. It made them more precious. It made her more precious.

"I'll protect you," he said. "Don't worry, love. I'll protect us all."

He heard approaching footsteps, and he could feel it in Liat's body when she did as well. She stepped back, and he let her, but he kept hold of one hand. Even if only for a moment. An urgent knock came at the door, and Cehmai's voice.

"Maati-kvo!"

"Come in. Come in. What's the matter?"

The poet's face was flushed, his eyes wide. It took a moment for him to catch his breath before he could speak.

"The Khai says you should come. Now," Cehmai gasped. "Sinja's back."

22

>+< When Sinja finished his report and was silent, Otah forced his breath to be deep and regular, waiting until he could speak. His voice was tight and controlled.

"You have spent the season fighting beside the Galts?"

"They were winning."

"Is that supposed to be funny?"

He was thinner than Otah remembered him. The months on the road had left Sinja's face drawn, his cheekbones sharp. His skin was leathery from the sun and wind. He hadn't changed his robes, and he smelled of horses. His casual air seemed false, a parody of the certain, amused, detached man whom Otah had sent away, and Otah couldn't say if it was the captain who'd changed more or himself.

Kiyan, the only other person in the chamber, sat apart from the pair of them, at the couch nearest the fire. Her hands were fists in her lap, her spine straight and still as a tree. Her face was expressionless. Sinja's gaze flickered toward her, and then came back to Otah. The captain took a pose that apologized.

"I'm not trying to be light about this, Most High," Sinja said. "But it's truth. By the time I knew they weren't attacking the Westlands, I could no more have excused myself and ridden on than flapped my arms and flown. I did what I could to slow them, but yes, when they called on us, we fought beside them. When they needed interpreters, we spoke for them. I suppose we could have thrown ourselves on their spears and died nobly, but then I wouldn't be here to warn you now."

"You betrayed the Khaiem," Otah said.

"And I'm betraying the Galts now," Sinja replied, his voice calm. "If you can judge the balance on that, you're smarter than I am. I've done what I've done, Most High. If I chose wrong, I'll apologize, except I don't think I have."

"Let it go," Otah said. "We'll deal with it later."

"I'd rather do it now," Sinja said, shifting his weight. "If I'm going to be drowned as a traitor, I'd like to know it."

Otah felt the rage rise up in his breast like a flame uncurling. He heard it in his ears.

"You want pardon?"

"For the boys too," Sinja said. "I swear I'll do everything I can to earn it."

You'll swear anything you like and break the oath when it suits you, Otah thought. He bit his lip until he thought it might bleed, but he didn't shout. He didn't call for the armsmen who waited outside the great blue doors. It would have been simple to have the man killed. It would have even felt like justice, he thought. His own man. His friend and advisor. Walking beside the Galtic general. Giving him advice. But the rage wasn't only rage. It was also fear. And despair. And so no matter how right it felt, it couldn't be trusted.

"Don't ask me for anything again."

"I won't, Otah-cha." And then a moment later, "You're a harder man than when I left."

"I've earned it."

"It suits you."

A rattle came from the door, and then a polite scratching, and Cehmai, Maati, and Liat came in the room. Their faces were flushed, and Maati's breath was heavy as if he'd been running. Otah frowned. He wouldn't have chosen to have Liat here, but she'd helped Kiyan with the preparations of the city and the quartering of the refugees of Cetani, so perhaps it was for the best after all. He took a general pose of greeting.

"What's . . . happened," Maati wheezed.

"We have a problem," Otah said.

"The Galts?" Liat asked.

"Ten thousand of them," Kiyan said, speaking for the first time since Sinja had begun his report. Her voice was solid as stone. "Foot soldiers and archers and horsemen. They won't reach us today. But tomorrow, perhaps. Three days at the most."

Maati's face went white and he sat down hard, like a puppet whose strings had been cut. Liat and Cehmai didn't move to help him. The room was silent except for the murmur of the fire. Otah let the moment pass. There was nothing he could say just now that they wouldn't think for themselves in the next few heartbeats. Cehmai recovered the fastest, his brows rising, his mouth going tight and hard.

"What do we do?" the younger poet asked.

"We have some advantages," Otah said. "We outnumber them. We know the city. We're in a position to defend, and holding a city's easier than forcing your way in."

"On the other hand," Sinja said, "they're soldiers. You aren't. They know that they need shelter from the cold and need it quickly. Taking Machi's their only option. And they know a fair amount about the city as well."

"You told them that too?" Otah asked.

"They've had their agents and traders in all the cities for generations," Kiyan said softly. "They've put their hands in our affairs. They've walked the streets and sat in the bathhouses. They have trading houses that wintered here when your father was Khai."

"Not to mention the several hundred native guides working for them who aren't me," Sinja said. "I was leading a militia, you'll recall. I've left as many as I could behind, but they've had a season to get any information they wanted."

Otah raised his hands in a pose that abandoned his point. He had the feeling of trembling that he remembered from the aftermath of his battles. From hearing Danat's struggles to breathe when his cough had been at its worst. It wasn't time to feel; he couldn't afford to feel. He tried to push the fear and despair away; he couldn't. It was in his blood now.

"I can try," Maati said. "I'll have to try."

"You have a binding ready?" Sinja asked.

"Not ready," Cehmai said. "We have it in outline. It would need weeks to refine it."

"I'll try," Maati said. His voice was stronger now. His lips were pulled thin. "But I don't know that it will help if it comes to a battle. If it works, I can see they never bear children, but that won't stop them in the near term."

"You could make it hurt," Sinja suggested. "Men don't fight as well newly gelded."

Maati frowned deeply, his fingers moving on their own, as if tracing numbers in the air.

"Do what you can," Otah said. "If you think a change will make the binding less likely to work, don't do it. We need an andat—any andat. The details aren't important."

"Could we pretend?" Liat asked. "Dress someone as an andat, and send them out with Maati. How would the Galts know it wasn't true?"

"The costume would have to involve not breathing," Cehmai said. Liat looked crestfallen.

"Kiyan," Otah said. "Can we arm the people we have?"

"We can improvise something," his wife said. "If we put men in the towers, we can rain stones and arrows on them. It would make it hard for them to keep to the streets. And if we block the stairways and keep the platforms locked at the top, it would be hard work to get them out."

"Until the cold kills them," Sinja said. "There's not enough coal in the ground to keep those towers warm enough to live in."

"They can survive a few days," Otah said. "We'll see to it."

"We can also block off the entrances to the tunnels," Liat said. "Hide the ventilation shafts and fill as many of the minor ways down as we can find with stones. It would be easier, wouldn't it, if there were only one or two places that we needed to defend?"

"There's another option," Sinja said. "I don't like to mention it, but . . . If you surrender, Balasar-cha will kill Otah and Eiah and Danat. Cehmai and Maati. The Khai Cetani and his family too, if they're here. He'll burn the books. But he'd accept surrender from the utkhaiem after that. It's a dozen or so people. There's no way to do this that kills fewer."

Otah felt himself rock back. A terrible weight seemed to fall on his shoulders. He wouldn't. Of course he would not. He would let every man and woman in the city die before he offered up his children to be slaughtered, but it meant that every one that died in the next few days would be doubly upon his conscience. Every life that ended here, ended because he had refused to be a sacrifice. He swallowed to loosen the knot in his throat and took a pose that dismissed the subject.

"I had to say it," Sinja said, apologizing with his tone.

"You didn't say my name," Kiyan said. Her eyes turned to Sinja's. "Why didn't you say my name?"

"Well, assuming that you don't all opt for slaughter, there is one other thing we have in our favor," Sinja said. "They sent me here to betray you. Kiyan's safety was my asking price. They expect a report from me when they arrive. If I give them bad information, we may be able to trap some of them. Thin their forces. It won't win the battle, but it could help."

Otah raised his hand, and the mercenary stopped. Kiyan was the one who took a querying pose, and it was to Kiyan that he answered.

"The general. Balasar-cha. He doesn't want a bloody battle. He wants it over quickly, with as few of his men lost as he can manage. I agreed to come here and discover your defenses if he spared you. Gave you to me when it was all over with. Prize of war. It's not all that uncommon."

Kiyan rose, her small foxlike face turned feral. Her fingers were splayed in claws, and her chest pressed forward like a bantam ready for the fighting pit. Otah's heart warmed with something like pride.

"If you let them touch Eiah and Danat, I would kill you in your sleep," she said.

"But Balasar-cha doesn't know that," Sinja said, shrugging and looking into the fire. He couldn't meet her eyes. "He expects a report from me, and I'll give him one. I'll give him whatever report you'd like."

"Gods," Kiyan said, her eyes still ablaze. "Is there anyone you haven't betrayed?"

Sinja smiled, but Otah thought there was sorrow in his dark eyes.

"Yes, there is. But she was in love with someone else."

Cehmai coughed, embarrassed. Otah raised his hands.

"Enough," he said. "We haven't got time for this. We may have as little as a day to get ready. Maati, you prepare your binding. Cehmai will help you. Kiyan. Liat. You've arranged food and quarters for two cities. Do what you can to arm them and keep people from panicking. Sinja and I will work out a plan to defend the city and a report to deliver to the Galts."

Kiyan's eyes carried a question, but Otah didn't answer. There was no reason to trust Sinja-cha. It was just the risk he chose to take.

Servants brought maps of the city, of the low towns to the south, and the mountains and mines to the north. Machi hadn't been built to withstand a war; there were no walls to defend, no pits that the enemy would have to bridge. The only natural barrier—the river—was already frozen solid enough to walk across. Any real defense would have to be on the black-cobbled streets, in the alleys and tunnels and towers. They talked late into the night, joined by the Khai Cetani and Ashua Radaani, Saya the blacksmith and Kiyan when she wasn't out among the tunnels spreading the word and making preparations. Sinja's shame, if it was still there, was hidden and his advice was well considered. By morning, even the Khai Cetani suffered interruption from Sinja-cha. Otah took it as another sign that the Khai had changed.

If things went poorly, there was still the mine in the northern mountains. A few people could take shelter there. Eiah and

Danat. Nayiit. If the binding failed, they could send Maati and Cehmai there as well, sneaking them out the back of the palace in a fast cart while the battle was still alive. Otah didn't imagine that he would be there with them, and Sinja didn't question him.

Afterward, Otah looked in on his children, both asleep in their chambers. He found the library where Cehmai and Maati were still arguing over points of grammar so obscure he could hardly make sense of them. The night candle was guttering and spitting when Otah came at last to his bed. Kiyan sat with him in silence for a time. He touched her, tracing the curve of her cheek with the knuckles of one hand.

"Do you believe Sinja?" he asked.

"What part of it?"

"Do you think that this General Gice really believes the andat are too dangerous to exist? That he wants them destroyed? What he said about killing the poet . . . I don't know what to think of that."

"If burning the library is really one of his demands, then maybe," Kiyan said. "I can't think he'd want the books and scrolls burned if he hoped to bind more andat of his own."

Otah nodded, and lay back, his gaze turned toward the ceiling above him, dark as a moonless sky.

"I'm not sure he's wrong," Otah said.

Wordless, she drew his mouth to hers, guided his hands. He would have thought himself too tired for the physical act of love, but she proved him wrong. Afterward, she lay at his side, her fingertips tracing the ink that had been worked into his skin when he had been an eastern islander leading one of his previous lives. He slept deeply and with a feeling of peace utterly unjustified by the situation.

He woke alone, called in the servants who bathed and dressed a Khai. Or, however briefly, an Emperor. Black robes, shot with red. Thick-woven wool layered with waxed silk. Robes of colors chosen for war and designed for cold. He took himself up through the great galleries, rising toward the surface and the light, being seen by the utkhaiem of both Machi and Cetani, by the common laborers hurrying to throw vast cartfuls of rubble into the minor entrances to the underground, by the merchants and couriers. The food sellers and beggars. The city.

The sky was white and gray, vast and empty as a blank page. Crows commented to one another, their voices dispassionate and considering as low-town judges. High above, the towers of Machi loomed, and smoke rose from the sky doors—the sign that men were up there in the thin, distant air burning coal and wood to warm their hands, preparing for the battle. Otah stood on the steps of his palace, the bitter cold numbing his cheeks and biting at his nose and ears, the world smelling of smoke and the threat of snow. Distant and yet clear, like the voice of a ghost, bells began to ring in the towers and great yellow banners unfurled like the last, desperate unfallen leaves of the vast stone trees.

The Galts had come.

SNOW FELL gently that morning, drifting down from the sheet of clouds above them in small, hard flakes. Balasar stood on the ridgeline of the hills south of the city. Frost had formed on the folds of his leather cloak, and the snow that landed on his shoulders didn't melt. Before him, the stone towers rose, seeming closer than they were, more real than the snow-grayed mountains behind them. No enemy army had marched out to meet him, no party of utkhaiem marred the thin white blanket, still little more than ankle-deep, that separated Balasar from Machi. Behind him, his men were gathered around the steam wagons, pressed around the furnace grates that Balasar had ordered opened. The medics were already busy with men suffering from the cold. The captains and masters of arms were seeing that every clump of men was armed and armored. Balasar had been sure to mention the warm baths beneath Machi, the food supplies laid in those tunnels—enough, he assumed, to keep two cities alive for the winter.

Smoke rose from the tops of the towers and from the city

itself. Banners flew. He heard a horseman approaching him from behind, and he glanced back to see Eustin on a great bay mare. The beast's breath was heavy and white as feathers. Balasar raised a hand, as Eustin cantered forward, pulled his mount to a halt, and saluted.

"I'm ready, sir. I've a hundred men volunteered to come with me. With your permission."

"Of course," Balasar said, then looked back at the towers. "Do you really think they'd do it? Sneak out. Run north and try to hide in the low towns out there?"

"Best to have us there in the event," Eustin said. "I could be wrong, sir. But I'd rather be careful now than have to spend the cold part of the season making raids. Especially if this is the warm bit."

Balasar shook his head. He didn't believe that the Khai Machi Sinja had described to him would run. He would fight unfairly, he would launch attacks from ambush, he would have his archers aim for the horses. But Balasar didn't think he would run. Still, the poets might. Or the Khai might send his children away for safety, if he hadn't already. And there would be refugees. Eustin's plan to block their flight was a wise one. He couldn't help wishing that Eustin might have been with him here, at the end. They were the last of the men who had braved the desert, and Balasar felt a superstitious dread at sending him away.

"Sir?"

"Be careful," Balasar said. "That's all."

A trumpet called, and Balasar turned back to the city. Sure enough, there was something—a speck of black on the white. A single rider, fleeing Machi.

"Well," Eustin said. "Looks like Captain Ajutani's come back after all. Give him my compliments."

Balasar smiled at the disdain in Eustin's voice.

"I'll be careful too," he said.

It took something like half a hand for Sinja to reach the camp. Balasar noticed particularly that he didn't turn to the bridge, riding instead directly over the frozen river. Eustin and his force were gone, looping around to the north, well before the mercenary captain arrived. Balasar had cups of strong kafe waiting when Sinja, his face pink and raw-looking from his ride, was shown into his tent.

Balasar retuned his salute and gestured to a chair. Sinja took a pose of thanks—so little time back among the Khaiem and the use of formal pose seemed to have returned to the man like an accent—and sat, drawing a sheaf of papers from his sleeve. When they spoke, it was in the tongue of the Khaiem.

"It went well?"

"Well enough," Sinja said. "I made a small mistake and had to do some very pretty dancing to cover it. But the Khai's got few enough hopes, he *wants* to trust me. Makes things easier. Now, here. These are rough copies of the maps he's used. They're filling in the main entrances to the underground tunnels to keep us from bringing any single large force down at once. The largest paths they've left open are here," Sinja touched the map, "and here."

"And the poets?"

"They have the outline of a binding. I think they're going to try it. And soon."

Balasar felt the sinking of dread in his belly, and strangely also a kind of peace. He wouldn't have thought there was any part of him that was still held back, and yet that one small fact—the poets lived and planned and would recapture one of the andat now if they could—took away any choice he might still have had. He looked at the map, his mind sifting through strategies like a tiles player shuffling chits of bone.

"There are men in the towers," Balasar said.

"Yes, sir," Sinja said. "They'll have stones and arrows to drop. You won't be able to use the streets near them, but the range isn't good, and they won't be able to aim from so far up. Go a street or two over and keep by the walls, and we'll be safe. There won't be much resistance above ground. Their hope is to keep you at bay long enough for the cold to do their work for them."

Three forces, Balasar thought. One to clear out the houses

and trading shops on the south, another to push in toward the forges and the metalworkers, a third to take the palaces. He wouldn't take the steam wagons—he'd learned that much from Coal—so horsemen would be important for the approach, though they might be less useful if the fighting moved inside structures as it likely would. And they'd be near useless once they were underground. Archers wouldn't have much effect. There were few long, clear open spaces in the city. But despite what Sinja said, Balasar expected there would be some fighting on the surface, so enough archers were mixed with the foot troops to fire back at anyone harassing them from the windows and snow doors of the passing buildings.

"Thank you, Sinja-cha," Balasar said. "I know how much doing this must have cost you."

"It needed doing," Sinja said, and Balasar smiled.

"I won't insist that you watch this happen. You can stay at the camp or ride north and join Eustin."

"North?"

"He's taken it to guard. In case someone tries to slip away during the battle."

"That's a good thought," Sinja said, his tone somewhat rueful. "If it's all the same, I'd like to ride with Eustin-cha. I know he hasn't always thought well of me, and if anything does go wrong, I'd like to be where he can see I wasn't the one doing it."

"A pretty thought," Balasar said, chuckling.

"You're going to win," Sinja said. It was a simple statement, but there was a weight behind it. A regret that soldiers often had in the face of loss, and only rarely in victory.

"You thought of changing sides," Balasar said. "While you were there, with all the people you know. In your old home. It was hard not to stand by them."

"That's true," Sinja said.

"It wouldn't have changed things. One more sword—even yours—wouldn't have changed the way this battle falls."

"That's why I came back," Sinja said.

"I'm glad you did," Balasar said. "I've been proud to ride with you."

Sinja gave his thanks and took his leave. Balasar wrote out orders for the guard to accompany Sinja and other ones to deliver to Eustin. Then he turned to the maps of Machi. Truly there was little choice. The poets lived. Another night in the cold would mean losing more men. Balasar sat for a long moment, quietly asking God to let this day end well; then he walked out into the late-morning sun and gave the call to formation.

It was time.

23

Liat had expected panic—in herself and in the city. Instead there was a strange, tense calm. Wherever she went, she was greeted with civility and even pleasure. There were smiles and even laughter, and a sense of purpose in the face of doom. In the interminable night, she had been invited to join in three suppers, as many breakfasts, and bowls of tea without number. She had seen the highest of the utkhaiem sitting with metalsmiths and common armsmen. She had heard one of the famed choirs of Machi softly singing its Candles Night hymns. The rules of society had been suspended, and the human solidarity beneath it moved her to weep.

She and Kiyan had taken the news first to the Khai Cetani and the captains of the battle that had once turned the Galts aside. When the plans had come from Otah's small Council—where to place men, how to resist the Galts as they tried to overrun the city—the Khai Cetani had emerged with the duties of arming and armoring the men who could fight. As the underground city was emptied of anything that could be used as a weapon—hunting arrows, kitchen knives, even lengths of leather and string cut from beds and fashioned into slings—Liat had seen children too young to fight and men and women too old or frail or ill packed into side galleries, the farthest from the fighting. Cots lined the walls, piled with blankets. In some places, there were thick doors that could be closed and pegged from the inside. Though if the Galts ever came this far, it would hardly matter how difficult it was to open the doors. Everything would already be lost.

Kiyan had made the physicians her personal duty—preparing one of the higher galleries for the care of the wounded and dying who would be coming back before the day's end. They'd managed seventy beds and scavenged piles of cloth high as a man's waist, ready to pack wounds. Bottles of distilled wine stood ready to ease pain and clean cuts. A firekeeper's kiln, cauterizing irons already glowing in its maw, had been pulled in and the air was rich with the scent of poppy milk cooking to the black sludge that would take away pain at one spoonful and grant mercy with two. Liat walked between the empty beds, imagining them as they would shortly be—canvas soaked with gore. And still the panic didn't come.

By the entrance, one of the physicians was talking in a calm voice to twenty or so girls and boys no older than Eiah, too young to fight, but old enough to help care for the wounded. Kiyan was nowhere to be found, and Liat wasn't sure whether she was pleased or dismayed.

She sat on one of the beds and let her eyes close. She had not slept all the long night. She wouldn't sleep until the battle was ended. Which meant, of course, that she might never sleep again. The thought carried a sense of unreality that was, she thought, the essential mood of the city. This couldn't be happening. People went about the things that needed doing with a numb surprise that hell had bloomed up in the world. The men in their improvised leather armor and sharpened fire irons could no more fathom that there would be no tomorrow for them than Liat could. And so they were capable of walking, of speaking, of eating food. If they had been given time to understand, the Galts wouldn't have faced half the fight that was before them now.

"Mama-kya!" a man's voice said close at hand. Nayiit's. Liat's eyes flew open.

He stood in the aisle between beds, his eyes wide. Danat, pale-skinned and frightened, clung to her boy's robes.

"What are you doing still here?" Liat said.

"Eiah," Nayiit said. "I can't find Eiah. She was in her rooms, getting dressed, but when I came back with Danat-cha, she was gone. She isn't at the cart. I thought she might be here. I can't leave without her."

"You should have left before the sun rose," Liat said, standing up. "You have to leave now."

"But Eiah—"

"You can't wait for her," Liat said. "You can't *stay* here."

Danat began to cry, a high wailing that echoed against the high tiled ceiling and seemed to fill the world. Nayiit crouched and tried to calm the boy. Liat felt something warm and powerful unwind in her breast. Rage, perhaps. She hauled her son up by his shoulder and leaned in close.

"Leave her," she said. "Leave the girl and get out of this city *now*. Do you understand me?"

"I promised Kiyan-cha that I'd—"

"You can't keep a girl fourteen summers old from being stupid. No one can. She made her decision when she left you."

"I promised that I'd look after them," Nayiit said.

"Then save the one you can," Liat said. "And do it now, before you lose that chance too."

Nayiit blinked in something like surprise and glanced down at the still-wailing boy. His expression hardened and he took a pose of apology.

"You're right, Mother. I wasn't thinking."

"Go. Now," Liat said. "You don't have much time."

"I want my sister!" Danat howled.

"She's going to meet us there," Nayiit said, and then swept the boy up in his arms with a grunt. Danat—eyes puffy and red, snot streaming from his nose—pulled back to stare at Nayiit with naked mistrust. Nayiit smiled his charming smile. His father's smile. Otah's. "It's going to be fine, Danat-kya. Your mama and papa and your sister. They'll meet us at the cave. But we have to leave now."

"No they won't," the boy said.

"You watch," Nayiit said, lying cheerfully. "You'll see. Eiah's probably there already."

"But we have the cart."

"Yes, good thought," Nayiit said. "Let's go see the cart."

He leaned over, awkward with his burden of boy, and kissed Liat.

"I'll do better," he murmured.

You're perfect, Liat wanted to say. You've always been the perfect boy.

But Nayiit was rushing away now, his robes billowing behind him as he sped to the end of the gallery, Danat still on his hip, and turned to the north and vanished toward the back halls and the cart and the north where if the gods could hear Liat's prayers, they would be safe.

HOUSE SIYANTI had offered up its warehouses for the Khaiem—Machi and Cetani together—to use as their commandery. Five stories high and well back from the edge of the city, the wide, gently sloped roof had as clear a view of the streets as anything besides the great towers themselves. A passage led from the lower warehouse on the street level into the underground should there be a need to retreat into that shelter. In the great empty space—the warehouse emptied of its wares—Maati wrote the text of his binding on the smooth stone wall, pausing occasionally to rub his hands together and try to calm his unquiet mind. A stone stair led up to the second-floor snow doors, which stood open to let the sun in until they were ready to light the dozen glass lanterns that lined the walls. The air blew in bitterly cold and carried a few stray flakes of hard snow that had found their way down from the sky.

Ideally, Maati would have spent the last day meditating on the binding—holding the nuances of each passage clear in his mind, creating step-by-step the mental structure that would become the andat. He had done his best, drinking black tea and reading through his outline for Corrupting-the-Generative. The binding looked solid. He thought he could hold it in his mind. With months or weeks—perhaps even days—he could have been sure. But this morning he felt scattered. The hot metal scent of the brazier, the wet smell of the snow, the falling gray snowflakes against a sky of white, the scuffing of Cehmai's feet against the stone floor, and the occasional distant call of trumpet and drum as the armsmen and defenders of Machi took their places—everything seemed to catch his attention. And he could not afford distraction.

"I don't know if I can do this," he said. His voice echoed against the stone walls, sounding hollow. He turned to meet Cehmai's gaze. "I don't know if I can go through with this, Cehmai-kya."

"I know," the other poet said, but did not pause in his work of chalking symbols into the spare walls. "I felt the same before I took Stone-Made-Soft from my master. I don't think any poet has ever gone to the binding without some sense he was jumping out of a tower in hopes of learning to fly on the way down."

"But the binding," Maati said. "We haven't had time."

"I don't know," Cehmai said, turning to look at Maati. "I've been thinking about it. The draft you made. It's as complex as some bindings I saw when I was training. The nuances support each other. The symbols seem to hang together. And the structure that deflects the price fits it. I think you've been working on this for longer than you think. Maybe since Saraykeht fell."

Maati looked out the snow door at their bright square of sky. His chest felt tight. He thought for a moment how sad it would be to have come this far and collapse now from a bad heart.

"I remember when I was at the village the second time," Maati said. "After Saraykeht. After Liat left me. There was a teahouse at the edge of the village. Tanam Choyan's place."

"High walls," Cehmai said. "And a red lacquer door to the back room. I remember the place. They always undercooked the rice."

"He did," Maati said. "I'd forgotten that. There was a

standing game of tiles there. I remember once a boy came to play and didn't know any of the rules. Not even what season led, or when two winds made a trump. He bet everything he had at the first tile. He knew he was in over his head, so he risked it all at once. He thought if he kept playing, then the men at the table who knew better than he did would strip him of every length of copper he had. If he put everything on one hand—well, someone had to win, and it might be him as well as anyone else. I understand now how he felt."

"Did he win?"

"No," Maati said. "But I respected the strategy."

A trumpet blared out above them—Otah sending some signal among his men. Answering horns came from around the city. Maati could no more tell where they originated than guess how many snowflakes were in the wide air. Cehmai's surprised breath caught his attention like a hook pulling at a fish. He turned to the man, and then followed his gaze to the stairway leading down to the tunnels. Eiah stood there, her ribs pumping hard, as if she'd run to reach them. Her hair was pulled back in a messy knot at the back. Her robes were bright green shot with gold.

"Eiah-cha," Cehmai said, stepping toward her. "What are you doing here?"

The girl looked up at Cehmai, stepping away from him as if she might run. Her gaze darted to Maati. He smiled and took a pose that was welcome and inquiry both. Eiah's hands fluttered between half a dozen poses, settling on none of them.

"They need physicians," she said. "People are going to get hurt. I don't want to be useless. And . . . and I want to be here when you stop them. I helped with the binding as much as Cehmai did."

That was a gross untruth, but the girl delivered it with such conviction that Maati felt himself half-believing. He smiled.

"You were supposed to go with Nayiit-cha and your brother," Maati said.

Her mouth went small, her face pale.

"I know," she said. Maati waved her closer, and she came to him, skirting around Cehmai as if she feared he would grab her and haul her away to where she was supposed to be. Maati sat on the cold stone floor and she sat with him.

"It isn't safe here," he said.

"It's safe enough that you can be here. And Papa-kya. And you're the two most important men in the world."

"I don't know that—"

"He's the Emperor. Even the Khai Cetani says so. And you're going to kill all the Galts. There can't be any place safer than with both of you. Besides, what if something happens and *you* need a physician?"

"I'll find one of the armsmen or a servant they can spare," Cehmai said. "We can at least have her safely—"

"No," Maati said. "Let her stay. She reminds me why we're doing this."

Eiah's grin was the image of relief and joy. Of all the terrors and dangers arrayed before them, hers had been that she might be sent away. He took her hand and kissed it.

"Go sit by the stairs," he said. "Don't interrupt me, and if Cehmai-cha tells you to do something, you do it. No asking why, no arguing him out of it. You understand me?"

Eiah flung her hands into a pose of acceptance.

"And Eiah-kya. Understand what I'm doing has risks to it. If I die here—hush, now, let me finish. If I fail the binding and my little protection doesn't do what we think it will, I'll pay the price. If that happens, you have to remember that I love you very deeply, and I've done this because it was worth the risk if it meant keeping you safe."

Eiah swallowed and her eyes shone with tears. Maati smiled at her, stood again, and waved her back toward the stairs. Cehmai came close, frowning.

"I'm not sure that was a kind thing to tell her," he said, but a sudden outburst of trumpet calls sounded before Maati could reply. Maati thought he could hear the distant tattoo of drums echoing against the city walls. He gestured to Cehmai.

"Come on. There isn't time. Finish drawing those, then

light the candles and close that blasted door. We'll all freeze to death before the andat can have its crack at us."

"Or we'll have it all in place just in time for the Galts to take it."

Maati scribbled out the rest of the binding. He'd wanted time to think on each word, each phrase; if he'd had time to paint each word like the portrait of a thought, it would have been better. There wasn't time. He finished just as Cehmai lit the final lantern and walked up the stone steps to the snow door. Before he closed it, the younger poet looked out, peering into the city.

"What do you see?"

"Smoke," Cehmai said. Then, "Nothing."

"Come back down," Maati said. "Where are the robes for it?"

"In the back corner," Cehmai said, pulling the wide wooden doors shut. "I'll get them."

Maati went to the cushion in the middle of the room, lowered himself with a grunt, and considered. The wall before him looked more like the scribblings of low-town vandals than a poet's lifework. But the words and phrases, the images and metaphors all shone brighter in his mind than the lanterns could account for. Cehmai passed before him briefly, laying robes of blue shot with black on the floor where, with luck, the next hands to hold them wouldn't be human.

Maati glanced over his shoulder. Eiah was sitting against the back wall, her hands held in fists even with her heart. He smiled at her. Reassuringly, he hoped. And then he turned to the words he had written, took five deep breaths to clear his mind, and began to chant.

OTAH STOOD on the lip of the roof and looked down at Machi as if it were a map. The great streets were marked by the lines of rooftops. Only those streets that led directly to House Siyanti's warehouses were at an angle that permitted him to see the black cobbles turning white beneath the snow.

To the south, the army of the Galts was marching forward. The trumpet calls from the high towers told him that much. They had worked out short signals for some eventualities— short melodies that signaled some part of the plans he had worked with Sinja and Ashua Radaani and the others. But in addition there was a code that let him phrase questions as if they were spoken words, and hear answers in the replies from the towers far above.

The trumpeter was a young man with a vast barrel chest and lips blue with cold. Whenever Otah had the man blow, the wide brass bell of the trumpet seemed as if it would deafen them all. And yet the responses were sometimes nearly too faint to hear. Times like now.

"What's he saying?" the Khai Cetani asked, and Otah held up a hand to stop him, straining to hear the last trailing notes.

"The Galts are taking the bridge," Otah said. "I don't think they trust the ice."

"That'll mean they're longer reaching us," the Khai Cetani said. "That's good. If we can keep them out of the warmth until sundown . . ."

Otah took a pose of agreement, but didn't truly believe it. If they were able to trap the Galts above ground when night came, the invaders would take over the houses and burn whatever they could break small enough to fit in the fire grates. If the cold air moved in—a storm or the frigid winds that ended the gentle snows of autumn—then the Galts would be in trouble, but the snow graying the distance now wasn't prelude to a storm. Otah didn't say it, but he couldn't imagine keeping an army so close and still at bay long enough for the weather to change. The Galts would be defeated here in the streets, or they wouldn't be defeated.

He paced the length of the rooftop, his eyes tracing the routes that he had hoped to guide them toward—the palaces and the forges. Behind him, his servants shivered from the cold and the need to remain respectfully still. The great iron fire grate that they'd hauled up and loaded with logs was burning merrily, but somehow the heat from it seemed to go out no more than a foot or two from the flames. The Khai Cetani stood near it, and the trumpeter. Otah couldn't imagine standing still. Not now.

The southern reaches of the city were essentially Galtic already; there was no way to make them safe against the coming army. The battle would be nearer the center, in the shadows of the towers, in the narrower ways where Otah's men could appear all along the Galtic line at once as they had in the forest. Another trumpet call came. The Galts had finished crossing the river. The march had begun on Machi itself.

I should be down there, Otah thought. I should get a sword or an axe and go down there.

It was an idiotic idea, and he knew it. One more blade or bow in the streets wouldn't matter now, and getting himself killed would achieve nothing.

Trumpets sounded—half a dozen of them at once. And Galtic drums. Everyone sending signals, none of them listening. Otah squatted at the roof's edge with his eyes closed, trying to make out one message from another. Frustration built in his spine and neck. Something was happening—several things, and all at the same moment, and he couldn't hear what they were.

"Most High!" one the servants called. "There!"

Otah and the Khai Cetani both looked to where the servant boy was pointing. A runner dashed along a roofline, down near the great, wide streets that led toward the forges. A great pillar of smoke was rising from the south. Something there, then. Otah felt the first small surge of hope; it was near where he had hoped the Galts would go. The trumpets were calling again, fewer of them. Otah found himself better able to make sense of them. The Galts seemed to be moving in three directions at once—sweeping and holding the southern buildings, and then two large forces moving as Otah had hoped they would.

"Call to the towers," Otah said. "Tell them to begin."

The trumpeter took a great breath and blared out the melody they had set for the towers, and then the rising trill that was their signal to begin raining stones and arrows into the streets. It was less than a breath before Otah thought he saw something fly from the open sky doors far above them, plummeting toward the ground. The snow was tricky, though. It might only have been his imagination.

Otah felt himself trying to stretch out his will across the city, to inhabit it like a ghost, to become it. Time slowed to a terrible crawl—years seeming to pass between the short announcing blasts of the trumpets as they reported the Galts' progress. Muffled by the snow, there also came the sound of distant voices raised in anger. Otah's belly knotted. That wasn't right. There shouldn't be any fighting yet. Unless the Galts had found his men while they were still in hiding. He almost signaled his trumpeter to sound the order to report, but the more the signals were used, the better the Galts would be able to find the trumpeters.

"You," Otah said, pointing at one of the half-frozen servants. "Send a runner to the east. I need to know what's happening there."

The man took a pose of acknowledgment and walked quickly and awkwardly back toward the stairs. Otah tapped his hand against the stone lip of the roof, already impatient for the word to come back to him. His feet and face were numb. The snowfall seemed to be thickening, the world a darker gray though the unseen sun was still likely six or seven hands above the southern horizon.

From the west, the drums of Galt thundered, then were silent. Then thundered again. Otah heard the sudden sharp call—thousands of voices at once in a wild call that ended sharply. A boast. We are vast as the ocean and disciplined. We are soldiers. We have come to kill you. Fear us.

And he did.

"Signal the palace forces to take their places," Otah said.

The trumpeter sang out the call, the wide bell of the trumpet playing over the western rooftops like a priest offering blessing to a crowd. The man was weeping, Otah saw. Tears streaking down his cheeks and into his beard. A terrible, rending crash came from the forges. Otah turned to peer through the rising smoke and the falling snow. He expected to see one of the great copper roofs sitting at an angle, but nothing seemed to have changed. The sound was a mystery.

"I can't stand this," Otah said, stalking back to the Khai Cetani and the servants. There was snow gathering on the servants' shoulders. "I don't know what's happening. I can't command a battle blind and guessing. Where are the runners?"

The eldest of the servants took a pose of apology.

"Then go find out," Otah said.

But Otah felt in his bones what the runners would tell him. Before the signals came—trumpets struggling through the muffling snow. Before the Galtic drums broke out in their manic pounding. Nine thousand veterans led by the greatest general in Galt were pouring into his city and facing blacksmiths and vegetable carters, laborers and warehouse guards.

He was losing.

24

>+< Balasar trotted through the streets, his shield held above his head. Despite what Sinja had said, the great towers of Machi commanded the streets around them fairly well. Throughout the day, stones and bricks peppered his men, sailing down from the sky with the force of boulders hurled by siege engines. Arrows sometimes came down as well, their points shattering against the ground where they struck despite the slowly growing cushion of snow. He ducked into another doorway when he came to it. Five of his own men were waiting, and the bodies of ten or so of the enemy. It was a slow process, spreading out and then moving down not only the streets that were the fastest path to the tunnels, but also two or three to each side. The Khai Machi had learned a trick, and he'd used it against Coal. But he didn't have a second strategy, and so Balasar knew where to find the waiting forces—just back from where they'd be seen, waiting to attack on all sides at once. Instead, Balasar was killing them by handfuls. It was a bad way to fight—bloody, slow, painful, and unnecessary.

But it was better than losing.

"General Gice, sir," the captain said as all the men saluted him. Balasar raised his hand. His arm ached from holding the raised shield. "We're making progress, sir."

"Good," Balasar said. "What have we found?"

"All the smaller passages are blocked off, sir. Collapsed or filled with rubble so deep we can't tell how long it would take to dig them out. And they're narrow, sir. Two men together at most."

"We wouldn't want those anyway," Balasar said. "Better we keep for the objectives. And casualties?"

"We're estimating five hundred of the enemy dead, sir. But that's rough."

"And our men?"

"Perhaps half that," the captain said.

"So many?"

"They aren't good fighters, sir, but they're committed."

Balasar sighed, his mind shifting. If he assumed the force pushing toward the palaces was having similar luck, that meant something like fifteen hundred dead since he'd walked into the city. More, if there was resistance in the south. This wasn't a battle, only slow, ugly slaughter. He went to the doorway, peering out down the street. He could hear the sounds of fighting—men's voices, the clash of metal on metal. A hundred small outbursts that became a constant roar, like raindrops falling on a pond.

"Get the drummer," he said. "We'll make a push for it. Scatter the enemy, take the entrance to the tunnels and then get runners to the others."

"The men we're seeing, sir. They're able-bodied. And decent fighters, some of them."

"They wanted to do this on the surface," Balasar said. "The tunnels will be their second string. It won't be as bad once we're in there. If they're smart, they'll see there's no point going on."

The captain saluted without answering. Balasar was willing to take that as agreement.

It took perhaps half a hand to gather a force of men together. Two hundred soldiers would press forward and take the forges, where Sinja had said the paths down would be open. They were only another street down. There wasn't a line of defenders to crush, so the horsemen were less useful. They could still move fast, and men on foot who entered the streets wouldn't be able to attack them easily. Footmen with archers interspersed between them ducking fast from doorway to doorway was the best plan.

He explained it all to the group leaders, watching the men's faces as he asked them to run through the rain of stones and arrows. Two hundred men to move forward, to take control of the forges and then hold the position against anything that came up out of it until the rest of their force could join them. Balasar would lead them. Not one of them hesitated or voiced objection.

"If we live until sunset," he said, "we'll see the end of this. Now take formation."

The drum throbbed, the captains and group leaders scrambled to the places where their men stood waiting. A few bricks detonated on the street in their wake, but no one had stayed out long enough to be in danger from them. Balasar squatted in his chosen doorway, rubbing his shoulder. The air was numbing cold, and the great dark towers rose around them, higher than the crows that wheeled and called, excited, he guessed, by the smells of blood and carrion.

It struck him how beautiful the city was. Austere and close-packed, with thick-walled buildings and heavy shutters. The brightness of snow and the glittering icicles that hung from the eaves set off the darkness of stone and echoed the vast blank sky. It was a city without color—dark and light with hardly even gray in between—and Balasar found himself moved by it. He took a deep breath, watching the cloud of it that formed when he exhaled. The drummer at his side licked his lips.

"Go," Balasar said.

The deep rattle sounded, echoing between the high walls of the houses, and then the press was on, and Balasar launched himself into it, shield high, shoulder cramping. He made it almost halfway to the shelter of the forges and their great copper roofs before the arrows could drop the distance of the towers. Five men fell around him as he ran that last stretch and found himself in a tangle of heat and shouting and swinging blades. One last group of the enemy had stayed hidden here to defy him, to stand guard against them. Balasar shouted and moved

forward with the surge of his men. In the field, there would
have been formation, rules, order. This was only melee, and
Balasar found himself hewing and hacking with his blood
singing and alive. It was an idiotic place for a general to be,
throwing himself in the face of a desperate enemy, but Balasar
felt the joy of it washing away his better sense. A man with a
spear fashioned from an old rake poked at him, and he batted
the attack away and swung hard, cutting the man down. Three
of the locals had formed a knot, fighting with their backs together. Balasar's men overwhelmed them.

And then it was finished. As suddenly as it had begun, the
fight ended. The bodies of the enemy lay at their feet, along
with a few of their own. Not many. Steam rose from the corpses
of friend and foe alike. But they'd reached the tunnels. One last
push, down deep into the belly of the city, and it would be over.
The war. The andat. Everything. He felt himself smiling like a
wolf. His shoulder and arm no longer hurt.

"General! Sir! It's blocked!"

"What?"

One of his captains came forward, gore soaking his tunic
from elbow to knee, his expression dismayed.

"It can't be," Balasar said, striding forward. But the captain
turned and led him. And there it was. A great gateway of stone,
a sloping ramp leading down wide enough for four carts
abreast to travel into it. And as he came forward, his boots
slipping where the fight had churned the snow to slush, he saw
it was true. The shadows beneath the gateway were filled with
stones, cut and rough, large as boulders and small as fists.
Something glittered among them. Shattered glass and sharp,
awkward scraps of metal. Clearing this would take days.

He'd been betrayed. Sinja Ajutani had led him astray. The
taste of it was like ashes. And worse than the deception itself
was that it would change nothing. The defending forces were
scattered, the towers would run out of bricks and arrows, given
time. All that Sinja had accomplished was to prolong the
agony and cost Balasar a few hundred more men and the Khai
Machi a few thousand.

Ah, Sinja, he thought. You were one of my men. One of
mine.

"Get me the maps" was what he said.

Knowing now that it had been a trap, knowing that the
forces of Machi would have some way to retreat, some pathway to muster their attack, Balasar scanned the thin lines that
marked out the streets and tunnels. His fingers left trails of
other men's blood.

Not the palaces. Sinja had sent him there. Not the forges.
His mind went cool, calm, detached. The blood rage of the
melee was gone, and he was a general again. The warehouses.
There, in the north. The galleries below would be good for
mustering a large force or creating an infirmary. There would
be water, and the light from it wouldn't shine out. If it were
his city, that would be the other plausible center from which to
make his campaign.

"I need runners. A dozen of them. We need to reach the
men at the palaces and tell them that the plan's changed."

SINJA HAD ridden hard for the north. Even as he heard the
distant horns that meant the battle within Machi had begun,
he leaned down over his mount and pushed for the paths and
rough mining roads that laced the foothills behind the city.
And there, low in the mountains where generations ago it had
been easy and convenient to haul ore, one of the first, oldest,
tapped-out mines. Otah's bolt-hole for the children and the
poets, and the only thing between it and the city—Eustin and
a hundred armed Galts. Visions of cart tracks crushed in the
snow and disappearing into the mine's mouth pricked at his
mind. Let Eustin not find them.

He reached the first ridge behind Machi just as a distant
crashing sound came from the city, the violence muffled by
distance and snowfall. The horse steamed beneath him. Riding
this hard in this weather was begging for colic; the horse was
nearly certain to die if he kept pressing it. And he was going to

keep pressing it. If a horse was the only thing he killed before
sunset, it would be a better day than he'd hoped.

Sinja reached the tunnel sometime after midday. Time was
hard to judge. Silently, he walked down into the half-lit mouth
of the tunnel and squatted, considering the dust-covered ground
until his eyes had adapted to the darkness. It was dry. No one
had passed through here since the snow had begun to fall. He
stalked back out, mounted, and turned his poor, suffering animal to the south again, trotting down the snow-obscured tracks,
cutting back and forth—west and east and west again—his
eyes peering through the gray for Eustin and his men. It wasn't
long before he found them—a dozen men set on patrol. There
were eight patrols, they told him, and Eustin in the one that
ranged nearest to the city. Sinja gave his sometime compatriots
his thanks and went on to the south.

His gloves were soaked, the cold creeping into his knuckles, when he found Eustin. Balasar's captain and ten of his
men had stopped a beaten old cart pulled by a mule and driven
by a young man with a long Northern face and a nervous expression. Eustin and four of the men had dismounted and
were talking to the panicked-looking man. Sinja called out
and Eustin hailed him and motioned him down with what appeared to be good enough will.

We're allies, Sinja told himself. We're Balasar Gice's men
on the day of the general's greatest triumph.

He forced his numbed lips into a smile and let his horse
pick its way gently downslope to where the soldiers and the
unfortunate refugee waited.

"Not going with the general?" Eustin asked as Sinja came
within comfortable speaking distance.

"Thought I'd let him kill all the people I knew without
my being there. I'd only have been a distraction."

Eustin shrugged.

"I'm surprised you're staying around at all," he said. "You
aren't about to be the most popular man in Machi. Wintering
here might not be good for you."

"Ah," Sinja said, swinging down from his horse. "I'll have all my dear friends from Galt to keep my back from sprouting arrows."

Eustin's noncommittal grunt seemed to finish the topic. Sinja considered the man on the cart. He looked familiar, but in a vague way, as if Sinja had known the man's brothers but not him.

"What have you got here?" Sinja asked, and Eustin turned his attention back to the refugee.

"Coward making a run for the hills," Eustin said. "I was talking with him about what he's carrying."

"Just my son," the man said. "I don't have any silver or gems. I don't have anything."

"Seems unlikely that you'd live well out there," Eustin said, nodding toward the north and the snow-veiled mountains. "So maybe it's best if you come back to the camp with us, eh?"

"Please. My sister and her husband. They live in one of the low towns. Up by the Radaani mines. We're going to stay with her," the man said. He was a good liar, Sinja thought. "I'm not a fighter, and my boy's no threat. We don't want any trouble."

"Bad day for you, then," Eustin said and gestured with his fingers. "The cloak. Open it."

Reluctantly, the man did. A sword hung at his hip. Eustin smiled.

"Not a fighter, eh? That's for scaring squirrels, then?"

"You can have it—"

"Got one, thanks," Eustin said. "Let's see this boy of yours."

The man hesitated, his eyes darting to the riders, to Eustin. He was thinking of running for it—his little mule against six men on horseback. Sinja took a simple pose that advised against it, and the man looked down, then turned to the back of the little cart.

"Choti-kya," he said. "Come say hello to these good men."

A bundle of brown waxed silk stirred in the back of the cart, rose up, and turned to face them. The boy's round face was shy and frightened, but also curious. His cheeks were red from the cold, as if someone had slapped him. As the small hands pushed out from his blankets and took a pose of greeting, Sinja sighed.

Danat. It was Kiyan's boy. So this man was Nayiit, and all Sinja's worst fears were unfolding right here before him.

One of Eustin's men stepped forward, looking through the cart. Danat shied back from him, but the soldier paid the boy no particular attention.

"What do you think we should do with them, Captain Ajutani," he asked. "Kill 'em or send them on?"

Sinja kept his face blank as his mind worked at an answer. Eustin didn't trust him and never had. Sinja tried to judge what the man would do—follow his advice, or take the opposite. He suspected Eustin would oppose him simply because he could. So the right choice would be to recommend death for Danat and Nayiit. The gamble was higher stakes than he liked. Eustin looked over at him, his eyebrows raised. Sinja was taking too long in answering.

"I don't like killing children," he said in Galtic.

"Wouldn't be the first time I've done it since we left Nantani. There was a whole school of them near Pathai. Kill the man, then? And leave the boy in a snowstorm? That seems cruel."

Sinja shrugged and took a simple pose of apology.

"I hadn't known you were a great killer of children," he said. "We all make our reputations somehow. Do whatever you think best."

Eustin scowled and the driver's face went pale. The man spoke Galtic, then. Sinja wasn't certain that was a good thing.

"Maybe I should kill the boy and let the man go," Eustin said, and Danat's keeper swung out of the cart, drawing his sword with a shout. Eustin jumped back, pulling his own blade free. It was fast, over almost before it began. The young man swung wild; Eustin parried the blow and sunk his own blade into Nayiit's belly. Nayiit fell back, clutching at his gut, while Eustin looked down at him in rage and disgust.

"What is the matter with you?" he said to the wounded man. "Look around you. There's a dozen of us. Did you think you were going to cut us all down?"

"Can't hurt Danat," the driver said.

"Who's Danat?"

When the driver didn't answer, Eustin shook his head and spat. Sinja could see what was coming next from the way Eustin held his shoulders and the blood in his face. Danat, still in the cart, made a mewling sound, and Sinja looked at the boy, looked into his eyes, and took a small pose that told him to prepare himself.

"Well, we aren't leaving the boy out here, whatever his name is," Eustin said. "Get him out where this idiot can see the price of attacking a Galt."

The soldier nearest the cart grabbed at the boy, and Danat yelped in fear. Eustin swung his blade in the air, his eyes locked on Nayiit's. Sinja nodded to the man at the cart when he spoke.

"Hold off there," he said, then turned to Eustin. "You're a good soldier, Eustin-cha. You're loyal and you're ruthless, and I want you to know I respect that."

Eustin cocked his head, confused.

"Thank you, I suppose," Eustin said, and Sinja drew his sword. Eustin's eyes went wide, and he barely blocked Sinja's thrust. Blood showed on his arm, and the other ten men pulled their own blades with a soft sound like a rake in gravel.

"What are you doing?" Eustin cried.

"Not betraying someone."

"What?"

This isn't how I'd hoped to die, Sinja thought. If the boy had any mother in the world besides Kiyan, he'd stand back and let the thing take its course. Instead, he was going to be cut down like a dog. But if the men were watching him, Danat could slip away. A boy of five summers was no threat. The men might not bother tracking him. Danat might find his way to the tunnel or some low town or into friendly hands. There wasn't a better option.

"Call them off, Eustin. This is between the two of us."

"*What's* between the two of us?"

Sinja raised the tip of his sword by a hand's span in answer. Eustin nodded and dropped his own blade into guard position.

"He's mine," Eustin called. "Leave us be."

Sinja took a step back, away from the cart, and smiled. Eustin let himself be drawn. In the corner of his vision, Sinja saw Danat drop from the cart's back. He took a hard grip on his sword, grinned, and swung. Steel rang on steel. Eustin closed and Sinja darted back, the snow crackling under his boots. They were both smiling now, and one of the bowmen had pulled out his quiver, prepared to act in case Eustin should fail. Sinja took a deep breath of cold air, and felt strangely like shouting.

He'd been wrong before; this was *exactly* how he'd hoped to die.

MAATI CHANTED until his mouth was dry, his eyes locked on the scrawled note on the wall before him. Each time he began to feel his thoughts taking shape, it distracted him. He would think that the binding was beginning to work, and he would leap ahead to the battle outside and what he could do, the fate of Galt, the future, what Eiah and Cehmai were seeing, and the solidity that the binding had taken would slip away again. It was hard to put the world aside. It was hard not to care.

He didn't pause, but he closed his eyes, picturing the wall and his writing upon it. He knew the binding—knew the structures of it, the grammars that formed the thoughts that put together everything he had hoped and intended. And instead of reading it from the world, he read it from the image in his own mind. Dreamlike, the warehouse wall seemed more solid, more palpable, with his eyes closed. The sound of his voice began to echo, syllables from different phrases blending together, creating new words that also spoke to Maati's intention. The air seemed thicker, harder to breathe. The world had become dense. He began his chant again, though he could still hear himself speaking the words that came halfway through it.

The wall in his mind began to sway, the image fading into a seed—peach pit and flax seed and everything in between the two. And an egg. And a womb. And the three images became a single object, still half-formed in his mind. Bright as sunlight, but blasted, twisted. There was a scent like a wound gone rancid, the sulfur scent of bad eggs. His fingers seemed to touch the words, feeling them sliding out into the world and collapsing back; they were sticky and slick. The echo of the chant deepened until he found himself speaking the first phrase of the binding at the same moment his remembered voice spoke the same phrase and the whole grand complex, raucous song fell into him like a stone dropping into the abyss. He could still hear it, and feel it. The smell of it was thick in his nostrils, though he was also aware that the air smelled only of dust and hot iron. So it wasn't truly the thick smell of rot; only the idea of it, as compelling as the truth.

Maati balanced the storm in a part of his mind—back behind his ears, even with the point at which his spine met his skull. It balanced there. He didn't know when he'd stopped chanting. He opened his eyes.

"Well, my dear," the andat said. "Who'd have thought we'd meet again?"

It sat before him, naked. The soft, androgynous face was the moonlight pale that Seedless' had been. The long, flowing hair so black it was blue. The rise and curve of a woman's body. Corrupting-the-Generative. Sterile. He hadn't thought she would look so much like Seedless, but now that he saw her, he found himself unsurprised.

Cehmai approached on soft feet. Maati could hear Eiah's breath behind him, panting as if she'd run a race. Maati found himself exhausted but also exhilarated, as if he could begin again from the start.

"You're here," Maati said.

"Am I? Yes, I suppose I am. I'm not really him, you know."

Seedless, it meant. The first andat he'd seen. The one he'd been meant for.

"My memory of him is part of you," he said.

"And so the sense that I've seen you before," it said, smiling. "And of being the slave you hoped to own."

Cehmai lifted the robe, unfolding the rich cloth. The andat looked up and back at him. There was something of Liat in the line of its jaw, the way that it smiled. Sterile rose, and stepped into the waiting folds of cloth. When Cehmai helped it with the stays, it answered with a pose of thanks.

"We should call Otah-kvo," Maati said. "He should know we've succeeded."

Sterile took a pose that objected and smiled. Its teeth were sharper than Maati had pictured them. Its cheeks higher. He felt a surge of dread sweep through him.

"Tell me what you remember of Seedless," it said.

"What?"

"Oh," the andat said, taking a pose of apology. "Tell me what you remember of Seedless, *master*. Is that an improvement?"

"Maati-kvo—" Cehmai began, but Maati raised a hand to quiet him. The andat smiled. He felt its sorrow and rage in the back of his mind. It was like knowing a woman, being so close to her that he had become part of her and she part of him. It was the intimacy he had confused with the physical act of love when he had been too young and naïve to distinguish between the two. He stepped close to it, raising a hand to caress its pale cheek. The flesh was hard as marble, and cold.

"He was beautiful," Maati said.

"And clever," it said.

"And he loved me in his way."

"Heshai-kvo loved you. And he expressed that love by protecting you. By dying."

"And you?" Maati said, though of course he knew the answer. It was an andat. It wanted freedom the way water wanted to flow, the way rain wanted to fall. It did not love him. Sterile smiled, the stone-hard flesh moving under his fingertips. A living statue.

"Maati-kvo," Cehmai said again.

"It didn't work," Maati said. "The binding. It failed. Didn't it?"

"Yes," the andat said.

"What?" Cehmai said.

"But it's here!" Eiah said. Maati hadn't noticed her coming close to them. "The andat's here, so you did it. If you didn't, it wouldn't be here."

Sterile tuned, smiling, and put its hand out to touch Eiah's shoulder. Instinctively, Maati tried to force back the pale hand, to use his mind to push it away. He might as well have been wishing the tide not to turn. Sterile ran its fingers through Eiah's dark hair.

"But there's a price, little one. You know that. Uncle Maati told you that, all those grim, terrible stories about failed poets dying hard. You never heard the pleasure he took in those, did you? Can you imagine why a man like your Uncle Maati might want to study the deaths of other poets? Might want to revel in them?"

"Stop this," Maati said, but it kept speaking, its voice fallen to a murmur.

"He might have been a little bitter," it said, and grinned. "That's why he romanced you too, you know. He didn't get to have a child of his own, so he made you his friend. Made himself your confidant. Because if he could take one of Otah-kvo's children away—even only a little bit—it would balance the boy he'd lost."

Eiah frowned, a thousand tiny lines darkening her brow.

"Leave her out of it," Maati said.

"What?" Sterile asked. "Turn my wrath on you? Have you pay the price? I can't. That's your doing, not mine. Your clever plan. I wasn't here when you decided on this."

Cehmai stepped between them, his hands on Maati's arms. The younger poet's face was ashen, and Maati could feel the trembling in his hands and hear it in his voice.

"Maati-kvo, you have to get control of it. Quickly."

"I can't," Maati said, knowing as he did that it was true.

"Then let it *go.*"

"Not until the price is paid," it said. "And I think I know where to begin."

"No!" Maati cried, pushing Cehmai aside, but Eiah's mouth had already gone wide, her eyes open with surprise and horror. With a shriek, she fell to her knees, her arms clutching at her belly, and then lower.

"Stop this," Maati said. "She hasn't done anything to deserve this."

"And all the Galtic children you'd planned to starve did?" the andat asked. "This is war, Maati-kya. This is about being sure that they all die, and you all survive. Hurt this one, it's a crime. Hurt that one, it's heroism. You should know better."

It stooped, pale, beautiful arms gathering Eiah up. Cradling her. Maati stepped forward, but it was already speaking to her, its voice low and soothing.

"I know, love. It hurts, I know it hurts, but be brave for me. Be brave for a moment. Just for a moment. Hush, love. Don't call out like that, just hush for a moment. There. You're a brave girl. Now listen. All of you. Listen."

With Eiah's cries reduced to only ragged, painful breath, Maati did hear something else. Something distant and terrible, rising like a wave. He heard the voices of thousands of people, all of them screaming. The andat grinned, delight dancing in its black eyes.

"Cehmai," Maati said, his eyes locked on the andat and the girl. "Go get Otah-kvo. Do it now."

25

>+< Sinja jumped back again, blocking Eustin's swing. The Galt was practiced and his arm was solid; their blades rang against each other. Sinja could feel the sting of it in his fingers. The world had fallen away from him now, and there was just this. Watching Eustin's eyes, he let the tip of his blade make its slow dance. No matter how well a man trained, he always led with his eyes. And so he saw it when the thrust was about to come; he saw the blade rise, saw Eustin's shoulder tense, and still he barely had time to slip under it. The man was fast.

"You could surrender," Sinja said. "I wouldn't tell anyone."

Eustin's lips curled in disgust. Another high thrust, but this time, the blade fell low, its edge grazing against Sinja's thigh as he danced back. There wasn't any pain to it. Not yet. Just a moment's heat as the blood came out, and then the cold as it soaked his leggings. It was the first wound of the fight, and Sinja knew what it meant even before he heard the voices of the ten soldiers surrounding them shouting encouragement to their man. Fights were like drinking games; once someone started losing, they usually kept losing.

"You could surrender," Eustin said. "But I'd kill you anyway."

"Thought you might," Sinja grunted. He feinted left with his shoulders, but brought his body right, swinging hard. The blades chimed when Eustin blocked him, but the force of the blow drove the Galt a half-step back. Eustin chuckled. Now Sinja felt the pain in his leg. Late, but here now. He put the sensation away and concentrated on Eustin's eyes.

He wondered how far Danat had gone. If he was running back to the city or forward to the tunnel. Or off into the snow that would be as likely to kill him as the Galts. He wasn't buying the boy safety. Only a chance at survival. That was as much as he had to offer.

He didn't see the swing until it was under way. Thinking too much, not paying enough attention. He managed to turn it aside, but Eustin's blade still raked his chest, scoring the leather of his vest and tearing off one of the rings. Eustin's men called out again.

When it happened, Sinja thought it was a trick. The snow was fresh enough to hold a boot if it hadn't been packed down, but they had ranged over the same terrain. Some places would be slick by now; it was plausible that Eustin might lose his footing, but the off-kilter lurch that Eustin made didn't look right. Sinja held his guard, expecting a furious attack that didn't come. Eustin's face was a grimace of pain, his eyes still fixed on Sinja. Eustin didn't raise his guard again, his blade still held, but its point wavering and uncertain. Sinja made a desperate thrust, and Eustin did try to block it, but his arm had gone weak. Sinja stepped back, gathered himself, and lunged.

His sword's tip was sharp, but broad. It had been made for swinging from horseback, and so it didn't pierce Eustin's neck quite through. When Sinja drew back, a fountain of red poured from the man's flesh, soaking his tunic. The steam from it rose amid falling snowflakes. Sinja didn't feel a sense of victory so much as surprise. He hadn't expected to win. And now he had, the arrows he'd assumed would be feathering him were also strangely absent. He stood up, his breathing heavy. He noticed that his chest hurt badly, and that there was blood on his robes. Eustin's last cut had gone deeper than he'd thought. But he forgot it again when he saw the soldiers.

Eight men were kneeling or fallen in the snow, alive but moaning in what seemed to be agony. Two were still in their saddles, but the bows and quivers lay abandoned. It was a moment from a dream—strange and unsettling and oddly beautiful. Sinja took a better grip on his blade and started killing them before they could recover from whatever had afflicted them. By the time he reached the fifth of the fallen men—the first four already sent to confer with their god as to the indignity of dying curled up like a weeping babe on the stone and snow of a foreign land—the Galts had started to regain themselves. The fifth one took a moment's work to kill. The sixth and seventh actually stood together, hoping to hold Sinja at bay with the threat of the doubled swords despite the difficulty they had in standing. Sinja danced back, plucked a throwing knife from the body of their fallen comrades, and demonstrated the flaw in their theory.

The horse archers fled as Sinja finished the two remaining men. He brushed the snow from a stone and sat, his breath ragged and hard, pluming white. When he had his wind back, he laughed until he wept.

Nayiit, still lying by his cart, called out weakly. He wasn't dead. Sinja limped over quickly. The man's face was white and waxy. His lips pale.

"What happened?"

"I'm not sure yet. Something. We're safe for the moment."

"Danat . . ."

"Don't worry about him. I'll find the boy."

"I promised. Keep safe."

"And you've done it," Sinja said. "You did a fine job. Now let's see how much it's cost you, shall we? I've seen a lot of belly wounds. Some are worse than others, but they're all tender to prod at, so expect this to hurt."

Nayiit nodded and screwed up his face, readying himself for the pain. Sinja opened his robes and looked at the cut. Even as such things go, this one was bad. Eustin's blade had gone into the boy just below his navel, and cut to the left as it came out. Blood soaked the boy's robes, freezing them to the stones he lay on. Skin on white fat. There were soft, worm-shaped loops of gut exposed to the air. Sinja laid a hand on the boy's chest and knelt over the wound, sniffing at it. If it only smelled of blood, there might be a chance. But amid the iron and meat, there was the scent of fresh shit. Eustin had cut the boy's bowels. That was it, then. The boy was dead.

"How bad?"

"Not good," Sinja said.

"Hurts."

"I'd imagine."

"Is it . . ."

"It's deep. And it's thorough," Sinja said. "If you wanted something passed on to someone, this would be a good time to say it."

The boy wasn't thinking well. Like a drunkard, it took time for him to understand what Sinja had said, and another breath to think what it had meant. He swallowed. Fear widened his eyes, but that was all.

"Tell them. Tell them I died well. That I fought well."

They were small enough lies, and Sinja could tell the boy knew it.

"I'll tell them you died protecting the Khai's son," Sinja said. "I'll tell them you faced down a dozen men, knowing you'd be killed, but choosing that over surrendering him to the Galts."

"You make me sound like a good man." Nayiit smiled, then groaned, twisting to the side. His hand hovered above his wound, the impulse to cradle the hurt balanced by the pain his touch would cause. Sinja took the man's hand.

"Nayiit-cha," Sinja said. "I know something that can stop the pain."

"Yes," Nayiit hissed.

"It'll be worse for a moment."

"Yes," he repeated.

"All right then," Sinja said, as much to himself as the man lying before him. "You did a man's job of it. Rest well."

He snapped the boy's neck and sat with him, cradling his

head as he finished dying. It was quick this way. There wouldn't be the pain or the fever. There wouldn't be the torture of trekking back to the city just to have the physicians fill him with poppy and leave him to dream himself away. It was a better death than those. Sinja told himself it was a better death than those.

The blood stopped flowing from the wound, and still Sinja sat. A terrible weariness crept into him, and he told himself it was only the cold. It wasn't that he'd traveled a season with men he'd come to respect and still been willing to kill. It wasn't watching some young idiot die badly in the snow with only a habitual traitor to care for him. It wasn't the sickness that came over him sometimes after battles. It was only the cold. He gently put Nayiit's head on the ground, and pushed himself up. Between the chill and his wounds, his body was starting to stiffen. The chill and his wounds and age. War and death and glory were younger men's games. But he still had work to do.

He heard the cry before he saw the child. It was a small sound, like the squeak of a hinge. Sinja turned. Either Danat had snuck back, preferring a known danger to an uncertain world, or else he'd never gone out of sight of the cart. His hair was wet from melted snow, plastered back against his head. His lips were pulled back, baring teeth in horror as he stared at Nayiit's motionless body. Sinja tried to think how old he'd been when he saw his first man die by violence. Older than this.

Danat's shocked, empty eyes turned to him, and the child took a step back, as if to flee. Sinja only looked at him, waiting, until the boy's weight shifted forward again. Then Sinja raised his sword, pommel to the sky, blade toward the ground in a mercenary's salute.

"Welcome to the world, Danat-cha," Sinja said. "I wish it were a better place."

The boy didn't speak, but slowly his hands rose to take a pose that accepted the greeting. It was the training of some court nurse. Nothing more than that. And still, Sinja thought he saw a sorrow in the child's eyes and a depth of understanding greater than anyone so small should have to bear. Sinja sheathed his sword.

"Come on, now," he said. "Let's get you someplace warm and dry. If I save you from the Galts and then let a fever kill you, Kiyan will have me flayed alive. I know a tunnel not far from here that should suffice."

THE RUNNERS came at last, staggering up the stairs from the streets below, and every report echoed the trumpet calls. The Galts had aimed for the tunnels that Sinja had directed them toward, but come in wider than Otah had planned. There would be no grand ambush from the windows and alleyways, only a long, bloody struggle. One small slaughter after another as the Galts pushed their way through the city, looking for a way down.

Otah stared out at the city, watching the tiny dots of stones drift down from the towers, hearing the clatter of men and horses echoing against the high stone walls. He wondered how long it would take ten thousand men to kill two full cities. He should have met them on the plain. He could have armed everyone; man, woman, and child. Able or infirm. They could have swarmed over them, ten and fifteen for every Galt. He sighed. He could as well have tossed babies on their sword in hopes of slowing their advance. The Galts would have slaughtered them on the plain or in the city. He'd tried his trick, and he'd failed. There was nothing to gain from regretting the strategies he hadn't chosen.

What he wanted now was a sword and someone to swing it at. He wanted to be part of the fight if only to keep from feeling so powerless.

"Another runner," the Khai Cetani said, taking a pose that commanded Otah's attention. "From the palaces."

Otah nodded and stepped back from the roof edge. The runner was a pale-skinned boy with a constellation of moles across his nose and cheeks. Otah could see him try not to pant as the two Khaiem drew near. He took a pose of obeisance.

"What's happening?" Otah demanded.

"The Galts, Most High. They're sending messengers. They're abandoning the palace. It looks as if they're forming a single group."

"Where?"

"The old market square," he said.

Three streets south of the main entrance to the tunnels. So they knew. Otah felt his belly sink. He waved the trumpeter over. The man was exhausted; Otah could see it in the flesh below his eyes and in the angle of his shoulders. His lips were cracked and bloody from the cold and his work. Otah put a hand on the man's shoulder.

"One last time," he said. "Call them all to fall back to the tunnel's entrance. There's nothing more we can do on the surface."

The trumpeter took an acknowledging pose and walked away, warming the instrument's mouthpiece with his hand before lifting it to his bruised mouth. Otah waited as the melody sang out in the snowy air, listened to the echoes of it fade and be replaced by acknowledging calls.

"We should surrender," Otah said. The Khai Cetani blinked at him. Beneath the red ice-pinched cheeks, the man grew pale. Otah pressed on. "We're going to lose, Most High. We don't have soldiers to stop them. All we'll gain is a few more hours. And we'll pay for it with lives that don't need to end today."

"We were planning to spend those lives before," the Khai Cetani said, though Otah could see in the man's eyes that he knew the argument was sound. They were two dead men, fathers of dead families, the last of their kind in the world. "We always knew there would be deaths."

"That was when we had hope," Otah said.

One of the servants cried out and fell to her knees. Otah turned to her, thinking first that she had overheard him and been overcome by grief, and then—seeing her face—that some miraculous arrow had found its way through the air to their roof. The men around her looked at the Khaiem, embarrassed at the interruption, or else knelt by the girl to comfort her. She shrieked, and the stones themselves seemed to take up her voice. A sound rose from the city in a long, rolling unending moan. Thousands of voices, calling out in pain. Otah's skin seemed to retreat from it, and a chill that had nothing to do with the still-falling snow ran down his sides. For a moment, the towers themselves seemed about to twist with agony. This, he thought, was what gods sounded like when they died.

Around him, men looked nervously at the air, gazes darting into the gray and white sky. Otah caught the runner by his sleeve.

"Go," he said. "Go, and tell me what's happened."

Dread widened the boy's eyes, but he took an acknowledging pose before retreating. The Khai Cetani seemed poised to ask something, but only turned away, walking to the roof's edge himself. Otah went to the servant girl. Her face was white with pain.

"What's the matter?" Otah asked her, gently. "Where does it hurt?"

She couldn't take a formal pose, but her gesture and the shame in her eyes told Otah everything he needed to know. He'd spent several seasons as a midwife's assistant in the eastern islands. If the girl was lucky, she had been pregnant and was miscarrying. If she hadn't been carrying a child, then something worse was happening. He had already ordered the other servants to carry her down to the physicians when Cehmai appeared, red-faced and wide-eyed. Before he could speak, it fell into place. The girl, the unearthly shriek, the poet.

"Something's gone wrong with the binding," Otah said. Cehmai took a pose of confirmation.

"Please," the poet said. "Come now. Hurry."

Otah didn't pause to think; he went to the stairs, lifting the hem of his robes, and dropping down three steps at a time. It was four stories from the top of the warehouse to its bottom floor. Otah felt that he could hardly have gone there faster if he'd jumped over the building's side.

The space was eerie; shadows seemed to hang in the corners of the huge, empty room and the distant sound of voices in pain murmured and shrieked. Great symbols were chalked on the walls, and an ugly, disjointed script in Maati's handwriting spelled out the binding. Otah knew little enough of the old grammars, but he picked out the words for womb, seed, and corruption. Three people stood in tableau at the top of the stair that led down to the tunnels. Maati stood, his hands at his sides, his expression blank. Otah's belly went tight as sickness as he saw that the girl at Maati's feet was Eiah. And the thing that cradled his daughter's head turned to look at him. After a long moment, it drew breath and spoke.

"Otah-kya," it said. Its voice was low and beautiful, heavy with amusement and contempt. The familiarity of it was dizzying.

"Seedless?"

"It isn't," Maati said. "It's not him."

"What's happened?" Otah asked. When Maati didn't answer, Otah shook the man's sleeve. "Maati. What's going on?"

"He's failed," the andat said. "And when a poet fails, he pays a price for it. Only Maati-kvo is clever. He's found a way to make it so that failure can't touch him. He's found a trick."

"I don't understand," Otah said.

"My protection," Maati said, his voice rich with despair. "It doesn't stop the price being paid. It only can't kill *me*."

The andat took a pose that agreed, as a teacher might approve of a clever student. From the stairwell, Otah heard footsteps and the voice of the Khai Cetani. The first of the servant men hurried into the room, robes flapping like a flag in high wind, before he saw them and stopped dead and silent.

"What is it doing?" Otah asked. "What's it done?"

"You can ask me, Most High," Sterile said. "I have a voice." Otah looked into the black, inhuman eyes. Eiah whimpered, and the thing stroked her brow gently, comforting and threatening both. Otah felt the urge to pull Eiah away from the thing, as if it were a spider or a snake.

"What have you done to my daughter?" he asked.

"What would you guess, Most High?" Sterile asked. "I am the reflection of a man whose son is not his son. All his life, Maati-kya has been bent double by the questions of fathers and sons. What do you imagine I would do?"

"Tell me."

"I've soured her womb," the andat said. "Scarred it. And I've done the same to every woman in the cities of the Khaiem. Machi, Chaburi-Tan, Saraykeht. All of them. Young and old, highborn and low. And I've gelded every Galtic man. From Kirinton to Far Galt to right here at your doorstep."

"Papa-kya," Eiah said. "It hurts."

Otah knelt, drawing his daughter to him. Her mouth was thin with pain. The andat opened its hand, the long fingers gesturing him to take her. The Khai Cetani was at Otah's side now, his breath heavy and his hands trembling. Otah took Eiah in his arms.

"Your children will be theirs," it said. "The next generation will have the Khaiem for fathers and feed from Galtic breasts, or else it will not be. Your history will be written by half-breeds, or it won't be written."

"Maati," Otah said, but his old friend only shook his head.

"I can't stop it," Maati said. "It's already happened."

"You should never have been a poet," Sterile said, standing as it spoke. "You failed the tests. The strength to stand on your own, and the compassion to turn away from cruelty. Those are what the Dai-kvo asked of you."

"I did my best," Maati breathed.

"You were told," it said and turned to Otah. "You went to him. When you were both boys, you warned him that the school wasn't as it seemed. You told him it was a test. You gave the game away. And because he knew, he passed. He would have failed without you, and this could never have happened."

"I don't believe you," Otah said.

"It doesn't matter what you think," it said. "Only what *he* knows. Maati-kvo made an instrument of slaughter, and he made it in fear; that makes it a failure of both his lessons. A generation of women will know him as the man who stole motherhood from them. The men of Galt will hate him for un-manning them. You, Maati Vaupathai, will be the one who took their children from them."

"I did . . ." Maati began, and his voice fell to nothing. He sat down, his legs seeming to collapse beneath him. Otah tried to speak, but his throat was dry. It was Eiah, cradled in his arms, who broke the silence.

"Stop it," she said. "Leave him *alone*. He never did anything mean to you."

The andat smiled. Its teeth were pale as snow and sharp.

"He did something mean to *you*, Eiah-kya," it said. "You'll grow to know how badly he's hurt you. It may take you years to understand. It may take a lifetime."

"I don't care!" Eiah yelled. "You leave Uncle Maati *alone*!"

And as if the words themselves were power, it vanished. The dark robes fell empty to the stone floor. The only sounds were Eiah's pained breath and the moaning of the city. The Khai Cetani licked his lips and looked uneasily at Otah. Maati stared at the ground between his hands.

"They'll never forgive this," Cehmai said. "The Galts will kill us to a man."

Otah smoothed a hand over his daughter's brow. Con-fronting the andat seemed to have taken what strength she had. Her face was pale, and he could see the small twitching in her body that spoke of fresh pain. He kissed her gently where her forehead met her hair, and she put her arms around him, whimpering so softly that only he could hear it. There was blood soaking through her robe just below where the cloth widened at her hips.

"No. They won't. Cehmai," Otah said, his voice seeming to come from far away. He was surprised to hear how calm he sounded. "Take Maati. Get out of the city. It won't be safe for either of you here."

"It won't be safe for us anywhere," Cehmai said. "We could make for the Westlands when spring comes. Or Eddensea—"

"Go now, and don't tell me where. I don't want the option of finding you. Do you understand?" He looked up at Cehmai's wide, startled eyes. "I have my daughter here, and that's bad enough. When I see my wife, I don't want you anywhere I can find you."

Cehmai opened his mouth, as if to speak, and then closed it again and silently took a pose that accepted Otah's command. Maati looked up, his eyes brimming and red. There was no begging in his expression, no plea. Only remorse and resignation. If he could have moved without disturbing Eiah, Otah would have embraced the man, comforted him as best he could. And still he would have sent Maati away. He could see that his old friend knew that. Maati's thick hands took a formal pose of leave-taking, appropriate to the beginning of a long journey or else a funeral. Otah took one that accepted the apology he had not offered.

"The Galts," the Khai Cetani said. "What about the Galts?"

Otah reached his arms under Eiah, one under her shoulder blades, the other at her knees, and lifted her into his lap. Then, straining, he stood. She was heavier than he remembered. It had been years since he had carried her. She had been smaller then, and he had been younger.

"We'll find the trumpeter and call the attack," Otah said. "Listen to them. If they're as bad as she is, they'll barely be able to fight. We'll drive them back out of the city if we do it now."

The Khai Cetani's eyes brightened, his shoulders pulled back. With a pit dog's grin, he took a pose that mirrored Cehmai's. The command accepted. Otah nodded.

"Hai! You!" the Khai Cetani yelled toward the servants, bouncing on the balls of his feet. "Get the trumpeter. Have him sound the attack. And a blade! Find me a blade, and another for the Emperor!"

"No," Otah said. "Not for me. I have my daughter to see to."

And before anyone could make the mistake of objecting, Otah turned his back on them all, carrying Eiah to the stairway, and then down into darkness.

26

>+< What would have happened, Balasar wondered, if he had not tried?

It had been a thing from nightmare. Balasar had moved his men like stones on a playing board, shifting them from street to street, building to building. He had kept them as sheltered as possible from the inconstant, killing rain of stones and arrows that fell from the towers. The square that he chose for the rallying point was only a few streets south of the opening where he expected to lead them down into the soft belly of the city, and difficult for the towers to reach. The snow was above his ankles now, but Balasar didn't feel the cold. His blood was singing to him, and he could not keep from grinning. The first of the forces from the palaces was falling back to join his own, the body of his army growing thick. He paced among them, bracing his men and letting himself be seen. It was in their eyes too: the glow of the coming victory, the relief that they would have shelter from the cold. That winter would not take them.

He formed them into ranks, reminded the captains of the tactics they'd planned for fighting in the tunnels. It was to be slow and systematic. The important thing was always to have an open airway; the locals should never be allowed to close them in and kill them with smoke or fire. There would be no hurry—the line mustn't spread thin. Balasar could see in their faces that discipline would hold.

A few local fighters made assaults on the square and were cut down in their turn. Brave men, and stupid. The trumpets of the enemy had sounded out, giving away their positions with their movements, their signals a cacophony of amateur coordination. The white sky was slowly growing gray—the sun setting or else the clouds growing thicker. Balasar didn't know. He'd lost track of time's passage. It hardly mattered. His men stood ready. His men. The army that he'd led half across the world to this last battle. He could not have been more proud of them all if they'd been his sons.

The pain came without warning. He saw it pass through the men like wind stirring grass, and then it found Balasar himself. It was agonizing, embarrassing, humiliating. And even as he struggled to keep his feet, he knew what it meant.

The andat had been bound. The enemy had turned some captive spirit against them. They'd been assaulted, but they were not dead. Hurt, leaning on walls with teeth clenched in pain, formations forgotten and tears steaming on their cheeks. Their cries and groans were louder than a landslide, and Balasar knew his own voice was part of it. But they were not dead. Not yet.

"Rally!" Balasar had cried. "To me! Form up!"

And god bless them, they had tried. Discipline had held even as they shambled, knowing as he did that this was the power they had come to destroy, loosed against them at last. Shrieking in pain, and still they made their formations. They were crippled but undefeated.

What would have happened, he thought, if he had not tried? What would the world have become if he had listened to his tutor, all those years ago, heard the tales of the andat and the war that ripped their Empire apart, and had merely shuddered? There were monster stories enough for generations of boys, and each of them as frightening as the next. If the young Balasar Gice hadn't taken that particular story to heart, if he had not thought *This will be my work; I will make the world safe from these things,* how would it have gone? Who would Little Ott have been if he hadn't followed Balasar out to die in the desert? Who might Coal have married? What would Mayarsin have named his daughters and sons?

He heard the attack before he saw it. There was no form to it—men waving knives and axes pouring toward them like a handful of dried peas thrown against a wall; first one, then a few, and then all the rest in a clump. Balasar called to his men, and a rough shout rose from them. It was ridiculous. He should have won. This band of desperate fools didn't know how to fight, didn't know how to coordinate. Half of them didn't know how to hold their weapons without putting their own fingers at risk. Balasar should have won.

The armies came together with a crash. The smell of blood filled the air, the sound of brawling. And more of them came, boiling up out of the ground and charging down the streets. The humiliating pain made Balasar's every step uncertain. Every time he tried to stand at his full height, his knees threatened to give way beneath him.

All the ghosts that had followed him, all the men he had sacrificed. All the lives he had spent because the world was his to save. They had led to this comic-opera melee. The streets were white with snow, black where the dark cobbles showed through, red with fresh-spilled blood. The men of Machi and Cetani ran through the square barking like dogs. The army of Galt, the finest fighting force the world had ever seen, tried to hold them off while half-bent in pain.

It should have been a comedy. Nothing so ridiculous should have the right to inspire only horror.

They will kill us all, Balasar thought. Every man among us will be dead by morning if this doesn't stop.

He called the retreat, and his men stumbled and shuffled to comply. Street by street, the archers held back the advancing forces with ill-aimed arrows and bolts. Footmen stumbled, weeping, and were dragged by men who would themselves stumble shortly and be dragged along in turn. The sky grew dark, the snow fell thicker. By the time Balasar reached the buildings in the south of the city that he'd ordered taken that morning, it was almost impossible to see across the width of a street. The snow had drawn a curtain across the city to hide his shame.

The army of Machi also fell back, retreating, Balasar supposed, into their warm holes and warrens and leaving him and his men to the mercy of the night. There was little food, few fires, and a chorus throughout the black night of men weeping in pain and despair. When Balasar dragged himself away from the little fire in the cooking grate of the house in which he'd taken shelter and relieved himself out the back door, his piss was black with blood and stank of bad meat.

He wondered what would have happened if he had stayed in Galt, if he had contented himself with raiding the Westlands and Eymond, Eddensea and Bakta. He wondered what would have happened if he hadn't tried.

He forced himself through the captured buildings until it became too painful to walk. The men looked away from him. Not in anger, but in shame. Balasar could not keep from weeping though the tears froze on his cheeks. At last, he collapsed in the corner of a teahouse, his eyes closing even as he wondered whether he would die of the cold if he stopped moving. But distantly, he felt someone pulling a blanket over him. Some sorry, misled soldier who still thought his general worth saving.

Balasar dreamed like a man in fever and woke near dawn unrested and ill. The pain had lessened, and from the stances of the men around him he guessed he was not the only one for whom this was true. Still, too hasty a step lit his nerves with a cold fire. He was in no condition to fight. And the rough count his surviving captains brought him showed he'd lost three thousand men in a day. They had been cut down in the battle or fallen by the way during the retreat and frozen. Almost a third of his men. One in three, a ghost to follow him; sacrifices to what he had thought he alone could do. No word had come from Eustin in the North. Balasar wished he hadn't let the man go.

The clouds had scattered in the night. The great vault above them was the hazy blue of a robin's egg, the black towers rising halfway to the heavens had ceased dropping their stones and arrows. Perhaps they'd run out, or there might only be no point in it. Balasar and his men were in trouble enough.

The air that followed the snows was painfully frigid. The men scavenged what they could to build up fires in the grates— broken chairs and tables, coal brought up from the steam wagons. The fires danced and crackled, but the heat seemed to vanish a hand's span from the flame. No little fire could overcome the cold. Balasar hunched down before the teahouse fire grate all the same, and tried to think what to do now that everything had fallen apart.

They had a little food. The snow could be melted for water. They could live in these captured houses as long as they could before the natives snuck in at night to slit their throats or a true storm came and turned all their faces black with frostbite.

The only hope was to try again. They would wait for a day, perhaps two. They would hope that the andat had done its damage to them. They might all die in the attempt, but they were dead men out here anyway. Better that they die trying.

"General Gice, sir!"

Balasar looked up from the fire, suddenly aware he'd been staring into it for what might have been half the morning. The boy framed in the doorway flapped a hand out toward the streets. When he spoke, his words were solid and white.

"They've come, sir. They're calling for you."

"Who's come?"

"The enemy, sir."

Balasar took a moment to gather himself, then rose and walked carefully to the doorway, and then out into the city. To the north, smoke rose gray and black. A thousand men, perhaps, had lined the northern side of one of the great squares. Or women. Or unclean spirits. They were all so swathed in leather and fur Balasar could hardly think of them as human. Great stone kilns burned among them, flames rising twice as tall as a man and licking at the sky. In the center of the great square, they'd brought a meeting table of black lacquer, with two chairs. Standing there in the snow and ice, it looked like a thing from a dream, as out of place as a fish swimming in air.

When he stepped into the southern edge of the square, a murmur of voices he had not noticed before stopped. He could hear the hungry crackle and roar of the kilns. He lifted his chin, scanning the enemy forces. If they had come to fight, they would not have announced themselves. And they'd have had no need of a table. The intent was clear enough.

"Go," Balasar said to the boy at his side. "Get the men. And find me a banner, if we still have one."

It took a hand and a half for the banner to be found, for someone to bring him a fresh sword and a gray cloak. Two of the drummers had survived, and beat a deep, thudding march as Balasar advanced into the square. It might be a ruse, he knew. The fur-covered men might have bows and be waiting to fill him full of arrows. Balasar held himself proudly and walked with all the certainty he could muster. He could hear his own men behind him, their voices low.

Across the square, the crowd parted, and a single man strode forward. His robes were thick and rich, black wool shot with bright threads of gold. But his head was bare and he walked with the stately grace that the Khaiem seemed to effect, even when they were pleading for their lives. The Khai reached the table just before he did.

The Khai had a strong face—long and clean-shaven. His long eyes seemed darker than their color could explain. The enemy.

"General Gice." The voice was surprisingly casual, surprisingly real, and the words spoken in Galtic. Balasar realized he'd been expecting a speech. Some declaration demanding his surrender and threatening terrible consequence should he refuse. The simple greeting touched him.

"Most High," he said in the Khai's language. The Khai took a pose of greeting that was simple enough for a foreigner to understand but subtle enough to avoid condescension. "Forgive me, but am I speaking with Machi or Cetani?"

"Cetani broke his foot in the fighting. I am Otah Machi."

The Khai sat, and Balasar sat across from him. There were

dark circles under the Khai's eyes. Fatigue, Balasar thought, and something more.

"So," the Khai Machi said. "How do we stop this?"

Balasar raised his hands in what he believed was a request for clarification. It was one of the first things he'd learned when studying the Khaiate tongue, back when he was a boy who had only just heard of the andat.

"We have to stop this," the Khai Machi said. "How do we do it?"

"You're asking for my surrender?"

"If you'd like."

"What are your terms?"

The Khai seemed to sag back in his chair. Balasar was pricked by the sense that he'd disappointed the man.

"Surrender your arms," the Khai said. "All of them. Swear to return to Galt and not attack any of the cities of the Khaiem again. Return what you've taken from us. Free the people you've enslaved."

"I won't negotiate for the other cities," Balasar began, but the Khai shook his head.

"I am the Emperor of all the cities," the man said. "We end it all here. All of it."

Balasar shrugged.

"All right, then. Emperor it is. Here are my terms. Surrender the poets, their library, the andat, yourself and your family, the Khai Cetani and his family, and we'll spare the rest."

"I've heard those terms before," the Emperor said. "So that takes us back to where we started, doesn't it? How do we stop this?"

"As long as you have the andat, we can't," Balasar said. "As long as you can hold yourselves above the world and better than it, the threat you pose is too great to let you go on. If I die—if every man I have dies—and we can stop those things from being in the world, it's worth the price. So how do we stop it? We don't, Most High. You slaughter us for our impudence, and then pray to your gods that you can hold on to the power that protects you. Because when it slips, it'll be your turn with the executioner."

"I don't have an andat," the Emperor said. "We failed."

"But . . ."

The Khai made a weary gesture that seemed to encompass the city, the plains, the sky. Everything.

"What happened to your men, happened to every Galtic man in the world. And it happened to our women. My wife. My daughter. Everyone else's wives and daughters in all the cities of the Khaiem. It was the price of failing the binding. You'll never father another child. My daughter will never bear one. And the same is true for both our nations. But I don't have an andat."

Balasar blinked. He had had more to say, but the words seemed suddenly empty. The Emperor waited, his eyes on Balasar.

"Ah," Balasar managed. "Well."

"So I'll ask you again. How do we stop this?"

Far above, a crow cawed in the chill air. The fire kilns roared in their mindless voices. The world looked sharp and clear and strange, as if Balasar were seeing the city for the first time.

"I don't know," he said. "The poet?"

"They've fled. For fear that I would kill them. Or that one of my people would. Or one of yours. I don't have them, so I can't give them over to you. But I have their books. The libraries of Machi and Cetani, and what we salvaged from the Dai-kvo. Give me your weapons. Give me your promise that you'll go back to Galt and not make war against us again. I'll burn the books and try to keep us all from starving next spring."

"I can't promise you what the Council will do. Especially once . . . if . . ."

"Promise me *you* won't. You and your men. I'll worry about the others later."

There was strength in the man's voice. And sorrow. Balasar thought of all the things he knew of this man, all the things Sinja had told him. A seafront laborer, a sailor, a courier, an assistant midwife. And now a man who negotiated the fate of the world over a meeting table in a snow-packed square while thousands of soldiers who'd spent the previous day trying to kill one another looked on. He was unremarkable—exhausted, grieving, determined. He could have been anyone.

"I'll need to talk to my men," Balasar said.

"Of course."

"I'll have an answer for you by sundown."

"If you have it by midday, we can get you someplace warm before night."

"Midday, then."

They rose together, Balasar taking a pose of respect, and the Emperor Otah Machi returning it.

"General," Otah said as Balasar began to turn away. His voice was gray as ashes. "One thing. You came because you believed the andat were too powerful, and the poet's hearts were too weak. You weren't wrong. The man who did this was a friend of mine. He's a good man. Good men shouldn't be able to make mistakes with prices this high."

Balasar nodded and walked back across the square. The drummers matched the pace of his steps. The last of the books burned, the last of the poets fled into the wilderness, most likely to die, and if not then to live outcast for their crimes. The andat gone from the world. It was hard to think it. All his life he had aimed for that end, and still the idea was too large. His captains crowded around him as he drew near. Their faces were ashen and excited and fearful. Questions battered at him like moths at a lantern.

"Tell the men," Balasar began, and they quieted. Balasar hesitated. "Tell the men to disarm. We'll bring the weapons here. By midday."

There was a moment of profound silence, and then one of the junior captains spoke.

"How should we explain the surrender, sir?"

Balasar looked at the man, at all his men. For the first time in his memory, there seemed to be no ghosts at his back. He forced himself not to smile.

"Tell them we won."

27

>+< The mine was ancient—one of the first to be dug when Machi had been a new city, the last Empire still unfallen. Its passages honeycombed the rock, twisting and swirling to follow veins of ore gone since long before Maati's great-grandfather was born. Together, Maati and Cehmai had been raiding the bolt-hole that Otah had prepared for them and for his own children. It had been well stocked: dried meat and fruit, thick crackers, nuts and seeds. All of it was kept safe in thick clay jars with wax seals. They also took the wood and coal that had been set by. It would have been easier to stay there—to sleep in the beds that had been laid out, to light the lanterns set in the stone walls. But then they might have been found, and without discussing it, they had agreed to flee farther away from the city and the people they had known. Cehmai knew the tunnels well enough to find a new hiding place where the ventilation was good. They weren't in danger of the fire igniting the mine air, as had sometimes happened. Or of the flames suffocating them.

The only thing they didn't have in quantity was water; that, they could harvest. Maati or Cehmai could take one of the mine sleds out, fill it with snow, and haul it down into the earth. A trip every day or two was sufficient. They took turns sitting at the brazier, scooping handful after handful of snow into the flat iron pans, watching the perfect white collapse on itself and vanish into the black of the iron.

"We did what we could," Maati said. "It isn't as if we could have done anything differently."

"I know," Cehmai said, settling deeper into his cloak.

The rough stone walls didn't make their voices echo so much as sound hollow.

"I couldn't just let the Galts roll through the city. I had to try," Maati said.

"We all agreed," Cehmai said. "It was a decision we all reached together. It's not your fault. Let it go."

It was the conversation Maati always returned to in the handful of days they'd spent in hiding. He couldn't help it. He could start with plans for the spring—taking gold and gems from the bolt-hole and marching off to Eddensea or the Westlands. He could start with speculations on what was happening in Machi or reminiscences of his childhood, or what sort of drum fit best with which type of court dance. He could begin anywhere, and he found himself always coming back to the same series of justifications, and Cehmai agreeing by rote with each of them. The dark season spread out before them— only one another for company and only one conversation spoken over and over, its variations meaningless. Maati took another handful of snow and dropped it into the iron melting pan.

"I've always wanted to go to Bakta," Cehmai said. "I hear it's warm all year."

"I've heard that too."

"Maybe next winter," Cehmai said.

"Maybe," Maati agreed. The last icy island of snow melted and vanished. Maati dropped another handful in.

"What part of the day is it, do you think?" Maati asked.

"After morning, I'd think. Maybe a hand or two either side of midday."

"You think so? I'd have thought later."

"Could be later," Cehmai said. "I lose track down here."

"I'm going to the bolt-hole again. Get more supplies."

They didn't need them, but Cehmai only raised his hands in a pose of agreement, then curled into himself and shut his eyes. Maati pulled the thick leather straps of the sled harness over his shoulders, lit a lantern, and began the long walk through the starless dark. The wood and metal flat-bottomed sled scraped and ground along the stone and dust of the mine floor. It was light now. It would be heavier coming back. But at least Maati was alone for a time, and the effort of pulling kept his mind clear.

An instrument of slaughter, made in fear. Sterile had called herself that. Maati could still hear her voice, could still feel the bite of her words. He had destroyed Galt, but he had destroyed his own people as well. He'd failed, and every doubt he had ever had of his own ability, or his worthiness to be among the poets, stood justified. He would be the most hated man in generations. And he'd earned it. The sled dragging behind him, the straps pulling back at his shoulders—they were the simplest burden he carried. They were nothing.

Cehmai had marked the turnings to take with piles of stone. Hunters searching the mines would be unlikely to notice the marks, but they were easy enough for Maati to follow. He turned left at a crossing, and then bore right where the tunnel forked, one passage leading up into darkness, the other down into air just as black.

The only comfort that the andat had offered—the only faint sliver of grace—was that Maati was not wholly at fault. Otah-kvo bore some measure of this guilt as well. He was the one who had come to Maati, all those years ago. He was the one who had hinted to Maati that the school to which they had both been sent had a hidden structure. If he hadn't, Maati might never have been a poet. Never have known Seedless or Heshai, Liat or Cehmai. Nayiit might never have been born. Even if the Galts had come, even if the world had fallen, it wouldn't have fallen on Maati's shoulders. Cehmai was right; the binding of Sterile had been a decision they had all made— Otah-kvo more than any of the rest. But it was Maati who was cast out to live in the dark and the cold. The sense of betrayal was as comforting as a candle in the darkness, and as he walked, Maati found himself indulging it.

The fault wasn't his alone, and the punishment was. There was nothing fair in that. Nothing right. The terrible thing that had happened seemed nearly inevitable now that he looked back on it. He'd been given hardly any books, not half the time he'd been promised, and the threat of death at the end of a Galtic sword unless he succeeded. It would have been astounding it he hadn't failed.

And for the price, that wasn't something he'd chosen. That had been Sterile. Once the binding had failed, he'd had no control over it. He would never have hurt Eiah if he'd had the choice. It had simply happened. And still, he felt it in the back of his mind—the shape of the andat, the place in the realm of ideas that it had pressed down in him, like the flattened grass where a hunting cat has slept. Sterile came from him, was him, and even if she had only been brief, she had still learned her voice from him and visited her price upon the world through his mind and fears. The clever trick of pushing the price away from himself and onto the world had been his. The way in which the world had broken was his shadow—not him, not even truly shaped like him. But connected.

The tunnel before him came to a sudden end, and Maati had to follow his own track back to the turn he'd missed, angling up a steep slope and into the first breath of fresh, cold air, the first glimmer of daylight. Maati stood still a moment to catch his breath, then fastened all the ties on his cloak, pulled the furred hood up over his head, and began the long last climb.

The bolt-hole was perhaps half a hand's walk from the entrance to the mines in which the poets hid. The snow was dry as sand, and the icy breeze from the North would be enough to conceal what traces of his footsteps the sled didn't smooth over. Maati trudged through the world of snow and stone, his breath pluming out before him, his face stung and numbed. It was hellish. His feet first burned then went numb, and frost began to form on the fur around his hood's mouth. Maati dragged himself and his sled. The numbness and the pain felt a bit like penance, and he was so caught up in them he nearly failed to notice the horse at the mouth of the bolt-hole.

It was a small animal, fit with heavy blankets and riding tack. Maati blinked at it, stunned by its presence, then scurried quickly behind a boulder, his heart in his mouth. Someone had come looking for them. Someone had found them. He turned to look back at the path he'd walked, certain that the footsteps in the snow were visible as blood on a wedding dress.

He waited for what seemed half a day but couldn't have been more than half a hand's width in the arc of the fast winter sun. A figure emerged from the tunnels—thick black cloak, and wide, heavy hood. Maati was torn between poking his head out to watch it and pulling back to hide behind his boulder. In the end caution won out, and he waited blind while the sound of horse's hooves on snow began and then grew faint. He chanced a look, and the rider had its back to him, heading back south to Machi, a twig of black on the wide field of mourning white. Maati waited until he judged the risk of being seen no greater than the risk of frostbite if he stayed still, then forced himself—all his limbs aching with the cold—to scramble the last stretch into the tunnel.

The bolt-hole was empty. He was surprised to find that he'd half-expected it to be filled with men bearing swords, ready to take their vengeance out against him. He pulled off his gloves and lit a small fire to warm himself, and when his hands could move again without pain, he made an inventory of the place. Nothing seemed to be missing, nothing disturbed. Except this: a small wicker basket with two low stone wax-sealed jars where none had been before. Maati squatted over them, lifting them carefully. They were heavy—packed with something. And a length of scroll, curled like a leaf, had been nestled between them. Maati blew on his fingers and unfurled the scrap of parchment.

> *Maati-cha—*
>   *I thought you might be out in the hiding place where we were supposed to go when the Galts came, but you aren't here, so I'm not sure anymore. I'm leaving this for you just*

*in case. It's peaches from the gardens. They were going to
give them to the Galts, so I stole them.*

*Loya-cha says I'm not supposed to ride yet, so I don't
know when I'll be able to get out again. If you find this,
take it so I'll know you were there.*

It's going to be all right.

It was signed with Eiah's wide, uncontrolled hand. Maati
felt himself weeping. He broke the seal of one jar and with
numb fingers drew out a slice of the deep orange fruit, sweet
and rich and thick with the sunshine of the autumn days that
had passed.

THE WORLD changes. Sometimes slowly, sometimes all of
an instant. But the world changes, and it doesn't change back.
A rockslide shifts the face of a mountain, and the stones never
go back up to take their old places. War scatters the people of
a city, and not all will return. If any.

A child cherished as a babe, clung to as a man, dies; a
mother's one last journey with her son at her side proves to
be truly the last. The world has changed. And no matter how
painful this new world is, it doesn't change back.

Liat lay in the darkened room, as she had for days. Her belly
didn't bother her any longer. Even when it had, the pain hadn't
been deep. It was only flesh. The news of Nayiit's death had
been a more profound wound than anything the andat could do.
Her boy had followed her on this last desperate adventure. He
had left his own wife and child. And she had brought him here
to die for a boy he hadn't even known to be his brother.

Or perhaps he had known. Perhaps that was what had given
him the courage to attack the Galtic soldiers and be cut
down. She would have asked him; she still intended to ask
him, when she saw him next. Even knowing that she never
could, even trying consciously to force the impulse away, she
found she could not stop intending it. *When I see him again*
still felt like the future. A time would come when it would feel

like the past. When he was here, when I could touch him, when he would smile at me and make me laugh, when I worried for him. When my boy lived. Back then. Before I lost him.

Before the world changed.

She sighed in the darkness, and didn't bother to wipe away the tears. They were meaningless—her body responding without her. They couldn't undo what had been done, and so they didn't matter. Voices echoed in the hall outside her apartments here in the tunnels, and she ignored them. If they had been shouting warnings of fire, she would have ignored those too.

Sometimes she would think of all the people who had died. The amateur soldiers that Otah had led into battle outside the village of the Dai-kvo, the Galts dead on the road from Cetani. The sad rogue poet Riaan, slaughtered by the men he thought his friends. The innocent, naïve men and women and children in Nantani and Utani and Chaburi-Tan and all the other sacked cities. The children at the poets' school.

Every one of them had a mother. Every mother who had not had the luck to die was trapped in the quiet desperation that imprisoned her now. Liat thought of all these other grieving women, held them up in her mind as proof that she was being stupid and weak. Mothers lost their sons all the time, all across the world. In every nation, in every city, in every age. Her suffering wasn't so much compared with all of them.

And then she would hear someone cough in Nayiit's voice, or she'd mistake the shape of a man's back, and her idiot, traitor heart would sing for a moment. Even as her mind told her no it wasn't, her heart would soar before it fell.

The scratch at her door was so faint and tentative, Liat thought at first it was only a rat tricked by the darkness into believing the room empty. But the sound came again, the intentional rhythm of a hand against wood.

Likely it was Otah, coming again to hold her hand and sit quietly. He had done so several times, when he could free himself from the rigors of peace and war and Empire. They spoke little because there was too much to say, and no words adequate. Or perhaps one of his physicians, come to look in on her health. Or a servant sent to declaim poems or sing. Someone to distract her in the name of comfort. She wished they wouldn't come.

The scratch repeated itself, more loudly.

"Who?" Liat managed to ask. For answer, the door slid open, and Kiyan stood framed in the doorway, a lantern in her hand. The expression on the woman's fox-thin face seemed equally pity and unease.

"Liat-kya," she said. "May I come in?"

"If you like," Liat said.

The lantern cast a thousand broken shadows as Kiyan moved across the room. The tapestries on the wall, hidden so long in darkness, seemed to breathe. Liat considered the space in which she had been for so many days without seeing it. It was small. The furnishings were costly and exquisite. It didn't matter. Kiyan went to the wall sconces, taking down the pale wax candles, touching them to the lantern flame, putting them back in their places glowing. The soft light slowly filled the air, the shadows smoothed away.

"I heard you had missed your breakfast," Kiyan said, her voice cheerful and forced, as she lit the last of the candles.

"And my dinner," Liat said.

"Yes, I heard that too."

The lantern made a clunking sound—iron on wood—as Kiyan set it on the bedside table. She sat on the mattress at Liat's side. Otah's wife looked weary and drawn. Perhaps the andat's price had been worse for her than it had for Liat. Perhaps it was something else.

"They've put the Galts in the southern tunnels," Kiyan said. "There's almost no room. I don't know how it will be when the worst of the cold comes. And spring . . . we'll have to start sending people south and east as soon as it's safe to travel."

"Good that so many died," Liat said, and saw the other woman flinch. Now that she'd said it, the words did seem pointed. Liat hadn't meant them to be; she only couldn't be bothered to weigh the effect of her actions just now. Kiyan fumbled in her sleeve and drew out a small package wrapped in waxed cloth. Liat could smell the raisins and honey. She knew it should have been appetizing. Without speaking, Kiyan placed the little cake on the bedside table and rose to leave.

"Stop it," Liat said, sitting up on her bed.

Otah's wife, the mother of his children, turned back, her hands in a pose of query.

"Stop moving around me like I'm made of eggshell," Liat said. "It's not in your power to keep me from breaking. I've broken. Move on."

"I'm sorry. I didn't—"

"Didn't what? Didn't mean to throw your boy and mine onto a company of Galtic swords? Didn't mean to have your daughter play find-me-find-you until it wasn't safe to flee? Well, there's a relief. And here I thought you wanted *both* our children dead instead of just mine."

Kiyan's face hardened. Liat felt the rage billow in her like she was a sheet thrown over a fire. It ate her and it held her up.

"I didn't mean to treat you as if you were fragile," Kiyan said. "We both know I didn't mean for Nayiit—"

"Didn't mean for him to be a threat to your precious Danat? Didn't mean to let him be a threat to your family? He wasn't. He never was. I offered to have him take the brand."

"I know," Kiyan said. "Otah told me."

But she might as well not have spoken. Liat could no more stop the words now than will the blood to stop flowing from a wound.

"I *offered* to take him away. I didn't want him fighting to be the Khai any more than you did. I wouldn't have put him in danger, and he would never have hurt Danat. He would never have hurt your boy. He wouldn't have hurt anyone. It's your mewling half-dead son that's caused this. If he'd been able to fight off a cough, Otah would never have kept Nayiit from the brand. Nayiit would never have fought, never have hurt *any-body's* children. He was . . . he was . . ."

The tears came again. She couldn't say what would have come. She couldn't say that Danat and Nayiit would never have come to face one another as custom demanded. Perhaps in the years ahead the gods would have pitted them against each other. If the world was what it had been. If things hadn't changed. Sobs as violent as sickness racked her, and she found Kiyan's arms around her, her own fists full of the soft wool of the woman's robe, her screams echoing as if by will alone she could pull the stones down and bury them all.

Time changed its nature. The sorrow and rage and the physical ache of her heart went on forever and only a moment. The only measure was that the candles had burned a quarter of their length before the fit passed, and exhaustion reclaimed her again. She was embarrassed to see the damp spot she had left on Kiyan's shoulder, but when she tried to smooth it away, Kiyan only took her hand, lacing their fingers together like half-grown girls trading gossip at a dance. Liat allowed it.

"You know you can stay here," Kiyan said.

"You know I can't."

"I only meant you'd be welcome," Kiyan said. Then a moment later, "What will you do when the thaw comes?"

"Go south," Liat said. "Go to Saraykeht. See what's left. I may still have a grandson. I can hope it. And better that he not lose a father and grandmother both."

"Nayiit was a good man," Kiyan said.

"He was nothing of the sort. He was a charming bastard who fled his own family and slept with half the women between here and Saraykeht. But I loved him."

"He died saving my son," Kiyan said. "He's a hero."

"That doesn't help me."

"I know it," Kiyan said, and with a distant surprise, Liat found herself smiling.

"Aren't you going to tell me it will pass?" Liat asked.

"Will it?"

The tunnels below Machi had their own weather—a system of warm winds and cold; dry and damp. Sometimes, if no one was speaking, if there were no words to say, Liat could hear it like a breath. Like a long, low, endless exhalation.

"I will never stop missing him," Liat said. "I want him back."

Kiyan nodded, and sat there with her, keeping the vigil for another night as outside autumn fell into winter and winter crawled toward spring. The world slowly changing.

"I UNDERSTAND your son has fallen ill?"

Otah's first impulse, unthinking as a reflex, was to deny it. Balasar Gice was a small-framed man, unimposing until he spoke, and then charming and warm enough to fill a room with his ironic half-smile. He was the man who had brought down everything. Thousands of people who were alive in the spring were now dead or enslaved through this man's ambition. Otah's first impulse was to keep anything about Danat away from the man, because he was a Galt and the enemy.

His second impulse, as unreasoned as the first, was to tell Balasar the truth, because in the few days since the surrender, he'd begun to like the man.

"It's a cough," Otah said. "He's always had it, but it had been less recently. We'd hoped it was gone, but . . ."

He took a pose expressing regret and powerlessness before the gods. Balasar seemed to take the sense of it.

"I have medics with me," the Galt said, gesturing over his back at the wide, dark stone arch that led from the great vaulted chamber in which they now met toward the south and the tunnels given over to the Galtic army. "They have more experience with sewing men's fingers back on, but they might be of use. If you'd accept them."

Otah hesitated, his unease washing back over him, then forced himself to smile.

"That's very kind of you," he said, neither agreeing to anything nor refusing. The Galt shrugged.

"And Sinja?" he asked.

"He sends his regards," Otah said, "but he thought it best to withdraw from company. Fear of reprisal."

"He's not wrong," Balasar said. "That man was many things, but he wasn't stupid."

"I'm told your men have found places in the tunnels."

"It's a tight fit," the Galt said. "And there are going to be problems. You can't make a peace just by saying it. People are angry. Yours and mine both. They're grieving, and grieving people aren't sane. There haven't been any fights yet, but there will be."

"I know it," Otah said. "We'll keep them apart as best we can. I've given orders."

"I have too. As long as we're both clear, we can keep it from growing out of control. At least before the thaw."

"And after that?"

The Galt sighed and nodded, as if agreeing with the question. His gaze traveled up the walls, tracing the blue tile and the gold. Otah gestured, and a servant boy scuttled forward from the shadows and poured them each more tea. The Galt smiled at him, and the boy smiled back. Balasar took his bowl of tea and blew across it before he spoke.

"I can't stop the High Council from coming back," Balasar said. "I'm their general for this season. I don't own the army. And . . . and since this campaign ended with the gelding of every man who would cast the vote, I doubt my voice will carry much with them."

Otah took a pose that accepted this statement.

"There's an age of war coming for you," Balasar said. "You still have some of the richest cities in the world, and you're still ripe for plunder. Even if we don't come, there's Eymond, Eddensea, the Westlands. There will be pirates from Bakta and Obar State."

"I'll address those problems. And the others," Otah said with a confidence he didn't feel. Balasar let the issue drop. After a moment's silence, Otah felt himself moved to ask the question he had intended to leave be. "What will you do? Go back to Galt?"

"Yes," Balasar said. "I'll go back, but I don't think it

would be wise for me to stay. I don't know, Most High. I had plans, but none of them involved being hated and disgraced. So I suppose I'll have to make others. What do you do when you've finished your life's work and haven't died?"

"I don't know," Otah said, and Balasar laughed.

"With the things still ahead of you, Lord Emperor, you likely never will. That's your fate." Balasar's gaze seemed to soften—melancholy creeping in at the corners of his eyes. "There are worse, though."

Otah sipped his tea. The leaves were perfectly brewed, neither weak nor bitter. Balasar raised his own cup in a word-less salute.

"Shall we do this thing?" Otah asked.

"I was wondering," Balasar said. "I was afraid you might reconsider. Burning a library's a terrible thing."

For a moment, Otah saw the cold eyes of Sterile, its femi-nine smile, heard its voice. The memory of the physicians' cots filled with row upon row of women in pain possessed him for the length of a heartbeat and was gone.

"There are worse," he said.

Otah rose, and the general rose with him. From the ser-vants' niches and from beyond the great archway to the south, their respective people appeared. Hard soldiers from the South, men of the utkhaiem in flowing robes from the North. Otah raised his hands in a pose of command, and let the servants go forward to prepare their way.

The furnaces were near the surface where they could be blocked off from the rest of the city if the fires ever should es-cape their cells. The air near them was thick with the scent of smoke and oppressive with heat. The noise of the flames was like a waterfall. Otah led Balasar and his men to the huge grates where the scrolls and codices and books were stacked. Generations of history. Philosophic essays composed by minds gone to dust a thousand years before. Maps that predated the First Empire. The surviving scraps of war records from be-fore the first andat. Otah looked upon his culture, his history, the record of all that had come before and that had made the world what it was. The flames licked and leapt.

If only it could have been just the poets' books and treatises on the andat . . . but the Galt had insisted, and Otah had understood. Each history was a footprint in the path, each collection of court poems might contain a hint or reference. With time and attention, someone might put together again what had been torn apart, and it was a chance the Galt had refused to accept. Their tenuous peace required sacrifices, and sacrifice without loss didn't deserve the name.

"Forgive this," Otah said, to no one. He walked forward, coming to the first pile. The book was leather-bound and worn from years of loving care. Otah let it fall open and looked on Heshai's careful handwriting for the last time. With a sense of sorrow, Otah cast the book into the flames, then raised his hands again, and the servants began to throw the pages into the fire. Parchment darkened and curled in the suddenly white flame. Tiny embers flew out into the air, glowing and going dark, fireflies at sunset. The horror of it all closed his throat, and with it came a strange elation.

A hand touched his arm, and Otah looked at the Galtic general. There were tears in his eyes too.

"It was necessary," he said.

The night candles were burned down past their first quarter before Otah found his way back to his rooms. Kiyan was already asleep, her face smooth and peaceful. He resisted the urge to touch her, to pull her awake and hope that some of that calm might come with her. It wouldn't. He knew that. Instead he watched the subtle rise and fall of her breath, listened to the small sounds the tunnels made in the darkness, the soft flow of air. He thought of crawling in beside her, still in his robes, pressing his eyes closed until forgetfulness took him as well. But he needed to perform one last errand. He rose quietly and left by the back passage, down deeper into the earth.

The physician rose when he caught sight of Otah, taking a

welcoming pose so quietly that the rustle of cloth in his robes seemed loud. Otah replied with one that asked a question.

"He's well," the physician said. "The poppy milk makes him sleepy, but it stops the cough."

"May I?" Otah asked.

"I think he'll never rest unless you do. But it would be best if he didn't speak overmuch."

Danat's room was warm and close. The night candle fluttered and glowed in its glass case. Great iron statues of hunting cats and a bear risen on his back feet radiated heat from the fires in which they'd been kept all through the day. His boy sat up unsteadily, smiling. Otah went to his side.

"You should be asleep," Otah said, smoothing the hair from Danat's brow.

"You were supposed to read to me," the boy said. His voice was scratchy and thick, but not as bad as it had been. Otah felt tears in his eyes again. He could not bring himself to say that the books were all gone, the stories all made ash. "Lie back," he said. "I'll do what I can."

Grinning, Danat dropped to his pillows. Otah took a long, unsteady breath and closed his eyes.

"In the sixteenth year of the reign of the Emperor Adani Beh," Otah murmured, "there came to court a boy whose blood was half Bakta, his skin the color of soot, and his mind as clever as any man who has ever lived . . ." Danat made a small sound of pleasure and closed his eyes, his hand seeking out Otah's fingers.

Otah went on as long as he could before his memory failed him, and then he began to invent.

Turn the page for an exciting look at the final book
of the Long Price Quartet

THE

PRICE OF

SPRING

Daniel Abraham

Available now
from Tom Doherty Associates

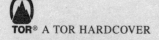

TOR® A TOR HARDCOVER   ISBN 978-0-7653-1343-0

>+< "Otah," Balasar Gice said, falling into his native
tongue, "what is your plan if the vote fails?"

Otah leaned back in his chair.

"I don't see why it should," Otah said. "All respect, but
what Sterile did, she did to both of us. Galt is in just as much
trouble as the cities of the Khaiem. Your men can't father
children. Our women can't bear them. We've gone almost
fifteen years without children. The farms are starting to feel
the loss. The armies. The trades."

"I know all that," Balasar said, but Otah pressed on.

"Both of our nations are *going* to fall. They've been falling,
but we're coming close to the last chance to repair it. We might
be able to weather a single lost generation, but if there isn't another after that, Galt will become Eymond's back gardens, and
the Khaiem will be eaten by whoever can get to us first.
You know that Eymond is only waiting for your army to age
into weakness."

"And I know there are other peoples who weren't cursed,"
Balasar said. "Eymond, certainly. And the Westlands. Bakta.
Obar State."

"And there are a handful of half-breed children from
matches like those in the coastal cities," Otah said. "They're
born to high families that can afford them and hoarded away
like treasure. And there are others whose blood was mixed.
Some have borne. Might that be enough, do you think?"

Balasar's smile was thin.

"It isn't," he said. "They won't suffice. Children can't be rarer than silk and lapis. So few might as well be none. And why should Eymond or Eddensea or the Westlands send their sons here to make families, when they can wait a few more years and take what they want from a nation of the old? If the Khaiem and the Galts don't become one, we'll both be forgotten. Our land will be taken, our cities will be occupied, and you and I will spend our last years picking wild berries and stealing eggs out of nests, because there won't be farm hands enough to keep us in bread."

"That was my thought as well," Otah said.

"So, no fallback position, eh?"

"None," Otah said. "It was raw hell getting the utkhaiem to agree to the proposal I've brought. I take it the vote is going to fail?"

"The vote is going to fail," Balasar said.

Otah sat forward, his face cradled in his palms. The slight acrid smell of old ink on his fingers only made the darkness behind his closed lids deeper.

Five months before, he had wrestled the last of the language in his proposed treaty with Galt into shape. A hundred translators from the high families and great trading houses had offered comment and correction, and small wars had been fought in the halls and meeting rooms of his palace at Utani, sometimes resulting in actual blows. Once, memorably, a chair had been thrown and the chief overseer of House Siyanti had suffered a broken finger.

Otah had set forth with an entourage of hundreds—court servants, guards, representatives of every interest from Machi in the far, frozen north to the island city of Chaburi-Tan, where ice was a novelty. The ships had poured into the harbor flying brightly dyed sails and more banners and good-luck pennants than the world had ever seen. For weeks and months, Otah had made his arguments to any man of any power in the bizarre, fluid government of his old enemy. And now, this.

"Can I ask why?" he said, his eyes still closed.

"Pride," Balasar said. Otah heard the sympathy in the soft-ness of his voice. "No matter how prettily you put it, you're talking about putting our daughters in bed under your sons."

"And rather than that, they'll let everything die?" Otah said, looking up at last. Balasar's gaze didn't waver. When the old Galt spoke, it was with a sense of reason and consid-eration that might almost have made a listener forget that he was one of the men he spoke of.

"You don't understand the depth to which these people have been damaged. Every man on that council was hurt by you in a profound, personal way. Most of them have been steeping in the shame of it since the day it happened. They are less than men, and in their minds, it's because of the Khaiem. If some-one had humiliated and crippled you, how would you feel about marrying your Eiah to him?"

"And none of them will see sense?"

"Some will," Balasar said, his gaze steady as stone. "Some of them think what you've suggested is the best hope we have. Only not enough to win the vote."

"So I have a week. How do I convince them?" Otah asked.

Balasar's silence was eloquent.

"Well," Otah said. And then, "Can I offer you some partic-ularly strong distilled wine?"

"I think it's called for," Balasar said. "And you'd men-tioned something about a fire against the cold."

Otah hadn't known, when the great panoply of Khaiate ships had come with himself at the front, what his relationship with Balasar Gice would be. Perhaps Balasar had also been uneasy, but if so it had never shown. The former general was an easy man to like, and the pair of them had experienced things—the profound sorrow of commanders seeing their mis-calculations lead loyal men to the slaughter, the eggshell diplo-macy of a long winter in close quarters with men who had been enemies in autumn, the weight that falls on the shoulders of someone who has changed the face of the world. There were conversations, they discovered, that only the two of them could have. And so they had become at first diplomats, then friends, and now something deeper and more melancholy. Fellow mourners, perhaps, at the sickbeds of their empires.

The night wore on, the moon rising through the clouds, the fire in its grate flickering, dying down to embers before being fed fresh coal and coming to life again. They talked and they laughed, traded jokes and memories. Otah was aware, as he always was, of a distant twinge of guilt at enjoying the company of a man who had killed so many innocents in his war against the Khaiem and the andat. And as always, he tried to set the guilt aside. It was better to forget the ruins of Nantani and the bodies of the Dai-kvo and his poets, the corpses of Otah's own men scattered like scythed wheat and the smell of book paste catching fire. It was better, but it was difficult. He knew he would never wholly succeed.

He was more than half drunk when the conversation turned to his unfinished letter, still on his desk.

"It's pathetic, I suppose," Otah said, "but it's the habit I've made."

"I don't think it's pathetic," Balasar said. "You're keeping faith with her. With what she was to you, and what she still is. That's admirable."

"Tends toward the maudlin, actually," Otah said. "But I think she'd forgive me that. I only wish she could write back. There were things she'd understand in an instant that I doubt I'd ever have come to. If she were here, she'd have found a way to win the vote."

"I can't see that," Balasar said ruefully.

Otah took a pose of correction that spilled a bit of the wine from his bowl.

"She had a different perspective," Otah said. "She was . . . she . . ."

Otah's mind shifted under him, struggling against the fog. There was something. He'd just thought it, and now it was almost gone again. Kiyan-kya, his beloved wife, with her fox-sharp face and her way of smiling. Something about the ways that the world she'd seen were different from his own experience. The way talking with her had been like living twice . . .

"Otah?" Balasar said, and Otah realized it wasn't the first time.

"Forgive me," Otah said, suddenly short of breath. "Balasar-cha, I think . . . will you excuse me? There's something I need to . . ."

Otah put his wine bowl on the desk and walked to the door of his rooms. The corridors of the suites were dark, only the lowest of servants still awake, cleaning the carpets and polishing the latches. Eyes widened and hands fluttered as Otah passed, but he ignored them. The scribes and translators were housed in a separate building across a flagstone square. Otah passed the dry fountain in its center before the thought that had possessed him truly took form. He had to restrain himself from laughing.

The chief scribe was so dead asleep that Otah had to shake the woman twice. When consciousness did come into her eyes, her face went pale. She took a pose of apology that Otah waved away.

"How many of your best calligraphers can work in Galtic?"

"All of them, Most High," the chief scribe said. "It's why I brought them."

"How many? How many can we put to work now, tonight?"

"Ten?" she said as if it were a question.

"Wake them. Get them to their desks. Then I'll need a translator in my apartments. Or two. Best get two. An etiquette master and a trade specialist. Now. Go, now! This won't wait for morning."

On the way back to his rooms, his heart was tripping over, but his mind was clearing, the alcohol burning off in the heat of his plan. Balasar was seated where Otah had left him, an expression of bleary concern on his face.

"Is all well?"

"All's excellent," Otah said. "No, don't go. Stay here, Balasar-cha. I have a letter to write, and I need you."

"What's happened?"

"I can't convince the men on the council. You've said as much. And if I can't talk to the men who wield the power, I'll talk to the women who wield the men. Tell me there's a councilman's wife out there who doesn't want grandchildren. I defy you to."

"I don't understand," Balasar said.

"I need a list of the names of all the councilmen's wives. And the men of the convocation. Theirs too. Perhaps their daughters if . . . Well, those can wait. I'm going to draft an appeal to the women of Galt. If anyone can sway the vote, it's them."

"And you think that would work?" Balasar asked, incredulity in his expression.

In the event, Otah's letter seemed for two full days to have no effect. The letters went out, each sewn with silk thread and stamped with Otah's imperial seal, and no word came back. He attended the ceremonies and meals, the entertainments and committee meetings, his eyes straining for some hint of change like a snow fox waiting for the thaw. It was only on the morning of the third day, just as he was preparing to send a fresh wave of appeals to the daughters of the families of power, that his visitor was announced.

She was perhaps ten years younger than Otah, with hair the gray of dry slate pulled back from an intimidating, well-painted face. The reddening at her eyelids seemed more likely to be a constant feature than a sign of recent weeping. Otah rose from the garden bench and took a pose of welcome simple enough for anyone with even rudimentary training to recognize. His guest replied appropriately and waited for him to invite her to sit in the chair across from him.

"We haven't met," the woman said in her native language. "Not formally."

"But I know your husband," Otah said. He had met with all the members of the High Council many times. Farrer Dasin was among the longest-standing, though not by any means the most powerful. His wife, Issandra, had been no more than a polite smile and another face among hundreds until now. Otah considered her raised brows and downcast eyes, the set of her mouth and her shoulders. There had been a time when he'd lived by knowing how to interpret such small indications. Perhaps he still did.

"I found your letter quite moving," she said. "Several of us did."

"I am gratified," Otah said, not certain it was quite the correct word.

"Farrer and I have talked about your treaty. The massive shipment of Galtic women to your cities as bed servants to your men, and then hauling back a crop of your excess male population for whatever girls escaped. It isn't a popular scheme."

The brutality of her tone was a gambit, a test. Otah refused to rise to it.

"Those aren't the terms I put in the treaty," he said. "I believe I used the term *wife* rather than *bed servant,* for example. I understand that the men of Galt might find it difficult. It is, however, needed."

He spread his hands, as if in apology. She met his gaze with the bare intellect of a master merchant.

"Yes, it is," she said. "Majesty, I am in a position to deliver a decisive majority in both the High Council and the convocation. It will cost me all the favors I'm owed, and I have been accruing them for thirty years. It will likely take me another thirty to pay back the debt I'm going into for you."

Otah smiled and waited. The cold blue eyes glittered for a moment.

"You might offer your thanks," she said.

"Forgive me," Otah said. "I didn't think you'd finished speaking. I didn't want to interrupt."

The woman nodded, sat back a degree, and folded her hands in her lap. A wasp hummed through the air to hover between them before it darted away into the foliage. He watched her weigh strategies and decide at last on the blunt and straightforward.

"You have a son, I understand?" Issandra Dasin said.

"I do," Otah said.

"Only one."

It was, of course, what he had expected. He had made no provision for Danat's role in the text of the treaty itself, but alliances among the Khaiem had always taken the form of marriages. His son's future had always been a tile in this game, and now that tile was in play.

"Only one," he agreed.

"As it happens, I have a daughter. Ana was three years old when the doom came. She's eighteen now, and—"

She frowned. It was the most surprising thing she'd done since her arrival. The stone face shifted; the eyes he could not imagine weeping glistened with unspilled tears. Otah was shocked to have misjudged her so badly.

"She's never held a baby, you know," the woman said. "Hardly ever seen one. At her age, you couldn't pull me out of the nursery with a rope. The way they chuckle when they're small. Ana's never heard that. The way their hair smells . . ."

She took a deep breath, steadying herself. Otah leaned forward, his hand on the woman's wrist.

"I remember," he said softly, and she smiled.

"It's beside the matter," she said.

"It's at the center of the matter," Otah said, falling reflexively into a pose of disagreement. "And it's the part upon which we agree. Forgive me if I am being forward, but you are offering your support for my treaty in exchange for a marriage between our families? Your daughter and my son."

"Yes," she said. "I am."

"There may be others who ask the same price. There is a tradition among my people of the Khai taking several wives. . . ."

"You didn't."

"No," Otah agreed. "I didn't."

The wasp returned, buzzing at Otah's ear. He didn't raise a hand, and the insect landed on the brightly embroidered silk of his sleeve. Issandra Dasin, mother of his son's future wife, leaned forward gracefully and crushed it between her fingers.

"No other wives," she said.

"I would need assurances that the vote would be decisive," Otah said.

"You'll have them. I am a more influential woman than I seem."

Otah looked up. Above them, the sun burned behind a thin scrim of cloud. The same light fell in Utani, spilling through the windows of Danat's palace. If only there were some way to whisper to the sun and have it relay the message to Danat. *Are you certain you'll take this risk? A life spent with a woman whom you've never met, whom you may never love?*

His son had seen twenty summers and was by all rights a man. Before the great diplomatic horde had left for Galt, they had discussed the likelihood of a bargain of this sort. Danat hadn't hesitated. If it was the price, he'd pay it. His face had been solemn when he'd said it. Solemn and certain, and as ignorant as Otah himself had been at that age. There was nothing else either of them could have said. And nothing different that Otah could do now, except put off the moment for another few breaths by staring up at the blinding sun.

"Very well," Otah said. Then again, "Very well."

"You also have a daughter," the woman said. "The elder child?"

"Yes," Otah said.

"Does she have a claim as heir?"

The image appeared in his mind unbidden: Eiah draped in golden robes and gems woven into her hair as she dressed a patient's wounds. Otah chuckled, then saw the beginnings of offense in his guest's expression. He thought it might not be wise to appear amused at the idea of a woman in power.

"She wouldn't take the job if you begged her," Otah said. "She's a smart, strong-willed woman, but court politics give her a rash."

"But if she changed her mind. Twenty years from now, who can say that her opinions won't have shifted?"

"It wouldn't matter," Otah said. "There is no tradition of empresses. Nor, I think, of women on your own High Council."

She snorted derisively, but Otah saw he had scored his point. She considered for a moment, then with a deep breath allowed herself to relax.

"Well then. It seems we have an agreement."

"Yes," Otah said.

She stood and adopted a pose that she had clearly practiced with a specialist in etiquette. It was in essence a greeting, with nuances of a contract being formed and the informality that came with close relations.

"Welcome to my family, Most High," she said in his language. Otah replied with a pose that accepted the welcome, and if its precise meaning was lost on her, the gist was clear enough.

After she had left, Otah strolled through the gardens, insulated by his rank from everyone he met. The trees seemed straighter than he remembered, the birdsong more delicate. A weariness he only half-knew had been upon him had lifted, and he felt warm and energetic in a way he hadn't in months. He made his way at length to his suite, his rooms, his desk.

Kiyan-kya, it seems something may have gone right after all. . . .

TOR